Once she was a shop girl.

Now she is a Countess, living in a fairy tale castle near Vienna. But Viola Erhmann's beautiful dream explodes with the advent of World War I. Torn from a secure and loving marriage, she must face the pitiless cruelty and savage desire of a man who will do anything to conquer her.

And across the channel in England, her son, James-Carlo, must abandon the shelter of an upper class school, fight for his manhood, and confront the secret of his true identity.

COUNTESS

A splendid drama of passionate loyalties, brutal ambitions and revenge, played out against a sweeping backdrop of empire, war, and aristocracy.

Josephine Edgar

Countess

WARNER BOOKS

A Warner Communications Company

WARNER BOOKS EDITION

Copyright © 1978 by Josephine Edgar
All rights reserved.

This Warner Books Edition is published by arrangement with
St. Martin's Press, 175 Fifth Avenue, New York, N.Y. 10010

Cover art by Elaine Quillo

Warner Books, Inc., 75 Rockefeller Plaza, New York, N.Y. 10019

 A Warner Communications Company

Printed in the United States of America

First Printing: July, 1981

10 9 8 7 6 5 4 3 2 1

Countess

PART ONE

COUNTESS VIOLA

CHAPTER ONE

The little castle called Die Kinderburg stood on a promontory rather higher than a hill, but smaller than a mountain, on a bend in the Danube some fifty kilometres from Vienna.

An ancient barbican had stood there since medieval times, the family fortress of the Erhmanns, the rich and powerful family to whom it and the land for miles around belonged. In the eighteenth century a charming little romantic castle had been built round and within the ancient walls, a place where the family could bring their children away from the heat of the city, and the threats of plague, cholera and typhus that haunted its insanitary slums. Die Kinderburg could be called a very small castle or a very large country house. It had a gingerbread prettiness of beams, and rosy tiled roofs, of castellated walls overgrown with vines and roses, all clustered about the towering old barbican and the pretty village of Kinderburg below. Its name, The Children's Castle, was apt. On this day in July of 1913 it looked like an illustration from a fairy-tale book.

A stone terrace ran along the south-west of the house, with the long french windows of the drawing- and dining-rooms opening out on to it. The terrace was a riot of bloom, large antique stone urns, imported from Italy by some romantically-minded countess of a past age, were filled with geraniums and petunias. In the turret rooms of the barbican lived a colony of white doves which fluttered and swooped about the terrace and towers, one of which inconsiderately deposited a dropping on the garden table at which the Countess sat writing a long letter to her friend, Mrs Betsy Lyttelton of Clapham Common, London.

In the last year of the nineteenth century, the year when the war with South Africa had broken out, two years before the great old Queen had died, she and Betsy had come to London,

3

two poor young shop-assistants, to find their fortune. Virtue, they say, has its own reward, and Betsy, so small, myopic and innocent, had married the Reverend Matthew Lyttelton, then a poor curate in London. Viola had had a different destiny. The mistress of the Earl of Louderdown, the mother of his illegitimate son, the wife of a rich, cruel man, whose death had caused a notorious scandal, and now the wife of Count Eugene Erhmann. Two women so different in every way it was difficult to relate the one with the other, but although they had not met for twelve years, they corresponded regularly, and their letters were still the simple, gossipy, not very well spelled letters of their girlhood.

'Oh, drat these mucky birds!' said the Countess inelegantly, and rang a small silver bell on the table by her side, bringing a uniformed manservant, who summoned a housemaid to bring water and cloth to clear the small mess. 'Well, it hasn't gone on my letter, any road. I suppose the children have been feeding them here again?'

Vatel shrugged and smiled indulgently. He was a Frenchman and had been in the Count's service for many years.

'The little mademoiselle has, milady. They come at her call.' It seemed to Vatel that his mistress grew more beautiful with the years. As she looked up at him, her long, golden-green eyes crinkled with laughter, the July sunshine shining on the burnished cloud of her red-gold hair.

To Viola Erhmann Vatel was a special friend. He knew all about her, right from the beginning, just as her husband Eugene knew about her. About her wild love affair with James-Carlo's father, about her disastrous first marriage, and the five-day scandal of her first husband's death. With them she had neither to conceal nor pretend. And, unlike the other servants, Vatel spoke English, which was a relief, because her German, in spite of painstaking efforts and highly paid teachers, was fluent but ungrammatical, although she spoke it with a charm that captivated Viennese society.

'I must tick that young lady off,' she said. She looked at a small gold and green enamel watch hung on a chain round her neck. 'Isn't it time they were back from their ride?' As she spoke, children's voices could be heard from below in the stableyards and then footsteps clattering up the winding stone steps to the terrace. 'Here they are. Vatel, would you ask them to bring tea out here? It's so warm and lovely. And Vatel – currant tea-cakes for James-Carlo.'

'Of course, milady.'

He went into the house, still very erect and spry. She knew he dyed his hair now. Dear Vatel, he must be nearly sixty. Eugene was over fifty, and Vatel had served him since his boyhood. Was Eugene too beginning to look older? To her he seemed eternal.

For a moment her face was serious, for her husband's health and happiness was her chief concern. Then she turned to her letter.

I must finish now, Betsy love, because the children are back for their tea. We are all well, though Eugene worries about the country, and I worry about him. He says we are trying to damp down a volcano. But here everything looks lovely and peaceful and the children are here on holiday with me. James-Carlo is so handsome and looks almost sixteen although he is only thirteen. Terry is a spoiled little monkey, and Lorenz – she hesitated over her second son, and added, *Lorenz is sweet but Eugene says I spoil him. My love to dear Matthew and tell him to watch that cough, and also to your little Amy. The photographs are grand. She looks so pretty but very sensible. It would be champion to see you all again, and perhaps one day I'll find my courage and come with Eugene on a visit to London. I must stop. All my dearest love. Vi.*

She sealed it and gave it to Vatel who had returned with the tea-trolley. He would stamp it for her and put it in the postbag. She remembered how she and Betsy used to run down to the pillar-box on the corner in Clapham, shawls round their heads against the cold winter rains, to post their letters.

The children came racing across the terrace to hug her. James-Carlo was always the first. He was only half a head shorter than his mother and she was a tall woman. He was a handsome, slender boy, bursting with vitality and a whippy strength. He enveloped her in a crushing embrace, knocking her straw hat awry, making her laugh and protest at his clumsiness, although her eyes were brimful of love. He was her favourite and she could not disguise it. Lorenz, his young half-brother, pulled furiously at his jacket and kicked at his ankles jealously.

The little girl, Theresa, like a living portrait by Gainsborough, watched her brothers with amused detachment. She wore a chestnut brown riding habit, looped to show boots of soft Spanish leather. Her cloud of red hair, fairer than her mother's, with high golden lights, was tied back severely from her perfect face. She was like her mother, but with a less generous beauty and the Erhmann mouth, controlled but passionate. She neatly moved aside as James-Carlo, turning to subdue Lorenz, nearly collided with her, then she went gracefully to her mother's side. Viola put an arm round her, stroked the bright hair, said: 'Well, my little picture, did you have a good ride?'

'Lovely, except for those appalling boys,' Theresa said, precisely. 'They squabble all the time. I rode with Gunther and let them go ahead.'

'All right, Miss Prig,' said James-Carlo. He returned to his mother, having easily reduced Lorenz to screams of 'Pax!' 'Not fair! Great bully!' and finally 'Mama, help me. Stop him!' when James-Carlo had held him down and tickled him into helpless and indignant laughter.

A large English tea was brought out, a lace cloth spread and a big pottery tea-pot. No elaborate samovars for Viola. 'Currant tea-cake,' said James-Carlo. 'Champion!'

The children spoke English fluently and correctly but James-Carlo liked to imitate his mother's West Riding idioms. He loved to make her laugh.

Theresa only mimicked her mother at family parties, and not just the Yorkshire Viola, but the Viennese Viola, with her broken ungrammatical German, half-academic, half-market woman, interspersed with West Riding expletives, but the German spoken in the sweet cultured accent called the *Schonbrunner deutsch*, Eugene's accent. Theresa was a gifted little mimic.

Viola sat down at the table and poured out tea, and presently Lorenz, watching her with greedy adoration, finger in mouth, sat beside her. His looks were all Erhmann – the fine-drawn distinguished fairness, but he was entirely without his father's charm and humour and showed no signs of inheriting his brilliant brains. He had an acute reading difficulty and Viola was inclined to over-indulge him because of the distress and guilt he roused in her heart. For Eugene she had wanted a son as splendid as James-Carlo, and it seemed terrible to her that he should love another man's son more than his own. Lorenz pushed aside the food she put before him, put his head against her arm, his big, pale blue eyes full of tears.

'Mama . . . he hurt me.'

'Mama,' mocked Theresa, 'why don't you love me as much as the others? Is it because Jimmy-C is big and tall, and Terry is a girl? Mama, why couldn't I have been a girl?'

'Shut up! You beast!'

'That's enough, Terry!' Viola said. 'You're too sharp by half. There's a difference between being funny and being downright nasty.'

'Well, Mama, he *is* such a baby. He's always whining about everything, and he cries before he's even hurt. I'm ashamed to have such a milk-sop for a brother.'

'Theresa, that is enough. I won't speak to you again. If I have to, you'll go upstairs to the nursery and not come down to see Papa before dinner.'

Theresa subsided, glowering as prettily as an angry kitten, but knowing her mother meant what she said. In a minute she had forgotten and went on with her tea, talking to James-Carlo. Viola put her arm round Lorenz, passed him a cake he especially liked, and in the circle of her arm he gazed triumphantly at the others.

I've got her now, he thought, *all to myself*, and he wished they would feel as jealous and left out as he would have done, but they ate and chatted, and laughed, so sure she loved them that they took it for granted. And in a few minutes, popping bits of cake into his mouth, his mother was talking with them over his head as though they were all grown-up, and he was a baby, although he was ten, and older than Theresa, who met his glance and, when her mother looked away, pulled a mocking cry-baby face at him.

He leaped to his feet, picked up a cake knife from the table and hurled it at her. James-Carlo jumped, caught it and dropped it as it nicked his hand. The blood ran down on to the lace cloth.

'Beasts, pigs!' roared Lorenz, and then in an explosion of German: 'English-pig, Jimmy-C! Beastly bullying English pig!'

He rushed away from the terrace and slammed into the house. Viola went to James-Carlo, mopping the cut with her handkerchief, deeply distressed. He kissed her, with a look so tender and devoted that her heart missed a beat. She would never forget his father while he could smile at her like that. The laughing, dark blue eyes with the thick black Irish lashes, Staffray lashes; the wide sweet smile, the perfect teeth. Only his nose was straight without the broken bridge that had given his father, James Staffray, such a piratical look.

'Mama, don't fuss,' he said, 'and don't go on at Lorenz. Terry's a little monkey.'

'But to throw a *knife!*'

'It was the nearest thing. It's only a silly little cake knife. He might have thrown a cream cake.' He burst out laughing. 'That would have been great – to see Miss Prig with cream all over her mug.' He kissed Viola's hand. 'Look, I'll go up and soothe the little beggar or he'll work himself up into a paddy. Don't *worry*, Mama.'

'Tell him, when he has stopped crying, he must come down and apologize to me,' said Viola firmly, 'or he stays up in his room this evening.'

'And to me?' asked Theresa pertly.

'No. Not to you, Terry. You asked for it. I shall tell Papa how naughty you have been.'

Theresa drooped; she was Eugene's favourite and she adored him. His rare displeasure could shrivel up her confident charm.

'I'm sorry, Mama. I just didn't think.'

'Well, happen you'll have to learn to think, love.'

8

'You're always crosser with me and Jimmy-C than you are with Lorenz,' Theresa grumbled, 'and he really is impossible.'

'Yes, well . . .' Viola said, and her words failed inadequately. How could she explain these things to Theresa? Her lovely face was so unexpectedly sad that Theresa threw herself at her, burying her face against the creamy lace on her mother's bosom, filled with love and remorse.

'Don't look sad. It's not your fault you have such horrid children. I do love you, Mrs Darling Viola.'

'Get on with you,' said Viola, sighing. The pert little face was truly repentent and loving. She said gently, 'Run and change. Jimmy-C will calm down Lorenz.'

'Can I put on my new dress?'

Viola smiled and sighed again. She knew what it was to want to look lovely for one's love and was aware of Theresa's passion for her father. 'I ought to say no – to punish you.'

'Oh, Mama . . . *please*.'

'All right.'

Theresa flew into the house.

Viola paced along the terrace. The light was westering, gilding the white wings of the circling doves. To the east the clustering woods stretched towards Vienna, west and south the mountains gleamed in the distance. She suddenly felt lonely.

Eugene had been away in St Petersburg during the first part of the children's holidays. These days, increasingly, the Ministry sought his advice. The Ministry, not the Government, for there was no real parliament. He was in St Petersburg ostensibly because of his own financial interests but she knew there was more to it than that. It was said that Russia was secretly encouraging the pan-slavic movement within the Austro-Hungarian Empire, and even shut a blind eye to anti-Habsburg terrorists training within her borders.

Viola did not know. She heard rumours, but Eugene did not speak to her about such things. The life of the rich in Vienna had not changed. Society was just as pleasant and the capital just as gay in spite of rumours of national bankruptcy and threats of war. It did not cross her mind that she or her children could ever

9

be in danger – Eugene would not permit it. The whole world would have to go bankrupt for him to be a poor man. But lately she had wished he did not look so tired and that he had not to travel so far and so often.

Down in the valley beyond the village nestling round its onion-domed church she heard the hoot of a motor-car horn. Only one family in the whole district possessed a motor-car. It must be Eugene's big open Daimler which he used to bring him quickly to and from Vienna.

She went through the drawing-room, pausing in the hall to look at herself in the porcelain-framed wall mirror, wreathed in cupids and roses. At thirty-four she was as beautiful as she had been at twenty, but she was no longer a beautiful girl. That flawless bloom of youth had started to go with James-Carlo's birth. Viola did not regret its passing. She would have sacrificed ten years of her life to have borne James-Carlo.

She cast a critical look at her pale lavender linen dress, elbow-sleeved and low-necked, its fashionable skirt draped to give the narrow hobble look. She took off her big peasant sun hat. Her hair was bound with a wide green velvet ribbon, into which she had pinned a small brooch, shaped like a viola flower, in amethysts and emeralds, the first present Eugene had given her. She had given up wearing heavily draped skirts, tight corsets and boned collars. Her flair for beautiful and elegant 'art nouveau' clothes made her one of the fashion leaders of Vienna.

'It is all very well for you,' her friend and neighbour, Baroness von Retz, said. 'Tall and slim as a reed. I would look permanently pregnant in some of the things you wear.'

Viola bent forward, examining the tiny lines the years and sunshine had etched at the corners of her heavily-lidded green eyes. 'Heck,' she said despondently, and then twinkled with laughter at her own vanity. The motor-car horn sounded imperiously from the entrance courtyard, and she lifted her skirt and ran across the Persian rugs and the shining parquet, across the stone-paved hall to the entrance, down the steps and into his arms.

'Ah, *liebchen*,' he said, 'I am sick of courts and kings. How good it is to be home.'

A mother and a mistress and a friend, thought Eugene, tying his evening tie while Vatel fussed about him, brushing imaginary specks of dust from the shoulders of his black moiré 'smoking'. At Die Kinderburg he and Viola dressed informally for dinner. Vatel still valeted him at home, although he had a younger man to travel with him. He watched his master's face in the mirror; three hours home and already the lines of anxiety had smoothed away from the long, firm mouth, half hidden by the fair, neatly trimmed beard, which gave him a royal look in a world where men were becoming increasingly clean-shaven. The Countess was certainly a woman who knew how to look after a man. Eugene's watchful grey eyes met his, and he smiled faintly, as though guessing his thoughts.

'Ah, Vatel. It is, as the Countess says, champion to be home.' Vatel smiled discreetly, and Eugene lapsed into French. 'Has everything gone well while I was away?'

'Perfectly, *m'sieur*.'

'And the children?'

'Angels, *m'sieur*.'

Eugene's long, shrewd mouth twitched, disbelievingly.

'Angels they are not. Come now, Vatel, I detect a certain subdued note.'

'It was nothing, *m'sieur*. Nothing. They ride every day. They helped with the cherry harvest in the village and Herr Lorenz fell out of a tree, and they have been fishing . . .'

'And Lorenz fell into the water, as usual, to be rescued by James-Carlo, who of course caught the largest fish. It is very hard to be the smaller brother of a boy like James-Carlo.'

'Yes, *m'sieur*. Very hard.'

Eugene sat down by his desk. The big room with its spectacular view of pine-clad mountains was a combined study and dressing-room. 'Now, you tell me. If it were pleasant the Countess would have told me. If it is unpleasant she will wait for the right moment. But if I have to deal with anything, it is better I

11

should be forewarned.'

'They have their little quarrels.' Vatel's voice was indulgent. He turned away, hanging Eugene's travelling clothes in the wardrobe. 'The little *mademoiselle* can be a tease.'

'She can be very provoking. So – it couldn't have been Jimmy-C. He would have put her up a tree or on top of the play-room cupboard and left her to cool off. Lorenz, of course? He lost his temper again? And did what?'

'He threw something at her . . . oh, it didn't hit her and James-Carlo caught it.'

'Caught what?'

'A cake knife.'

'Ach!'

'Only quite small . . .'

'And supposing a dangerous hunting knife had been there, he would have thrown that – the nearest thing to hand.'

Vatel shrugged.

'Was anyone hurt?'

'*M'sieu*, James-Carlo had a small cut on his hand and the Countess was a little upset.'

'So.' Vatel looked apologetic. It had delighted him to see his master relaxed, but now the two deep lines serrated his forehead again. 'Vatel, does young Lorenz remind you of someone?' Vatel spread his hands, his eyes blank, but he did not deceive Eugene. 'Yes. My cousin, Prince Alberich. Old blood can be dangerous, Vatel.'

'*M'sieu*, Herr Lorenz will grow up; it is just that he is a little jealous.'

'Yes. Right. But he must learn not to throw knives. Thank you, Vatel.'

Eugene sat at his desk, thinking about his little son. He had cause for jealousy, that was true. A handsome, confident, co-ordinated elder brother, a seductive charmer for a sister. Lorenz tried and tried, but he could not compete, and one could not always expect the other children to be indulgent. As his mother was. Too indulgent . . . too guilty about her love for the elder boy: a son anyone would want, a boy whom he loved

12

himself because he was so easy to admire and love.

He knew he was to blame. His inescapable self-honesty told him he had been unable to conceal how much he loved Theresa, who had all her mother's charm and seductive wiles, and how much he loved Staffray's fine son, Jimmy-C. James-Carlo Corbett. So uncomplicated, good-looking, good-natured. So physically attractive, playing games, riding, running, dancing, like a beautifully articulated machine. Alert and competent, almost arrogantly modest ('I'm no great-shakes' – his favourite self-deprecation); not brilliant. But strong, honest and sensible. Poor Lorenz, so babyish for his ten years, so light-boned and unco-ordinated, so apt to lose his temper in fits of frustrated jealousy, no match for his half-brother, quite unable to outwit his mischievous imp of a sister.

But he would have to punish him. He must not be allowed to blackmail people with his weaknesses.

'And that was all, Vatel?'

'A little name-calling.'

'What names?'

'Pig. English pig.'

'Ach, Christ,' said Eugene in disgust. 'Where do they hear such things?'

The door opened and Viola came in, wearing a dinner gown of flowing cream-coloured chiffon, two big apricot-coloured roses fastened in the fine puffs of tulle that framed her lovely shoulders. She smiled at him, her eyes glinting, her cheeks just flushed from the love they had made together during the three hours since he had been home, renewing his desire so sharply he was amused and dismayed. He should be grateful she was not an unscrupulous woman – she had such sexual power over him. But, if she had been, she would not have been Viola.

'Are you ready, love?' Vatel bowed and left the room. 'We have such beautiful trout that Jimmy caught this morning up at the High Falls.' She went to his side, searching his face. 'Vatel told you about the row?'

'But you would have told me later.'

'Yes. Poor lamb. Theresa was a little bitch. I made her say she

13

was sorry . . . and she *was* truly sorry.'

'And you made him say he was sorry to you, and you gave him a gentle little lecture and many kisses – enough reward to encourage him to behave badly, and Jimmy-C jollied him out of his bad mood and gave him sweets. So now Lorenz swells like the frog in the fable, his filthy behaviour getting him all the attention he craves for? He – he is like my Cousin Alberich.'

'I did not know you had a cousin. You have never spoken of him before.'

'No. He no longer lives in Austria . . .' Eugene hesitated. 'We quarrelled many years ago.'

'Tell me. Even if you don't want to. Lorenz is my little boy too. How is he like your cousin?'

'Alberich had greater estates than mine. A grander pedigree, a principality. His mother was noble, mine was a commoner and a Jewess. And yet he was so jealous of me.'

'Because you did everything better than he could – like Jimmy?'

'I suppose so. I swear I never tried.'

'Neither does my James-Carlo. In fact, he muffs things sometimes, deliberately, when Lorenz is there. But I do love Lorenz, Eugene . . . so much.'

He took her hands and kissed them. 'So much but not enough. Not as much as you do James. And not as much as I love my *leibchen*, Terry. And he knows and with a child's terrible tyranny he demands compensation, more than either of us can give him: Your tender indulgence humiliates him further.'

'But what can we do?'

'Yes, what can we do to make him believe in himself?'

'*Families*!' exclaimed Viola. '*Children*! Sometimes I think I was lucky to be a bastard without a penny to my name and my mother in an early grave. It makes you stand on your own feet. I never looked to anyone for owt.' She met his tenderly mocking eyes. 'Until I met you, love, and you've spoiled me silly, making me as soft as young Lorenz.' He could smell the faint scent of gardenia about her, and the fine red-gold hair touched his lips. 'It's your first night home, love. I wanted it to be perfect . . .'

14

'It has been,' he assured her. 'We won't have quarrels. But I must speak to the boy.'

The children were waiting in the drawing-room when they went down, Theresa a picture-book beauty in pale lemon crepe-de-chine, tucked and gathered, a big pale tea-rose fastened in the band that held her hair atop her head like a Spanish dancer. Like her mother, she had a flair for clothes, but with a slightly theatrical touch which he hoped she would grow out of. Excellent for an actress, but not quite *comme il faut* for a young Austrian lady. James-Carlo looked very handsome and incredibly grown-up in his first dinner-suit. He had a small plaster on his hand, and when Eugene commented upon it, he smiled his big white smile and said, 'Oh, it's nothing, sir. I scratched it this afternoon.'

'White lie, Jimmy,' said Eugene, and patted his shoulder lovingly, just as Lorenz came into the room. He wore an immaculate white sailor-suit, and his thin, delicate little neck rose from the collar like a fragile stem. He saw his father and Jimmy smile together, and his big, light-grey eyes glowered sullenly. He went to his father and stood apprehensively beside his chair.

Eugene bent and kissed him, and stood back, looking down into the sullen young face. What put a sparkle into eyes? The lines of the face? The personality of the individual? Lorenz would never have a sparkle.

'Well, Lorenz, I hear you have been very naughty.' The big eyes started like a hare's and he glanced round suspiciously. Who had betrayed him? 'Knives,' continued his father quietly, 'table knives are not for throwing – they are for eating with.'

'Papa,' burst out Theresa, 'it was all my fault. I was a beast.'

'It was an accident,' explained James-Carlo. 'Lorry did not mean to hurt anyone, he just got mad at us.'

'Lorenz?'

'I am very sorry, sir, for losing my temper,' Lorenz said, stiffly. 'I am sorry, Mama. I am sorry, Jimmy and Terry.'

'And for calling James-Carlo an English pig.'

'Oh,' said James-Carlo quickly, 'forget that. I get called that at school all the time. I hit them for the pig but I'm proud of

15

being English.' He became aware that his parents were both looking at him with concern in their eyes.

'Who calls you these things?' asked Eugene.

'Oh, boys . . .'

'The boys who will go on to military academies?'

'Mostly, yes.'

'The boys whose fathers are in the army?'

James grinned, shrugged, disconcerted at his father's bleak expression. 'Well, yes, I suppose so . . . they seem to think that, if you don't go on to one of those schools, you don't want to be a soldier. I'd love to be a soldier, but . . .' he stopped, his cheeks scarlet.

'Not an Austrian soldier?' said Eugene slowly.

'Who is not our friend and ally must be our enemy,' Lorenz shouted shrilly, like a little parrot.

'If I do not beat you for bad behaviour, I could beat you for that!' said Eugene savagely.

'Please, love . . . he's only a baby,' said Viola.

'Dad,' protested James-Carlo, sometimes in intimacy he used the English word. 'it's not his fault. We hear this sort of thing at school. He imitates the hotheads. I don't care a fig. But – Mama has told me my father was a brave English soldier and gentleman, so I would like to be a soldier. But it seems to me that here the officers think that everyone who is not an officer is so much dirt . . . even their own troopers. I don't want to be like that. Surely, if there is a war, an officer depends upon his men? How can he if they all hate him? All ranks have to fight and die together, and in danger they are all equal.'

There was a long silence. Eugene nodded, and sat down on a settee. Viola went and sat beside him.

'You will learn nothing like that in an Austrian military academy,' he said drily. 'In England it is not the custom to send the sons of gentlemen to military academies at your age. They usually go to a boys' school – your own father, I believe, went to Rugby. Then when they are eighteen, if they want a military career, they go to a military college, provided they can pass the necessary entrance examination. You could do this if you

16

wished.'

'You mean – finish my education in England?'

'Yes. Think about it.'

'Lorry.' He turned on Lorenz, who quailed before the grave glance. He dare not make a scene before his father as he would have before his mother. 'I love you and I've never beaten you yet, but if I hear you have lost your temper, insulted people, or have been thoughtlessly violent, I shall. Do you understand?'

'Yes,' Lorenz said sullenly. 'Yes, Papa.'

'Well, now, it is over. Let us forget it.' Eugene pressed Viola's hand, and looked at Theresa's anticipatory face with a falsely puzzled air. 'Everyone seems to be waiting. I wonder what for?'

'The presents. The presents from Russia!' shouted Theresa, climbing on his knee. 'Have you bought me a diamond tiara?'

Lorenz sidled over to his mother's side, and put his head against her shoulder. His thumb went to his mouth and she gently removed it. He hated it because she looked sorry for him. She was never sorry for Jimmy-C. She laughed at his clowning, and her eyes always lit up with admiration and love. He was three years younger than Jimmy – he wanted to tell her that when he was thirteen he too would be big and strong, but she would only smile, and say, 'Of course you will, love,' but she did not really believe it. She treated him like a baby.

So he behaved like a baby. He sulked disparagingly over his present, a beautiful painted sleigh, and said he did not like playing in the snow, and why couldn't he have a cossack saddle and a sable cap like James-Carlo? There was a small ermine muff and stole for Theresa and a signed photograph of the great dancer Kschessinska. For Viola there was a gold box which opened when they wound a handle, when a tiny gold and enamelled bird popped up on a spring and sang like a nightingale. It had been made by the Russian court jeweller, Fabergé, and was a curio of great value. Viola loved the absurdly expensive toy, and let the children wind it up and listen to the little singing bird. But after Lorenz had handled it she found he had broken the spring. She put it away without telling Eugene. She never knew whether Lorenz did these small, sly, destructive

17

things deliberately or not, but she could not bear that he should be punished again.

When Viola and Eugene lay together in their big carved and gilded bed, neither of them could sleep. Through the window they could see the stars shining among the pine-clad peaks. After the children had gone upstairs they had walked through the echoing courtyards, through the rose gardens, by the fountains. Once again they had made passionate and tender love, but they could not sleep.

'Viola,' Eugene said suddenly, 'have you ever thought of sending James-Carlo to school in England?'

'Not until tonight.'

She had not been back to England since their marriage. Eugene had settled money on the boy and he would be very handsomely provided for. But he had not adopted him. James-Carlo was a British subject, and Eugene had thought it better to wait until the boy was old enough to choose his own nationality.

'He is such a very English boy, Viola,' he said to her. 'He has the little frills of manner and speech of the Viennese, but he remains so solidly English. He would be happy in an English public school. He would excel at the sports and the easy fellowship. The sort of school his own father went to. He could well become a leader of men. That remark he made – that, if there is a war, all ranks have to fight and die together, was very shrewd.'

'You are his father now.'

'I love him very much, but he is not like me. I am an Austrian. He is the image of Staffray.' He felt her soft, warm body stiffen. The name was rarely spoken between them: she had hoped he had forgotten how much she had loved the other man. The love of her youth. 'I've told him to think about it. You must too. You don't want him to go to a military academy, to be baited for his Englishness and to be bullied into conformity. To be turned out a Junker. The sort of officer material they expect. You heard what the boy himself said about it.'

'Of course I don't. But there are other schools.'

'James-Carlo is no intellectual. My little Terry is more creative and artistic. Jimmy-C has a good intelligence and a – a

18

splendid character. He's kind and honest, and of course physically he is already superb.'

She smiled with pleasure against his shoulder in the darkness. 'And what else?'

'He can do everything better than Lorenz. It might be better to separate them.'

'Lorenz will grow out of his jealousy.'

'Look at them, my darling. Jimmy could be taken for sixteen. There is already down on his cheeks. Lorry has – he has certain inadequacies. It might be better to separate them in these growing years.'

'But – where should I send him?'

'To a good preparatory school for a year, where he could take the entrance examination for a public school. We could ask Grant Eckersley.' Eckersley was his London stockbroker. 'He's been through that mill and has boys that age.'

'It is so far away, Eugene.'

'He would come home for holidays. We could go to England to visit him.'

'But one hears so many rumours. Supposing there was a war?'

He drew her close to him, pressed her head against his chest.

'Things are a little easier. I did not find so much belligerence in Russia, although they draw closer to France. But if it should ever come to war, which God forbid, he would be better off in England. He is still a British subject. I do not think they would trouble a boy of his age, but in wartime people are not rational.'

'You mean – they would send him to prison?'

'They might intern him. As a foreign national. But I don't think so. Don't worry about it, *leibchen*. There is no urgency. For a moment the sabre-rattling has quietened down. Talk with Jimmy about it. Calmly. There is plenty of time. Sleep now.'

Presently she slept, but Eugene was still awake, thinking of Europe, the countries playing out their deadly power game. Italy and Russia were both moving towards the entente, isolating the two central powers. Austria with its army like Virgil's *Monstrum horrendum, informe, ingens cui lumen ademptum* – ill-

19

shapen, huge – and completely out of date; Germany with a large, efficient and deadly modern force which had not yet been tested. If war broke out it would mean horror for the people of Europe whichever side was victorious, and he knew his own country, rife with dissension, hollow with internal strife, would collapse like a house of cards.

It was the day of the von Retz harvest picnic and Lotte von Retz was chasing about like a scalded cat confusing the issue by changing her mind every half hour. Would the long hot spell last? Or would the heat break in a storm? Would it, therefore, be better to set the luncheon on the big terrace of the von Retz hunting lodge, which was called, picturesquely, Die Adlerburg, or should they risk it and load up the drays and house wagons and transfer the whole feast to the charming sylvan glade where the family always held the harvest picnic when the weather was good?

Although Lotte herself possessed the bluest of blue blood (she had been a Schausenhardt before her marriage) her husband's family did not. Their wealth had been founded by a Czech merchant who had speculated in land and property in Vienna after Napoleon's armies had reeled back from Russia in 1812, and had made a great fortune. His son had been granted the condescending von with which the Austrian Court rewarded useful parvenus, and his grandson, Lotte's husband, was created Baron von Retz, further than which the *nouveau riche* could not rise.

Lotte was a society friend of Viola's, a superficial little woman, nice, pleasant when nothing disturbed her, and very flirtatious in the lively Viennese manner. Fundamentally she was rather stupid. She had been educated to be an aristocratic and fashionable young lady, which meant she thought that she and her kind had a right to every privilege without lifting a finger, and to regard the Schausenhardt blood as only secondary to that of the Hapsburgs.

Her stout, second-generation Baron adored her, and she

accepted his adoration as she had accepted his fortune, as her right. She understood why he held her family in such respect, but she wished he would not be so obvious about it. If her brother, the Lieutenant Prince Friedrich Schausenhardt, thought Die Adlerburg a typical merchant's week-end house, pretentious and vulgar, she infinitely preferred it to the draughty, ancient and uncomfortable *schloss* in which she had been born. There was every comfort and luxury, and even the servants had decent rooms in which to sleep, not mice-infested attics.

If anyone had pointed out to Lotte that it was not very sensitive to give a picnic for thirty people with enough expensive food and drink to serve well over a hundred, before peasants who could not afford to buy their children shoes, and barely feed them through the winter once their small-holdings were snowbound, she would have been amazed.

'Nonsense, poor things, they love it,' she said to Viola. 'They love to see our pretty dresses and the children enjoying themselves and riding on the haycarts. It's the high spot of the year – that and Christmas. And we give them a feast and a dance in the evening, and they can take away the left-overs. Would you believe it that the only time those children see *tortes* and *strudels* are at the haymaking picnic?'

'Yes,' Viola said, 'I would.'

'Oh, Viola, you are as bad as your Eugene.' Lotte had tossed her black curls. 'I don't see how such a rich man can be such a radical! If he goes on giving more land to his peasants and paying such exorbitant wages he will have us all in the poorhouse.'

It was no use talking to Lotte. Viola wondered if anyone who had not known what real hunger could do to you could understand.

But on the morning of the picnic Lotte had not only the anxiety of her party, but her brother, Prince Friedrich, had arrived unexpectedly – he said for a day of rough shooting, but Lotte knew better. Friedrich only came to see his relations when he wanted to borrow money and borrowing was a polite way of

21

putting it because they never saw it again. She admired him. She thought that his ideas were probably quite right; she thought him very handsome with his fine military bearing and cold, prominent, blue eyes. But Lotte was incurably frivolous, and she did not really enjoy his company. So long as her world was secure she and her husband went through life with a smiling hedonism and the Viennese *gemütlichkeit* – a word which did not exist in her brother's vocabulary. Of course, he was an officer in the Imperial Guard which she supposed gave him the right to be stiff and stuck up, but she preferred his absence to his company.

He was twenty-eight, the product of an aristocratic caste system and military academy. He was proud and arrogant, he hated his poverty and lived as extravagantly as he felt one of his noble birth was entitled to do. He despised any race but his own, any caste but his own, regarding anyone who worked for a living as belonging to the lower orders. He was obsessively resentful of such people having riches. He was fanatically patriotic and pro-Empire. The irredentists – the Serbs and Czechs who wanted self-determination – were, in his opinion, vassal states; lower breeds who should be kept in their places by force if necessary.

He lounged in a chair, smoking a cigarette through a long holder, watching Lotte bustling about with her lists. He was dressed in riding breeches, a cream-coloured silk shirt with a high Russian neck and long riding boots made of the softest Spanish leather. An expensive tweed jacket with trimmings of green suede hung over the chair, with his felt hunting hat, tufted with chamois. But even out of uniform and lounging, no one could have mistaken him for anything but an officer of the Imperial Army. He caught Lotte's hand as she passed, her taffeta underskirts rustling.

'Oh Freddi,' she protested, 'I'll never be ready. I don't know why you've come today. You hate children and today is the children's day. All the neighbours' children come for miles around and we have games and rides on the haycarts. Not at all your kind of thing.'

'I have no intention of coming. I shall take a gun into the high meadows.'

'Why can't you come next week?'

'Next week I am on duty at the Schönbrunn, and I have something special to ask you . . .'

'Yes,' sighed Lotte, 'I was afraid you might. I suppose it is money again. Why can't you marry a nice rich girl, Freddi, like I married a nice rich man? You know very well Gottfried would be delighted to put up the marriage bond for you.'

An officer in the Imperial Army had to put up a thirty-thousand kronen bond before permission to marry was granted. Lotte knew very well her husband would part with twice that amount to have Friedrich off his back.

'If you think I would marry into a Czech merchant family . . .'

'Gottfried is not a Czech.'

'Well, his great-grandfather was.' She looked down into the sullen, handsome face, the cold blue eyes, full of self-contempt because he had to ask for money, and said kindly, 'Oh, well, I will ask Gottfried, and I know he will come across, but you are extravagant and very ungrateful. How much? Five thousand? Really, Freddi, you are *too* bad!'

'I've a bond to meet. The filthy Jews won't give you a minute's grace. They're afraid there will be war and they'll lose their money. They ought to clear all that rabble out of the country.'

'And then who would lend you money?' she teased. 'All the rich girls are too common for you and all the girls of good family too poor. If you are staying today, behave yourself. The harvest picnic is an old tradition in Gottfried's family and I won't have you spoiling things.'

'Tradition,' Friedrich said scornfully. 'What does von Retz know about tradition? Who is coming to this *bauernfest*?'

'The usual neighbours. Viola Erhmann is bringing her children – Eugene has had to go away again to Italy. One hardly sees him these days now he is a diplomat.'

'A fine rabble you mix with.'

'Rabble!' Lotte stared. 'You're crazy. Eugene Erhmann is from an older family than ours. The Erhmanns have owned Die

23

Kinderburg and the land round it since I don't know how long . . . since before we came from Prussia in the sixteenth century.'

'We should have stayed there. This country is going to the dogs. Erhmann's mother was a Jewess.'

'She was a Mendel from Cologne – they are international bankers.'

'What does that matter? You can see it in Erhmann. He prefers to play the exchanges rather than be a gentleman and an officer like his forefathers were. He has one foot in the Leopoldstadt and the other in the Schönbrunn. And I am told his wife was an English whore.'

Lotte went scarlet.

'I'll have you know,' she said furiously, 'that Viola Erhmann is one of my dearest friends, the nicest and the most beautiful woman I have ever met. If you are going to talk like that you can go, and you can try and borrow money elsewhere, because I certainly will not ask Gottfried to help you if all you can do is to insult him and our friends!'

He saw he had gone too far. 'Now, little sister,' he said caressingly, 'I am sorry. I apologize.'

'That's easy enough. Don't soft-soap me. And you don't know what you are talking about, because you have never met Viola. Wait until you do, then you'll soon change your tune.'

'Look, Lotte, I get so desperate. I get edgy and say things I don't mean. I see junior officers with more money and better horses than I have. In my regiment it is important. I get passed over for promotion because I can't afford to live up to my rank. I'm close to the court, but in reality I'm a beggar. Sometimes, Lotte, I feel it would be easier just to shoot myself and have done with it. I mean it.'

A shadow crossed her face. There was an unstable strain in their blood. Knowing his frantic rages, his wild and unpredictable behaviour, she was afraid he might carry out his threats one day.

'Now, Freddi, *liebling*,' she said coaxingly, 'you mustn't say such awful things. Be good. Go out shooting and don't come back until dinner-time. Or, if you decide to join us at the water

24

glade, be nice and polite to all the ladies, and as charming as you can be *when* you want to.'

Baron Gottfried von Retz came into the room, a stout, beaming man of forty, adoring his children and his pretty wife, happy to spend his life getting richer so that he could make them all happy. If Friedrich's unexpected presence was unwelcome he gave no sign but extended his hand affably.

'Freddi, my dear boy, how nice that you have come to our little feast. The weather will hold, Lotte. The carts are all ready and I have told them to start packing the food and tables. We should make a start if we are to be at the water glade in time to welcome our guests.'

The small von Retz children were brought in by their nurse, the two little girls befrilled and beribboned in the height of expensive fashion, the two little boys in spotless, white-starched sailor suits. They all rushed to their father to be lifted and kissed, and made awed bows and curtseys to their tall and rather alarming Uncle Friedrich.

Friedrich behaved pleasantly; he wanted the five thousand kronen badly. He said he might walk along to the water glade around midday. He wanted to get a train back to Vienna in the evening.

Lotte and Gottfried and the children, accompanied by the nurse, footmen and maidservants set off in open carriages, followed by a train of carts loaded with wine and beer and ice boxes, and every kind of cold delicacy from grouse to salmon, and an impedimenta of trestles and benches, cushions and parasols, all so necessary to Lotte's idea of a picnic, to drive the five miles to the beautiful glade where a waterfall splashed down a rock face into a trout stream running through a cool green glade, the traditional place for the harvest picnic.

Left alone, Friedrich helped himself to a brandy, and went to the gun room, took a light sporting rifle and a game-bag, had a pony saddled and set off up the winding mountain road. An Irish setter of impeccable lineage and training ran by his side. It was pleasant to imagine that all these things were his. It was the sort of place his birth gave him the right to own. What sort of place was Austria becoming, when a Schausenhardt could be a beggar, and Gottfried von Retz so rich? A fat Czech who, if his grandfather had not speculated luckily, would be behind a corn chandler's counter in a back street in Prague.

The mountain air was so clear that he could see the distant snow peaks above the serrated ridges of pine, and here on the uplands he passed through small villages, where the peasants pulled off their hats as he passed. The vines were ripening on the lower slopes. Down in the valley he could hear the voices of the haymakers as they bent over their scythes.

He got a couple of rabbits and a hare. He was a fine shot. By midday he was hungry and thought about the splendid picnic which had been packed up at Die Adlerburg that morning. He was above the beautiful rocky valley where the waterfall fell in a mist of rainbows, and from below he could hear the sound of voices and children's laughter. He was tempted to join them.

He set the sturdy little pony at the steep lane and came out at the opposite side of the stream, where a row of broad stepping-stones went across the water. He turned his pony loose to graze and started across, just as a woman came running barefooted down the opposite bank, a troupe of children about her. Parents and nurses stood higher up the bank, calling in laughing protest.

'Viola, they'll all get soaked. Whoever heard of such a thing? What about your dress?'

But the red-haired woman paid no heed. She wore a crisp and simple white muslin dress, and a big straw hat like the peasants wore in the hayfield. She helped the children take off their shoes and stockings, and gathering her flowing skirts from her long, slender legs, waded into the water, laughing, throwing back her head so that the sun caught the long lovely line of her throat. The children splashed in gleefully, shouting about her.

Friedrich stared, fascinated, as she played with the children, a child herself among them. He could not guess her age — it could be twenty-five or thirty-five. The tall handsome boy by her side, laughing with her, but watchful in case she slipped, was obviously her son. He put his hands on her waist and lifted her over some stones, and Friedrich felt a pang of jealousy.

He crossed the stream and went up the bank to his sister, who was watching comprehendingly. His face was burning. His eyes blazing.

'Who is she, Lotte? I've got to meet her. I've got to know her. She is exquisite.'

Lotte took his arm and led him down to the water's edge, calling across to the red-haired woman. 'Viola, Viola . . . come and meet my brother.'

Viola turned and waded to the bank, tall and slender, swaying like a reed, smiling her gentle, soft, sensuous smile.

'Viola, this is my brother, Lieutenant Prince Schausenhardt, and, Freddi, this is Countess Erhmann.'

His throat constricted and his mouth was dry with desire. He remembered things he had heard bandied about the mess by officers, indiscreet with drink. That Erhmann's wife had been the mistress of an English nobleman before their marriage. That there had been a scandal in London. This slow, smiling, copper-haired goddess, brimming with laughter, was the most desirable woman he had ever seen in his life. If what he had heard was true, according to his code she was not unassailable, and watching her smiling in the sunshine, apparently unconscious of his burning glance, he swore he would make her his mistress, if he had to kill Erhmann to do so.

He took her outstretched hand. 'I kiss your hand, gracious lady,' he said, and when he did, sought to retain it, but with a brief indifferent smile Viola released her hand, and turned away.

CHAPTER TWO

Prince Friedrich Schausenhardt lived in a rented apartment, three first-floor rooms with a squint-eyed view of the Stadtpark across the Schubertring. The address was quite impressive although he considered it a slum compared with what he had been used to in his youth and early twenties. He looked back bitterly on those days when he had still owned the family *palais* on the Herrengasse, with three carriages, a stable full of fine horses and a retinue of servants. Now his orderly looked after him.

Although he was only in his late twenties Friedrich had spent the considerable fortune he had inherited on coming of age, taking extensive leaves in Paris and the French Riviera, a famous and splendid figure at the gaming tables, the racecourses and restaurants of the fashionable European world. Now all that was left was the ancient and dilapidated Schloss Schausenhardt, near the border of Bavaria, and there he had sold the timber, the surrounding land and mortgaged everything that would raise a kronen.

The *palais* in Vienna had been bought by his brother-in-law and converted into large and luxurious apartments, one of which, on the *étage noble*, Gottfried and Lotte occupied as their own residence.

Gottfried had imagined, hopefully, that the considerable price he paid for the huge old house would keep his mother-in-law for the rest of her life and, invested, provide Friedrich with an income. But, as anyone could have told him, Friedrich went through his portion in twelve months and had already so depleted his mother's capital that she had been forced to give up her own apartment and live with them.

The Princess Adela was in Vienna now. Normally Friedrich found it a complete bore to have his mother in Vienna. To pay duty visits, to kiss the hands of the dreary old crones and the even drearier old gentlemen who came to drink coffee with her, all, of course, of the highest pedigree. The Hoffähig, court-worthy, and, as he told his friend, Lieutenant Johann Hoch-burg, all of them as old as the Emperor himself.

Johann was a pleasant well-born fellow, younger than Frie-drich, very impressed by the wild elegance of his friend's repu-tation. He lounged in a deep chair watching Friedrich's orderly help him into his highly polished boots. Every button on the skin-tight uniform gleamed. Friedrich stood while the man carefully adjusted the tasselled black and yellow striped silk waistbelt of an officer of the Imperial Guard. If Prince Friedrich's bulging blue eyes were blood-shot with dissipation he still retained the fine figure of a horseman. The orderly flicked a whisk over his shoulders for any vestige of dust or dan-druff that might have escaped his notice, sprayed his master with expensive cologne then presented him with his cap and gloves.

'Put them down, you idiot,' said Friedrich irritably. 'Where are the flowers for my mother?'

'In the hall, Herr Leutnant.'

'Right, get out now.'

'So you are going to your sister's again?' teased Johann. 'To kiss the old ladies' hands? To hear how the Emperor loved them madly sixty years ago? Come on now, Freddi, who is it at the von Retz place? A pretty maidservant? A governess? One of the new season's fillies with a good dowry? I hear their mamas are lining them up there for your inspection.' Friedrich did not an-swer. 'One of your sister's married friends?' He saw that he had hit the target. Friedrich's expression changed. He sat down, fixed a cigarette in a long amber holder, and lit it. His hand shook slightly as he did so.

'If you must know, it's Erhmann's wife. She's driving me insane.'

'You mean you're driving yourself insane because you can't have her? All Vienna is in love with her and I believe has been since Erhmann brought her here from London thirteen years ago. I've met her. She is a beautiful woman, such fun, and so nice . . .'

'They tell me she was once an Englishman's whore.'

Johann coloured, rose, bristling indignantly.

'In Vienna they say anything. Something some plain spiteful woman has cooked up. I don't believe it. She is not a coquette, but she is not a stiff and starched hypocrite like so many of our smart ladies. They carry their noses in the air and run off to take their knickers down for a lover the minute their husband's back is turned. The Countess is charming. She and Erhmann are devoted to each other.'

Friedrich raised tormented eyes. Johann was surprised. There was something demonic about his suffering.

'There is no one more virtuous than a reformed whore,' he said heavily. 'I cannot understand her. She will not look at me. Is she cold or heartless? Frigid or mercenary? I suppose if I had Erhmann's money bags it would be different.'

Johann put on his gloves, picked up his riding whip, flicking his polished boots wearily. His friend's extraordinarily paranoic egotism was beginning to bore him. He could not bear defeat, especially by a woman.

'Has it never occurred to your Highness,' Johann mocked, 'that the beautiful Countess might not like you? Come off it, old boy. If you were as rich as Rothschild it wouldn't make any difference. You know perfectly well that if you succeeded, and she became your mistress, you'd discard her immediately. You always do. Frankly I don't think all the sighs and roses, the sufferings and rages in the world will impress that lady. You're wasting your time. I'm going round to the stables to get my nag and put her through some schooling. Are you going to the ball at the Italian Embassy tonight?'

'If I hear she is going I shall go,' said Friedrich. 'That is why I am going to my sister's place. She might be there – or I shall learn where she will be this evening. I go everywhere she goes. I never dance or speak with another woman. I stand and look at Viola Erhmann. She never seems to notice.'

'Jesu!' Johann burst out laughing. The idea of that accomplished rake, Prince Friedrich Schausenhardt, standing gazing at a woman like a moon-calf tickled him. 'Well, if you don't seduce the lady she'll die laughing.'

It was rumoured that Schausenhardt's methods of seduction could be vicious and violent as well as romantically persistent, but this would not be the case with a woman of Viola Erhmann's standing. Like Friedrich, Johann was well-born but impecunious, living on debts, a small income and his officer's pay. He had enjoyed going out with the Prince, accompanied by theatre girls and occasionally the more elegant whores, making the round of the luxurious cafés and always ending up at the gaming tables, but his patience with Friedrich's moods was becoming a little strained.

'Well,' said Johann, 'if you're going to play the moping Romeo I'm off. I don't believe you'll stand a chance with the beautiful English *frau*. If you follow her around with that desperate look, she is bound to become interested, even if she just thinks you're crazy.'

Friedrich rose, with the restless energy of a caged animal. The thought of Viola haunted him night and day. Those green-gold eyes that looked at him so vaguely, the pleasant nod, as though trying to remember who he was; the breath of scent as she passed with that swaying walk that drove him mad.

'Maybe there is another man,' he said. 'There must be another man if she is so indifferent.'

'There is. Her husband. It is said she worships him, and why not? A charming fellow – the most civilized man in Vienna.'

'A half-Jew.'

'For God's sake, Freddi, Erhmann is of the sixteen-quarterings.'

'He can be descended from Charlemagne for all I care. His mother was a Jewess and he refused to lend me money.'

'It was an insult for you to ask him. He's not a money lender from the ghetto. He raises loans for empires and royal houses, not for the likes of us. All right – glare! Time was when you lived in the Herrengasse and kept three carriages. What securities can you offer now? A good night at the tables?'

'We shall quarrel if you speak to me like that.'

'Oh, forget it. I don't want to quarrel with you, but sometimes, Freddi, I think you live in a dream. Well, I'll see you tonight at the Embassy Ball and if it's very boring we'll get off as soon as the Royals leave. We might have a few drinks together afterwards. *Auf wiedersehen*.'.

When he had gone Friedrich poured himself a drink and sat thinking of Viola. Every day he sent her roses. Every day a polite note came from Erhmann's secretary. 'The Countess thanks you for your charming gift of flowers.' Nothing personal. No invitation. Nothing. The flowers he knew would be sent to a hospital.

She had been charming to him at the picnic at Adlerburg, but she had been charming to everyone, and indeed she had been far more interested in the children than in him. Particularly that tall boy of hers who had looked at him watchfully, as though he guessed his feelings, and was warning him away from his mother. But the second boy, Lorenz, had followed him about like a puppy, gazing at him with admiring eyes. Firing questions.

'Are you really the best shot in the regiment, Prince Friedrich?'

'Did you really win the regimental Steeplechase?'

'Have you really fought hundreds of duels, and won every time?'

'Why do you want to know all these things?' Friedrich asked with a smile, not because he liked children, but he wanted Viola to smile on him.

'I want to be a soldier,' Lorenz had said boastfully, standing to attention. 'Like my grandpa. All our family were soldiers until Papa. I don't want to be a financier. I don't want to go to silly old Iggy's. I want to go to a soldiers' school and ride a charger, and guard the Emperor, and fight for my country.'

'Well said!' Friedrich smiled.

Viola drew the child to her, kissed him, sent him on a trivial errand. He was astounded at the expression in her eyes.

'You don't want him to be a soldier?'

'I want him to be a good man, and do whatever he is good at,' she said gravely. 'I don't want him to waste his life in dreams.'

She had risen and left him, since when he had only seen her at a distance in her carriage, at balls and receptions or at Lotte's with her children. He could not believe he meant no more than any fashionable young officer who admired her. He was Prince Friedrich Schausenhardt. He was no nearer possessing her than that first day in Adlerburg.

The orderly called a *fiacre* and Friedrich drove round to his sister's home. He went straight up to his mother's drawing-room and presented her with the posy.

Princess Adela was delighted. Freddi was really being such a sweet and attentive boy, bringing her flowers almost every day and not pestering her for money, although she knew his debts were very large.

She served him coffee and he stood behind her chair with a gilded Meissen cup in his powerful, brutal-looking hands and surveyed the company with his restless eyes. His mother had taken to inviting rich friends with marriageable daughters to her afternoons, because, like the rest of the family, she always hoped that her darling boy would marry well and cease to be a drain on her resources.

The aristocratic maidens paraded for his choice were either very young or very plain and they fidgeted on their gilt chairs and eyed the lieutenant, standing there very erect and straight-backed. His black hair was closely cropped, so that, above the gold laced collar of his jacket, it looked like navy blue bristle. His eyes moved over them with an insolence that seemed to strip the frills of fashion from their maiden bodies and set their hearts beating like anvil blows.

They all had heard that he was dreadfully wicked, which only made them yearn for him the more, until they met his eyes, when they would be a little afraid. His eyes were a pale milky blue, which gave him the disconcerting blank stare of a statue, but in anger or desire the pupils could expand into a hot, black intensity. Beneath the clipped moustache his lips were red and sensual, the lower lip full and slightly protruding. His mother said this was inherited from a Habsburg ancestor.

33

The girls fluttered and chattered, drifting together like young does seeking protection from the predator snapping at their heels. They could not know he was incapable of love. Indeed for him the word had an overt meaning, the highest excess of sexual abandonment and he read the promise of such abandon in every undulant movement of Viola's tall and graceful body.

It was hot in the drawing-room, full of the chatter and the smell of women. His uniform collar was tight and his highly polished boots hot. He thought the debutantes looked like so many calves as they chewed politely on their cream cakes and picked over the silver salvers of crystallized fruits that were offered to them. He could stand it no longer. No woman on earth was worth such boredom. He would send a message to Johann that he was cutting the ball and they would have a night on the town together. Get a couple of girls, take them back to his place.

He began to make his farewells, clicking his heels, bending over the wrinkled and jewelled hands of the grandmamas. Just as he reached the door Lotte von Retz entered, very chic in red, with an absurdly large white hat that had an enormous red quill across the turned-up brim, held by a jewelled buckle. She wore a long stole of white ermine, and her skirts were so tight about her little black and white buttoned boots that she could not make a full step. Her spoiled, pretty children were with her, and everyone made a great fuss of them, exclaiming over their growth and beauty and feeding them with sweets. They greeted their Uncle Friedrich warily, having experienced the edge of his ungovernable temper.

'Oh Lotte,' screeched one of the old *gräfins,* looking like a parrot in her high feathered hat, 'are you going to the ball at the Italian Embassy tonight?'

'Of course. We are taking Viola Erhmann with us. Eugene was coming but he has to dine with the Italian Foreign Minister who is visiting. They are supposed to come on later, but who knows these days? I tell Eugene he should not let anyone have any money, then they could not afford to have wars.'

'We cannot afford not to teach the Serbs a lesson!' flashed Friedrich.

34

'Oh Freddi, don't snap at me. I know nothing about politics. God forbid! But it *is* nice of you to come and see Mama. Shall you be going tonight?'

'Of course.'

Lotte's eyes twinkled. She was quite aware of his infatuation. Indeed all Viennese society was talking about it. It was a great joke.

'See you there, *liebling.*' She kissed him heartily, and he kissed her hand. 'Keep one dance for your poor old married sister. *Auf wiedersehen.*'

He went out, down the grand stairway and through the massive porch framed by writhing stone caryatids supporting the stone arch with its carved Schausenhardt shield, and out into the windy autumn air. There was a smell of distant snow. On such an evening Vienna glittered, opening its heart for pleasure, careless, frivolous, gay, ignoring the threatening rumours of insurrection and war. He did not know where he was going. He only knew that in a few short hours he would hold Viola in his arms in a waltz, see the little laughter lines about her lips, a few inches from his own, smell the gardenia scent which rose from the lace veiling her lovely breasts. The sweat broke out under the tight band of his uniform cap and desire rose unbearably at the very thought of her.

Tonight Erhmann would not be there. There would be an hour, perhaps two, when he could lay siege to her, pleading, imploring, protesting, lying, with all the dominating skill which he could so well use if he wished. So far he had not had the chance to speak, she was so adroit at keeping him at a distance. But tonight, he told himself, it would be different. Like all women, without her husband's presence, she would drop her guard.

In her big dressing-room in the eighteenth-century *palais* on the Prinz Eugenstrasse Viola was dressing for the Embassy Ball. Her hair was already dressed, brushed into a spun silk cloud, and her gown of apricot satin hung ready, free of its dust cover, for her to slip into at the last minute. Over her camisole and petticoat she wore a voluminous gown of sky-blue silk, woven in Damascus, with a silver pattern of tiny birds and animals, one of the many gifts Eugene had brought back to her from his travels. The three children were there with her. Lorenz and Theresa were rifling through her jewel case to the protesting horror of Anya, her lady's maid. Theresa had a long pair of chandelier earrings in her small ears, and three diamond swallows pinned down the front of her nursery overall. James-Carlo sat on a small stool near his mother's feet, as he did nearly every evening, telling about school, and what he had been doing, and listening to her talk about her day.

A small frown ruffled his smooth forehead, for although he kept up a good all-round standard of work he did not like the school any more than Lorenz, although for different reasons. There were no sports. It was run by Jesuits and was very academical and austere. The long days in the stuffy classroom stifled him. Eugene had chosen the school in preference to a military establishment, against all the rules of his breed and class. He disliked the arrogant, thoughtless chauvinism that was bred in the military schools; he disliked the extreme racialism and nationalism, and the exaltation of an aristocratic army caste who claimed privilege by right. But he also thought children, particularly boys, should not be educated privately when they grew older, learning nothing of any world outside their homes. But James-Carlo was not his son, and he too came from a family of serving soldiers.

'Mama, I am sure it would be easier to learn at Iggy's if they opened the windows.'

'We freeze now,' said Lorenz. 'If they did that we should freeze to death.' He did not mean to be funny, but was gratified when his mother and James laughed.

'The place stinks!' said James disgustedly.

'Stinks? What of?' asked Viola.

'Of boys, cabbage, pee and priests' robes,' he said positively.

Viola pulled a horrified face.

'Besides, it's deuced awkward for me not being a Catholic. Do

36

you know I'm the only non-Catholic boy in the school?'

He had been baptized into the Church of England by Matthew Lyttelton before he left England as a very small baby. Eugene's two children had been baptized, as was the custom in his family, into the Catholic Church. The school had only admitted James-Carlo because of Eugene's great wealth and position.

'Do you know when old Father Strawberry-nose takes catechism he looks at me and says all dissenters will burn in hell with Martin Luther? I think he looks forward to seeing me frying.'

'Oh, Jimmy-C, don't exaggerate. He's a nice man and a real good teacher.'

James-Carlo looked down his perfect aristocratic nose. 'If you would condescend to sit still, *Frau Gräfin*?' The maid spoke crossly. Viola held her head still and erect while her maid fixed a small tiara of rose diamonds and angelskin coral in her cloud of red hair. The pretty rosy ornament was set with invisible tremblers so that the diamonds quivered and caught the light in their facets as she moved her head. Theresa clapped her hands with delight.

'Mama, how lovely! You look like the picture of Our Lady in the Elisabeth Kirche.'

'I shan't fry in hell with Jimmy,' said Lorenz smugly, 'or Martin Luther. I'm a Catholic. I shall go straight to heaven.'

Which made Viola laugh until her tiara shook and glittered, and set Anya scolding, and the other two children giggling, for Lorenz hated the Academy of St Ignatius even more than James.

'What else are you wearing?' demanded Theresa. 'A diamond collar?'

'Oh no, they're too scratchy,' said Viola. 'I'll wear my pearls.'

'You always wear those old pearls,' protested Lorenz.

The children all knew that the long string of pearls she so often wore had been given to her by James-Carlo's father. She and Jimmy had a little ritual from his baby days. When the pearls were round her neck she would slip the long loop over his

37

head, drawing his face towards her so that she could kiss him.

Lorenz watched, full of trembling jealousy. *She was going to do it. She did it every night. She never did it to him.* Thoughtlessly Viola lifted the long string of perfectly matched pearls and dropped them over Jimmy's fair head.

Lorenz threw himself at them, just as they fell about Jimmy's collar, screaming at her. 'Don't do it! Don't do that silly thing! It's stupid, silly, beastly! Don't do it! I can't bear it!'

They drew back, sharply. He caught and tugged at the long necklace which broke. The pearls were knotted so only two creamy, irridescent globes rolled across the carpet, pursued by Anya. Lorenz threw himself on the carpet at Viola's feet, sobbing and thumping the floor with his fists.

A shadow touched Viola's face. They had never been broken before. An omen? A little angrily she pulled Lorenz to his feet.

'Now, now, such tantrums. What for? Do you want to be linked to me too? Anya, put them carefully in their box and get the jeweller to collect them for re-stringing.' She looked at her younger son's flushed, tear-stained, unhappy face and suddenly pulled him against her perfumed shoulder. Her little German whom she could not understand. 'Ah, *mein liebling*,' she said in German. 'Try to be a happy boy. Do not doubt that I love you.'

'You love him more,' he said helplessly.

Jimmy had risen, and was seated some way away, impatient but tolerant. Theresa had no such tolerance.

'*Don't* let's have all that old stuff again. It's enough to drive Mama crazy. Mama, darling, what will you wear instead?' she asked.

'Find me something.'

'Ooh, yes! Are you wearing your tiara because the Emperor will be there?'

'The Emperor won't be there. He's too old for balls. The Archduke Franz Ferdinand and the Archduchess will be there, I expect.'

'Is she pretty?'

'The Archduchess? Not very. Not chic. But I'm told she is very nice.'

'Duchesses should be beautiful. Why does Papa sometimes call you Duchess?'

Viola looked up sharply. It was odd how sometimes the past jumped out on her, the breaking of the pearls, and now the old nickname. Before she could reply Theresa had forgotten, finding a gold chain so thin it was almost invisible and a delicate pendant to match the tiara. 'Wear this, Mama . . . it's so pretty . . .' She came to put it about her mother's slender neck, only to have it whipped away by Anya in case she should disturb the beautifully dressed hair.

'Jimmy-C,' said Viola, 'have you thought about what Papa suggested? That you might go to school in England, if you wished?'

'I'd say yes right away, except that I *would* be such a long way from you, Mama.'

'Yes,' she sighed. 'We wouldn't like that. But there would be holidays of course. Well, we'll see.'

She rose and went behind a large Japanese screen and took off her robe, while Anya held the apricot satin gown for her to step into, drawing it up over her arms and fastening the innumerable tiny hidden hooks-and-eyes that cunningly held the bodice in shape about her shoulders and breasts, and the draped skirt which gave her the fashionable narrow hemline without impeding her movement. A very small train, like a fish-tail, embroidered with rhinestones, fell from the waist. She came out, a gleaming, shining, slender figure just as Eugene entered the room, spare and elegant in his black evening clothes, a golden order on a blue ribbon about his neck.

'Here's Papa. Hallo, my love. Children, now a quick good night kiss, and off to your supper, or we shall be late.'

The children bowed formally, kissing Eugene's hand. Then Jimmy and Theresa hugged him uninhibitedly. He noticed Lorenz's sullen, tear-stained eyes, but asked for no explanation, kissing him affectionately. No one mentioned the pearls. Viola promised she would go up to say a final good night before she went out, and they trooped off to the nursery quarters.

'You look magnificent, Viola,' said Eugene. He took her into

39

his arms and Anya squeaked in protest. He would crush the *Frau Gräfin*. His shirt buttons would catch in her hair and his orders tear her lace.

'Anya, please don't fuss. Just go down and see if the carriage is waiting. Come back in ten minutes.' As soon as the maid had gone, Viola pushed Eugene into a comfortable chair and sat down on his knee, her arms about his neck. 'That woman! I'm sure she thinks we will leap into bed the minute her back is turned and my hair will be ruined for the evening.'

'Your hair and my dignity. And of course she's quite right.' He delicately pulled back the tulle edging on the décolleté of her dress and kissed the curve of the white breast beneath. 'It's what I would like to do more than anything in the world.'

'Me too,' said Viola. She caught her breath a little as the skilful fingers moved beneath her bodice. 'And then get dressed, but not dressed up, and drive out to one of those little inns we used to go to. The ones where they pop a whole chicken into boiling oil and serve it with salad and new bread. I'm beginning to wonder if those days haven't gone forever. Oh, my dear love, why are we always so grand these days? Why can't we stay out at Kinderburg or live on the farm in Italy? Why don't we have some fun? Are we getting old?'

'You'll never get old. We stay in the city because of my business interests, and because the boys have to go to school. Once you did not find dressing up and being grand such a bore,' he teased her.

'Well, I suppose I'm used to it now.'

'You do it too well. Bright brains get bored with things they master quickly. I know how you feel.' He turned his head into the smooth warmth of her neck and noticed she was not wearing her pearls. 'Be a little patient, beloved. This year we are walking along a precipice – the next eighteen months will decide. If we are still at peace you and I may dance into old age together. If not, no one in Europe will have much fun for a very long while. And the Empire may cease to exist.'

She opened fearful eyes. 'That could be called treason!'

'Yes. Nevertheless it is true. But let's not be gloomy. Tonight you are going to dance.'

'At an Embassy ball. Everyone clicking and bowing and hand-kissing and gracious-ladying. D'you remember the first time we danced together in London?'

'I do. At Franconeri's restaurant with Grant Eckersley and those pretty girls from the Gaiety? I found you that night only to lose you.'

She rose, moved round the chair, slipped her arms round his neck. He held her hands against his face. 'Can't we sneak off somewhere later? The Royals are sure to go about eleven.'

'I can't promise anything.'

'If I didn't go to this ball it wouldn't matter a ha'porth. But if you didn't meet San Giuliano and Count Sturgk I suppose the peace of Europe might collapse. I just wish you weren't so important.'

'I'm not. But countries need money to fight and I happen to be one of the people who know about money. God knows our armies need a lot of equipping. The availability of money can delay things – sometimes prevent them. At least it can make time for thinking instead of sabre rattling.'

'I sometimes think Lotte is right when she says you shouldn't give any of them money to buy guns.'

'If I didn't, someone else might, or worse, someone would give more to the other side. It's like a balancing act. One day they'll drop the whole lot.'

He looked so despondent that she was afraid.

'I hate to see you look so tired, Gene. Try and call for me tonight.'

'I will. But have a happy time with your friends. In a week or two we'll try and get away together . . . to Italy. Would you like that?'

'More than anything in the world.'

Anya tapped discreetly and came in to say the carriage was waiting. The Erhmanns kept two carriages as well as the Daimler and the electric brougham. Eugene helped Viola into her furs, smooth Russian sables. He liked to see her dressed like a queen. He liked her in a simple print gown at Die Kinderburg or at the farmhouse they had bought above Lake Como. He adored her in her Arab robes, or naked in the moonlight like a laughing nymph. He closed his arms tightly round the slim body in the sleek furs, sending Anya into twitters of apprehension.

'You're a lovely girl.'

'Girl! I'm nearly thirty-five. And beginning to get crow's-feet. Anya, ask the secretary to write the usual notes for the flowers and then send them to the hospital.'

'Yes, *Frau Gräfin*.'

Eugene went over to the side table where the day's floral tributes lay, bouquets of greeting and thanks, official and unofficial. Schausenhardt's two dozen flaming red roses were conspicuous. Eugene read the card, his brows twitching distastefully. 'With passionate devotion. I didn't know you knew Schausenhardt well, Viola.'

'I don't,' said Viola flatly. 'He's just another of these daft young swaggerers that buzz about like . . . like . . .'

'Bees round a honeypot. You swat one and another comes to take its place.'

'Right. And he's one I'd really like to swat.'

Eugene hesitated. Prince Friedrich Schausenhardt was unprincipled and unpredictable. He had been in unpleasant scandals and more than one society woman had been ruined socially by his behaviour. But he did not want to bother Viola with warnings and he had great faith in her common sense.

'Not wearing your pearls?'

'The string broke. I'm having them mended.' She put her hand through his arm. 'Come, we must hurry if we are to say good night to the children before we go.'

They went up in the lift to the nursery floor – an elaborate gilt cage hissing up its shaft at the rear of the house. The sound made Viola remember the little wooden cylinders containing money and change which hissed along the wires when she had worked in the shop in Oxford Street. Involuntarily she shivered, and in answer to his glance, said: 'Suddenly I thought of Netherby.'

42

'*Liebchen*, that part of your life is well and truly buried.'

'I know. But sometimes the past seems very near. I don't know why.' But she did know. It was speaking of Schausenhardt, a man she disliked, and who gave her the same sense of unpredictable cruelty as had Netherby.

The children had just finished their evening meal.

'Why don't you wear a white uniform at parties or when you go to Schönbrunn, like Prince Friedrich?' demanded Lorenz, who adored the glitter of uniforms. In spite of the Order about his father's neck he found the elegant black evening suit boringly unmilitary.

'And when have you seen the Prince in uniform?'

'At Tante Lotte's when he's been taking her to a ball. He's splendid. He guards the Emperor. Why don't you guard the Emperor, Papa?'

'I do,' Eugene said drily. 'It's not only soldiers who look after him, Lorry.'

'A soldier in the Imperial Guard is the only thing for a gentleman,' said Lorenz importantly. Viola touched his round fair head on the thin delicate-looking neck. Her unsoldierly little soldier.

'My English teacher says it's a Fred Karno's army,' said James-Carlo. His teacher was a sharp-tongued gentleman with an Oxford degree, not in holy orders. Viola gave a little, suppressed laugh. She was the only one who understood the allusion. 'What does that mean, Mama?'

'I'm sure I don't know, love,' she lied.

'I wouldn't like to be like Prince Friedrich,' said James-Carlo. 'I think officers should set an example to their men. He's rude to servants. I can't stick people who are rude to people who can't answer back.' Viola could hear Staffray in every scornful word. She glanced at Eugene and said, 'Well, you'd best keep those opinions to yourself, love. Especially at Tante Lotte's. He is her brother.'

'I'm not an idiot, Mama.'

'No, and you're not so tactful either. And –' she lifted the thin golden chain with the beautiful pendant, dropped it over

43

Lorenz's round fair head, and smiled as his eyes shone with delight – 'little pigs have big ears.' She lifted the necklace, and bent to kiss Theresa where she nestled in her father's arms. '*And* little parrots have noisy, nosy beaks.' The two younger children stared, puzzled, but James Carlo understood and looked abashed, and apprehensive. Imagine if that idiot Lorry repeated this at Tante Lotte's! He felt quite hot at the very idea. 'Now we must go. Good night. Say your prayers. Be good children.'

Vatel was waiting in the hall with Eugene's evening cape, hat and gloves, and the carriage stood waiting in the courtyard, the two fine horses moving their heads and jingling the polished harness. The coachman lifted Viola's train inside and spread the carriage rug over their knees. It was a beautiful chill evening with a brilliant dark blue sky, the lights twinkling through the trees.

'What is this Fred Karno's army?' asked Eugene.

'Oh, Karno is an English comic. He runs a company of clowns. Everything falls down or comes to pieces when it is touched. Nothing works properly.'

He looked grim. 'An apt comment! Gold laced uniforms, plumed helmets, old-fashioned guns. No mechanization. No real armament – not compared with the other powers. Russia is the same. Archdukes running things instead of experts. You're right, that Jimmy of yours must learn to be tactful.'

She had been about to tell him of Schausenhardt, his tiresome pursuit of her, but now did not want to trouble him with such a triviality. There were always young men about her, she had always been able to control them. But in Schausenhardt's presence there was a feeling of threat. He was like a good-looking horse or dog with a vicious streak.

'Will you come in and say hallo to Lotte?' she asked when they drew up outside the von Retz mansion.

'No. I have no time. Tell her I kiss her gracious hand.' He spoke the flowery Viennese phrase with a touch of mockery. Then seriously: 'Viola, we must get away together. Perhaps next month.'

'Oh, Gene, love, if we could.'

44

He watched the graceful figure sway up the wide steps into the portico as he drove away. In Lotte's drawing-room, Prince Friedrich was waiting, magnificent in his dress uniform, watching the door for her entrance, the pupils of his pale eyes so dilated they were almost black.

'I will permit you to accompany us if you are a good boy,' Lotte had said to him. 'But no scenes, Freddi. This is an Embassy ball, not a *kaffeehaus*. Besides Viola hates scenes. She is very English in that respect.'

So he behaved. He rode with them to the Embassy in the von Retz carriage, sitting next to Viola in an agony of controlled desire. He could feel her knee against his beneath the carriage rug and smell the scent of gardenias that emanated from her silky furs every time she moved. He could see her profile against the passing lights, and the glitter and tremble of the jewels in her hair. He listened to her voice, deep with a crisp note of mockery and the flat West Riding vowels which she never troubled to correct, quite different from Lotte's musical Viennese court accent. He could not believe she was indifferent to his feelings but the two women and Gottfried gossiped away as though he was not there. He felt he could have thrown Lotte and the benign Gottfried on to the road and driven away with Viola, a captive in his arms. A hundred years ago his ancestors would have done just that. But he had to sit beside her, silently enduring the agonizing temptation of her presence.

At the reception she went with Gottfried and Lotte while he followed discreetly a few paces behind. A few genuine words of regret were murmured by their host concerning Eugene's absence and then they passed onward into the beautiful white and gold ballroom, banked with flowers, brilliant with the colours of the uniforms and the gold lacings, the glitter of Orders and jewels and the dresses. The orchestra was playing an entr' acte from an operetta, the guests were lining the ballroom waiting for the Royal party to arrive, which they did, as always, dead on time. The National Anthem was played, their Royal Highnesses, with the Ambassador and his wife, followed by ladies and officials of the court, walked in procession down the room. The lines of women curtseyed as they passed like rows of flowers swaying in a breeze.

'Well, thank goodness that's over. I am longing to dance,' whispered Lotte. The Royal party mounted to a small balcony overlooking the ballroom where gilt chairs were set for them. The Archduke gave the signal for the ball to start, and immediately the violins dipped into a Strauss waltz. 'What a stuffy provincial the Archduchess is, a typical Czech.'

Viola looked across at the plain, unsmiling woman who was an Archduchess but would never be an Empress, and felt sorry for her.

'You really are an awful snob, Lotte,' teased Viola. 'You criticize the poor Archduchess, but you make a friend of me. I'm as common as they come, and you know it.'

'But you are so chic, Viola, amusing and charming. You *look* like a duchess while the Archduchess looks like a housekeeper.'

Like a duchess? Twice that evening – the old name, and the old memories when all fashionable London had known her as Duchess, young Lord Staffray's mistress. Jimmy Staffray. Her fingers rose to her throat but the pearls were not there. Watching her strange expression Schausenhardt felt utterly excluded. The beautiful eyes looked through him and did not see him.

'Countess!' he said roughly.

The heavy, long-lashed lids lifted, and she gave a hesitant, half-apologetic smile.

'Prince Friedrich, I *am* so sorry. I was miles away. Back in my youth.'

Lotte put her hand on her husband's arm.

'Dear Gottfried, shall we dance? The first of the evening together, as usual?'

'Yes, my angel,' said Gottfried, beaming with uxorious pride, 'while I still have the breath.'

They skimmed on to the floor, for in spite of his weight Gottfried danced like a true Viennese. Before Friedrich could claim Viola, a young attaché approached her, saying his Excellency would like her and her party to join his table at supper. Friedrich could have killed him. The room was full of girls who longed to dance with him, and one or two women who would have died for a glance but he stood watching her shining satin-clad figure, desiring her so much that he wanted to destroy her. Never in his whole life had he felt like this for a woman.

Presently Lieutenant Hochburg greeted him, very immaculate, rosy and smiling, his small fair moustache twisted into upturned points, obviously enjoying himself.

'Why, Freddi, what's up now? Smile, man. You are at the ball and in your lady's party. The champagne is excellent. And Countess Erhmann has promised me a dance.'

'She has what?' demanded Friedrich furiously. 'How?'

'She has promised to dance with me. How? I just asked her. She's so nice and kind.'

A second waltz had started. Gottfried came up with Viola on his arm. He was puffing, mopping his brow with his silk handkerchief.

'Please, Freddi, finish this dance with Viola. Lotte has waltzed me to exhaustion. I shall have a heart attack.'

'Nonsense, Gottfried, you are just trying to get rid of me,' teased Viola.

'Countess,' Friedrich brought his heels together, 'may I have the honour of this dance?'

She had been perfectly aware of his eyes following her about the room like a hunter stalking his prey. Without being flagrantly discourteous she could not refuse him.

'Why, of course,' she said, and put her hand on his arm.

Immediately she was aware of the appalling tension, the muscles under the smooth white cloth of his sleeve were knotted as though he was holding a fighting horse in check. When he put his hand on her waist she could feel it burning through his white glove, through the silk of her dress. It was as though he had fever. His eyes, so near, were devouring her features, dwelling on her lips, on the puffs of tulle above her breasts. She looked up and said solemnly, 'Are you counting my new wrinkles, Prince Friedrich? Or calculating my age from the condition of my teeth?'

He did not smile and her heart sank. How could one manage

a man who could not laugh? A man who refused to accept rejection? Usually she found it quite easy to turn ardent young men adroitly aside and would-be lovers into admirers, friends or companions.

'Do not laugh at me,' he said. 'I cannot take my eyes from you. Since I met you at Adlerburg I have thought of nothing else. I cannot sleep or eat for thinking of you. Why are you so cruel to me?'

'Oh, heck,' said Viola, thinking aloud. 'Have I to listen to that sort of old rubbish!'

He went white, then coloured. She could see the bluish skin crimson under his short cropped hair.

'You insult me.'

'Oh, I forgot you spoke English. I'm sorry.'

'Why should you avoid me?' he said accusingly.

'Well, it's quite obvious, isn't it?' she said flatly. 'I thought you were working up to being a nuisance, and it looks as though I was right.'

'You talk like a shop-girl!'

She burst out laughing. 'Well, that's just what I was, lad,' she said, 'so it's not so surprising. I don't think I want to dance with you any more.'

Viola had laughed. She was not ashamed of once being a shop girl, but she was also Eugene's wife, conscious of his position and dignity. The indifference in her eyes withered him. 'Now, will you take me back to your sister and her husband?'

She was going away from him again, not angry, just a little irritated; not flattered, good-humoured, tactfully concealing her distaste. Nothing had been said, arranged, accepted. He was no further than he had been that morning.

'You mock me,' he burst out. 'You treat me like a fool.'

'No, indeed, Prince Friedrich.' Her gloved hand rested on his arm as etiquette demanded after the dance. She put her head on one side and smiled, and the long green eyes softened good-humouredly as though he were an unreasonable child. 'If you make a scene you will cause a scandal which will be painful to me and to my husband. And to your sister and her husband.

48

And your mother, and do you no good at all. I know it is the code among young officers to ruffle like bantam cocks if their masculine reputation is questioned, and I find the whole idea daft, conceited and unreasonable. You must learn not to be a nuisance. You're Lotte's brother and I'm very fond of her. I don't want to upset her — or you, for that matter. But if you can't behave I shall not call at her house again. And I shall tell her why.'

'You lecture like a schoolmarm!' he sneered.

'And like a naughty schoolboy you deserve a good caning!' she replied tartly. The seductive eyes flashed. 'You cannot intimidate me, or flatter me, and I will not let you persecute me. So perhaps you will behave like a gentleman and not like a street bully.'

They were walking towards the supper-room. She smiled and nodded to acquaintances as she passed, as though she were exchanging the mildest pleasantries with him.

'Am I so repulsive then?'

'You are making yourself so to me. I can't do with a man who can't see when he's not wanted! Ah, here is that nice Hochburg boy coming to claim his dance . . . there is just one before supper.'

Johann came eagerly, proffering his arm, beaming pinkly, clicking his heels smartly. 'Countess, I kiss your gracious hand. It is our dance, I believe.'

'Oh, yes, and it is the cotillon, and I am told, Johnny Hochburg, that you dance it better than anyone in Vienna.'

She sailed away, her hand on Hochburg's wrist, joining the line of the cotillon with its proud parade, and the small dip as they changed step to the beat of the music.

Friedrich felt empty, drained. Useless. He meant nothing to her. If he were the commonest private soldier or the cheapest little city clerk, or a Jewboy from the exchange, he could not mean less. One day, he thought, I'll make her notice me. Her and all the breed of fools and nonentities who wanted to pull him down.

His egotism made him imagine that the whole room was

49

aware of his humiliation. Every lifted fan and questioning glance was a barb in the skin of his paranoic pride. He stalked out towards the entrance hall, his head stiff and high, glaring at anyone who attempted to speak or to greet him, so that they turned aside, baffled and sometimes offended.

As he went down the grand staircase he passed Eugene who was mounting to the reception floor in the company of a group of beribboned ministers and diplomats. Their eyes met and Eugene bowed with casual politeness, but Friedrich knew he knew of his feelings for Viola, knew he had failed with her, and that she would tell him all that had passed. They might even laugh at him together.

The Italian Ambassador greeted Eugene with pleasure, then seeing Friedrich departing, turned to him in concern.

'Prince Friedrich, going so soon? But the Archduke has not yet left.'

It was against protocol for an officer to leave before the Royal party.

'I am not well,' Friedrich lied. 'I am sorry. I will send my apologies.' Without waiting for a reply, he plunged down the stairs, retrieved his cape and plumed dress-cap and went out into the night.

He walked through the streets, his anger boiling within him. At Viola, his poverty and his debts. He had been brought up to believe that the privileges of his rank and fortune were limitless, and he had gambled away his fortune. More than anyone he hated Erhmann. He hated his immense wealth, his aristocratic indifference, and the fact that he owned Viola, and the scapegoat to blame for his own failures was Erhmann's money and his Jewish blood. The country was corrupt, he told himself. They should, like some had said, trace non-German blood back to the third and fourth generation and then put them back into the ghetto.

He took a *fiacre* and drove to a house he knew and picked out a girl with red hair. Upstairs he took her with such cruel ferocity that she screamed with pain and fear and the house bullies had to drag him away from her, for he was tearing at her hair and breasts. Afterwards, in his apartment, he was frightened, for he knew that in his drunkenness it was Viola he had been trying to destroy.

CHAPTER THREE

The Academy of St Ignatius for the primary education of young gentlemen, familiarly known as Iggy's, closed at four o'clock in the afternoon, and at that time parents and upper servants could be seen waiting to collect the various pupils to walk or drive them home. There were a good many carriages on this particular day for the skies were lowering and full of rain and only a sharp westerly wind kept the clouds moving and the weather from turning to storms.

The boys came out very sedately in twos and threes, carrying their books, wearing their peaked student caps, until they reached the outer archway when, having passed the black-gowned ushers whose bleak eyes watched for any over-exuberance, they tumbled down the steps into the street in a wrestling, shouting explosion of vitality.

James-Carlo walked with two of the older boys, watchful of Lorenz running ahead with Albrecht von Retz. He was three classes ahead of his half-brother and steered clear of him at school, leaving him to fight his own battles unless they became desperate.

Lorenz was a boastful and provocative boy, but when attacked would scream for his big brother. James-Carlo would go to his aid, sorting the matter out with calm strength and taking no sides. In spite of the disadvantages of being a Protestant and English, he was extremely popular at school, and met the rare examples of prejudice or malice with calm indifference. Also, he was a very strong boy indeed, not to be provoked. The smaller boys were inclined to regard him with a passionate admiration which infuriated Lorenz.

But today the younger boy was neither kicking, nor spitting, nor calling names. Outside, the von Retz carriage stood at the kerb with a footman waiting to open the crested door. Albrecht leaped in and began to jump up and down to make the springs bounce and Lorenz immediately joined him, disturbing the horses which stamped and shifted, and annoying the coachman.

James-Carlo shrugged and sighed, bade his companions good-bye and went to get Lorenz out of the carriage. His mother had said that for a special treat she and Theresa would meet the boys with the electric brougham and drive them to Demel's for *jause*, the Viennese equivalent of afternoon tea, consisting of hot chocolate or coffee and expensive, rich cream cakes. Viola could not bear it herself, but the children enjoyed it occasionally, especially Theresa, who liked to look at the smart society ladies and famous actresses.

James-Carlo could see neither Viola nor the brougham. A few heavy spots of rain fell from the darkling clouds. He went up to the von Retz carriage and called to Lorenz.

'Come out of it, Lorry, and you, Albrecht, stop bouncing. You'll have the horses bolting if you go on like that.'

'*Herr Graf*,' said the footman, 'your mother, the Countess, telephoned to the Baroness. She is visiting near the Gloriette and the brougham has broken down. She says you are to come back to the Herrengasse with the young master for tea, and that your mother will call for you there as soon as possible.'

'Oh, very well. Though we could easily have walked home. Move over, Lorry, and make room for me. We're going to Tante Lotte's for tea.'

'Will you play with us, Jimmy?' pleaded Albrecht. 'Can we play at sleigh runs down the grand staircase?'

'Well, we'll see what your mother says,' said James-Carlo diplomatically. Sleigh runs consisted of sliding down the wide stairs on large kitchen trays. He was getting a bit big for it himself, and it was a little dangerous for the younger children – also it was hard on marble steps and polished banisters. Now he could ski and toboggan properly he preferred to wait for the snow. This year Papa had promised to take him up to the high slopes.

The footman had put up the hood and by the time they were jingling past the Hofburg the rain had exploded over the city.

Water was spurting out of the tramlines as the tramcars went along and the streets emptying into the cafés and shops. Coachmen and footmen donned oilskins and pulled down their hats. As they drove into the entrance court of the von Retz mansion, lightning struck viciously across the sky and the air reverberated with the noise of thunder. The three boys jumped down and bolted up the steps into the house.

Lotte had a drawing-room full of callers but she welcomed the two Erhmann boys affectionately. She had an especially weak spot for James-Carlo. 'Already,' she would say, 'he is so handsome and every inch a man.'

Her sparkling black eyes smiled at him as a servant helped him out of his overcoat and took his cap. He was extraordinarily tall and well-built for his age, and when he saw her looking at him, his handsome face lit up with an instant response that delighted her.

It was a very pretty thing to be admired by such a charming child who in a very short time would be a handsome stripling and then a personable young man. Lotte wished he was her son, but, alas, all her children were plump and short like herself and Gottfried. James-Carlo was like Viola only in manner. He had the same common sense, the same charming good-humour, and the same plain-spoken, amusing way with him. Lotte often speculated as to who his father might be. He must have been devastatingly attractive, and if Jimmy-C's lordly manner was anything to go by, an aristocrat.

Viola always seemed to attract handsome men. Eugene had been the most eligible man in Vienna, and the best-looking, and the cleverest. He was as well-bred as her own family, and almost as rich as the Rothschilds. Elegant, amusing and charming. It was really too bad! And her own brother, Prince Friedrich, was off his head about Viola, although that had not done him much good, for it was buzzed around the drawing-rooms that she had sent him off with a flea in his ear after the ball at the Italian Embassy. He had not been near the Herrengasse since and she had been told he was back at his old ways of gambling, drinking and whoring. She hoped her mother would not find out. If he made a scandal, and he had often been near it, he might have to leave the regiment. And then what would become of him? Lotte *knew* what would become of him: Gottfried would have to keep him.

Gottfried was the dearest old chap in the world, but she wished he was a little better-looking. It had once been a comfort to believe a good-looking husband was a liability in Vienna, where flirting and love affairs were the chief preoccupation of married women. But Eugene Erhmann adored Viola and for him no other woman existed. Lotte sighed again with good-natured envy, and when the two young boys, Lorenz and her own Albrecht, went tearing up to the nursery floor, she stopped James-Carlo as he went to follow them, and was touched and amused by his quick blush. He was much fairer than Viola, with crisp, curly, golden hair. Only the deft grace of his movements, and the softly sensual droop of his dark-lashed eyelids stamped him as her boy.

'*Ach*, Jimmy-C,' she said, taking his arm, 'don't run away. You get bigger and bonnier every time I see you. You will break a few hearts in years to come.'

'I hope not,' he said, mischievously straight-faced. 'Broken-hearted people are always crying. In books and plays about love everyone is always unhappy. Now, if *I* was in love with a pretty lady like you, Tante Lotte, I would be happy all the time. I think Onkel Gottfried must always be blissfully happy.'

Lotte burst out laughing.

'What a wicked little gallant you are already! I'm not going to let you go. You're too big for nursery tea. You must come into the drawing-room as my cavalier and talk to all the pretty ladies in there.' James-Carlo, who was very fond of pretty ladies, was only too delighted to oblige.

Outside, the fury of the storm continued and once or twice he glanced anxiously out at the rain-lashed streets, thinking of his mother.

'I hope,' he said to the old Princess, 'my mother is all right in this storm. She has gone to call on friends in the Gloriettegasse, and the electric brougham has broken down.'

Princess Adela, who looked to him as though she was made of the same choux pastry as the éclair she was forking into her mouth, light, blown-up and beige-coloured, patted his hand, which, politely, he did not withdraw. He was aware that women did like to touch him, although in this case he did not care for it very much.

'How sweet he is, this child,' she said to Lotte, 'worrying about his Mama. I wish my son was so considerate. He hasn't been near me for days. A week or so ago it was all bouquets and calls, and now, not so much as a message. I hope it isn't a woman.'

'I'm sure your Mama will be quite all right,' said Lotte hurriedly, turning the conversation away from Friedrich. 'She will be sheltering with her friends.'

'In my opinion,' boomed Princess Adela, 'a pair of good horses will always beat these mechanical contraptions. They are always breaking down.'

'That is quite true,' agreed James-Carlo. 'The electric brougham is very unreliable in wet weather. But the Daimler, that's a whizzer, and Papa says the motor car has a great future. He is going to teach me to drive when I am older.'

The butler came across to Lotte's side.

'The Countess Erhmann is on the telephone again, Prinzessin. She is still out at the Gloriettegasse.'

'Come, Jimmy-C,' said Lotte, 'you shall speak to your Mama on the telephone.'

'Telephone,' snorted the old Princess, taking a large piece of cream and orange torte. 'More contraptions!'

To be on the telephone was very chic, and very few people had as yet had it installed. Most rich people still sent their servants scurrying about the city with notes and messages or hired the red-capped and usually red-nosed public messengers. The Erhmann mansion was one of the first to acquire this new means of instant communication, because it was necessary for Eugene to be in constant touch with the money markets of the world. But it was Lotte's new toy. She chatted breathlessly to Viola for a few minutes, and then handed the receiver to James.

'Isn't it wonderful! She might be in the next room.'

'Hallo, Mama!'

'Oh, Jimmy-C, love,' said Viola's deep lilting voice, 'isn't it awful? They say the brougham will soon be all right, but we dare not start off in the rain. I will be home as soon as I can and Tante Lotte has said very kindly that she will send you home in her carriage as soon as this storm is over.'

'Mama, there is no need. If it stops we can easily walk home. Or go on the tramway. Lorenz would like that.'

The idea that upper-class children could not go through the city unaccompanied was something that had begun to irk him considerably. It was all very well for the small ones and the girls. He was quite certain that he could take Lorenz safely across the streets, or indeed anywhere.

'Oh, Jimmy,' Viola said doubtfully. 'It must be a mile.'

'What's a mile? You know we sometimes walk ten miles when we're at Kinderburg. It's stupid that they should have to get the horses out and harnessed up again for us. Please say yes.'

'What would Papa say if you were run over?'

'We shan't be! Oh, Mama, don't be so daft! We-ell! That's what you say to me. Don't worry. I'll hold Lorry's hand all the way.'

'Well, don't speak to any strangers or linger. Straight home.'

'Yes, Mama. Of course, Mama, absolutely, you silly little worrying old Mama.'

He put down the receiver, beaming his wide bright smile.

'Mama says we can go home alone.'

Lotte protested, saying she would send a footman or page with them, but he loftily refused.

'It is perfectly absurd, Prinzessin,' he said grandiloquently, 'to make those poor chaps bring the carriages out. They were soaked coming here. We shall be home in no time. I know the way perfectly well.'

'Well, very well. Come and finish your tea. The rain has not stopped yet.'

It was nearly five when the clouds rolled clear and a red and stormy late sun painted the roofs and towers of the city. James-

Carlo fetched Lorenz from the nursery to the obvious relief of the von Retz nursemaid. He had been playing up when he found that his half-brother had been asked to tea in the drawing-room. Not that he liked the drawing-room and being polite to ladies, but he could not bear to be overlooked. But James-Carlo put him quickly into his overcoat and buttoned up his leather gaiters and gloves, put his cap on straight, and took him firmly by the hand.

'Mama has said we can go home alone.'

'On a tramway?'

'If you are very good.'

They made their adieux and he thanked Lotte very formally and kissed her hand, and they went out into the early evening. After the storm everything was painted a ruddy gold, like his mother's hair. They took a tramcar for part of the way, sitting behind the driver, and watching his nonchalent twirls of the control through the glass. They alighted at the Kartnering because they wanted to look at a bicycle shop they had glimpsed when passing. It was really very exciting to be on their own in the city. The lights were going on everywhere, strings of them along the Ring, the pavements were drying in the wind, waiters were turning down and drying the café chairs, flower-sellers and newspaper vendors uncovering their wares again.

They found the bicycle shop. Here, in Vienna, they were not permitted to ride their bikes, but kept them at Die Kinderburg where they were allowed complete liberty. The bicycles in the window were the new British BSAs and Lorenz, for once good and contented, happy to hold James-Carlo's hand, chattered away eagerly. It was only when other people were present his envy became demonstrable.

James-Carlo glanced at his watch and began to hurry Lorenz homeward. They were passing a fashionable *kaffeehaus*, one patronized by army men, when a group of officers came out, laughing and talking loudly, a little unsteady after a long afternoon session.

'Prince Friedrich!' shouted Lorenz delightedly, recognizing his idol, Lotte's splendidly uniformed brother.

Schausenhardt turned round, fixed a monocle and stared blankly at the two boys. Recognition dawned. 'My God,' he said, 'it's the beautiful Countess's boys. What are you two sprats doing out alone?'

'We are walking home,' said Lorenz proudly, 'from Tante Lotte's. Why don't you ever come there now?'

His round eyes were alight with admiration. He was soldier-mad and Schausenhardt was his idol. An officer, a prince, someone who often saw the Emperor. The officers with him, of whom Lieutenant Hochburg was one, glanced at each other. They knew very well why Schausenhardt had ceased to haunt his sister's drawing-room.

'Good evening, Prince Friedrich,' said James-Carlo, distantly polite. He did not like Schausenhardt. 'Our mother was to call for us, but her brougham broke down, so she gave us permission to come home alone. We must hurry now, before it gets dark.'

'Well, I'll take you,' said Schausenhardt, dropping his monocle, focusing a little muzzily on the grave young face. 'I'll get a *fiacre* and drive you.'

'No, thank you very much, gracious sir,' said James-Carlo, and though he used the extravagant Viennese phrase, his dark blue eyes were chilled with disdain. 'It is only a step now, and we enjoy walking.'

The edge of Schausenhardt's unstable temper sharpened. The young bastard was looking at him just as his mother did.

'Well, something then – let me give you a treat? How about an ice-cream? Or some pastries? Schoolboys like stuffing themselves, don't they, even if they go to a Jesuit school?'

James-Carlo recognized the jibe and stiffened perceptibly but Lorenz burst out childishly, 'Oh yes. Iggy's is a horrid old school. I want to go to a military school but Papa says it might make us into snobs and bullies . . .' He glared at James-Carlo whose boot tapped him sharply on the ankle.

'Does he, by God!' said Schausenhardt, with sudden ferocity, turning on James-Carlo. 'And what do you say, young Eng-lischer?'

'I think we should go home. My mother will worry if we are

not there when she returns.'

'Come on, Freddi,' said Lieutenant Hochburg in exasperation. 'Let the kids go home.'

'Not without my treat,' insisted Schausenhardt. His two strong hands closed on the boys' shoulders and he propelled them back towards the café. The other officers exchanged glances and indifferent shrugs, but followed. Hochburg anxiously. He knew what the Prince could do if he was thwarted in any way.

The restaurant was empty, the waiters setting the tables for the evening, but a few people were sitting at the marble-topped tables in the bar. Schausenhardt called to a waiter to bring champagne and ices and some lemonade for the boys.

James-Carlo was filled with the apprehensive instinct that warns of imminent danger. He knew quite well that the Prince was not buying ice-creams because he liked them. He resented his overbearing manner and was aware that he was by no means sober, and that in manner and class he represented everything his step-father despised.

The waiter hurried with the order. He too glanced apprehensively at the Prince, knowing him of old.

'I am very sorry,' said Lorenz after a manful gulp at the ice-cream, 'but I have just eaten an enormous tea at Tante Lotte's. I have no more room.'

'Well, some champagne, then,' said Schausenhardt. 'Fill up the glasses, man.'

'Lorenz,' said James-Carlo, 'please don't drink that. Papa would not like it.'

'What's this?' mocked Schausenhardt. 'Does he act nursemaid to you, young Erhmann? Don't you like champagne?'

'Of course I do,' said Lorenz, who did not, but he was going to prove before these officers that he was every bit as good as Jimmy-C. Schausenhardt stood him up on a chair and put a glass into his hand and told him to drink up. He took a sip and the bubbles started him sneezing, and because Schausenhardt and one or two of the other officers laughed, he laughed too and swallowed it down, on top of the cream cakes he had eaten at

Lotte's. He began to hiccough.

'A toast,' shouted Schausenhardt, filling the glass again. He was sitting astride a chair grinning up at the little boy. He raised his own glass. 'Success to the army, defeat to all enemies of the Emperor and death to the Jews and half-Jews.'

'Success to the army, defeat to all enemies of the Emperor, and . . .' James-Carlo took the glass out of his hand and lifted him down to the floor before he could finish.

'Freddi,' said Johan Hochburg furiously, 'you're out of your mind. They're only kids. Send them home. You go too far.'

The other men glanced at each other uneasily. The Prince was quite capable of wrecking the place in a temper. He ignored them. He put Lorenz back on the chair. The little boy was feeling sick and beginning to feel frightened. Friedrich straddled his chair again.

'To the toast of Vienna,' he said. 'The beautiful, the cruel, the tantalizing Countess Erhmann. The English whore!'

James-Carlo knocked the glass out of his hand and hit him across the mouth. The blow drew blood and nearly sent him off the chair. He rose to his feet, wiping the wine out of his eyes. 'Why, you little bastard, I'll whip the daylights out of you . . .' Hochburg and the others closed on him, restraining him by force.

'Are you raving mad, Freddi,' shouted Hochburg. 'It is a child you are talking to. You insulted his mother.'

'If I were a grown man,' said James-Carlo, and he was deathly white, not with fear, but with a consuming rage and disgust, 'I would challenge him and kill him for speaking like that of my mother. He is supposed to be a Prince, but he is really scum. Lorenz!' He took hold of the little boy's hand. The child was green with cream cake and champagne, quite unaware of Schausenhardt's foul insinuations. But he knew that Jimmy-C was terribly angry.

'Don't hit me, Jimmy,' he cried.

'Have I ever, you stupid little worm?' said James-Carlo and marched him out into the street where he immediately vomited. James-Carlo held him over the gutter, wiped his face gently, took his hand and dragged him off towards the Prinz Eugen-strasse.

Friedrich Schausenhardt stood, swaying slightly, grinning maliciously round him.

'You disgust me,' said Hochburg and walked out. The other officers followed him.

Hochburg ran after the two boys and caught up with them.

'James-Carlo,' he said, 'I apologize.'

'It is not you who has offended me, Herr Lieutenant.'

'I apologise because an officer of my regiment has behaved in such a manner. I can only say, as an excuse, that he was not sober.'

'My father says a gentleman should not take drink if he cannot hold it.'

'Your father is right. May I have your permission to see you safely home?'

'You can do what you like. I am perfectly capable of seeing myself and my brother home.'

He marched on at a great pace, dragging the tearful Lorenz along with him, across the Ring towards the Belvedere. When they reached the house the electric brougham had just arrived and Viola was alighting. She stood on the pavement regarding the small procession with surprise.

With a loud wail the whey-faced Lorenz threw himself into her arms.

She had never seen such an expression on James-Carlo's face before. He was deathly white. His lovely mouth was set in a hard line, his dark blue eyes bright with fury and unshed tears. He walked up to her, stopped, and instead of his usual affec-tionate, boyish hug, took her hand, bent over it formally, and marched past her up the steps and into the house.

Lieutenant Hochburg, his nice pink face extraordinarily dis-tressed, saluted and bowed.

'Good heavens,' cried Viola, 'what on earth has happened?'

'I am so sorry, Countess. James-Carlo has been upset – by a fellow officer of mine. I was going to say a friend, but I cannot say that now. His behaviour was inexcusable.'

'Ah,' said Viola. 'Prince Friedrich Schausenhardt. Lorenz, *be* quiet! You are not dead. Go upstairs to the nursery at once and tell Nanny to wash your face.'

Lorenz departed, wailing that James-Carlo had been horrid to him, and he had not done anything naughty.

'Now,' said Viola, leading the way indoors, 'you'd better come in, Johnny, and tell me all about it. Exactly what happened, and what was said.'

A pretty baroque parlour opened off the great drawing-room which she used as a private sitting-room and for evenings when she and Eugene were alone. There was a big cream and gold porcelain stove, the walls were painted with flowers and fruit and exotic birds and the polished floors strewn with golden Afghan rugs. She threw down her gloves and unpinned her hat. After the storm the low, ruddy sunset lit the pretty room, slanting across the trees outside. Young Lieutenant Hochburg was filled with melancholy romanticism. All his life he would remember the amber, rose and golden lights, the tawny chrysanthemums and apricot roses, and the tall woman with the cloud of bronze hair, her beauty like the beauty of a golden summer day.

'Well, now, what happened?'

He told her, haltingly, ashamed of his friend. Ashamed of his presence at the scene. Ashamed for his regiment, for the insult to her and to Erhmann, and most of all for the baiting of James-Carlo. But, standing stiffly, his cap under his arm, he told her the exact truth. When he told her that James-Carlo had hit Schausenhardt across the face she gave a little spurt of dismayed laughter.

'Well, thank heaven he's only a lad and not twenty-one,' she said, 'or we'd have a duel on our hands.'

'It is a duty I shall take over for him,' said Hochburg stiffly.

'You do, my lad, and I'll see your Colonel hears about it.' Viola was suddenly very cross, very West Riding and forthright. 'You do, that's all. Happen he'll clap you both in jail – Freddi too. You know there are penalties for duelling.'

'In certain cases a blind eye is turned, Countess.'

'*Not* in this case. *Be sure of that.* I can't stand this cockbird quarrelling and challenging among you young officers. Over women, over your pride, over prestige, then ending up shooting at each other. It's just plain daft.' She gave him her hand, saying frankly, 'Thank you for telling me so honestly. I know it wasn't easy. And thank you for apologizing to Jimmy-C. It'll go a long way to calming him down. Now, please forget it. Did you enjoy the ball at the Embassy?'

She switched to social chat. Told him how she had been caught in the rain that day, and that she was going to the opera that night. How she hoped to get away with her husband for a short holiday in Italy, and how much she loved Italy. He listened, charmed, amused, but when she dismissed him and he bent punctiliously over her hand he said sternly, 'Nevertheless, I shall never speak to Prince Friedrich again. Except in the course of duty. *Auf wiedersehen*, Countess.'

When Eugene came in half-an-hour later she had not turned on the lights, but was sitting in the dusk by the window, her chin on her hands, gazing across the Belvedere Gardens. He was startled by the expression in her eyes.

'What is it, my dearest?'

'The past has come up to hit me. I, foolishly, gave the boys permission to walk home from Lotte's. They met Prince Friedrich on the way, he took them into a *kaffeehaus*. He was drunk. He said things. He called Jimmy-C a bastard, he spoke of half-Jews, and he called me a whore.' Eugene rose, she put her hand out, pulling him down on the little settee beside her. 'No, Eugene. James-Carlo hit him over the face, and I've already spent half an hour talking that nice Hochburg boy out of challenging him to a duel. I want no scandals and shooting matches.'

'Nevertheless,' Eugene said icily, 'I shall have to deal with Schausenhardt. He has gone too far. I will not have you persecuted or my children baited in public.'

'In many people's eyes what he says is true. What he said about James-Carlo – I was not married to his father.'

'And about me,' he said. 'My mother was a Mendel. I am

proud of it. But only a paranoic brute would turn these facts into insults.'

'I think we must do as you suggest. Send James-Carlo to England to school. I had thought Prince Friedrich was just another foolish officer whom I could manage, but I am beginning to think that he is mad. A man who would behave so to children must be. Eugene, it must not happen again.'

'It will not.'

'I cannot have it gossiped about, perhaps by Jimmy's schoolfriends. It would be better for him to be away from Vienna, and, as you suggested, to be educated at an English school as an English boy.'

'My dearest, I will see this braggart makes no more trouble for you in Vienna. There is a crazy streak in that family. Just as there is a weak streak in my own.' She knew he was thinking of Lorenz and her hand tightened on his. 'But I think you are right. James-Carlo grows very fast towards manhood, and as he grows he becomes more English.'

'You'll come with me to London? To find a school? To arrange everything?'

'*Liebchen*, I cannot. Not if we are to take our holiday in Italy together.'

'I'm not giving that up,' she said firmly. She had to get him away from the harrowing responsibilities of the political scene, if only for a while. He needed the break, and she needed to be alone with him. 'I can go alone.'

'You're not afraid to return to England?'

The beautiful eyes were a little wistful, a little apprehensive.

'Of seeing the old places? Of stirring old memories? Aye, a bit perhaps. It's bound to be so.'

He wondered if she was frightened of meeting James Staffray, Lord Louderdown as he was now. Meeting him and discovering she still loved him, and the old passion still smouldered over the years. It was what he himself was afraid of, but it was a risk he had to take.

'Don't be frightened, dear one. Everything will be arranged for you. You will take Vatel with you, and your maid. I will be in touch with Eckersley and get him to see to everything for you. He has boys of his own, and knows about schools. Just remember all the time how much I love you and how much the children need you. Perhaps my foolish little Lorenz more than most. You need not stay long – just to see the boy settled. And you may see Betsy Lyttelton again.'

Her eyes lit with pleasure.

'That would be grand. I've been longing to see her. Can we go soon? So that we can go to Italy before the snows begin.'

'If the world goes up in flames, sweetheart, we will go away to Como together first. I promise. Just now, things are a little easier . . . since the Italian Minister's visit. I promise we shall go away together.'

In the intermission that evening Eugene sought out the War Minister who was present. The two men walked slowly together along the arcaded balcony overlooking the magnificent foyer of the Staatsoper.

'There's a young officer I wish to speak to you about, Minister,' said Eugene. 'Prince Friedrich Schausenhardt.'

'Oh, yes. A fine old family, but I believe a wild fellow. Are you pulling strings, my dear Eugene? You want promotion for him?'

'That would be splendid,' said Eugene gravely. 'Promotion that would include a new posting. As far from Vienna as possible. Galicia, perhaps?'

The Minister raised his brows. Galicia was the farthest and dullest posting a soldier could have. In the bleak north, close to the Russian border. But Eugene's smiling face gave nothing away.

'Well, why not?' said the Minister. 'No doubt you have your reasons.'

'He has been an insufferable nuisance to my wife,' replied Eugene frankly. 'She is taking a trip to England to put her young son to school there. His father was English. When she returns we are taking a short holiday in Italy. I would find it convenient if this matter could be arranged before she returns to Vienna for the Christmas season.'

'My dear fellow, I do understand. These young bloods must

66

be a devilish nuisance to a woman like Viola. I sometimes think she is too good-looking – or, perhaps, too nice. But I am sure I can arrange Prince Schausenhardt's new posting before her return.'

'I should be most grateful,' said Eugene.

They shook hands and he went back to his box to join Viola and hear the second act of *Die Rosenkavalier*. Viola sat looking out over the audience, and there was an ineffable touch of sadness about her. Since the scene with Schausenhardt James-Carlo had been a little too polite and considerate to her. The sudden boyish hugs, the shared jokes, the mutual laughter had gone. He did not come and sit at her feet any more and tell her about his day. He appeared to be glad to be going to England but did not discuss the project with eager enthusiasm. A shadow had fallen between them.

As the house lights faded Eugene took her hand.

'Do not fret, *liebchen*, he will get over it.'

She shook her head, without speaking. The thought that the boy's love for her could be damaged by Schausenhardt's ugly tongue was more than she could bear.

When they returned home Viola went straight upstairs while Eugene went into the library to look through the messages and post that had come in during the evening. He was slitting the envelopes and glancing through the contents when the door opened quietly and he saw James-Carlo standing on the threshold, a dressing-gown over his night-shirt. Since the scene with Schausenhardt, his ebullience had been a little blurred.

'Jimmy-C,' Eugene said welcomingly, 'come in and sit down.' He lit a cigar and went over to the tray of drinks on a small sideboard, deliberately behaving as though the boy was a grown man and that it was the most natural thing in the world that he should come down at one o'clock in the morning to speak to him. 'A drink? I'm having a night-cap. How about you? A little port?'

'No, thank you, Papa. I wanted to ask you something.'

'Well, go ahead. Are you worried about going to England to school?'

'No, I'll manage that all right.' The touch of lordly confidence brought a smile to Eugene's lips. 'No, it's . . .' He hesitated, squared his shoulders, then said, 'Papa, what is a whore? I know it's a bad woman. But – in what *way* bad?'

'Ah.' Eugene caught his breath, suddenly back over thirty years, remembering the bafflements and distresses of adolescence, and the awful embarrassment of *not* knowing what every grown-up apparently knew. The smiles and glances which can make a budding man feel such a fool.

'A whore, James-Carlo,' he said steadily, 'is a woman who sells herself – her body – for money.'

The boy went very red.

'Why did that beast Schausenhardt call my mother the English whore?'

'Because Prince Friedrich is a man who cannot bear to be denied anything he wants. Your mother dislikes him and his ways and did not conceal her displeasure. Therefore he can only think of hurting her – getting his own back, you would say. Hurting her and her family as much as he can. He has managed to hurt you.'

'I could have killed him. I will one day.'

'Nonsense! You would then be a murderer and your mother and I would really be upset. We can ignore the sort of filth a crazy fool like Schausenhardt speaks in his cups. James-Carlo, there is one reason that I am very glad you are going to England. You are an honourable boy and if there is one thing I detest about my own country it is this so-called code of honour among Austrian officers. It is the code of privileged cads. To attempt to take a woman's honour, and then consider yourself wronged because she refuses your advances. To make it a duty to attempt to kill a man over a quarrel. To despise civilians. To ill-treat inferiors. It is unspeakable.'

James-Carlo looked down at his scarlet morocco bedroom slippers.

'I still want to kill him,' he said.

Eugene shook his head and sighed. 'Jimmy-C, when you are older you will understand that a man like that is already dead. It is his own self-disgust that drives him to such things.'

James-Carlo did not answer. Eugene realized he was choked with suppressed tears. He could no longer take him on his knee as he once would have done, but he put down his cigar and went and sat by his side, put his arm about him, and after a few more seconds of battle James-Carlo put his curly head down on Eugene's shoulder and wept. Eugene rocked him gently, his heart torn for this son who was not his son.

'I'm sorry,' said James-Carlo, sitting up and sniffing. 'I'm sorry to behave like a baby, Papa.'

'It's not only babies who cry. Now, tell me what else you want to know. Because there is something else, isn't there?'

'I'd rather not.'

'Because you think it is disloyal to your mother?'

The surge of colour beneath the boy's transparently fair skin betrayed him.

'You want to know if there is any justification for Schausenhardt's remark?'

James-Carlo nodded shamefacedly. He had been going through agonies of self-accusation. To him Viola was not only his lovely, affectionate, adored mother, but also an icon-like figure, like, as little Theresa had said, the pictures of the Queen of Heaven.

'There is no justification at all,' said Eugene gravely. 'A woman who loves and is not married to the man she loves is not a whore. Your mother loved your own father very splendidly, and believe me, there is nothing more splendid than a great love. She was very young, and quite alone, and very brave, and the man she loved was away in South Africa at the war. She would not tell him about you at first. That their love was going to bring a baby into the world. She thought he had enough to face out there.'

'And he was killed?'

Eugene did not hesitate. No one had ever told James-Carlo directly that his father was dead. It was a white lie, an evasive defence born of Viola's love for him, which she had neither denied nor clarified.

'No. Mama has let you think that. She did not want to hurt you. She did not want anyone to know. And she knew I was proud to call you my son. She is too kind, James-Carlo, to those she loves. To your father, to you, to me, to Theresa and most of all to Lorenz. It is her one weakness. It was her choice not to marry your father although *he* wanted to marry her. She knew it would not do. His family objected. He was a great aristocrat. She was afraid the marriage would not make him happy and she only wanted his happiness.'

'But you too are a great aristocrat.'

Eugene laughed. 'Oh, Jimmy-C, but a very different kind. And I was not such a young man, and not answerable to any family. It was my father who had that battle, when he married my mother, who was Jewish. My marriage was a matter in which I would not have tolerated any interference – but, I had no one left to interfere. No parents.'

James-Carlo gave one of those long shuddering sighs that small children give after drinking or crying, and stood up. Eugene could almost see him sloughing off childhood like a snake's skin.

'I want you to know, sir,' he said very formally and sincerely, 'that if I could have anything I wish, I would wish that you were my real father.'

Eugene felt his eyes prick with tear. 'Oh, Jimmy-C . . .' He turned his head away momentarily, then put his arm round the boy's shoulder. 'Thank you. Now, go up to Mama, and never take a scrap of your love from her, she needs it so much. Oh, and one other thing. When you are in England, at school, we think it best that you should be known by your mother's maiden name, which is Corbett. You may not like this, but there is feeling between our countries and Erhmann is not really your name. There is no point in provoking trouble.'

'It is not running away?'

'No, my dear boy, it is not. It is what is called being diplomatic.'

James-Carlo smiled his big, bright, heart-warming smile, the beautiful lips curling with joy and relief. 'Good night, Papa.'

He raced upstairs and hammered at Viola's boudoir door and when Anya admitted him, shot across the room, fell on his knees at Viola's feet and enveloped her in a crushing embrace.

'Mama, Papa has been telling me all about you and my real father, and I think you were very brave and absolutely splendiferous and I am prouder of you than anyone can be, so there!'

Viola laughed, and tried not to cry, and waved Anya out of the room. A great wave of gratitude swept over her. Eugene, as always, had made everything right for her again. He always did.

It was early September when Viola and Jimmy left for London. It was a happy journey for both of them, but for James-Carlo it was sheer bliss. Never, since Lorenz had been born, had he had his mother to himself for any length of time. Not that he was jealous, for there was not a spark of envy in his nature. Although he was three years older than Lorenz he had matured fast, his voice was tending to drop into alarming depths and his silken cheeks were beginning to show the faintest golden down. He and Viola had a very special relationship. They never spoke of it. In fact, they both felt a little guilty about it, but they knew they loved each other more than anyone else in the world. And on this journey to England there was just the two of them, so that they could talk about anything, and laugh at their private jokes, and not feel they were excluding anyone else or hurting them by doing so.

Then there was his excitement at travelling on the great transcontinental express, watching Austria and the Danube, the forests and the mountains sliding eastward as they went westward through Germany and into France. In Germany he noticed many railway sidings filled with army equipment, and soldiers in grey-green battledress. In Paris they broke their journey for two nights, and if the rest of Europe was sabre-rattling, at least there was no evidence of it here. They stayed at The Ritz and went out to see the sights. James-Carlo was filled with pride. His mother was the most beautiful woman anywhere. He even managed not to yawn waiting for her, nodding sleepily on a spindly gilt chair while she was fitted at Worth and Patou. She treated him as a grown-up man. Not sending him to bed early, but letting him wear his new dinner jacket, allowing him to accompany her to the theatre and to restaurants, to Longchamps and the opera, allowing him to read the menu to her.

'Your French is so good, darling, and I haven't a word.'

Allowing him to pay bills and cabmen, buy programmes, call taxis and hand her in. Of course Vatel was there in the background to see to the more important responsibilities like hotel bills, booking theatre seats and train accommodation, and tipping the very important looking hall-porters and *maîtres d'hôtel*.

James-Carlo loved it. He did not know then how near to tears her happiness was, because she could see James Staffray in every action and word of his son.

She took him to the Comédie Française, the art galleries, and the usual tourist round of the Eiffel Tower, Montmartre and Notre Dame. On their last night they went to the Folies Bergère and had supper at The Cascade. He had asked her to take him to the Folies. A chap at school, he said, had told him it was a splendid show. Poker-faced, she told Vatel to get seats, and without a raise of his eyebrows, the Frenchman bowed and said, 'Certainly, milady.'

The show was glittering and splendid. Sometimes James-Carlo burst out with laughter at the comedians and was glad his mother did not speak French. He was astounded to see that many of the ladies on the stage wore sparkling headdresses and very little else. Every so often Viola glanced sideways at the flushed young face.

'You are a bit young for this sort of show, Jimmy-C,' she said gently, 'but I'm sure that if you were here with Papa he would have taken you, if you had asked. The only difference between people without clothes is that some are pretty and some are not.'

'These ladies are very, very pretty indeed,' said James-Carlo fervently, so that she was shaken with tender laughter. He was James all over again, all the bold beauty, all the fun, all the lordly good looks. And he had Eugene's sensitive perception

72

and perfect manners. Her fine boy. Her gradely lad. He could not have had two better fathers.

When the train hissed into Victoria station, he held her hand. He knew that in some obscure way she was frightened, but could not understand why. She looked superb, wearing a thin, dark chocolate brown suit from Paris, and a small hat trimmed with closely packed velvety orange flowers and autumn berries. Her throat and shoulders were wrapped in a long sable stole. He felt her hand shake.

'There's nothing to be afraid of,' he assured her. 'I'm here, Mama.'

'Aye, love, bless you. But I'm not really afraid. It's just that the old times were hard times and I had forgotten them.'

When the train ran through the shabby outer suburbs, she had recognized old landmarks. This was the London of her scandalous youth, where she had loved, queened it, suffered and nearly starved. Now she was returning after thirteen years. This great boy beside her had then been a baby on her lap.

A suite had been booked for them at the Ritz Hotel and Vatel went ahead to contact the hired motor car which had been ordered to meet them at the station. Her maid, clutching Viola's jewel case, saw to the unloading of the luggage. Eugene's London stockbroker and long-time friend, Grant Eckersley, had fixed an interview for her at Marsham Abbey Preparatory School where his own boys had been pupils. James-Carlo was old to go to a preparatory school, but it was thought that a senior year there would enable him to sit for the entrance examination to one of the public schools.

Viola looked round the station – the entrance to London. Somewhere in England, perhaps in London, even perhaps quite close in Belgrave Square, at Staffray House, James Staffray, the Earl of Louderdown, James-Carlo's father, might be, unaware of her presence here. He was married now, she knew, with children of his own.

She remembered how once she had stood for hours on a London station platform, waiting for just a glimpse of him, and he had been carried past her on a stretcher, wounded and semi-conscious, back from the South African war. Then she had felt her heart break. Her heart would not break now but she prayed that their paths would not cross. Loving and being in love were two such different things.

'Just remember what you mean to the children and how much I love you.' How good Eugene was to her. As she stepped out of the train her veil was down, and the rich furs bunched about her face, almost as though she expected to see Staffray's tall, soldierly, one-armed figure waiting at the station.

But, of course, he was not there. Why should he be? There was, however, another figure, dearly familiar. A small, incredibly neat little woman, peering myopically through her spectacles at the carriage windows, and holding a small girl by the hand.

'Mother,' said James-Carlo, 'there's a little lady waving at you.' She looked to him like an upper-servant of some kind.

To his astonishment his mother gave a whoop of delight and went racing down the platform, skirts flying, and swept the little woman up into her arms.

'Vi . . . oh, Vi . . . how splendid you look!'

'Betsy, my Betsy love, how grand to see you.' She held the little woman at arms' length, knocking her little straw hat askew, gazing at her with loving eyes. 'You're just the same. A little peg-top doll.'

But Betsy had changed. There was a shadowy touch of anxiety about her big short-sighted eyes and the pretty wild rose colour had faded from her cheeks. 'Is everything all right, love?' Viola asked. 'Are you all well?'

'I'm fine,' said Betsy, 'but Matthew has been poorly. He had a bad cough and chest last winter and doesn't seem to shake it off.' She looked at Viola's tall figure with admiration and not a trace of envy. She was so beautifully dressed, so expensively and discreetly bejewelled and befurred. So full of health and vitality. 'You're a real grand lady now, Vi,' she said.

Viola had bent to speak to the little girl.

'And is this my little namesake? Amy Viola? Just fancy,

James-Carlo. Betsy used to give you your bottle when you were a baby. And this little girl is named for me.'

James-Carlo bowed and politely took Betsy's hand. He thought he had never seen anything so miniature as the small girl, Amy. With her high forehead from which the straight light brown hair was taken back in a band, her pink cheeks and large bright eyes she was like the child Alice-in-Wonderland in the stories Theresa read at home. He took the tiny hand, bent over it, clicking his heels in the formal Viennese manner, whereupon Amy's huge eyes opened even wider, and she turned her face against her mother's arm, shaking with laughter.

The hired limousine drove them to the Ritz and he listened in bewilderment while the two grown women gossiped, giggled and recalled their youth. A past world which he had never known. The West Riding accent in his mother's voice became more pronounced than he had ever heard it as she talked to Betsy, crying in a young girl's voice of past acquaintances and adventures.

'And, Betsy – all the folk in the shop – what happened to them? Katy Martin? Married and keeps a pub? That would suit her.'

'She's ever so fat now, Vi!'

'Never? She used to be so skinny. And old Yellow-belly? Miss . . . what's her name? Heath.' They were both talking at once, amid gusts of reminiscent laughter. 'Dead? Well, rest her soul, she never had any fun down here. And that prison warder of a housekeeper, Mrs Harding . . . do you *remember* that tapioca pudding? *And* the cocoa made with warm water.'

Thirteen years of separation, trying to cover everything in a few minutes, questions and answers, flying to and fro. Little Amy seemed equally bewildered. She gazed at the beautiful lady who talked and laughed and cried a little and smelled so lovely, and at the big handsome boy who winked at her and made her hide her face again, and most of all at the motor car she was riding in, for she had never been in one before.

At the entrance to the hotel Betsy Lyttelton took one look into the cream and gilt cavern with the gilded decorative swags of fruit and leaves, the golden nymphs and the marble fountain, at the imposing waiters and uniformed doormen and went pink with fear.

'Oh, I *couldn't*, Vi. No, love, really, I'd much rather not. You tell the chap to drive us down to the Embankment where we get our tram.'

'Still the same Betsy. No one is going to eat you. We'll have dinner up in our suite, just ourselves.'

'Nay, love, I wouldn't feel right. You bring the lad out to our place to dinner on Sunday.'

'Roast beef and Yorkshire? Promise!'

'I promise. Matthew will be glad to see you again. But I'd rather not come in there, I'd not know where to look.'

Viola kissed them both, and told the driver to take them back to Clapham, all the way home.

'What was the lady so frightened of, Mama?' asked James-Carlo, when they were upstairs in their suite. 'It's only an hotel.'

'Ay, love, it is to you,' said Viola. 'But you've been brought up like a little prince.'

'You're such a grand lady at home . . . you were different just now.'

'That's how I *was*, Jimmy-C. Being a grand lady, well . . . I've learned all that, and Papa has taught me too. I'm not ashamed of it. Are you?'

'No, indeed,' he said stoutly. 'I think you're very clever.'

On Sunday they drove out to see Betsy and Matthew and James-Carlo was fascinated with the little house at Clapham Common. But the cottage cast a shadow over Viola. It was where she had been most unhappy and the small, confined, immaculately kept rooms brought it all back to mind. The place was crowded with bitter memories and she longed to escape once again into her own rich and spacious world. She was relieved when, after the midday meal, Matthew suggested they should go for a walk.

'We usually do on fine Sunday afternoons. Amy likes to feed the ducks.'

The district had changed a little, there was a great deal more

76

traffic and the electric trams now went clanging and sparking right along the south side of the Common. Betsy said she wished they could move out farther into the country, the district was going down. She looked at her small pale husband anxiously, the grey eyes behind her spectacles moist with tender anxiety. Ahead James-Carlo had taken Amy on his back and was galloping with her wildly, her hat slipping, and her long light brown hair flying, while she clutched him round the neck, squeaking with fear and delight.

'He's a fine boy,' said Matthew.

'Yes.' She had spoken about her other two children, Lorenz and Theresa, and showed their photographs.

They walked in silence across the grass. Viola said suddenly, 'Do you ever see Jimmy Staffray now, Matthew?'

Matthew winced. He could never get used to Viola's casualness, and she laughed, and added: 'I suppose I should say Lord Louderdown?'

'I haven't seen him for years,' Matthew said stiffly. 'He was kind enough to ask me to Louderdown to officiate at the baptism of his children. He married Lady Florence Mountjoy. There are twins, you know, a boy and a girl. Bellairs who is, of course, Lord Staffray, and the Lady Lucinda Staffray. They must be nearly eleven now. I have not seen him since, although I read about him in the newspapers. At the moment he is deeply engaged in the territorial army which, of course, we all pray will never be wanted. I wanted to be an army padre, and he would have found me something, but my health will not permit it. He is kind to us at Christmas. Always a magnificent hamper and a bird from the home farm. Always a most gracious personal note. But I don't see him.'

'They say his marriage is not too happy,' said Betsy.

'Betsy,' Matthew said warningly, 'we do not know. It is only gossip you hear.' He ran his finger round his hard clerical collar and looked as embarrassed as when she had said something particularly outrageous when she was a girl. 'Viola, I hope you are not going to renew your acquaintanceship with Lord Louderdown again. I feel it would be most unwise.'

Viola pulled her furs about her face as though she was cold. She looked at Matthew with wise, mocking eyes.

'It was a sight more than an acquaintanceship, Matthew, love, or that great lad of mine wouldn't be running along there now. But don't worry. Since Jimmy-C was born there has never been anything I have longed for more than to show James his bonny son. He's never seen him. But I would never do it. He's married and, in spite of what Betsy says, happily I hope. And I'm married to a man in a million, whom I love dearly. I'm only here for a short while. I am going to see the school and if I like it, and if they'll take Jimmy, then I shall be off back to Vienna. Don't worry, Matthew. You ought to remember I was never one to play a double game. I'm not going to see Lord Louderdown.'

Grant Eckersley called for them the following day and took them to Marylebone to take the train for Marsham Abbey School. He spoke very well of it. It was organized on more modern lines than the old-fashioned spartan prep schools. It was warm and comfortable with appreciation of the fact that small boys away at school for the first time missed their homes.

'Sometimes I wonder if it's too nice,' he said. He was a big, cheerful, hearty man with a fine silky moustache. 'My two are at Rugby now, and from their letters you'd think they were at Borstal. Still, no doubt they'll get used to it.'

He eyed Viola with a wary admiration, remembering her notorious past, yet giving her all the respect he thought due to Eugene's wife. Eugene was his wealthiest client although he only handled personal investments. The firm of Mendel-Erhmann & Sons were merchant bankers and only dealt through international banking firms.

'My wife has asked me to say, Countess,' he said presently, 'that she would be delighted if you would dine with us one evening.'

Viola's heavy white eyelids lifted with the old, familiar glance, so seductive, so mischievous, reminding him of the time when she had set the town alight thirteen years ago. She knew that Mrs Eckersley must have thought the matter over very seriously to take such a step. On the continent Viola had lived down her reputation with Eugene's support and her own splendid self-assurance. He wondered if she had any ambition to conquer London society and thought that, with Eugene's millions behind her, she might well do so for she was as beautiful as ever.

'I would like to meet your wife very much,' she said. 'I need her advice about buying Jimmy-C the right clothes – that is, if they accept him at Marsham.'

'I am sure they will,' he said heartily. 'We must fix up for you to come to us before you return.'

Marsham was a tiny village cradled in the Chilterns, a mere collection of farms and cottages around an old church. The nearby school, a popular and exclusive preparatory one for young gentlemen, dominated the village.

Eckersley had ordered a taxi which took them to their destination. Marsham Abbey was an imposing neo-Gothic Victorian building standing in acres of playing fields, a wide stream running through its grounds. The Headmaster, Mr Ransome, was an urbane and kindly man. If he found the Countess Erhmann's West Riding accent a little unusual, he succumbed to her beauty and charm. Her title and the reputation of her wealth and position in European society were impressive.

After his wife had given them tea, the Headmaster suggested she might take James-Carlo out while he had a private chat with the Countess and Mr Eckersley.

James-Carlo walked with Mrs Ransome along the wide stone cloisters and up the stone stairway to the dormitory above. The whole place seemed empty and echoing, the light, airy, clean dormitory with ten narrow beds like a hospital ward, so foreign compared with the comfort and warmth, the beautiful furnishings, food and luxury in which he had been brought up, that for a moment his heart failed him.

Mrs Ransome saw the expression in his eyes, and said understandingly, 'You'll feel it a little at first – everyone does until they make friends. You mustn't compare it with home – it isn't home. It's school, and you'll find it has nice things too, and that

79

they make home things seem even nicer when you've been away.'

He responded with a smile of such charming gratitude that she felt certain misgivings. This one, with that smile and those beautiful eyes, was not going to steer an easy course through life.

'Thank you, *gnädige frau*. That was a very nice thing to say. I am sure that when I meet other boys and start games, I shall be quite happy. And the holidays will not be so far away.'

'No. And you do not call me *gnädige frau*, or even gracious lady, or kiss my hand, or any other lady's hand, Corbett. You call me Mrs Ransome. If a lady offers her hand, you take it; if she doesn't, you just say "How d'you do". That is when you are being introduced. You must learn English ways.'

'And the ladies don't mind?' asked Jimmy, astounded.

She laughed. 'Well, keep it that way at school, Maybe out of school, it might be appreciated – but when you are a lot older.'

Mystified, Jimmy followed her round a tour of the playing fields and classrooms, the chapel and refrectory, and there was a little hollow feeling in his heart.

They spent the next few days, under Mrs Eckersley's guidance, visiting special stores where Jimmy was fitted out with every sort of garment for school and sports, every kind of boot and shoe, three of every kind of underwear, six marked sheets, and six marked pillows, towels, and a large black trunk with a padlock, and a mysterious box which was known as a tuck-box. It was arranged that Vatel would travel to England at the end of the term and escort him home to Vienna for Christmas. At the half-term holiday he would go to stay with the Eckersleys, who had a seaside house, or, if anything should happen to prevent that, he could go to the Lytteltons at Clapham Common. James-Carlo looked a bit glum at that. The cottage, though immaculately neat and clean, seemed to him the sort of place a groom might live in.

'You mustn't be stuck-up, Jimmy,' scolded Viola. 'Aunt Betsy is my oldest and dearest friend. She may be poor compared with Papa, and her home may not be what you are used to, but I won't have her hurt by you looking down your nose. Understand?'

'I wouldn't, Mama, you know. She's very nice,' he protested. 'But there is only that little Amy. No boys to play with. And no horses, and no bicycles.'

'The half-term is only a few days.'

He put his arms round her like a lover, 'But you won't be there, Mama darling, darling *liebchen*.'

In the evenings they went out and saw London, visiting the theatres, the opera and the music hall, the restaurants she used to go to years ago.

'I went here with your father once,' she said.

'Did you have a lovely time?'

She smiled, and shook her head. 'There is a time when everything seems rose-coloured, Jimmy, when you are very young and in love.'

The day finally came when he had to go to school. She took him to the station, a strange new boy in school clothes, his bonny thick fair hair cut very short under the small peaked cap. The platform was full of strange boys and parents, mostly mothers. He was proud that not one of the mothers was as beautiful or as well-dressed as his.

She kissed him good-bye, and he realized it was not a done thing, but would not tell her so. He stood, very stiff and tall, blinking a little.

'Don't cry, Mama, and give my love to Papa and the others. I'll write every week. *Auf wiedersehen*. Good-bye, Vatel.'

'*Au revoir, m'sieu* Jimmy. Until *Noel*.'

'Goodbye, my darling. Christmas will soon be here.'

The train went out, leaving her tall slender figure, so elegant in its wine-coloured velvet, the beautiful face framed in the rich, shining furs, and Vatel, so small, dark-coated and subservient, standing beside her.

She waited until the train disappeared and then she cried a little on the way back to the hotel. It was true it would soon be Christmas. But Viola felt an aching emptiness, as she had felt once when his father, Lord Staffray, James Staffray, now the

Earl of Louderdown, had sailed to the war in South Africa. A feeling of an ending, and of a beginning of something unknown and unplanned.

That evening she took the train to Dover with Vatel to catch the cross-channel boat. From Paris she went straight to Italy and Lake Como, where Eugene would be waiting for her at La Faenza, their quiet country home above the blue lake. She longed for him – she needed comfort, and he who loved her so absolutely would understand.

It was a week later that Grant Eckersley came into his wife's boudoir with an expression of concern on his genial face.

'I say, darling, I've made the most awful gaffe. I've just learned that Staffray's young son started at Marsham this term. I had no idea. Just the one boy of all boys Jimmy Corbett ought not to meet.'

'Oh, Granty!' his wife exclaimed in horror. 'What will you do? They are . . . well, I mean . . .'

'They are half-brothers,' exploded Grant, mopping his big red face. 'That's the long and short of it. And they don't know it.'

'Is there any reason why they should find out?'

'I don't think so. I don't know. Young Jimmy is older by two years. He won't be at the school long – he'll go on to a public school at the end of next year.' He jingled the money in his pockets in a disconsolate way. 'How was I to know? It's a good school. We've always found it so. I didn't think of asking for a list of the new pupils . . . our lad did not mention it.'

'Well, he wouldn't know anyway. You'd have thought Mr Ransome would have mentioned it – well, the Earl of Louderdown's boy . . . it's something to talk about.'

'Old Ransome isn't like that.'

'Well, there's nothing you can do now, is there?' she said sagely. She crocheted a few more stitches of her edging. 'I think it would be more tactful if we said nothing . . . there is no reason why *anyone* should know *anything* about it.'

So it was that James-Carlo, finding his way in the new world of boarding school, in a new country among strangers, met Bellairs Staffray, his half-brother. There was two years between them but they instantly struck up a friendship, drawn to each other by a deep mutual sympathy, which boy-like, they never sought to define.

CHAPTER FOUR

Eugene met Viola at Milan, and they went straight to their Italian farm on the outskirts of a village high above Lake Como, a building of creamy stone and old terracotta bricks, surrounded by upland meadows and wine slopes over the twin-pronged lake where the tourists' paddle-boats looked like match-sticks floating on a blue surface and the eagles hovered in the mountain winds.

The autumn weather was exquisite, the air light and golden, spiced with an evening chill. They were just in time to see the last of the grapes brought in and to make a small *festa* for the vine gatherers who had come in from the neighbouring valleys. It was only a small vineyard, well-sloped towards the sun. The wine was sweet and golden, a desert wine, just enough for their own cellars and to give to neighbours and friends.

For four wonderful weeks they stayed there alone together, walking or riding along the high mule tracks, sailing on the lake, sitting in the sunshine, and in the still silence of the mountains finding a new dimension to their love. It seemed as though, in returning to England, she had been going back to a past which might have claimed her, and her return to him was different from past reunions, bringing them so close, so vividly aware of each other, that a glance or touch of their hands could set their senses singing, and their blood afire. They were so completely lost in each other there was barely any need to speak.

Viola wore simple gowns, the fine clothes ordered in Paris were sent straight to Vienna. They ate simple peasant food. After dinner, when the servants went back to the village and they were quite alone, they found a new depth of physical passion, an inexhaustible mutual desire that startled and stirred Eugene to his very soul. The flare of a flame before extinction? He did not know. Sophisticated and highly experienced he had never believed that the physical manifestations of human love could rise to such transcendental peaks. But during those late autumn days and star-filled nights, with the blue lake below and the mountains to the north beginning to wear their winter snows, he knew that it could be true – that two people could be transported into an unbelievable mutual ecstasy.

No wires, telephone messages or mail were allowed to come through from his office. Only the children's letters. James-Carlo seemed very happy. School was fine. He had made many friends. Rugby was a splendid game. The games master said he was a 'natural' whatever that meant. Lessons were all right. He was spending half-term with Mr and Mrs Eckersley. He was longing for Christmas at Die Kinderburg.

They went back to Vienna at the end of October and Christmas did not seem too far away. The war shadows had retreated, and the children were well. Theresa was taking professional dancing lessons. She had rebelled against the polite afternoon academy, partnering white-collared small boys in waltzes and polkas. She wanted to learn real dancing like the ladies in the ballet. To the horrified consternation of Lotte von Retz and her friends, Eugene permitted it.

'Among the daughters of ballet girls and shopkeepers,' they chattered. 'He must be mad.'

Lorenz was sent away to a school in the Tyrol where the discipline was firm but kind, and there was no Jimmy-C to rescue him from the results of his tantrums, and no Mama to rock him in her arms and comfort him for the consequences of his own weakness and jealousy. The Headmaster was a clever and enlightened educator, and Eugene hoped the boy would become more independent and self-reliant.

Prince Friedrich Schausenhardt had been posted to the Russian frontier in Galicia. Lotte von Retz told Viola about it on her return to Vienna.

'He was furious about it,' said Lotte, 'but he had promotion and it will keep him out of mischief for a while. I can tell you I am glad to have him out of the way. He can't spend much money out there, except for gambling, of course, but the officers can't afford to play for the high stakes that they do in the clubs in Vienna.'

It was a calm and happy time. Soon James-Carlo and Lorenz would be home, and they would all go to Die Kinderburg for Christmas.

At the end of November Viola found that she was pregnant — she was overjoyed and, seeing her radiant delight, Eugene kept his anxieties to himself. It seemed to him that the Central Powers were plunging towards war, and neither their rulers nor their military advisers had any conception of the havoc such a war would cause. Germany, with unprecedented instruments of destruction, Austria with her enormous man-power, were both ruled by men conditioned by the nineteenth century. And Russia was doomed, helpless as one of its own great land-owners, unable to cope with the changing times. What would such a war produce in Europe? What kind of life for these children? For this new child, yet unborn, which Viola was preparing for with such passionate delight. As her pregnancy advanced there was a look about her like a Renaissance madonna, of the earth earthy, and yet touched with golden light. They seemed to have come through into a new world of love; Eugene was almost glad when the intensity of their feeling relaxed. One had to come down from the peaks. The beauty of the aftermath was touched with a poignant sadness, like Vienna itself, dreaming its old dreams while the war clouds gathered.

Perhaps it was because they were so unalike that Bellairs Staffray and James-Carlo became such good friends. It was a warm, deeply affectionate friendship, without a trace of the devoted hysteria, known as a 'pash' which bedevils segregated education. They complemented each other. Bellairs was inclined to be secretive, hiding his creativity and artistic ability behind a mocking, humorous façade. His mother was an out-door woman, born and bred in the shires, and she wanted her boy to be the same. She had no patience with what she called his 'art-and-crafty' nonsense. His father, kindly, tolerant and detached, now increasingly busy with the Territorial Army and the recruitment of volunteers, had little interest in such things.

It was a disappointment to them both that Lucinda, the girl, was keener and more adept at country pursuits than the boy, with no sentimental nonsense about her.

Bellairs had disgraced himself by turning green and vomiting when he was blooded at his first kill, and nothing could induce him to follow the hounds afterwards. He was a good rider and became a competent horseman, but he loathed hunting, and began instinctively to avoid hunting people. Before he went to Marsham his one confidante was his grandmother, the Dowager Countess, looking at her books and reproductions of the great masters, longing to go to Italy and Paris and see these things for himself.

But at Marsham he found James-Carlo, who in his charming, good-natured manner seemed to understand everything, and inordinately admire his talent.

'Why the devil should you hunt if you don't like it, Belly?' he said mildly. 'It's a messy business from what I've heard. And, anyway, you can do other things so much better. What does it matter? It'd be a pretty dull world if everyone liked the same things.'

'I wish you'd tell my people that,' said Bellairs gloomily.

At the end of the Christmas term Lord Louderdown drove from London to collect Bellairs for the holidays. He sat in front beside the chauffeur, loving the power and speed of his new motor car, but resentful of the fact that because of his disability he could not drive. Over the years he had come to terms with it. It was, thank God, his left arm that had gone. He could ride and shoot, and he was CO of his local Yeomanry. The majority of territorial commanders were over retirement age, and his men thought themselves lucky to have such a young and experienced officer in charge. As the car hummed along the road he hoped that Bellairs would like it. He was fond of his son in a casual sort of way, but wished for his own sake that the boy was less squeamish.

Lord Louderdown never thought about the emotional aspect of being a father, but then he rarely questioned his motives, bred as he was from centuries of privilege. He never intellectualized about himself. It would have been bad form.

After the wild oats of youth a gentleman married, settled down and had children. It was one's duty to one's family. Of course one loved the little beggars when they came along and did one's best for them. Neither Lord Louderdown nor his wife, Florence, had ever held their babies after they were born, nursed them when they were sick, or comforted them when they cried. His children had been reared by nurses, governesses and grooms until Bellairs had come to Marsham Abbey School. A last-minute decision, following a row with his mother over his absolute refusal to ride out with the hounds.

Florence had not come today, she was busy with Christmas shopping and preparing for the exodus from Belgrave Square to Louderdown for Christmas. Besides, she was still a horse woman, militantly anti-motor car. But Lucinda was with him. Florence had prophesied breakdown and disaster, including pneumonia from exposure, but goggled, wrapped and gloved like Arctic explorers they had started, and arrived at the school trouble-free and in extraordinarily good time.

The car created quite a sensation and most of the boys and many of the masters came out to inspect it. Lucinda, delighted to be the centre of attention, leaned negligently back, raising her goggles with aristocratic indifference. She was a tall, strong child, with classically fair good looks and regular features. She had inherited none of the endearing Irish charm of Bellairs or the warm-hearted simplicity of the Staffrays. She was her mother's child, single-minded, possessive, arrogantly aware of her position. She had the looks and Bellairs the charm – they were most unidentical twins.

Bellairs appeared, already coated and muffled for the journey. He approached diffidently, greeted his father and his sister, and stared at the big maroon-coloured car, the uniformed chauffeur, gaitered and goggled against the wind, and gave an impressed whistle.

'Good-oh,' he exclaimed. 'It looks absolutely spiffing, Dad. I must tell my friend, Jimmy-C. He's crazy about cars.'

He turned as a tall, fair boy came out of the entrance, and

called across. 'I say, Jimmy-C, come and look at our motor car!'

The handsome boy came over to them. He was wearing a heavy travelling coat of continental cut with a collar of shining, expensive fur. His fair, fresh face against the soft, dark luxury of the fur stirred a violent recognition in James Louderdown. He watched as the boy approached, bewildered, uncomprehending, by this unlooked-for and completely incomprehensible emotion. He had never seen or heard of the boy before. Why should the smiling blue eyes and frank smile mean anything to him?

'Dad, this is my friend, Corbett.'

The name struck James Louderdown like a blow. He felt the door of painful past memories being wrenched open. He did not speak or make any move.

'We call him Jimmy-C,' Bellairs continued, 'because his name is James-Carlo. Jimmy, this is my father, Lord Louderdown – and this is my sister, Lucinda.'

'How do you do, sir,' said James-Carlo very correctly.

Louderdown felt his heart twist in his breast, the world about him lurch and steady again. He felt the colour drain from his cheeks, and put a hand out on to the car to steady himself. Only one other person he had ever known had possessed those heavy white lids, lifting them so slowly that it seemed the lashes weighed them down. But her eyes had been golden green and this boy's were blue, bright blue like his own. Corbett? His own son. Half-brother to this boy and girl of his.

Jimmy-C had turned his smile on Lucinda, who was pretending to be indifferent to his charm, queening it scornfully in the back of the big car.

'How do you do, Miss Lucy.'

'The Lady Lucinda Staffray,' corrected Lucinda coldly.

The boy grinned, bowed, and said, 'I kiss your hand, and offer you a thousand apologies, gracious and beautiful lady,' teasing her with the flowery Viennese manner, which made her colour and toss her head furiously and set Bellairs off into hooting laughter.

'What did you say your name was?' asked Louderdown. His

throat seemed constricted.

'Corbett, sir. James-Carlo Corbett.'

'And how old are you?'

Jimmy frowned with slight hauteur, not understanding and slightly resenting the inquisition.

'I am thirteen. I was born in England.'

'And you live in Vienna?'

'Yes, sir. My step-father is Count Eugene Erhmann.'

'The financier?'

'Yes, sir. Of Mendel-Erhmann and Sons.'

'And do you want to go into finance, young man?'

Again the heart-breakingly familiar smile.

'*No*, sir! I'm going to be a soldier, like my own father.'

'Your father is dead?' asked James.

He saw the momentary hesitation and defensive colour in the boy's cheeks and wondered how much he knew, how much he had been told.

'No, sir,' Jimmy said stoutly. He drew in his breath and gazed straight into James's eyes. 'My mother and father separated before I was born. But she told me he was a fine man and a great soldier.'

James turned away, and Bellairs, still full of the new car and his new and valued friend, went on, 'Jimmy is going all the way to Vienna for the Christmas hols. I tell him he ought to have an airship and fly.'

'I might one day,' said James-Carlo. 'Papa says people will be flying all over the world soon.'

'Your people live in Vienna?' asked James.

'Yes.' Again Jimmy frowned. It occurred to him that Lord Louderdown was trying to find out if he was a suitable friend for Bellairs, and he resented it. As though he guessed his thoughts, James put a tentative hand on his shoulder, and for the first time smiled.

'I'm sorry, I'm asking a lot of questions.'

'It's all right, sir,' Jimmy said, mollified. 'Yes, we live in Vienna near the Belvedere. And we have a country place higher on the Danube. Die Kinderburg. It's a castle. But it's only a

90

little castle. I expect that is why it was called the children's castle.'

'Well,' said James easily, 'I'm very pleased to meet Bell's friend. And what do you think of the car?'

'It's absolutely ripping. We have one at home. It's a Daimler. But Papa is buying a Mercedes too. What do you get out of this one, sir?'

'On the open road we do about forty miles an hour.' James was amused at the boy's knowledge. 'But of course it can do a great deal more. Unfortunately I cannot drive myself. It is impossible.'

James-Carlo looked at his empty sleeve with sympathy but without embarrassment. 'That's the most frightful hard cheese. Couldn't they make you a gear adaption so that you could?'

James glanced at the chauffeur.

'I think it might be possible, my lord,' the man said at once. 'It's worth enquiring into, anyhow.'

'It's a splendid idea. I'll go into it with the makers. So you're a car expert, my boy?'

'Well, not really, sir, but I do like mechanics. Papa lets me drive the Daimler in the grounds of Die Kinderburg – that is, if he is with me, or the chauffeur. And the chauffeur lets me help clean and service it.'

In a few minutes the two men and James-Carlo were talking cars. Bellairs stood back, proud of his friend's knowledge and his father's interest. Lucinda was sulking, and when she sulked her eyes glowered. She hated to be set aside and yet she was fascinated by the handsome, assured boy who seemed to have put her usually aloof father under a spell.

A little elderly dark man, carrying a valise, came out of the schoolhouse. He also wore a coat with a fur collar. A black Homburg hat was jammed down on to his jet black hair. He carried the stamp of the upper-servant in his pale face and his determined yet obsequious manner. His bright black eyes went from the Earl of Louderdown to James-Carlo's eager, handsome face. He waited a courteous minute, and then interrupted the conversation determinedly.

'If you will pardon me, my lord, but *M'sieu* Jimmy must go now. We have to catch our train to Dover from London, and the taxi is waiting to take us to the station.'

Louderdown found he could not bear to let the boy go. He had never seen him before. Over the long years he thought he had forgotten, or rather pretended he had forgotten he had this son. Now he wanted to extend the moment of meeting, to notice every small resemblance. Not just the lift of the heavy eyelids, the ready infectious laugh, head thrown back, lips open over teeth like split almonds, the odd mixture of seductive charm and practicality, the lack of sentimentality. He wanted to delay the boy, as though he could photograph every feature on to his memory.

'I'm motoring back to London,' he said easily. 'Can't Jimmy drive with us?'

James-Carlo's eyes lit up eagerly.

'I regret it, my lord,' said Vatel with all the authority of an old and trusted servant, very much in charge. 'But the luggage is already at the station.'

But James could not give up. 'I promise I'll have him at Victoria in time to meet you at the boat train.'

But Vatel was not to be shaken. He was a servant, but he was not James's servant. There was a watchful anxiety in the old shrewd eyes, a watchdog who sees his charge threatened.

He knows, thought James. *Of course he knows. He was probably there in London with Erhmann when Netherby died. When it all happened. The scandal and the newspaper headlines. Erhmann had been there and Viola had left England with him immediately afterwards.*

But he could not give up yet.

'The car is running splendidly,' he said, glancing invitingly at the boy. 'It would be fun for us all.'

'Vatel, please? I'm sure Mama would not mind.'

'I am desolated,' Vatel said stonily, 'but without the permission of the Count and Countess, I could not allow such a thing, milord. If you were to have a breakdown – or perhaps an accident, I would hold myself responsible. Besides, we have our train and boat connections to make. At this time of the year, we might be seriously delayed.'

James-Carlo swallowed his disappointment and gave in with considerable tact. He liked Lord Louderdown, and Belly was his best friend, and it would have been tophole to go speeding down to London in the splendid car. But he knew Vatel was right.

'I think I should go now, sir. I have a long journey and if we missed any of the connections my mother would be very anxious. But thank you, anyhow.'

'I'm sorry.' The disappointment was abysmal. It was ridiculous. Irrational. He smiled, a little stiffly. 'Just as you wish. Bellairs will be disappointed. Another time, perhaps.'

'I do hope so, sir. It was very good of you to ask me. Good-bye, old Bellyache.' Jimmy made a feint at Bellairs' stomach and they indulged in a brief, affectionate tussle. 'And good-bye to your little ladyship. I shall know how to address you next time we meet.'

Lucinda had recovered her poise.

'What do you do in Austria at Christmas?' she demanded.

'Go to church. Eat, dance, sing carols. All the village children come to the castle for their presents.'

'You live in a castle?'

'I told your father, a very little castle. But very old. Mama says it's a fairy-tale castle. And of course, if we get good snow, we ski.'

'What's that? Ski?'

'Really, Lucinda,' said Bellairs loftily, 'you are an ignoramus. *Girls!*'

'Well, why should I know about his beastly ski-thing? Doesn't he *hunt*?'

James-Carlo smiled good-temperedly which irritated her even more. As though he thought her a silly little girl, and that he was quite accustomed to dealing with such small fry.

'It's great fun. One day you and Bellyache shall come with me and I'll teach you. This Christmas Papa has promised to take me up into the high snows.' His eyes lit up at the thought. 'It is where only the very good skiers go. There is no one there. Just the shelter huts occasionally. You take food. He says there are miles and miles of glittering snow, everything silent except the wind.'

'It sounds horrible to me,' said Lucinda.

'It sounds great to me,' said Bellairs, his poetic imagination caught by the idea of a white, silent world.

'Does your mother ski?' asked Lord Louderdown unexpectedly.

James-Carlo burst out laughing. 'No fear, sir! She's a pussycat lady. She stays warm at Die Kinderburg before the fire, waiting for us to come home.'

It was so evocative – the silk-clad, lovely woman waiting in the evening light. He could see her, see her waiting there in the warmth for the men to come back from the snows.

'It must take a deal of pluck to go so high.'

'Papa is very brave,' said James-Carlo simply. He turned to Vatel, who was touching his arm. 'I'm coming, Vatel. You are a fuss-pot. Good-bye again, everyone.'

He went with the valet to the waiting taxi, putting his arm affectionately round the thin black-clad figure in the beaver-collared coat. He was already half-a-head taller than the devoted little man.

They watched the taxi drive away and got into their own car in silence, Bellairs thinking what spiffing fun it would have been if Jimmy could have driven back to London with them. Lucinda remembering the mocking, dark-blue eyes and feeling the first stirrings of adolescent desire. James thinking numbly as the road to London wound away before them, 'That's *my* boy. *My boy and Viola's*. Shall I ever have the chance really to know him? Shall I ever see him again?'

At Die Kinderburg the Christmas holidays whirled past in fairy-tale guise with a heavy snowfall and crisp frosty weather. There was sledding and ski-ing parties, snowmen, ice slides, and the big tree to drag in from the woods, erect in the great hall where its green crest touched the carved roof beams, and its decorations glittering in the lights from the chandeliers. James-Carlo, now taller than ever, incredibly lordly and self-assured, organized the children, the von Retz family and Lorenz and Theresa, teaching them to play rugby along the corridors, and fives in the stableyard. His English was losing its foreign precision and had become sprinkled with fascinating new expressions, so that the Austrian children filled the house with shouts of 'Holy mackerel!' 'Rotten cheese, old boy!' 'Stick to it, mugwump!'

Viola and Eugene told the children about the new baby on Christmas Eve, just before the village children came up to receive their presents and sing carols about the crib in the great hall.

'I hope it's a girl,' said Theresa, nestling like a kitten in her father's arms. 'Boys are no good for pretend games. They always have to be throwing something.'

'You won't love it more than you love me, will you?' Lorenz asked Viola anxiously, so that she kissed him with swift compunction, knowing that already she loved the unborn child more. Lorenz was growing too, almost as tall as James-Carlo now, but spindly, a little unco-ordinated and, to his despair, he had to wear spectacles. He wanted so much to be strong, handsome and of martial bearing.

It was after the children had gone upstairs, chattering in excited anticipation for the day ahead, the Christmas feast, their presents, the sleigh ride through the woods to the von Retz house where Lotte was to give a big party to local friends and neighbours, that Eugene told Viola what Vatel had so tentatively reported to him, with shrugging disclaimers and anxious hopes that he was not presuming in informing milord the Count about this matter.

He saw the startled apprehension fill her eyes as she sat in the firelight.

'You mean – that James's son is at the *same* school? But how could that happen? Grant Eckersley had two sons at Marsham. Surely they must have known about this? I mean, Grant knew all about the old days, about me – and James Staffray. If he knew that James's other son was there, how could he have recommended this particular school?' She was pale and angry.

'I telephoned Grant in London after Vatel told me. He was most upset. Apparently the Staffray boy did not start at Marsham until this term. It was a last-minute decision, as it was with Jimmy-C. The school happened to have vacant places, Grant said, and I think he might be right, that the less said the better. Jimmy will only be there a year at most. If we make a fuss, and remove him, it will draw attention to the situation.'

'I don't like it. It could cause a scandal, for them – and for us. I won't have my Jimmy humiliated.' Her beautiful mouth set stubbornly. 'It's not his fault that he's a bastard.'

'Ah, Viola, Viola, my love, the only way to avoid humiliation is to know the truth and not be ashamed. And no one can tell him the whole truth but you. He knows he is illegitimate – but you and his father are the only ones to tell him more.'

When James-Carlo came in to say good night Viola questioned him. How did he feel now about being so far away from home? Had he been lonely? Or unhappy? Would he like to stay in Austria now? If he did not like Marsham, something else could be arranged. Papa could easily see to that.

His face fell, his eyes filled with horror.

'Oh, no, Mama. It's a splendid school. I don't want to come back here.'

She gave a faltering little laugh.

'You are not very flattering, Jimmy-C.'

'Mama, of course I miss you and Papa and everyone. But it's great at school. When I get back I'll make the house team for sure, and we hope Cloisters will win the Inter-School. This next term is *the* rugger term. I mean they sort us out, and I'll know whether I'll get my place or not, and when I go on to a big school, I'll have been playing a whole season. They will want to know if I was any good at Marsham, and also I will have had one term of cricket, which I want to do . . .'

'Right, right, right.' She put her hand across his lips, laughing, feeling like crying because he had already gone from her into this new and masculine world. 'Ah dear, lads and games!

Of course we won't take you away unless you want it.' She wanted to add: 'Keep away from the Staffray boy. Don't be too friendly.' But what would she have said when he asked her why? She did bring the name in, lightly, and was overwhelmed by his enthusiasm and laughter. 'He's a great chap, really, Mama. You'd like him. He'd make you laugh. If a chap doesn't like games and is very clever they call him a swot or a sissy or a master's pet, but not with old Bellyache. He never loses his temper, and he makes them look utter fools. I'd thump them, but he just says something in his drawling sort of voice, and then everyone's laughing at them.'

'A lad to be reckoned with.'

'We both are. United we stand, together we fall. That's our motto.'

After dinner she told Eugene.

'You were right. He's mad about the school. He loves the games, the company of English boys, and everything about it. It's as though he's found his sort of place.' Her eyes lit reminiscently. 'You remember that first time we met and you took me to Frascati's? This is for me, I thought. Music, and fun, and good food, and fine company, and a fine gentleman looking after me. My world. Well, this boy's world is Jimmy's and he loves it. I can't take him away now.'

'We must not anticipate disaster, darling.' He touched her hair, remembering that first evening together and the brash, beautiful eager child she had been. 'The boy is obviously in the right place and, as Grant says, the less said, the easier it will be. After all, he will only be there for this year. The Headmaster writes to say he will certainly pass his public school entrance examination. He tells me young Staffray is down for Rugby, where his father went. We will send Jimmy elsewhere. As far away as possible. These boyish friendships are often very transitory and it will in all probability die a natural death if no fuss is made. If we withdraw him now it will mean explanations and disclosures that I would rather avoid.'

When Jimmy returned to school Viola and Eugene drove him to the station. Viola held his hand. He did not mind in Vienna.

At Marsham he would have been self-conscious at this demonstration of affection before his school fellows. He was learning the British code. But he wished his mother did not look so sad at the approaching parting, it made a lump come to his own throat, for her gaiety was so much part of his love for her. England seemed such a long way away.

'You won't miss me so much, Mama, when this new nipper comes along,' he said, blinking determinedly. 'It will be something for you to fuss over.'

She smiled, controlling her tears. He was her first-born, her handsome, beloved boy – she could not imagine loving any other child so much. Eugene drew her hand through his arm and they stood watching the transcontinental express carry him away.

'He no longer considers himself a nipper,' said Eugene, in dry amusement. 'In his own opinion he is very much a man, and so, for his age, he is. Don't look so sad, *liebchen*, Easter will soon be here and he will be with us again.'

But at Easter Vatel was ill with rheumatism and could not travel, and although James-Carlo insisted that he could travel alone, Eugene would not allow it. Europe was full of troop movements, and trains were being held up and delayed. The Easter holiday, after all, was only four weeks. So James-Carlo conquered his disappointment and it was arranged for him to go to the Eckersleys.

Once again Lord Louderdown motored to Marsham Abbey School to collect his son for the Easter vacation. The countryside was beautiful with an early spring, the new shrill green of beech and hawthorn, and in the coverts about Louderdown the bluebells ran in scented azure streams. It was a new car which he had had custom built, with the gears on the right hand side, so that he could drive it himself. It was a sweetly purring job built by a chap called Rolls. He took his chauffeur mechanic with him and when they had collected Bellairs they were going to make the long trip to Louderdown by road.

As they went through Marsham village he saw the school

building on the hill between the trees, and the bitter-sweet memory of the other boy came back to him. He was both angry and amused at the strength of his own feelings. Feelings were an indulgence he had not allowed himself for many years. Once an avalanche of emotion had swept him away and he had determined that such a thing would not happen again. He had regulated his life to service and convention. If he could no longer be a soldier he could be a good landlord and a patriotic Englishman, a dutiful husband and father, and a devoted son. But now he was like a man obsessed with a woman again, but it was not a woman, it was a boy. His own boy whom he could neither acknowledge nor claim. He hoped that when he arrived at the school James-Carlo would already have departed for Vienna.

Bellairs came anxiously to meet him, his sensitive face with its long clown's mouth full of apprehension in case his request should be refused.

'Something wrong, old man?' asked James kindly.

'Dad, it's awfully hard cheese for Jimmy-C. He can't go home for the hols. He was going to the seaside with the Eckersleys but Mrs Eckersley's father has been taken ill. So he'll have to stay here. Couldn't he come home with us, sir? We'll be no trouble, honestly. It would be really splendid if he could.'

Four weeks? What could it matter? If there were dangers in the situation, he did not want to see them.

As James-Carlo approached he extended a welcoming hand.

'Hallo, Corbett. I hear you're going to be marooned at school for the Easter break?'

'Yes, sir. It's pretty beastly. But Bellairs shouldn't bother you about it. I'll be quite all right here. I've got my bike, and there are lots of things to do really.'

'What's the trouble then?'

'It's two troubles – well, it's three really. I can't go home because poor old Vatel has gone all rheumaticky and Papa won't let me travel alone.'

'Quite right,' said James.

James-Carlo looked as though he disagreed. 'Mrs Eckersley's father has died. I would have gone to Clapham to

Mrs Lyttelton, but she writes to say Mr Lyttelton is very ill, and I must not come for my own sake. She has sent her own little girl to Yorkshire to relatives.'

Mrs Lyttelton? Of *course*. Matthew Lyttelton's funny little wife who had once been such a close friend of Viola's. Matthew ill? He had never been strong, poor fellow.

'Mr Lyttelton was at school with me,' he said. 'Is he seriously ill?'

'I'm afraid it's consumption, sir.'

'Oh lord, poor little Matty.'

James was appalled. He had not seen Matthew Lyttelton for many years, merely keeping in touch in a patronizing generous way. For many reasons. The Reverend Matthew Lyttelton's way of life was not his. They had little in common. And the Lytteltons were a link with Viola and a time of his life which he had tried hard to forget. But, *consumption*! And that poor little woman, his wife. Would she manage? He must get in touch at once and see if there was anything within his power that would help.

'I'll go and see them,' he said. 'Of course it would not be safe for you to go there.' The temptation to take the boy to Louderdown was irresistible. What harm could it do? 'Well, would you like to come back with us, as Bellairs suggested?'

The handsome face lit with delighted gratitude.

'That would be absolutely splendid, sir!'

'Right,' said James briskly. 'I'll speak to the Head.'

The Headmaster put up no opposition. He would have had to keep staff on at school if the boy had stayed. Bags were hurriedly packed and they set off on the long drive along the great north road to Yorkshire. The car behaved perfectly. They reached Louderdown in the early evening, driving up to the massive carved entrance porch with a triumphant tooting of the horn. Lord Louderdown put an arm round James-Carlo's shoulder and led him through the entrance hall into the great hall.

It was panelled in carved oak. It soared up three storeys to a high moulded ceiling, where the gilt on the swathes of entwined plaster foliage and armorial bearings glinted in the light of the chandeliers. There was a huge carved marble chimney piece, where logs burned, and two spoiled house dogs, mastiffs, flopped, ears spread across their massive paws. Portraits of long-dead Staffrays lined the walls. James-Carlo looked round at the painted effigies of his ancestors, unknowing and irreverent.

'Holy smoke!' he said. 'They look a stuffy old lot, Belly. Are they all your ancestors?'

'Yes,' groaned Bellairs, 'every blessed one of them, and what's more, Granny expects me to know all their names and their putrid histories.'

Lucinda came running down the grand staircase, breeched and booted like a boy, her fair hair flying. Too tall for the schoolgirl clothes her mother insisted upon, for the twins would not be twelve until the early autumn, she looked her best in riding clothes. She was already physically maturing, already conscious of unknown urgencies and self conscious about her small, swelling breasts. She stopped in surprise when she saw Jimmy-C standing with her father in the hall. Her colour rose, she half-turned as though to flee, then came down the rest of the way very slowly, heart beating, eyes haughty, very much on her dignity.

As the holiday days flew by she became very much aware of Jimmy's fascination – and not just to herself. Both her father and Bellairs valued him, relaxing and joking in his company. He seemed to draw Bellairs and his father closer together. Even her mother, averse to anything so alien as a boy reared in Vienna with a step-father who was a merchant banker of Jewish descent, was immediately seduced by his frank good looks, his courteous manners, and his ability to ride, or shoot or fish and master all the country pursuits she valued so highly.

Lucinda began to rival Bellairs for Jimmy's company. She was too young and unlearned to understand the confused yearnings of her adolescent body and mind. Conscious of her birth and title she possessed an arrogance that demanded the first and best. She despised the second-rate. During the crowded spring days of 1914 Jimmy came to symbolize everything she wanted from life, and she wove around his image a

101

web of fantasized desires. She fell in love; a child with a child. No one knew it. She did not even know it herself.

There was plenty to do at Louderdown. Lord Louderdown, splendid in uniform, and magnificently mounted, reviewed the local Yeomanry. There were parties. There were the ponies and horses to ride upon, the wonderful motor car which under supervision they were allowed to drive within the grounds, and there was the open moorland on which to wander and climb, and the Louder where the trout basked in the pools and the otters played. But one day Jimmy asked permission to go over to Low Ayrton to see Amy Lyttelton.

Low Ayrton was one of those depressed north country towns from which the mining industry has receded, leaving it grey and bleak and surrounded by slag heaps, neither in the country nor in the town and weighted with lack of industry and employment. The mineral rights had brought affluence to the nineteenth-century Staffrays, but the coal seams had been worked out years ago.

Amy was staying with some cousins of her father, the local teacher and his wife, religious, rather gloomy people, with no children of their own. When the children were shown into the parlour she looked very small and pale, much younger than her ten years. Jimmy remembered her as a gay and rather cheeky little person, given to fits of giggling at his high-flown continental manners. His tender heart was melted by her loneliness. She quite obviously missed her parents and the gentle, loving atmosphere of her own home. He embraced her, scooping her up into his arms like a long-lost puppy, and immediately insisted that they take her out with them for the day.

They had the car, a chauffeur, and he had plenty of money. They would go to Harrogate, they would have lunch, they would go to the cinema, or take a drive, and have tea, and give Amy a real treat.

Lucinda had never known people who lived in a small, terraced house, and to her Amy in her starched pinafore seemed to be what she called a 'village child'. The cousins, over-awed by three young aristocrats, a chauffeur and a Rolls Royce, were

102

very impressed. Lucinda listened stiffly to Jimmy's enthusiastic arrangements. She could not understand why he should exert all his considerable charm to persuade these boring people to let Amy come with them for the day, nor why he should *want* to do so. Bellairs, of course, agreed with Jimmy. The boys always stuck together.

'What on earth do you want to take *her* out for?' she demanded, when Amy was whisked away to change her dress.

'Her mother and my mother are great friends.'

'Good Lord,' drawled Lucinda, 'how very odd!'

'Oh, come off it, Lucy,' said Bellairs, 'you are the most frightful pip when you get all uppitty and titled-ladyish. It's nothing to be proud of, you know. It's nothing to do with you. You might have been born in a Hottentot village and be as black as boot polish.'

'Well, I wasn't!' This reasoning was too subtle for Lucinda.

'Well, I'm the eldest by ten minutes, and I say Jimmy can bring Amy if he wants to, she's a nice little kid.'

They had a splendid day, but Lucinda hated Amy. She could not bear the way the boys made a pet of her. The way Jimmy held her hand, sat her on his knee by the window so that she could see over the hedges as they passed, and before they left Harrogate bought her presents. A big box of chocolates. Postcards to send home to her mother. A little gold bracelet with a coral heart attached. The grave, smiling way he talked to her, not teasing her at all. Lucinda was simmering with fury by the time they had returned Amy to her guardians and driven home.

'Well, did you have a nice day?' her mother asked.

'We had a stupid day!' she stormed. 'The boys would take this silly kid everywhere. Even to the cinema.'

Jimmy looked at her gravely. 'She's very little,' he said, 'and she's away from her people. That's bad enough when you're as old as I am. And her father is very ill, and may not get better. I shall go and see her again before I go back to school, but there's no need for you to come, Lucy.'

Lucinda banged away to her room and wept. His tenderness unnerved her, and she wished, secretly, that he would cherish *her* like that horrible little Amy and hold *her* within the circle of his arms.

Shortly after the boys returned to school Lord Louderdown received a letter from Vienna.

It was courteous but explicit. Eugene wrote that he and his wife both felt that the situation was fraught with danger. Either the children should be told of their relationship, or the friendship should be broken. They could understand that it might be difficult for Lord Louderdown to take on himself such an explanation, and they would respect his feelings. But no more invitations to Louderdown should be extended. Count Erhmann was making sure that, when James-Carlo left Marsham, he would be entered at a different public school from Rugby, where Bellairs would be going. James-Carlo would, in any case, be leaving Marsham at the end of the following summer term. If no frank explanation could be forthcoming it might be better gently to discourage the friendship, and let it die a natural death. James-Carlo's mother had now no objection to his knowing the truth, so the decision to tell him therefore rested entirely with his natural father.

A very urbane, discreet and firm letter, and it sent James Staffray, Earl of Louderdown, into a fine ancestral rage. Damn the man's impertinence! How dared anyone dictate to him whether or not he should see his own son! What possible harm was there in childhood friendship? For God's sake, they *were* only children. For a wild moment he thought of telling Florence the truth, and insisting that the children should be told and that James-Carlo should be acknowledged. But it would not do, and he knew it. He could not tell her. She was a woman who lived within the laws of society; who had a proudly possessive conception of her position as his wife. She would be insulted and horrified. She would neither understand nor forgive him.

But the motto on the Staffray crest was 'What I Have I Hold'. And the thought of allowing this newly-found and beloved boy to drift out of his life for ever was unbearable. Even if he had forfeited his rights to fatherhood when he had let Viola go out of his life to Vienna and a new marriage, the boy was still his one link with a passionate but brief happiness.

He wrote back that he understood completely. Circumstances forbade him to acknowledge James-Carlo—at least until he was older – so he would comply with their wishes. There was no need for the friendship to continue after the summer term had ended. In his heart he knew Eugene Erhmann was right.

But he also knew that somehow and in some way he would not, and could not, let Jimmy go out of his life forever.

It seemed to Viola that Easter was the most beautiful she had known, and the beauty seemed to accentuate her mixed mood of happiness and sadness. Happiness because her relationship with Eugene had reached a new depth of fulfilment; sadness because James-Carlo was not home and the summer holidays were so far away. She was radiant in her new pregnancy. It was a confirmation that she and Eugene had come into a harbour both safe and beautiful. His other two children had been conceived in gratitude and affection, but this new baby, like James-Carlo, had been conceived in love.

They spent the holidays in Die Kinderburg with the two children, and when they returned to Vienna the lilacs in the Michaeler Platz were in full bloom. The threats of war rose and faded, and if Eugene felt they were living on borrowed time he kept his anxieties from Viola.

Her pregnancy gave her an excuse to avoid society and except for visits to friends, particularly Lotte von Retz, she did not go out a great deal. She heard of Prince Friedrich through his sister. No leave was being granted. Training and manoeuvres were intensified. Young Johann Hochburg was also away with the regiment.

'If this goes on,' complained Lotte, 'there won't be an officer left in Vienna to dance with. Friedrich writes to Mama sometimes, and to me, always wanting money. What he finds to spend it upon in Galicia I *don't* know. He seems very bitter about being posted there, although they did make him a Captain. He thinks some influential enemy arranged it. He's always quoting from a book by a man called Otto Weininger, *Geschlect und Charakter*, which I've never heard of, but apparently it says that women and Jews are the cause of all our evils.' Lotte burst out laughing. 'I don't see how Freddi could do without either. If he didn't borrow money from the Jews he couldn't afford his women.'

Viola listened while her kind but feather-brained friend rattled on. She never thought of Friedrich now, except with a shiver of repugnance and gratitude that Eugene had so tactfully removed him from her life.

On the 28th of June that year the Archduke Franz Ferdinand – heir to the throne of Austria and his wife Sophie were murdered in Sarajevo, and the news became headlines all over the world. Bellairs Staffray read it in *The Times*, sitting under an oak tree by the playing fields at Marsham Abbey School. He had been excused games that day because he was not feeling well, having awakened that morning with a severe headache. But as he had no temperature, Matron had allowed him to watch the house match.

He lay languidly in the shade with his back against the big tree watching the play, particularly James-Carlo who was hitting the bowling all over the pitch. Having knocked up a fast twenty-five to the delighted roars of the juniors, he skied one and was caught ignominiously and deservedly and came off grinning at his own discomfiture, dropped down beside Bellairs in the shade, and began to take off his pads.

'Hard cheese,' Bellairs commiserated.

In his whites, bronzed a smooth golden tan, his crisp curly hair bleached by the summer sun, Jimmy was the picture of a schoolboy hero. There was something about him that fascinated the younger boy. A familiarity in his boyish confidence, the authoritative way he turned his head, his charmingly unaffected kindness to less fortunate people. Watching him now he thought suddenly, *He's like my Dad. He really is awfully like Dad*. And the thought made his friend seem even closer.

'My own stupid fault,' said James-Carlo indifferently. 'I was showing off. How's the head, old man?'

'Bloody awful. I do feel darned peculiar. I've got a sore throat now. D'you think I've got a foul and incurable disease?'

'Yes, I should think so. Just in time for the hols. It's probably bubonic plague. Tell your people to let me know when the funeral is.'

Normally they would have indulged in a thumping, rolling scrap, but today Bellairs had not the energy. He picked up *The Times* again but the print hurt his eyes.

'What's all this about that Archduke Whosit in your part of the world? The chap who has been murdered?'

'Where?' James-Carlo took the paper and read the headlines. '*Crummy*! That's absolutely frightful! The Emperor is as old as Methusalah. He might die any minute. I wonder who'll be Emperor now!'

'Did you know him?' It was not an incongruous question. Bellairs belonged to a family familiar with Royalty.

'Who, the Archduke? I didn't. Papa did. Couldn't stand him. Said he was full of the obsessions of the second-rate.'

'Did he, by jove!' Bellairs sat up and opened his heavy eyes, impressed. 'That's a damned perceptive remark. Your father must be a very interesting man, Jimmy.'

'He is,' said James. 'You know when we were learning about Leonardo, and it said he was a *universal* man? Well, that's like Papa. He can do such a lot of things. He can ride, and fence and shoot, he reads like mad, he knows all about pictures and such things, and all about money. That's why he's so rich. I'm not a bit like him, but then, I'm not really his son, as I told you. I'm all right, not a duffer, but not like him. But then neither is Lorenz. He *is* a bit of a duffer, poor old man. I expect Theresa is the cleverest of us all, but it's not much use to a girl, is it?'

Bellairs thought this over.

'I suppose it isn't, though I can't see why not. I wouldn't like to marry a girl who only thought of horses and dogs and shooting things, like our Lucy, for instance.' He could have added 'like my mother' but it would have offended the code. Mothers

107

were beyond criticism. 'You know I'd quite like a brainy wife – someone like Granny who is so interesting.'

'I've never met your grandmother.'

'She's a Bellairs. That's where I got the name from. She always lives in the South of France. Dad's been trying to get her home since there's been so much war talk. But she won't come. She's a very stiff-necked and determined old bird, but she knows all about art and ever so many artists. And she was very beautiful when she was young. I'd like to marry someone like that. Have you ever thought about the sort of person you'd like to marry?'

'Yes. Someone like my mother. All lovely and silky and smoodgy. Papa calls her Queen of All Silky Things. It's from a book.'

'How lovely,' said Bellairs. 'It's a lovely thing to say.' He lay back on the grass. 'I say, I do feel rotten, Jimmy. I think I'm going to be sick.' He got to his feet and to James-Carlo's consternation went behind the oak tree and vomited. He came slowly back wiping his lips, and then suddenly heeled over on the grass. James-Carlo knelt, lifted him against his shoulder, and called to a passing boy to fetch Matron or a master.

Bellairs had not fainted but he was flushed and burning, and before evening Marsham Abbey had its first case of the virulent epidemic of scarlet fever which swept through the school. By the end of the week the boys were going down one by one and the school was in quarantine. James-Carlo took the infection two weeks later, and at the end of term he was recovering but still quarantined and too weak to move. He was one of a whole group of boys detained in the sick bay. The Headmaster wrote to Vienna that he was unfit to travel. Lord Louderdown, arriving to collect the recovered Bellairs, insisted autocratically that he should be allowed to see him. He told the anxious boy not to worry.

'But the newspapers say there will be a war – supposing I couldn't get home?'

The illness had temporarily marred his splendid vitality. The thin pale face and shadowed eyes made him look unusually childish and vulnerable. The budding young buck had been replaced by an anxious boy, not quite fourteen. Louderdown longed to comfort him.

'Don't you worry, young Jimmy, we'll get you home if we can. You just get better.'

James-Carlo looked over the playing fields, silent now and empty. The well boys had gone home. The convalescing lay in the sick bay with him.

He was English, and yet, unlike the other boys, his heart was in Austria with his beloved mother, his respected step-father, his young half-brother and sister. When he heard some of the English boys speak of the arrogant pigs of Germans, he knew what they meant. He thought of Prince Friedrich whom he hated, who represented Austrian military power. He was like the bullying, moustached German Kaiser Wilhelm in the cartoons in *Punch*. But he knew all Austrians were not like that, just as he knew all the English were not effete and idle aristocrats, taking their superiority for granted, as his schoolmates in Vienna had said. The thought made his head ache.

'I wouldn't want to fight the Austrians, sir, but I could never fight the British. I suppose if I had to fight, I would fight for the British.'

James Louderdown laughed. 'Jimmy, you won't have to fight anyone. It may still blow over. In a week you may be travelling across Europe for the summer holidays.'

'I hope so, sir.'

Louderdown had an impulse to stoop and kiss the broad white forehead, but instead he ruffled the boy's fair hair, friendly, fatherly, but detached.

'Stop fretting, Jimmy-C. Be sure we'll take care of you. It hasn't happened yet, and it may not. Within a fortnight you'll probably be home in Vienna with your mother fussing over you.'

Like many Austrians of prestige and power, Eugene helplessly watched his country slide into war. There had been no government since March. The only power was in the hands of the Army and the Emperor and the Army was pressing the frail old man towards open conflict. On the 28th July he capitulated, Austria declared war on Serbia and the first troops crossed the border. In the streets of Vienna people were cheering and acclaiming the Emperor with fervent enthusiasm. Eugene came home grey-faced with fatigue.

'They've gone mad,' he said to Viola. 'The poor old man has signed the death-warrant of the Empire. They think it's *our* war, local, between Serbia and Austria. They don't see it's like a powder trail, one explosion setting off the next. Yesterday the British Navy cancelled all leave.'

'You mean Britain will fight?'

'If Germany goes to war with Russia they cannot avoid it.'

'Eugene, what shall we do about Jimmy?' Viola was terrified. 'What *shall* we do?'

'We must talk about it. I had hoped it would not happen. I had hoped, as a last resort, he would be home with us already, and we could ask him what he felt himself. There may still be time to get him home, although communications are disrupted right across Europe. If you really want him home, I will see what I can do.'

'I want to do what is best. Eugene, help me. You're so wise.'

He shook his head wearily. He had aged during the day.

'It needs more than wisdom, my dearest. It needs a miracle. Jimmy is in England, he is English and his real father, who obviously cares for him, is there. I have resources in England. He will not want. But if war breaks out he will be cut off from us. He has Eckersley, who is a good friend of mine. He has your little friend, Betsy Lyttelton, who is loving and loyal to you. Physically and materially he will be as safe as he would be here, perhaps safer. He *feels* himself to be British. Legally he *is* British. He is a brave boy with charm. People like him. He adores you and will feel the separation, and will want to please you. You are the only one who can decide, Viola.'

She put her hands to her back, arching her spine beneath the weight of the child which was almost due. Her lovely eyes were shadowed with dark rings. She longed for him to take the decision. All her life she had been quick to decide and for the first time she felt utterly helpless.

'Viola, my love, if it was one of the other two, I would make the decision. But he is your boy, not mine.'

Vatel came in, his thin pale face agitated. '*M'sieu le Comte*, Lord Louderdown is on the telephone from London. He says not to delay – he has had permission to use a government line and may not be able to hold it for long.'

'You must answer it, Viola. He too is naturally anxious about the boy.'

She rose, stretched out her hand, said, 'Aye, well, if I must. I must. But come with me, love.'

They went into the library and she lifted the crackling, buzzing receiver to her ear.

'James?' she said. 'This is Viola.'

'Viola?'

James strived to control his emotions as over the years he heard her voice again. Faint, faraway on the other side of Europe against a background of other voices crackling and chattering faintly in the background. The words which rose to his lips were the words he had never spoken to any other woman but her, and which he must not speak now. I love you. I want you. I have never ceased to think about you.

'What is it? Is it my boy? Is he all right?'

'He is much better, and could leave England tomorrow. This is what I want to say. The Embassy staffs have not yet left. I could use my influence and he could travel with them. It is a question of what you want.'

'Eugene and I have talked. We think . . .' her voice broke on tears, 'we think it better for him to stay in England.'

Relief swept over James. It was so deep he felt guilty. Whatever happened in Europe, at least he would have the boy.

'Viola, you are British too. I could arrange for you to come home, if you wished, before the frontiers close. You could come here and bring your children. Then you would all be together.'

'Thank you. But Eugene cannot leave. His duty is to his

country. I am his wife. I would not dream of leaving him.'

'You must do as you wish.'

'I would like you to speak to my husband.'

'Of course.'

The two men had never met, never seen or spoken to each other before. Their only link was the woman whom they both loved.

'Lord Louderdown,' said Eugene, 'perhaps by tomorrow we shall be enemies.'

James Louderdown was startled by the cool, perfect English.

'The circumstances under which I wrote to you recently are now changed. Will you keep an eye on the boy for us? He is very dear to us both. You cannot, perhaps do not wish, to acknowledge him as your son, but he has only the Eckersleys and Mr and Mrs Lyttelton in England. We will write – it will be possible through Switzerland or America. Money for him is no problem. Eckersley will see to that. You will watch over him? He is the centre of Viola's life.'

'Of course.' James's voice was unsteady. 'No harm shall come to him if I can prevent it.'

'Well, good-bye then, Lord Louderdown. It has not yet begun. We can still pray for a miracle. Perhaps I should say *auf wiedersehen*.'

The line went dead with a crackle of static.

Viola was standing by the window, leaning her head against the pane, looking out at the trees in the Belvedere Gardens. The summer all over Europe had been long and hot and the grass was beginning to scorch and the leaves to yellow. The sunlight fell on the amber red cloud of her hair, and her long loose gown of geranium red silk. She turned and came across into his arms like a child seeking comfort and reassurance, which for the first time in their life together he was unable to give her.

In the early hours of the following morning, just as the dawn was beginning to gild the steeples and domes of the city with golden light, her baby was born, a little girl, small and vigorous, squalling and red-faced.

'She's beautiful,' said Viola.

'She's as pink as a boiled shrimp,' said Eugene. 'Shall we call her Shrimp?'

'Shrimp isn't very pretty,' said Theresa in defence of her new sister. 'She's as pretty as Mama's corals.' So they called her Coralie.

The capital was seething with rumours. Everyone who had anyone in the armed forces, and every family had, was frantic for news of them, because all leave had been cancelled. Lotte von Retz called with bouquets and congratulations to see the new baby, for whom she was to stand Godmother, bringing a magnificent French doll made by Jumeau in Paris, with a delicate bisque complexion and huge melting glass eyes.

'Of course she won't be able to play with it for ages,' she said, 'but we won't be able to buy these French dolls if we start fighting the French. It's a pity you're not up, Viola, we might go shopping together. Personally I'm going to buy in as many ribbons and gloves and things as I can while the shops still have them.'

'Lotte,' protested Viola in horrified amusement, 'there is a *war*! People are being *killed*.'

'Oh, yes, well,' said Lotte, 'but people are always being killed in earthquakes and things, and it won't be long. Friedrich says so.'

'You have seen your brother?'

'Yes. He is here for a short leave. He has further promotion – he is a Major now. And he is being transferred to the Serbian front.'

The news from Serbia was not good. Unexpectedly the Serbians were making a fighting stand.

'Freddi says this Serbian thing is only a flash in the pan. He says if anyone else starts we shall be sure to win, with Germany on our side . . . oh, don't look like that, Viola, James-Carlo will be all right. He's too young to be near any fighting, and everyone says it will all be settled and over in a shake.'

Friedrich was only in Vienna for three days and his time was taken up with military affairs. There was a war. Soldiers were needed. Officers were heroes. He had an occupation at last. He stood in Lotte's drawing room, no longer in his elegantly tailored, skin-tight walking-out uniform, but in a workmanlike pike grey, his new Major's insignia on his collar, carrying his jaunty field cap. He was surrounded by adoring girls, by twittering matrons, and elderly retired officers, all hanging on his every word. He was authoritative. Of course there would be war. The damned Russians had been provoking it for years. The border was a hotbed of terrorist camps with dissentients from everywhere in the Empire. Of course the Central Powers would win. The Kaiser and the Emperor were not fools. Germany had a great young military ruler, and Austria had an old and very wise one. They had given the Serbs every chance – now the country was united against these trouble-makers, organized by the Russians and financed by the Jews. He had no evidence whatsoever for his statements. His answer to any positive question was, 'Of course it's common knowledge.' It was popular opinion. Austria was not to blame – so some other power must be.

Lotte and his mother were in tears when he left, and Gottfried pressed a generous gift of money into his hands. Lotte went with him to the front door, and when she kissed him he asked the question he had been determined not to ask.

'Do you see anything of Countess Erhmann now?'

'Why, yes,' Lotte said, not surprised. She knew that dear Freddi was 'sweet on' Viola. It was very pleasant to have a handsome officer trailing his coat for one, and now, she was sure, Viola would forgive him for whatever it was he was supposed to have done. 'She is just up after the new baby. I'm to be Godmother – they are calling her Charlotte Coralie. Why don't you go round and see her?'

She kissed him good-bye and watched his tall, upright figure marching away. She did not think that he might be going to death and danger, Lotte never thought of such unpleasant things until they happened, and then, of course, there was nothing to be done about it.

Friedrich reached the corner of his street on the Schubert Ring and turned suddenly, crossed the road and went in the direction of the Belvedere. His intentions were not clear to himself. He had nursed a vicious hatred of Erhmann during the long, boring months in the dreary, cold, rainy provincial barracks in Galicia, for he had learned that he was responsible for his exile from Vienna. He had nursed imaginary revenge. The knowledge that Viola had had another child by Eugene Erhmann filled him with jealousy; that she was devoted to, and was possessed by, another man was unbearable. The fact that if Eugene was his enemy, the enmity was of his own making, did not cross his mind.

He walked along the railings of the Schwarzenberg Park, looking across the road and as he did, he saw her.

He would have known that walk anywhere, the subtle sway of the slender hips, the fine carriage of her head. She was dressed as always, with impeccable elegance and taste, but unlike most fashionable ladies she was pushing a perambulator, a nursemaid walking by her side; she was bending, smiling, obviously talking a mother's loving nonsense to the baby inside. A little girl, and the boy Lorenz ran ahead. He stopped and watched, his heart racing, and as he did so a Daimler motor car stopped and Erhmann alighted and went up to her, kissing her hand, speaking to the children, a smiling, united, family group, so domestic, so exclusive, so unaware of him. Eugene handed her into the motor, and she wound a long veil round her hat, and they waved to the children and drove off. Friedrich turned on his heel. She was not even aware of his existence. She looked at Erhmann, that damned Jewish banker, as though he were a king.

Four days later Germany declared war on Russia, the following day on France and Belgium, and the might of the German Army rolled across Belgium into France. England declared war on the Central powers. Prince Friedrich Schausenhardt was by then with his regiment.

In the capitals of the great powers people crowded into the streets, waving flags, wild with excitement at this introduction to their own destruction, and it would be five years before Viola saw James-Carlo again.

PART TWO

THE CHILDREN AT
LOUDERDOWN

CHAPTER FIVE

Like everyone else, including the vicar and the congregation, Amy had been impressed by the presence of the Earl of Louderdown at her father's funeral. The tall, soldierly, one-armed man wearing the uniform of a Major, as Commander-in-Chief of the Louderdown Yeomanry, would have been conspicuous anywhere and in the local parish church he created a sensation. Particularly as he was accompanied by James-Carlo – the boy from Austria – the son of her mother's beautiful friend, of whom her father had gently and unhappily disapproved, and who had swept briefly through their lives three years before.

The handsome fair boy was nearly as tall as the Earl himself now, and as they marched down the aisle, shoulder to shoulder, their presence, the Earl's obvious and genuine distress was commented upon. During Matthew's illness Lord Louderdown had visited him regularly, and spared no money in the effort to save his life and to spare Betsy the anxiety of expense.

There was actually a piece in the local paper mentioning that the Earl had been at school with her father.

'The Reverend Matthew Lyttelton,' it said, 'leaves a wife and one daughter. He was a regular churchgoer at the Parish Church, and in spite of his arduous duties as the Editor of the Churchman's Review he often assisted at the services. He will be greatly missed.'

Amy cried when she read this. Her father had been away ill in a sanatorium so long, many local people had forgotten him. But her mother, her dear, brave, simple, ignorant little mother was truly bereft.

After the burial service Lord Louderdown offered Betsy his arm and escorted her from the graveside. She had been speechless with grief, and now she was overwhelmed with embarrassment, and rather incoherently refused to be driven home in his car.

'No, your lordship, really, sir, it's nowt but a step,' she protested. 'The air will do me good. It was nice of folk to send so many flowers, but the scent was a bit over-facing. I'll walk if you won't mind.'

She was even more embarrassed when he insisted upon escorting her across the common to the cottage, matching his soldierly stride to her small steps. She had only prepared a simple tea with ham sandwiches and home-made cakes for the mourners. She thought in dismay of the low ceilings and wondered if they would accommodate his lordship's high and noble head.

Amy and James-Carlo fell in decorously a few paces behind. James-Carlo stooped so that he could see her small, pale face hidden beneath the brim of her unbecoming black beaver hat, and to his surprise found that, in spite of eyes red-rimmed with weeping, she was choked with suppressed laughter.

'Are you all right, little Amy?' he asked in concern.

'Yes, oh, yes, quite all right . . . but they do look funny, don't they? Mother and his lordship.'

James glanced ahead, and saw what she meant. In the spring sunshine the two figures were comically incongruous. Betsy had to stretch up to take Lord Louderdown's arm, and he had to stoop to listen to her words. By his side she looked like a little girl dressed in women's clothes.

'We must look just as funny – the long and the short of it. You're so tiny.' Seeing the pert resentment in her eyes, he added hurriedly; 'Although you *have* grown since I saw you last. At Low Ayrton. You were only a baby then.'

'I was ten,' Amy said furiously.

'Go *on*!' he teased. 'I thought you were about three. I remember when we first met when I came to London and Mother and I came here to lunch. You did nothing but giggle at me – and I gave you a piggy-back.'

'Well,' she conceded, 'then I was a bit younger. And you made me giggle. Always bowing and kissing people's hands and clicking your heels. Thank goodness you've stopped all that.'

'Well, you learn not to in England. They don't do those things. Or they pretend they don't. But I'll tell you something, most ladies really do like it,' he added with a touch of swagger. 'And Bellairs used to say that most chaps would like to do it, but it made them feel fools. That's the difference in being brought up on the continent. You're supposed to let girls know you think they're rippers.'

'I still think it's silly,' said Amy disapprovingly. 'Well, I suppose it's all right with splendid ladies like your mother, but it's a bit daft with people like Mother and me. Is your mother still in Germany?'

'In Austria. I shan't see her again until the war is over.'

'Oh, poor you.'

'I miss her terribly. D'you know sometimes I wake up and I swear I can smell gardenias and hear the rustle of her silk skirts. For a minute I'm certain she's in the room.'

'I expect that's when she's thinking of you. If you think hard enough you can make people think of you. I used to do it with Daddy, when he was at the sanatorium. Then he would write and say he had been thinking of me, and it was always the same time.'

'You're a funny little thing. A bit spooky. Like a little witch. Or a fairy.'

'Do you get letters from your mother?'

'Yes, through America. They write to New York, and Father's brokers send the letters to me. She says she is all right. She's in the country at Die Kinderburg with the kids. There's more food there. They are very short of food in the towns.'

'She was a very beautiful lady.'

The warm colour flushed up beneath his smooth, golden brown skin where there was already the faint fair down of a budding beard.

'There is no one in the whole world like her. I came here today because Lord Louderdown felt my mother would want me to represent her at your father's funeral, as they were such old friends. He met me at Marylebone. He's going to take me to lunch, and then I shall get the train back to school.'

'Do you like school?'

'Yes. I'm at a new school. It's topping. But I miss Bellairs. I wish I could have gone to the same school. I don't see him now.'

'Lord Louderdown is very kind,' Amy said thoughtfully, 'but I don't know why he is so kind to us. I know he went to school with my father and he paid ever so much money to send him to a sanatorium. If it hadn't been for the war he would have sent him to Switzerland. But they weren't really friends, not like your mother and mine. They're *real* friends.'

'Oh, he's just kind to everyone. It's his way. I've been marooned here by the war and he's very kind to me.'

Amy was still puzzled. She knew that, in spite of the affection between them, her father had not really approved of the Earl, nor of James-Carlo's beautiful mother. She supposed he had his reasons – one of those maddening reasons which grown-ups never explain. She did not like puzzles. She liked to know where she stood. They reached the cottage and the chauffeur had driven Lord Louderdown's car round. It had a badge on the windscreen – something, James-Carlo told her, to do with the War Office. The two children crossed the road and stood listening.

'Do the air raids worry you and the little girl, Mrs Lyttelton?' Louderdown was enquiring.

'They're frightening at times. We've had other things to fret about.'

'We saw a Zeppelin come down,' said Amy. 'Everyone cheered, but I thought it was horrid. Men were being burned up.'

Louderdown was touched by her perceptive sensitivity. She was very like Matthew. She had his extraordinarily beautiful clear grey eyes. Poor little Matty's only good feature. Light, silvery grey, the irises ringed in black, the light brown lashes long and silky, giving them a gentle, soft expression. Yet she had something else that neither of her parents possessed. A spunky, North Country directness. She was sharp, although she was such a dainty little thing. The rest of the mourners were approaching.

'A few folk are coming into the house for a bite,' Betsy said.

Reaction was setting in, and she wanted to be alone with her grief. 'People from the church and the office. If you would care to step in, your lordship, you would be welcome.'

He shook his head. 'Thank you, no. I have to get young Jimmy back to school. But you will be hearing from me, and don't forget, if there is any way in which I can help, don't hesitate to let me know. Good day to you. Good-bye, little Amy.'

The two tall, magnificent beings from another world got into the car and were driven away. Betsy's short-sighted eyes were red-rimmed from crying, and she was thin and tired from months of anxiety, numb with loss. But now she smiled to herself, shaking her head, thinking that whatever dear Matthew had thought, she could not go on disapproving of someone as kind and generous as his lordship. And it was all many years ago.

That year the London streets were full of khaki-clad men as the pressure for enlistment increased. The nights were bright with searchlights and noisy with the coughing roar of anti-aircraft guns and occasionally the sickening crump of bombs.

The Zeppelins throbbed through the night skies; making moonlight nights a terror as they followed the silver stream of the Thames up from the coast into the heart of London. Betsy made up a bed in the cellar and at the first howl of the sirens she and Amy would light a candle and go down, huddling together, each stubbornly refusing to let the other see any sign of the fear in their hearts.

Food and fuel were getting very short and a great deal of Betsy's time was taken up joining queues for bread, meat or coals. It was a relief that spring was coming when there would be fresh vegetables and no need of fires. But they were luckier than most. Every month brought a gift of game, poultry and fruit from Louderdown. Money was becoming Betsy's major anxiety. They had been thrifty and Matthew had been insured, but her small capital would not last for ever. Amy was so close to her that Betsy confided in her, forgetting she was no longer a child.

'I think I'll have to find a job, love. Happen I can get back into a shop now all the young ones are in munitions.'

'You hated it. You always told me you did. You can't add up. Besides, you'll get too tired.'

'I'd manage. But who's to do the work and the shopping if I'm out all day? The house is my own, thanks to your Aunt Viola.'

Amy had often heard about the magnificent gift of the freehold of the cottage which Viola had given to her parents when she had left England, which had, in a stroke, brought them from the verge of poverty to simple comfort.

'To tell you the truth,' Betsy faltered, 'I'm scared at having to go out to work again. I'd never have kept my job but for Vi helping me. Some of the customers were right over-facing. All the gentry's not kind like Lord Louderdown.'

Amy threw passionately protective arms about her.

'You shan't do anything you're afraid of. I won't have it. I'll soon be fourteen and then I can leave school and get a job.'

'You'll do nowt o' sort,' said Betsy. 'You're a right bright lass at school, not like me, and I promised your father you should have a real good education. Leave school at fourteen indeed! He'd never rest. He'd haunt me.'

Amy's arms closed tighter. As she grew older she was developing a touchy defensiveness about her little mother. She knew that people considered Mr Lyttelton had married beneath him but that her mother had no resentment about it. That he had been a gentleman while she was only a poor working lass was part of the miracle of their happiness.

'Well, at least we haven't a soldier to worry about,' said Amy. 'Nearly all the girls at school have someone in France.'

'At least there's a *chance* they'll come back. Not like my Matthew. I sometimes envy them. Nay, that's wicked o' me. I sometimes think, Amy, that I talk to you too much about my troubles . . .'

'You must always tell me everything. I'll work very hard at school and one day I'll get a good job and look after you like Father did. But, Mother, why don't you write to Lord Louderdown? He said he'd do anything to help. Why don't you ask and see if he can think of something?'

'Eh, I daren't,' said Betsy.

'Oh, go on! I'll help you with the spelling.'

So on a late April afternoon when Amy came back from school, she saw the big car with the war office badge on the windscreen standing outside the cottage and when she opened the front door, she was at once conscious of an alien masculine presence. The smell of cigars and eau de cologne, the murmur of a deep, authoritative voice. Her mother called from the front parlour.

Lord Louderdown was sitting on the small horsehair sofa and his huge, important and self-assured presence filled the room. James himself felt as though he was in Lilliput. When he stood up his head knocked the ceiling. He had to bend double through each doorway. Old Matty's widow in her black bombazine and the little clear-eyed girl who came in so quietly both seemed as undersized as the house.

Amy saw that her mother's eyes were bright with relief and knew that Lord Louderdown had come in answer to their letter. Betsy drew her to her side.

'Well, love, here's news for you. We're going to live in the country. Up in Yorkshire, near where both your father and I came from. You'll like that, won't you? No more air-raids?'

Lord Louderdown rose, bending apprehensively before his curly, greying head touched the ceiling.

'Well, then, it's all settled. I'm delighted that you can help me, Mrs Lyttelton. I'll get my agent to see about letting this house for you. I'm having Park Cottage refurbished. I would be grateful if you could take over there before the school holidays begin in July.'

'I'll be there, your lordship. And thank you.'

'And good-bye, little Amy.'

'Good-bye, sir.'

Betsy showed him to the door, and when she came back, took off her spectacles, polished them, and put them back again, hugged Amy, and said, 'Eh, love, you were right about him helping us, but I never thought of owt like this.'

'Tell me, tell me! What did he say?'

'He's giving us a house. Up in Yorkshire.'

'But why?'

Betsy glanced uneasily at the questioning eyes. How much *could* she tell Amy? And now, out of Lord Louderdown's masterful presence, she wondered once more if she was doing right.

'I know that poor Matty disapproved very strongly about my affair with Viola, Mrs Lyttelton, and perhaps he was right,' Lord Louderdown had said. 'But we were young and foolish and very much in love.' The handsome bright blue eyes had been appealing, boyish, a little abashed, as though he were asking for her forgiveness and understanding. It made her feel rather splendid that this great man, a peer of the realm, should talk to her like this. She had forgotten Matthew's solemn words about condoning immorality. No woman could resist James Staffray when he was so winningly persuasive. Certainly not Betsy Lyttelton. He outlined his plans.

'God knows when the boy will see his family again, the way this war is developing, but I promised to keep an eye on him and I will. With Eckersley in France, Mrs Eckersley is too distraught to take on the responsibility, therefore he would have to spend the holidays here with you. I must tell you I care deeply about his safety. I have come to love him. I have a boy and girl whom I also love – but Jimmy is different. I suppose – because he is Viola's boy. I cannot acknowledge him publicly, nor tell him that he is my son, or what he has come to mean to me. I suppose Matthew would say that is a just punishment for my sins. But I can have him under my care and safeguard his health while he is in England, during the school holidays. But I, and Viola and her husband, do not want him to continue his friendship with my children. Unless they can be told of the relationship, it would not be right. And circumstances forbid me to tell any of them.'

Tense and daring Betsy said, 'I will look after Mr Jimmy faithfully, your lordship. But I cannot choose his friends. He's been brought up a gentleman, and he would not let me interfere with that, I'll be bound.'

'I don't think there will be any need. The house I have chosen is at least fifteen miles from Louderdown. My children have their own interests when they are at home for the holidays. Since the boys have been to different schools they have not met. I don't want to make any fuss; just to let the schoolboy friendship die a natural death. I will not tell them that he is in Yorkshire.'

'It may not be my place to say so, my lord, but won't they all *have* to know the truth one day?'

His charming smile vanished, and he glared at her presumption, but the short-sighted grey eyes behind the thick-lensed glasses met his bravely, and it was he who turned away first. He shrugged slightly, disclaiming responsibility.

'That is not for me to say. One day, please God, the war will be over, things will return to normal and he will re-join his mother and step-father in Austria. Then, with a continent between us, they may not think it necessary he should ever know. But now, if you would make a small home for him where he can spend the school holidays, I should be grateful. He will be under my care, but not involved with my household, and his mother will be happy to know her oldest friend is caring for him.' He paused. 'Will you help me, Betsy – if you will *allow* me to call you Betsy?'

'Thank you, my lord.' Betsy's cheeks went pink, like a girl's but her glance did not falter. 'And your – and Lady Louderdown? Does she know – about Mr Jimmy?'

This time the imperious glance was intimidating.

'No. And she must not. It would hurt her bitterly. It would do the boy no good and my marriage a great deal of harm. It all happened before I met her, and there is no reason why it should be dragged out again – she does not deserve that of me.' His deep voice softened appealingly, 'Therefore, I ask you, Betsy, to help me in this matter. It will not even be a white lie – our two families will not meet. There should be no reason for them to do so.'

His charming smile melted her prejudices. Her timid and cautious soul caught a glimpse of the arrogant yet endearing youngster who had set Viola on fire eighteen years ago. She told Lord Louderdown that she would be happy and grateful to do as he wished.

James Louderdown was well-satisfied. He had never considered himself a devious man and did not think he was being so now. It was not his fault the way things had fallen out – the war, the boy's isolation, Eckersley joining the army and poor little Matty Lyttelton's tragic death, leaving this sad little woman woefully unprovided for. None of these things were of his doing. Was he therefore to leave his splendid boy to spend every school holiday in that miserable little cottage in Clapham? In danger each night from the German bombers? When he could be safe and comfortable near Louderdown, under his guardianship. He would have to be discreet, of course. But it should not be difficult.

With his usual lordly optimism James thought the arrangement with Mrs Lyttelton would work very well. Park Cottage *was* empty. He was doing the Eckersleys a favour in letting it to keep their marooned young charge out of London. It was fifteen miles from the great house; there was no reason why his wife Florence, or anyone, should suspect the truth about James-Carlo Corbett.

Betsy and Amy went through the turmoil of moving. Gentlemen from a West End agency, more used to dealing with mansions in Knightsbridge than cottages in Clapham, descended upon them, arranging for the cottage to be let furnished, so that when the day came for them to go to Yorkshire they had only to pack their clothes and personal effects. First-class seats were booked on the express. Betsy had never returned to Leeds since she and Viola had left it on that memorable evening in their girlhood when they had gone to London to seek their fortunes and met the Reverend Matthew Lyttelton and James, then still Lord Staffray, on the train. And Betsy had never in her whole life travelled first-class before.

She sat very primly in the corner seat of the well-upholstered carriage, regarding the other occupants with nervous trepidation. Both she and Amy were still in mourning, the girl's pale smooth face and clear grey eyes were watchful and critical beneath the brim of her black hat. Amy did not feel in the least out of place.

She was well aware that her mother's clothes, accent and manner, stamped her as irrevocably working-class and the awareness was already making her a radical. She was scornful of people who made such judgements. She thought her little mother splendidly brave and kind and loving and wished she was not so timid and humble. A condescending gentleman sitting next to her started a conversation with her about the book she was reading. Obviously he thought Betsy was a servant in charge of her. When he said indulgently, 'I suppose your Mummy will be meeting you in Leeds, little lady?' Amy flashed, 'The lady sitting opposite *is* my mother!' so fiercely that he retired abashed behind his newspaper.

She could not help feeling compensated when a uniformed chauffeur met them at Leeds with a hired limousine motor car.

Betsy stared out of the window at the city of her birth, at the shameless bronze nymphs outside the soot-blackened town hall and the busy streets clanging with tram-cars. It seemed smaller than she remembered. They drove past Hardcastle's, the store where she and Viola had once worked, and then north through factories, rows of small houses, affluent suburbs and finally into the country.

Yorkshire was glorious with early summer. The only sign of wartime were the girls in the breeches and green smocks of the Land Army working in the fields. The grey stone villages along the winding Louder were peaceful and very beautiful. The big house could be glimpsed across the parks and fields.

'Is that Louderdown House?' asked Amy.

'Aye. Grand place. Her ladyship has allowed it to be used as a convalescent home for the wounded. There's plenty there now and some'll not work again, never mind fight. Poor beggars.'

Some twenty minutes later they entered a typical greystone Yorkshire village.

'This is Great Louder. The house is beyond. The river's scarcely more than a beck here.'

They passed through the village, over a humped-back bridge

where the small Louderwater chuckled over stones, and turned along a side road.

'Here we are. Yon's the house, missus. You carry on in and I'll bring the bags. No, there's nowt to pay.'

To Betsy the pleasant red brick house was a mansion. There was a letter waiting for her from Lord Louderdown, telling her that James-Carlo would arrive from school in two weeks' time. He knew she would take good care of the boy, and if she needed anything or was in any difficulties she was to write to him at his club in London. Not to the house.

'It's as though Jimmy's a sort of Royalty, isn't it?' said Amy.

'Well, the lad's always been brought up grand.'

'I wonder why Lord Louderdown wants you to write to his club when his house is so near?'

'Well, now they're calling chaps up, there's nowt to do with the territorials and yeomanry. He's working in London at the War Office, so he won't be up in Yorkshire much. Besides, happen he wants to keep the whole thing quiet . . .' She stopped, conscious of Amy's alertly questioning eyes. 'I mean, it's easier for him to deal with things in London. We'd best have a look at the bedrooms.' She looked round at the pleasant sitting-room with its chintz-covered furniture and Turkey carpet. There were daffodils in vases, and tea was laid on a white crocheted cloth. 'I'll have to get used to taking tea in the parlour. Your Dad would have liked that. He always hoped to get a better place for you than the old cottage, although it will always be home to me . . .' and behind her spectacles her big eyes filled with tears.

Two weeks later the station cab drew up delivering James-Carlo and his school trunk at the door. He raced into greet them, affectionately, but beautifully mannered, filling the house with his big, bonny good looks and laughter, running from room to room, approving everything. It seemed to Amy that in truth the prince had come home.

The summer James-Carlo was sixteen and the Staffray twins

130

had their fourteenth birthdays, the war took over everything. The United States declared war, so that there were no more letters from Austria and Jimmy heard no more from home. Grant Eckersley was killed at Ypres. Lord Louderdown was in London at the War Office. Lady Louderdown was fully occupied with her war work up and down the country, raising money for her convalescent home for the local wounded. Everybody was so busy that, during the holidays, the children were forgotten, left to their own devices.

The reunion between Bellairs and Jimmy was rapturous. They both happened to be fishing the Upper Louder, saw each other from opposite banks, and waded across with shouts of joy. The friendship was instantly and closely renewed. The fifteen miles between Park Cottage and Louderdown House meant little to active youngsters with ponies and bicycles. From the beginning they suspected something, some vague, unspecified thing, was amiss.

'I can't understand why Dad did not tell us he had let the cottage to Eckersley for you,' said Bellairs. 'I mean, he knew we were friends at Marsham.'

The four of them were together on the high moors, surrounded by tinkling waterways and the sound of lark song. Lucinda, Amy, Bellairs and Jimmy-C. Their questioning gaze went from one to the other, and it was Jimmy who came up with the explanation.

'I think it's because I'm illegitimate,' he said a little self-consciously.

They all stared at him, surprised, Amy not quite sure what he meant.

'You see I don't know who my father was, but I know he and my mother were not married. This was before she married Papa, Count Erhmann, of course. But a lot of people are very shocked by this – particularly people like yours, Bell, who can go back to William the Conk. They couldn't help our meeting at school, so were nice about it, but they don't want it to go on. That's what *I* think it's all about.'

It was so simple they were all impressed. Lady Louderdown

131

had always rigidly vetted the twins' friends into those who were and those who were not what she called 'possible'.

'You're a bastard!' Bellairs shouted hilariously, and rolled about laughing.

'Well, I know, but I've never felt any different from anyone else,' Jimmy said protestingly.

'Why should you? But we'd better not talk about it – I mean, about seeing each other,' Bellairs said shrewdly. 'We don't want them interfering. We'll have a secret society. No one will know.'

So they clasped hands, swore secrecy and undying allegiance, and met often, well away from their homes. Lady Louderdown did not know. Betsy was unsuspectingly happy that Jimmy and Amy appeared to be good friends and were off out from under her feet every fine day. So long as the children were in to meals, and home before dark, no one made any enquiries – and no one, at all, realized that they were growing up.

They explored the miles of paddock, moorland, lake, crag and fell. They chased the imaginary fantasies of adolescence in a hundred adventures, and James-Carlo was the undisputed leader, already as tall as a man, and overflowing with the untiring vitality of his years. Lucinda quarrelled with him fiercely, provoking him to draw attention to herself, obsessed with the handsome boy. She was jealous of his exuberant affection for the others. The girls at her school raved over matinée idols, gym mistresses and soldier cousins, but Lucinda, with her mother's possessive single-mindedness, thought only of James-Carlo. She wanted to cut the others out, she wanted him to share every minute with her; she longed for him to dismiss Amy and Bellairs, to break the foursome into a passionately devoted companionship with her alone. He never did. He did not even want to. She was not at all his idea of a desirable girl. To him she was an overgrown, bossy schoolgirl. His night dreams were filled with the pretty actresses he had seen on the London stage.

It was always particularly galling to Lucinda that Amy tagged along everywhere with them, and that neither of the boys ever dreamed of leaving her behind. Because she was so small the boys treated her like a mascot or pet. She could not ride, climb and swim like they could, but she had a quick, bright intelligence. She could plan games, get them out of scrapes, make them laugh. James-Carlo, tormented by the turgescences of adolescence, sometimes found Lucinda irritatingly disturbing and demanding, but Amy he simply accepted, a little sister, a monkey, a little clever clown. He protected and coddled her, laughed at her and teased her, carrying her across the rough moors on his back, riding with her up in front on his pony, safe between his arms and strong knees.

Away over the North Sea the two armies were paralysed in a terrible deadlock, the fronts swaying backwards and forwards in offensives which only lost or recaptured a few miles of shell-torn farmland. The barrages killed and maimed, the toll of the dead and wounded rose every day. In Louderdown there was hardly a family not wearing the black armband of bereavement.

All through the summer term of 1917 Amy was longing for the holidays when James-Carlo would be with them again to form their secret and magic company. Life seemed extraordinarily dull without him. But when the longed-for day arrived, and the old station growler clopped up to the gate, it was a different Jimmy who alighted. No big boy rushed up the path to embrace her and her mother, raced round, stealing cake from the pantry, knocking things over, singing rude school songs at the top of an uneven broken voice. Who was this stranger in the smoothly tailored lounge suit and the barbered casque of well-brushed hair who instructed the cabman to bring in his luggage, tipped him with casual graciousness? She had forgotten the sophisticated young cosmopolitan from Vienna who had now suddenly reappeared, armed with the self-confidence of an English public schoolboy.

He took Betsy's thin shoulders in his hands, stooped, for by now she only came up to his shoulder, kissed her tenderly and courteously on each cheek.

'Aunt Betsy! It's good to be back.'

'It's great to see you,' said the startled Betsy, adding helplessly: 'Mr James-Carlo.'

'Please, Aunt Betsy, *Jimmy*, still!' he protested.

'Jimmy. That's a fine new suit you're wearing.'

Jimmy cast an approving squint down his handsome person.

'Well, Lord Louderdown said I needed some clothes, so he introduced me to his tailor, and we ordered several things. I've been going to dances and parties in town.' He turned. 'And little Amy? How are you?'

Her big grey eyes lit derisively.

'None the better for seeing you, you great stuck-up idiot!' she said, and burst out laughing. Jimmy's superiority cracked and he made a grab for her, but she evaded him like a kitten, flying down the path through the kitchen garden, Jimmy in full pursuit, oblivious of the danger of gooseberry thorns to the new, grown-up expensive Savile Row suit.

'Eh, he's nowt but a lad after all,' said Betsy thankfully, but she knew in her heart that it was no longer true. That the days when he would vacillate between childhood and manhood were already numbered.

To Amy and Bellairs, longing for the reunion of the holidays, the change in him was an unwelcome shock, but to Lucinda it was a revelation that set her senses tingling like taut wires. The young man was more exciting than the boy had ever been, but as unattainable as ever. She began to hate her schoolgirl clothes – she wanted to be a woman for him to notice, but the days when the four friends rode out across the moors were limited. The deep pools where the trout lurked were just as tempting, the larks sang and the tributaries of the Loudwater fell over the stone moorland terraces in fringes of crystal, but James-Carlo Corbett had other fish to fry, and there were many days when the disconsolate trio were left without their leader.

Lady Louderdown, run off her feet as the casualty lists lengthened and her convalescent home was stretched to capacity, stopped her pony-trap in the village one day to talk to the local doctor who was standing outside his surgery with a tall, fair young man who was vaguely familiar to her. The doctor came over to her, calling over his shoulder, 'Don't go away, Jimmy. Come here. This is Lady Louderdown. This young fellow, your ladyship, is home from school for the summer, and very rightly he thinks he is big enough and old enough to do some war work. I said I was sure you could do with some help at the convalescent home.'

Recognition came into the rather cold blue eyes, so like Lucinda's.

'Of course I know you. Weren't you at Marsham with Bellairs? You came one Easter, when you could not get home? What is your name?'

'James Corbett, Lady Louderdown.'

'Well, you're certainly a lot bigger and taller than when I saw you last. I hardly recognized you. Do you live here?'

'During the holidays at Great Louder. You see I'm not a kid any longer. I felt I should do something to help during the hols. I'm a sort of nothing, you know, not old enough to join up, and yet big enough to be of some use.'

'Well, I am sure there are many ways in which you could help us. Come up to the house tomorrow, and we'll see.'

'Thank you. I'll be delighted.'

He arrived, cycling the fifteen miles, the next morning. Bellairs ran into him in the outer courtyard.

'Hey, Jimmy-C, what are you doing here?'

Jimmy explained.

'What about the secret society?'

'Oh,' said Jimmy loftily, 'I can't be bothered with that sort of thing now. I've got some real work to do.'

'Oh' said Bellairs, a little hurt. Jimmy's physical maturity was beginning to make him feel a little gauche. 'Well, I suppose so. Better not let on, though, about our meeting in the hols.'

'Do you think I'm daft?' said Jimmy, sounding, although he did not realize it, very like his mother.

Jimmy worked devotedly. He was ashamed to be so big and strong and not be serving England as an Englishman should serve. It seemed to him sometimes that Austria had been a dream. His lovely mother, his step-father and half-brother and sisters, the little castle of Die Kinderburg smiling at its reflection in the Danube . . . all a dream. At first he was torn by the war news. His pleasure at any British success was always

135

undermined with fear that those dear ones at home should be suffering. The stories of food-shortage and hunger, of rioting soldiers swarming back from the Russian front filled him with dismay. He did not let himself think of his mother and family. He only thought of being a soldier, of helping to end the holocaust, of bringing peace back to the world. He hid his feelings under the insouciant gaiety of a young and attractive man. The English school and English friends had left their mark already, curbing his spontaneity. It was bad form to show your feelings. You faced up to things with calm and cheek, like taking six of the best with a grin, and kept the hidden fears buried.

And there were other distractions. Girls. Girls in the village to flirt with. The younger nurses at Louderdown House to take out to dinner on their days off, and afterwards to the theatre or music hall in Leeds, or to a Saturday tea dance, the latest craze. Viola's training gave him a head start, that 'darling Corbett boy' was in great demand. The laughter, the kisses, and sometimes more than kisses, for he was his father's son, kept at bay the stalking fears in his heart.

In September the twins were fifteen, and Lady Louderdown organized a flannel dance, partly as a celebration because she thought it was time they attended a few grown-up occasions, and partly to raise money for the convalescent home.

There would be the usual tombolas, side-shows and fortune-tellers, but the most important feature of the dance was that it would be on the great double terrace of Louderdown in the moonlight. Everyone was praying it would be fine. James-Carlo was going.

He came down into the garden where Betsy was sitting with her mending, and Amy was lying on the grass, her thick smooth hair flopping over a book. She looked up when he appeared and her eyebrows rose sardonically.

Betsy's expression was much more indulgent. She had come to love the boy, tended to spoil and forgive him anything, much to Amy's irritation. Betsy insisted that he was still a boy, therefore not to be expected to be tidy or punctual; that he was a *gentleman* and therefore had the right to be served, and that he was in effect *the master* since it was on account of him that they were able to live in this nice house in the country safe from air-raids and free from many of the wartime shortages. These arguments cut no ice with Amy.

Jimmy was wearing spotless whites, and his school cricket blazer, a silk scarf in his school colours knotted at his throat, his crisp hair was plastered down with brilliantine into the flat and shiny mode. Amy sat up, threw back her hair, and said, 'I suppose you think all the girls will fall in love with you?'

'Why not?' said Jimmy airily. 'It's not much use my doing myself up like a dog's dinner if they don't.'

'Ugh!' said Amy disgustedly. 'You're getting more conceited every minute. You're like the frog in the fable that swelled until it burst.'

He was on her before she could move, picked her up and threw her up in the air just as he had done when he had first met her when, because of her smallness, he had thought her so much younger than her nine years. She was still so light that she made him think of a small bird or a baby rabbit as she tried to wriggle free. He held her firmly, laughing at her helplessness, and her face became scarlet, her muscles tightened with surprising strength, she grabbed at his immaculately brushed head, spitting fury like a tiger kit.

'Put me down! Put me down at once, you great oaf!' she shrieked and, suddenly, he did, looking at her teasingly.

'Is the little kitty cross, then?' he mocked. 'Jimmy's baby girl!'

She lifted her hand and would have hit him if he had not caught her wrist. The colour faded from her cheeks, and the clear eyes stared into his. 'I find you offensive!' she said.

He dropped her hand sharply, his fair cheeks reddening. Amy smoothed her long hair, and angrily twitched the shoulders of her white pinafore into place. It was starched and frilled and Betsy insisted on her wearing it at home. She loathed the garment. Symbol of childhood, symbol of the working-class 'village' girl.

'Now then, that's enough,' Betsy admonished. 'She's getting

137

too big to tease, Jimmy.'

'She's still very small,' Jimmy said uncertainly.

'And, Amy, you shouldn't call him names.'

'I shall damn well call him what I like!'

He laughed, but now Betsy was really cross.

'Bad words!' Teasing and tantrums were one thing, but swearing was another. 'What *would* your father have said?'

'He's not here, worse luck. If he were he would probably take Mr Stuck-up Corbett down a peg or two.' Amy's eyes were frosty with offended dignity. 'When he learns to behave like a gentleman then I will treat him like one.' She marched out of the house.

He ran out after her, his handsome eyes rueful and apologetic, deeply touched by her small defiant anger. When he caught up with her he saw there were tears in her eyes.

'I was a beast. I'm sorry, Tidge. Forgive me?'

'Don't call me by that ridiculous name.'

He bowed, very much the great gentleman, his eyes laughing. 'Will the excellent and beautiful lady ever forgive me? I lay my apologies and my heart at your feet.'

'Oh, shut up!' said Amy but she began to laugh. He put his arm round her and drew her back to the garden.

'Look, we're friends again, Aunt Betsy.' He sat down on the grass beside her. Betsy rose, anxiously fussing, fetched a rug and spread it on the grass.

'Now, you sit on this, Mr Jimmy, and don't mess up those new flannels. They're terrible to get clean if you get grass stains on them.'

He moved obligingly and she went back to her chair, watching him uneasily. She was quite sure he should not go the dance. Undoubtedly the Louderdown children would be there, and they would meet again. But there was no way in which she could prevent his going. Over the months she had by her very nature become his housekeeper, not in any sense his guardian, and, as she had warned his father, he would either ignore or resent any interference. It was, however, getting near to the end of the holidays, and it was just this one occasion. And she had been told he had been working devotedly at the convalescent home. A lad of his age needed some fun occasionally, and there was not a great deal of outlet, here in the country. But the uneasiness would not go.

'It'll be your first real grown-up dance then, Mr Jimmy?'

'Well, sort of,' Jimmy said noncommittally. He was far too sophisticated to tell Betsy and Amy about his forays into the West End with his senior schoolfellows. Parties at Romano's and the Savoy with pretty girls, and visits to the music halls and theatres. 'It sounds as though it's going to be fun for a country hop,' he went on condescendingly. 'There won't be much in the food line, but they're making claret cup, and there will be champagne to drink Lord Staffray's and Lady Lucinda's health. I'm longing to have champagne again.'

'Why can't I go?' Amy asked suddenly.

'Because you're not asked and you're too young,' her mother said flatly. 'I was talking to Mrs Braithwaite who knows the Nanny over at Louderdown. They're too old for a nanny, of course, but she stays on as a maid for Lady Lucinda. She says that Lady Lucinda's got a really lovely new dress from her mother's dressmaker in London – Lucille she's called, but she's really a society person.'

'Oh, why can't I go?' wailed Amy, thumping the grass with her fist. 'I can dance, can't I, Jimmy?'

On wet afternoons he had taught her in the hall to the sound of the thumping pianola. Tangoes, Turkey-trots and fox-trots. The new tunes. *You Made Me Love You, I didn't wanna do it, Mammy.* Dreamy waltzes and hesitations. *My Little Grey Home in the West.* She danced like a sprite, following him perfectly.

'She could come, Aunt Betsy. Why not?'

But with Amy, Betsy had every right to be firm. She did not believe in fraternizing with the gentry. In the old days she would say to Viola that she hoped she knew her place, and Viola would laugh, and say, 'So do I, love. At the top.' But she was not letting Amy get ideas above her station.

'The dance is for ladies and gentlemen,' she said.

'You mean I'm not good enough?' Amy drew her shoulders

139

angrily from James-Carlo's encircling arm. In spite of the plastering of brilliantine, his hair was beginning to curl and crisp again, gilded delectably by the evening light.

'Oh, don't talk rot, Tidge,' he said, and turned all his charm on Betsy. 'It's not an invitation thing, Aunt Betsy, even if it is the twins' birthday. It's for the wounded soldiers. I'll buy Amy a ticket. It's for charity, for the home. The more the merrier. No one will mind.'

'It goes on until after twelve. That is too late for her. Amy must know her place. I said no, and I mean no, Mr James-Carlo.'

When Betsy called him Mr James-Carlo it meant she was as cross as she could manage to be. The last golden rim of the sun went down behind the distant beach copse. Jimmy rose and wheeled his bicycle out of the shed.

'I'd better get over there,' he said. 'It's to start at sunset.' He pulled Amy to her feet. 'Walk with me as far as the bridge, Tidge.'

She walked with him down the road to where the Louder water rushed below a stone bridge. She stood, head bent, hands behind her back, kicking at a stone. He looked down at the pretty rebellious face with its high, thoughtful forehead and wide-set grey eyes.

'What's up, Tidge?'

'*Amy!*'

'Amy, then.'

'Mother thinks I'm not good enough. She thinks of ladies and gentlemen, not of people. She thinks you're born like that and there you stay.'

'You're good enough for anything, and people *can* be. Look at my mother. She was a shop-girl once with your mother.' He could not bear Amy to be distressed. 'When the war is over and I see Mama again, I will ask her to give a ball for you. With my sister. You'll both be old enough then. And I'll ask her to buy you a beautiful dress and she knows all about dresses.' She was listening eagerly, and he spoiled the whole thing by adding: 'You'll have to grow a bit, you know.'

140

'Oh, you beast. I am five feet.'

'You're a pretty little one, and I'm sorry I hurt your feelings, and I promise to try not to call you Tidge any more. Give me a kiss.'

He bent down and she put her arms round his neck and kissed him, innocently and sweetly. He felt curiously relieved. She was his little pet. He did not want her growing up too soon. He pedalled off in the direction of Louderdown, and Amy went back into the house, hands folded behind her back, eyes thoughtful. She took off the hated white pinafore . . . and put it on the table.

'I'm not wearing this thing again,' she said.

The south front of Louderdown House was built on a wide double terrace, two stone-paved shelves, linked by shallow stone steps, descending to the lawns which ran between enormous cedar trees down to the encircling river.

Jimmy left his bicycle under the tree and walked up the lawns towards the house. He saw Bellairs and Lucinda standing on the lower terrace waiting for him.

At fifteen the twins were an attractive couple, both achieving the Staffray height, slender and tall as twin saplings. Bellairs was graceful and diffident, already, like Jimmy, a bit of a dandy, wearing his clothes with an air. But beside Jimmy he looked narrow-shouldered and boyish, languid and scholarly compared with Jimmy's whippy strength and vitality.

Lucinda leaped down the steps with her long, coltish strides, and then, remembering her first grown-up evening dress, halted abruptly, nervously eyeing her idol, awaiting his judgment.

The dress was of very pale pink chiffon, petalled flounces over a satin base and it fluttered about her as she moved. A string of single pearls gleamed round the base of her long, strong throat. She was wearing her first pair of silk stockings, white ones, and her rather large slender feet were clad in satin shoes to match her dress.

Like James-Carlo, Bellairs was wearing a white shirt and

flannels and his school blazer.

'Look at ower Lucy, then,' he crowed, affecting a heavy West Riding accent. 'By gum, lad, but yon lass is a sight for sore eyes.'

But James-Carlo did not laugh. He was amazed. He thought Lucinda looked beautiful. He had never seen her in anything but shapeless schoolgirl garments or riding clothes, and the subtle chiffons of a great dressmaker had transformed her. She was almost like one of those dream-ladies in the musical comedies in London.

'It's really beautiful, Lucinda,' he said. He lifted the sash of fringed satin of a darker, coral pink, feeling it, its softness bringing back surging memories. 'I love nice clothes, and I love girls in nice clothes. My mother always had such lovely clothes. You really do look tophole, Lucy.'

She blushed with pleasure. Her thick waving hair with its golden highlights was very like his own, but allowed to grow to waist length it was thick and unmanageable. It was her despair and her Nanny's pride. Tonight it was tied back with a wide moiré ribbon which matched her dress. She held it up and away from her neck, her raised arms lifting her fine young breasts. She was standing a little above him, looking down in a strange, brilliant, inviting way. He could see her lithe figure, taut beneath the silk and chiffon, the faint shadow of her nipples, and the sweet, lean length of her waist. He wanted to put out his hand and touch her. To feel her through the silk, and was possessed by a sudden tormenting desire.

'Nanny wouldn't let me put it up. Nor would Mummy,' she grumbled. 'They said fifteen is too young. I don't think it matters how old you *are*, only how old you *look*. I hate my hair. The minute I can I am going to have it bobbed like the American girls.'

'It would suit you,' he said.

He had always admired her strength and skill; she could ride as well as he could, climb and run like the wind on her fine, long legs. She could play the foils and shoot straight. The remark that 'Lady Lucinda should have been the boy' was always being heard about the estate. Not that the shy and amusing Bellairs

142

was in the least effeminate . . . he just did not run to the Staffray pattern. But tonight Lucinda was transformed, tonight she was a real girl, and as a girl she was a temptation. Son of his father, it was as natural for Jimmy to be drawn to her as it was for him to breathe. It was midsummer, and the band was tuning up on the lower terrace which was already crowded. Soon the moon would be rising. He put his arms round his two friends and they went up towards the house. But the arm he put round Lucinda's shoulder slipped down until it was pressing against her ribs, just below her breast. She could feel the warm, strong fingers as though they were drawn on the bodice of her beautiful new dress, and he could feel the quickening of her heart.

As they reached the top of the terrace, the band began to play the first dance, and there was the soft, scraping sound of feet moving over the stone terrace in a waltz. Above the beech copse the first pale light of the yet unrisen moon began to yellow the sky.

James Louderdown was standing on the terrace with his wife receiving the local people – he had travelled up from London at her request, because the affair was a money-raising event for her convalescent home. He saw Jimmy coming up the lower terrace between the twins and was startled to see them together, and to see how grown-up they all looked.

When he had met Jimmy in London he had kept the conversation away from his family, and he had been relieved that, apart from a casually polite enquiry, Jimmy had not pressed the subject. He never visited Jimmy at Louderdown, and neither Bellairs nor Lucinda had mentioned him on the rare occasions when their father was there. Now the boys were at different schools they both had new friends. He thought that the friendship had faded, as young friendships so often do, and that the separation had been achieved without painful disclosures or heartache. So he was startled and disturbed to see the three of them together and Lucinda in her pale, fluttering Lucille dress looking so lovely, so feminine for the first time, losing her abrasive boyishness, soft-eyed, malleable, forgetting her pride of position in the tremulous discovery of being a girl.

He turned to Florence. 'Isn't the boy with the children James-Carlo Corbett? He used to be a pal of Bell's at Marsham.' The lie came to him easily – in such situations it was the gentleman's duty not to arouse suspicion or create a contretemps. 'I didn't realize they were still friends?'

'Well, I don't think they are,' Florence said, aside, between greetings. 'How nice to see you. So glad you could make it. Yes, we are lucky, it *is* such a lovely night. 'It seems the Eckersleys took a house for him over at Great Louder, so he would be out of the raids during the holidays. Doctor Shaw brought him to me, because he wanted some war work during the holidays.'

'You mean – he's working *here*, at the home?'

'Yes. Every day. He has been a great help to me. He's been a real stalwart at the hospital. There's nothing he can't turn his hand to. Of course he's dying to be a soldier, like they all are, except Bellairs.'

'They're all too young,' he said harshly.

'Yes, but he has army blood, or so he tells me. I told him perhaps, when he leaves school, you'll help to get him into a good regiment. Jimmy-C!' she called and he came quickly and kissed her hand as he had been taught to as a small boy in Vienna. 'I'm so glad you could come, Jimmy. You know my husband, of course. He brought you here one Easter from Marsham.'

'Yes, indeed,' Jimmy held out his hand to James and his quick, smiling, conniving glance told James he would not mention their meetings in London. James was touched and amused. They were one of a kind, allies, gentlemen, men of the world, respecting each other's code.

'May I dance with Lucinda, Lady Louderdown?'

'Of course, she's obviously dying to. Bellairs, aren't you going to dance?'

Bellairs pulled a comical face and said, 'I suppose I must do my duty for the war effort. I shall go and ask Matron to dance with me.'

He went over and bravely asked the square-set lady with iron grey curls to waltz with him.

James watched Jimmy and Lucinda dancing together. They

were laughing and she was stumbling and clinging to him, because she was not a good dancer and did not know all the new steps as he did.

Perhaps he was worrying unnecessarily. After they went back to school for the autumn term he would tactfully make other arrangements before Christmas. He might have to tell Jimmy the truth, and his heart filled with joy and trepidation at the thought of telling the boy he was his father. Would he be glad? Would he understand?

But tonight he must remember his duty as a host. He went along the row of chairs and invalid carriages, chatting to the wounded men who had been allowed to stay up to watch. He spoke to them with a deep and sympathetic understanding, and they, seeing his empty sleeve, knew it was sincere. Some of those who had recovered were dancing. They would soon be sent back to the hellish deadlock of the Western front. If James had been whole he would have been out there too, helping to get the damned thing over, stop the slaughter and get life back to normal again. As he talked to them he realized more keenly than ever that this war was not like the war he had known – this was a vile, stinking, lice-ridden slough of despair. It was unbearable to think that Jimmy was already seventeen and within a year would be of an age to fight.

His attention was caught by a girl standing alone watching the dancers, particularly Lucinda and Jimmy. He recognized her as a neighbour's daughter. Her father had been a gentleman farmer from a manor a few miles away before he had joined up. There was something distraught about the girl as she stood there, her eyes fixed intensely upon Jimmy. He wondered if she was in love with the boy.

Florence came to his side.

'Not dancing?'

'I can't do this new American stuff – what do they call it? The Turkey Trot.'

'Something out of a barnyard. Lucy seems to be doing quite well with young Corbett. She's getting so tall – and quite a figure already.' She was seized with sudden half-amused anxiety. 'You don't think she's being a bit forward tonight? Perhaps the new dress has gone to her head. I do hope she's not going to be one of those girls who bloom precociously, at least not until the war ends, and I can get her away to a good finishing school. Girls are such a headache until you have them safely married. Especially girls in Lucy's position.'

'Don't worry. She's only a child.'

'Yes.' Florence was doubtful. 'She doesn't look it tonight. That dress was definitely a mistake. She'd have been safer in her muslin, but she went *on* so about it. He is a wonderful-looking boy. He reminds me of you a little, James . . .' She saw his face cloud. 'Is something wrong?'

'No. No, my dear. By the way, who is that girl just along the terrace, I forget her name. She's local, isn't she?'

'Yes. She's the Mansons' daughter, from Great Louder. I was surprised that she came. Both her brother and father have recently been killed.'

'The poor child,' said James compassionately. 'I'll have a word with her.'

He went along the terrace to the girl and said gently, 'Miss Manson, we are so glad you decided to come. Would you care to dance?'

He was taken back by the hostile glare. She brushed her untidy hair from her eyes with a quick, nervous gesture. *She hates me*, thought James. *Poor child. She hates me because I am still alive.*

'No, thank you, Lord Louderdown,' she said in a loud, unnatural voice. 'I do not care to dance. I only came because my Aunt insisted that it might be good for me.' She turned her back on him and walked away.

James's mother, the dowager Countess, sat in her wheelchair, her handsome, withered face broodingly watching the dancers. She had only been persuaded to return to England from her house at Cap Ferrat at the outbreak of war and had shivered through two bleak Yorkshire winters. But tonight it was fine and warm, a perfect summer night, so she had wrapped a shawl of lacy wool about her head and allowed Bellairs to wheel her out to watch the dancing which she viewed with rigid disapproval.

146

Arthritis had crippled and aged her, and the war had taken her away from the continental life she loved. Now she had captured her beloved Bellairs, named after her family, who was so like her.

She looked along the terrace to where James stood speaking to some guests. He had never travelled abroad with her. He could not tell a Botticelli if he saw one. But he was so tall, soldierly, so splendid to look at – even more so now he was in his forties. The women, she supposed, were chasing him as they always had. He was safely married now, thank God. Florence was a nice woman, with the right background, a good hostess and popular with the county. It was enough.

She clutched her grandson's hand until her rings cut into his knuckles. He was still a boy. At his age his father already looked a man – and behaved like one.

'Darling boy,' she said, 'why don't you dance?'

'I'm not awfully good at it, Granny.'

He wished he could dance like Jimmy and that all the girls were crazy about him. Look at Lucinda – looking as though she was swooning with delight. She had a snapshot of Jimmy pasted in her prayer book so that she could look at it in church and had made him swear never to tell anyone.

'Who is that young fellow dancing with your sister?' his grandmother asked peremptorily.

'That's Jimmy-C. My friend. He used to be at Marsham with me.'

'He is extremely handsome.'

'He's jolly nice.'

'Bring him up here and introduce him.'

Bellairs went down the steps to the lower terrace. His grandmother's order had to be instantly obeyed. Even his father gave in to her. He stopped Jimmy and Lucinda as they one-stepped near enough for him to shout above the music.

'I say, Jimmy, Gran wants to meet you.'

'Oh, fudge!' said Lucinda crossly, 'Can't she wait?'

Bellairs' shoulders shot up comically.

'Have you ever known her to? Have a heart, Jimmy, just come

147

and say hallo or something, but don't mention Vienna. She thinks all Germans should be exterminated. As a matter of fact,' he added as they went up the steps, 'she thinks all the people who won't let her have her own way should be exterminated, although she'd have the vapours if she saw a mouse in a trap. It's just her manner. She's a great old bird, really.'

'She'd have twenty-five fits and disinherit you if she heard you call her that,' said Lucinda. She was walking close to Jimmy and their hands were still clasped, hidden in the folds of her dress. She was flushed with happiness and triumph, shedding her childhood like an outgrown cocoon. For the moment her obsessive jealousy slept, she and Jimmy had already left Bellairs and Amy behind in childhood.

She slid her hand out of Jimmy's as they approached her grandmother's chair.

'Gran, this is my friend, Jimmy Corbett,' said Bellairs. 'Jimmy, this is my grandmother, the Dowager Countess.'

Across the terrace James watched the introduction with dismay. His mother regarded the handsome youngster, her still beautiful eyes suspicious and observant in her raddled old face. Would she not instantly see, as he had seen, the likeness in the boy to himself? The likeness to Viola in the slow, smiling lift of the heavy eyelids? But his mother smiled as the boy bent courteously over her hand, and kindled as she could still kindle when a good-looking man flattered her.

'I haven't met you before, young man.'

'That's been the most awful hard luck for me, Countess.'

She laughed, snapped a fan with a glitter of diamond rings, pulled her fine shawl up about her face to hide the wrinkles.

'You are already a wicked flirt, I can see. How old are you, boy?'

'I'm seventeen, ma'am.'

'Oh, ho! Indeed. And what will you be like when you are twenty-seven?'

At last the moon, the colour of a huge, pale orange, slid up over the trees of the home-park, slowing turning silver as it climbed the night sky, drenching the country and the house in

148

stark black shadows and brilliant white light. It was greeted by a splatter of applause. Lord Louderdown stepped forward, raising his hand, and calling for silence.

'Ladies and gentlemen, this is the last dance before supper. As it is so hot, most of you will, I am sure, like to picnic out here on the lawn which for once we can do, in spite of the black-out, having this lovely moonlight to see our food by. After supper, if you will come to the upper terrace, we will cut the birthday cake and drink to the health of the twins – and may you all be here to drink the same toast when they are twenty-one. So take your partners for what, I am told, is called a Ladies Excuse-me Dance. A fox-trot.'

'What in the name of heaven is an Excuse-me Dance?' asked the old Countess.

'Oh, it's great fun, Countess. You all take partners, but if another girl taps your shoulder you have to change partners and dance with her. Or vice-versa, if it's a gentleman's excuse-me. They do it all the time in America – they call it cutting-in. Only the boys do it there, of course.'

'Really?' drawled the Countess. 'And this – *fox*-trot?'

'Oh, that's another American sort of dance.'

'*Extraordinary* customs! Wheel me indoors, Bellairs, darling, and call Castle to get me to bed.'

The maid came and wheeled her to the room on the ground floor which had been made into her bedroom. The young maid was called Castle, as all her maids were, whatever their real names, to save her the trouble of memorizing a new name. 'There's a boy out there, Castle, who reminds me of someone. I can't think who. Corbett, he's called.'

'Yes, milady. I know who you mean.' Castle had been watching the dancing. 'Young Mr Corbett. Well, he certainly was a hit with all the young ladies. Lady Lucinda was really taken with him.'

'Nonsense!' said the old lady. 'I hope Lady Lucinda knows her position better than that. She is still a school-girl.'

'Yes, m'lady.' Castle pulled a mocking little face behind the old woman's back. Lady Lucinda was properly sweet on young

Corbett, as all the staff knew. Always hanging about the hospital since he had come to work there.

Settled in bed, the old lady could not concentrate on her book. The boy's face kept rising before her. There had been something about that endearing smile. When he had bowed over her hand, raising his eyes to meet her glance he had stirred her memory with the slow, sweet lift of the heavily fringed lids. The girl who had nearly wrecked James's life? That girl, who had looked at her so fearlessly, not intimidated by her rank, looked at her with beautiful cool green-gold eyes. But the boy's eyes were blue – blue as James's.

The Countess stirred uneasily and felt nervous palpitations flicker through her breast. It was a memory she endeavoured to suppress over the years. Corbett? Names evaded her nowadays. Faces stayed in her memory. The girl had been married, surely? There had been a disgusting newspaper scandal. She had been suspected of causing the death of her elderly husband and James had wanted, quixotically, to go to her aid. A sordid, horrible business. Netherby – that was the name. She remembered now. But there had been a child. A boy. Supposedly James's son.

The Countess was wide awake now, the humiliating memory very vivid, remembering how she had lost her dignity, wept and railed, and the girl had just stood, listening, and when she had demanded her price for giving up James, had said simply, 'Oh, a high one. Just to know he will be happier without me.'

The Countess reached for her drops. She was imagining things. It was years ago. James was married now with children of his own. Outside she could hear the band faintly in the distance, and the high voices of young people, laughing and talking. She took her drops, and lay back, waiting for sleep to come.

The Excuse-Me Dance was being encored. Jimmy was dancing with one of the pretty young nurses, pacing rhythmically to the new ragtime which all the young people loved.

'Oh, you beautiful doll, you great big beautiful doll . . .' he sang blithely. He felt a tap on his shoulder, and turned, smiling – new girls had been claiming him for a partner every few minutes. A thin girl whom he did not know stood looking at him with a dark, tragic, unsmiling face.

'Good-bye, and thank you so much,' he said to his partner, and put his arm round the girl who had just claimed him. Smiling into her sad eyes, 'It's nearly the end of the tune. Come on. Can you do this thing? It's quite easy. You just sort of walk to the rhythm, and change step . . . I'll show you . . .'

But she made no attempt to dance. She brought her hand from her bag and thrust a large white feather at him.

'How can you laugh,' she cried, 'with all these wounded men around you? Why aren't you in uniform too? You're young and strong! You ought to be fighting for your country. I've been told you're from Austria, so I suppose you want those beastly Huns to win! You are a traitor as well as a coward!'

Her voice, stifled with feeling, did not carry very far. Only three people heard it. Lord Louderdown standing just above on the upper terrace, and Bellairs near him, carrying a tray loaded with sandwiches, sausage rolls, waiting for the dancing to stop. And Lucinda, dancing nearby with a portly hunting man, her eyes yearning over her partner's shoulder at Jimmy's handsome head.

James put his good hand on the balustrade and vaulted over, dropping down beside Jimmy and the Manson girl. He put his arm round the boy's shoulder and said to the hysterical girl, 'You have made a mistake, Miss Manson. Jimmy is as British as you and me. And he is only seventeen yet, and has another whole year at school.'

'Oh,' she cried, and began to weep. 'I'm sorry. I thought you were so much older.'

'It doesn't matter in the least,' said Jimmy. He was white to the lips and stiff with humiliation.

'Oh, I've made a fool of myself. I'm sorry . . .' She fled away down the terrace.

'Florence,' James said to his wife – she was standing on the upper terrace – 'send someone after that poor girl. One of the

151

nurses. She is in great distress.' He patted Jimmy's shoulder, 'Now, Jimmy-C, don't take on so. It's only because you look three years older than your age.'

'I can't go around in shorts because of that,' Jimmy said furiously. 'It has happened before.'

James's heart bled for him. At the same age he had been looking forward to Sandhurst. He knew just how he felt.

'The poor girl has recently lost both her father and her brother in France.'

'I'm sorry – but that isn't my fault.'

'You'll have to carry your birth certificate with you, framed on your chest,' said Bellairs coming down with his tray. 'I say, I've got us some eats. Let's take them down to the lawn.'

Jimmy relaxed, and James released him with a friendly pat.

'That's better. Now cut along and get your supper.'

Lucinda joined them, and the three of them went across the terrace and down to the lawn.

They sat on a bank before the black shadows of the great cedars. In the moonlight the grass was grey, the Loudwater a glittering snake, the mere a sheet of silver. They all felt a little heady from the champagne which Bellairs had appropriated.

'Can you keep a secret?' asked Jimmy.

They looked at him scornfully, but he insisted. 'Swear!'

'By yonder blessed moon,' said Bellairs, 'of course we won't tell. Don't be a solemn idiot, Jimmy-C.'

'I've decided. I'm going to enlist.'

'Jimmy!' they both exclaimed, Bellairs horrified, Lucinda filled with pride and exultation. This was how a hero should behave. She could have killed that crazy Manson girl.

'I think it's splendid!' she said.

'I think you're off your crumpet!' said Bellairs. 'What good will it do anyone if you get yourself killed? The whole thing sickens me. All those soldiers shooting each other's heads off, and the front hasn't changed more than a few miles. That poor Manson girl, going nuts with grief. It's just wholesale slaughter.'

'*Bellairs*! That's defeatist talk,' said Lucinda fiercely. 'It's

152

cowardly. All Englishmen should be proud to give their lives for their country.'

'But not damn well throw them away,' he answered, 'and that's what Jimmy would be doing.'

'That stupid girl should have given *you* a white feather.'

'She wasn't stupid,' said Jimmy seriously, 'she just did not think. But I think I ought to go. It has happened to me before, you know. I *look* army age. If I'm fit enough, and big enough, I *ought* to go. But I can't if you can't keep a secret.'

'I'm damn well not going to keep it,' Bellairs said flatly.

'I will, I will, darling Jimmy,' breathed Lucinda adoringly. 'I won't breathe a word. I shall be so proud of you.'

'Well, you can both shut up, because, if I go, I shan't tell either of you now. You're both still kids. I shall just disappear one day.'

He was very sincere. He felt big and old enough to fight. He had been training arduously in his OTC. He felt an Englishman in every fibre of his being. Besides, he wanted to end the war and find his mother again.

Bellairs collected the plates and glasses, put them on the tray, and rose. 'I'll take these back. But I think you're an idiot, Jimmy.'

Lucinda thrust her hand into Jimmy's as they rose, and drew him under the black shadows of the huge cedar tree. Her mind was ablaze with glory. Her young body alight with a desire she did not understand. Her imagination aflame.

'You won't give up, will you, Jimmy? At school all the senior girls have heroes they write to. You'll be mine. The finest of the lot. I do love you, Jimmy.'

She put her arms round his neck, pressed against him. He was not inexperienced – there had been the parties in London with schoolfellows and theatre girls, but he had never looked upon Lucinda as anything but a schoolgirl before. His arms closed round her automatically and his lips took hers with a practised competence that drove her crazy. She responded with a passion that surprised and aroused him unbearably.

Bellairs' voice calling from the terrace told them to hurry.

153

The cake was going to be cut. Toasts to be drunk. They drew apart, Lucinda's senses reeling, Jimmy struggling to regain his self-control.

'Lucy, darling Lucy, we mustn't do this.'

'Why not? Why not? If we love each other?'

He held her away from him, trying to make his voice light, to laugh, to subdue the hard urgency of his desire.

'Lucy, you're only a kid.'

'I'm not, I'm not. I love you. I love you most dreadfully. We can be engaged. We are engaged now, aren't we?'

'You're too young to be engaged.'

'I am *not*! Practically all the girls at school are secretly engaged. I shall keep it a secret. I shall write to you and send you parcels when you're at the front, when you're my own brave soldier boy, fighting for England. I shall be so proud of you. A ring, give me your ring – I ought to have a ring.'

She seized his hand and drew the small gold signet ring from his little finger. She held his hand against the full curve of her breast, then against her lips. 'Can I have this, Jimmy, to keep until you buy me a real engagement ring? I won't let anyone see it. I promise.'

He held her away when she would have thrown herself into his arms again, and ruffled her hair, much as he would have Amy's, ashamed of himself. He had been as sexually aroused as though she were a grown woman. For a moment she had driven him wild. She was only a kid for all her height and full young breasts. She was the sister of his best friend. A lady. Sacrosanct.

'Oh Lucy, don't be so serious. We've years to be engaged. And your father didn't even want us to be friends – remember?' This time he managed a real laugh. 'On account of my being a bastard, like Belly said. Come on, we must go. It's your birthday. They're going to drink your health. Bell's calling us.'

But he let her take the ring, and she thrust it on to the third finger of her right hand, feeling she had committed herself to him for ever.

154

They came out from the dark shadow under the cedars and ran up the lawn to the terraces, and as she reached the top terrace, wild-eyed and very beautiful, Bellairs took her hand and led her forward. Her father raised his glass and proposed their health.

Jimmy did not find it difficult to enlist. He gave his age as eighteen and his occupation as a student. The need for recruits was so urgent that no particular questions were asked. He was summoned to Catterick, and early one morning he packed a haversack and caught a train to York. A lad brought Betsy a letter in the early evening. For a moment she could not understand, and when she did, panic overwhelmed her. She had not expected anything like this. Jimmy was Viola's boy, but he was the Earl's boy too, and he was under army age, and had another year at school. Someone had to advise her. She knew Lord Louderdown was still at the big house, so she left Amy at Park Cottage, hired a trap in the village and set off to Louderdown. James was dining with the family before leaving for London the following day when the butler told him a Mrs Lyttelton from Great Louder wanted to speak to him.

Florence raised her brows. 'Who on earth is she? Did you tell her we were dining?'

'Yes, my lady, but she is in quite a state. It seems that young Mr Corbett, who works for you, has run off and enlisted.'

James shot to his feet and instantly left the room. Florence was puzzled, slightly affronted. Bellairs and Lucinda glanced at each other apprehensively. The old Countess leaned back in her chair, pressing her hand to her heart. Presently James came back. He seemed to have aged in the few minutes he had been out of the room.

'The damned young fool!' he said. 'He sent a note from the station. He didn't say where he was going, but my guess is Catterick. Most of the chaps drafted from the village go there first.'

'Well, there's not much we can do about it, is there?' said Florence, and suddenly realized that it was not just a matter of a boy running off to the war. This boy meant something special to James.

'He told Lucy and me at the flannel dance,' said Bellairs. He was a little white. 'He was sick of people taking him for army age. But I thought he'd given up the idea.'

'I didn't. I knew he'd go. He's a hero!' said Lucinda. Her eyes blazed with love and pride. Her fingers groped through the silk of her dress to feel the hidden ring hanging on a silk ribbon between her breasts. She was astounded when her father turned on her in fury.

'You are both bigger fools than Jimmy is. Why the hell didn't you tell me then? I could have talked him out of it. With things as they are now, the boy could be drafted to France within a few months.'

'There is no need to swear, James,' Florence said. She glanced round, grateful that the only servant present was Bradman, an old and trusted retainer of her mother-in-law's. The old Countess was deadly white, shrunken in her armchair, her eyes staring out beneath her white lace shawl with horrified disbelief. James seemed not to notice her distress.

He had recovered his composure, but he did not return to the table. 'I am going into the study to telephone. Colonel Tallis is the CO at Catterick. He was with me on the Modder. He'll let me know if the boy turns up there.' He went from the room. Florence, stony-faced, motioned for Bradman to remove the plates and bring the desert.

'Such a fuss over a silly boy. He'll be back at the end of the week, I don't doubt.'

'He won't. He won't. He's too brave. He's the bravest, most wonderful boy in the whole world. I love him!' cried Lucinda.

'Don't be a goose,' her mother said coldly.

There was a sharp, clattering sound as the old Countess fell forward, her arm sliding across the table, sending china and cutlery skating across the polished surface. Bradman rushed to her side, lifting her back into her chair. Florence rose in alarm.

'Mama. Mama. What is it?'

The old lady opened her eyes – they seemed to glare out of

dark caverns in her white face. She clutched Florence's wrist.

'Mama, let me get you some brandy. Bradman, go and get Castle.'

'No.' With an effort the old lady straightened herself. Bradman, devoted, nearly as old as herself, hovered nearby, desperately anxious. 'No. Not Castle. Bradman, go and get my chair. Florence, accompany me to my room. I must speak with you. No one else.'

'Yes, Mama. Children, finish your dinner. If Daddy returns tell him Grandmama is not well and I have gone with her to her room.'

'No!' The old Countess cried. The twins were struck silent by her awful gaze. 'Tell him I have gone to bed and will not see anyone else tonight.'

Long distance calls in wartime were difficult, even for the Earl of Louderdown, and it took some time for James to get through and locate Colonel Tallis, who said he would ring back if the boy had arrived at the camp.

The library door opened and Florence came in, her blue taffeta gown rustling stiffly as she crossed the room. One look at her face told him that she knew. He rose and went towards her, but she made a quick, evasive gesture. Her eyes burned with condemnation.

'I have been talking to your mother. She has been telling me the reason for this scene – young Corbett's mother. Your ex-mistress. The Netherby woman.'

'Countess Erhmann,' he said stiffly.

'Countess or not, she was a common shopgirl and he is your son!'

His smile was ironic. Experience should have warned her, but it did not. James might be sorry, but he was never ashamed.

'A most *uncommon* shopgirl, I assure you, my dear. You must have been aware of the matter before we married.'

'I had heard there had been a scandal. My mother made light of it. Most men have had these trivial affairs.'

'Your mother no doubt had her reasons. Perhaps she should have been more explicit. It was not a trivial affair with Viola Corbett. She must have known about it, as all London did.'

Florence would not have listened at the time, she had been so mad to marry James Louderdown. If her mother had told her he was the devil from hell, she would not have listened. But now, being told after all these years, that the boy was his, the boy whom she had thought so charming, been so grateful for his help, the thought drove her to fury.

'I suppose she was good-looking as well as loose – such women always are. Did she send him here? Would this Count Erhmann no longer support her bastard?'

James shook his head.

'No. The boy is legally English and wished to be educated in England. Because of the war, he could not get back to them. He is my boy. I was responsible for his safety. I gave my word to her.'

'You have seen her?'

'No. It was over the telephone. The day before the frontiers closed.'

He unlocked his small private safe and took out an enlarged snapshot, already yellowing with age, of a young girl sitting in a hammock beneath summer trees. She was wearing a long gown, like a kimono, loose, silken, flowing over her splendid, uncorseted body. One bare, exquisite foot was pressed into the grass as though she had just arrested the swinging hammock to have the photograph taken. The girl was not just beautiful. She was voluptuous, endowed with a sweet, sensuous grace. The eyes that smiled out of the picture were the eyes of the handsome Corbett boy. Florence threw it down with a gesture of disgust.

'Was this taken in your love nest?'

'It was taken at a house we rented at Aldershot before I left for South Africa. I carried it with me during all those days before I was wounded at the Modder River before Kimberley. Afterwards – after we parted, it was all I had of her. I did not know she was pregnant when I left England. She kept it from me. I was very ill after I lost my arm. My parents separated us. When

I found her again she had married the man Netherby, in order to support the boy. Netherby died – suddenly, and she left England and married Eugene Erhmann. Neither of us expected this to happen. I am deeply sorry, Florence. I tried to keep it from you.'

He wished that she would fly into one of her jealous rages as she did at his rare and random infidelities. But she sat like a stone and he could not touch her.

'Now I know what it is,' she cried. 'Why you never loved me. Why you could not bring yourself to love me, or even try to pretend.'

'Florence, I have always cared for you.'

'Cared? A fine word. The word for a racehorse, not for your wife.' Her flash of fury reminded him of the passionate girl who had pursued him with such single-minded obsession sixteen years ago. Embarrassing him, amusing and intriguing him, so that in the end he had capitulated. 'When you made love to me it was as though you were being unfaithful to her. Never once since our marriage have you stayed with me until morning. I have never once awakened by your side. You had always to leave me as though I was the whore and this slut of yours your wife.'

'Florence, it was a long time ago.' His lordship was slightly irritated. 'You have known about other women, and forgiven me. Are you not building it all into a tragedy?'

'This is different. They *were* trivialities. Like I am to you. Like my children are compared with this bastard you have brought into our lives.' Her anger suddenly burst its bounds. She sprang out of her chair, banging the library table with her fists, banging the photograph as though she was killing something. 'How *could* you bring him here, so near your home? How *could* you permit our children to make a friend of him? Lucy already has a schoolgirl's infatuation for him. Do you want to involve her in incest? Because that is what it would be. He is her half-brother. It is disgusting that she should flirt with him in her ignorance.'

James's face was shadowed. 'You are right, and I was terribly wrong. I thought them all still children. I thought Park Cottage was a safe distance away. I thought the friendship between Bell and Jimmy was over once they went to different schools. They did not speak of each other any more. But, Florence, James Carlo is still my son and I love him, and I loved his mother. He is a splendid boy, and when I arranged for him to have Park Cottage, I only thought of his safety.'

'But *not* of ours! Not that our children would be contaminated by his presence. Do they mean nothing to you?'

'Of course,' he said painfully. But she could see that his regret was for her pain and humiliation, for the children's involvement in a dangerous situation. Not for the past. That if he could have obliterated it he would not, that it was still too precious, like his handsome, bastard son. 'The children will now have to be told the truth, Florence. It is the only way.'

'No. I will not tell them. Nor allow you to. I cannot tell such a thing to a fifteen-year-old. I have never spoken of such things to Lucinda.'

'For heaven's sake! It might be better if you had. To whom else can the child speak if not to her mother?'

'How can I tell her her father loved a whore and that her first girlish love is the son of that affair? Her own half-brother. It would humiliate and shock her. You must be mad to suggest that she should be told. It must be stopped and broken up at once. No word must get out to anyone. What a fine scandal it would make for society to gossip about! Children talk, they confide to schoolfriends, even to servants. How would I feel, with people, your generation of our friends, being sorry for me? Nothing must be said. This boy must never return here, and never see the children again. What reason you give him or them is nothing to me. It is your fault, you brought him into our lives, you must get him out of them again.'

'I will see to it.'

'And – when he has gone, if we are to continue to share a married life, I must ask you never to see or speak with him again.'

James picked up the photograph on the desk and returned it to the safe. She watched him, fumbling slightly with the keys because of his single hand. She saw the unbending masculine arrogance of his breed that nothing could break, except love, a love

160

that she now knew had never been and never could be for her. She twisted her hands together tightly, afraid that she might cry out with pain and the utter sense of loss. She wanted to hurt him, to break him, to bring him down. She wanted to destroy the unknown woman in Vienna, destroy her and her boy and their memory for ever.

'I certainly cannot promise you that, Florence,' he said quietly. 'Your position as my wife will never be questioned. Our personal life can continue, if you wish it to do so.'

'You mean by that, I suppose, that if you need a woman in bed I will do as well as any.'

The barb sank deep, because it was true. True, but unfair.

'Florence, you know I would never allow your position as my wife to be damaged in any way, and you know I care for you. I give you my word that, if it is in my power, James-Carlo will never cross your path or the children's again. Not if I can possibly prevent it. I will tell him the truth and I know he will understand and respect my wishes. If you will not be honest with our children, nor permit me to be, the consequences are on your head. When the war is over, Jimmy will return to his mother and step-father in Vienna. But until then, so long as he is under age, I must be a surrogate guardian in view of poor Eckersley's death. I promised his mother – I cannot break my promise.'

'A promise to her is sacred? My feelings mean nothing. Well, I hope you can't get him out of the Army. I hope he is drafted to the front and the Huns he was brought up among kill him. I hope he never returns – either to you or to his mother!'

'You are hysterical,' he said coldly. 'You do not know what you are saying. You had better go to your room until you have recovered your senses.' The telephone rang, and he lifted the receiver. 'Yes, Louderdown speaking. Colonel Tallis? Boy? Jimmy arrived at Catterick early this evening? Thank you. I will be there tomorrow to see you.'

When he put down the receiver Florence was no longer in the room.

CHAPTER SIX

James-Carlo had only been a soldier for twenty-four hours when Lord Louderdown arrived at Catterick. Together with a mixed group of lads, nervous and raw, defensively making jokes, and a sprinkling of unhappy older men forced out of the protection of their reserved occupations, he was kitted out and assigned a bed in a long corrugated iron shed, smelling strongly of disinfectant and damp khaki. The big push of 1917 had ended in stalemate, and there were rumours that a huge new German offensive was being mounted. Every man the Army could get was needed. There were few eager heroes these days. The appalling casualty lists spoke for themselves.

Jimmy had given Betsy Lyttelton as his next of kin, and Park Cottage as his address. He felt that Count and Countess Eugene Erhmann, Prinz Eugenstrasse, Vienna, was an unlikely address for a British Tommy.

He experienced his first hours of square bashing, embarrassingly conspicuous as he smartly obeyed the commands, his OTC training standing him in good stead. He was in the mess hall eating lead-coloured bread and margarine with plum and apple jam washed down by mugs of hot strong tea, and getting to know the fellows in his unit, when an orderly came in and spoke to the sergeant who immediately bellowed his name across the trestle tables. Unperturbed, Jimmy marched smartly across.

'Corbett? You're wanted at HQ.' The sergeant eyed him curiously, noting his height and good looks and his well-bred public school voice. The type of boy who usually went straight from school to OTC training units. 'Run off from school to be a soldier, sonny boy?'

Jimmy grinned, not in the least intimidated.

'Something like that, Sergeant.'

'Gawstrewth, there's one born every minute. Right, follow the orderly. Quick march.'

Jimmy guessed that Lord Louderdown was behind the summons. He should have enlisted in another county to cover his tracks. Betsy would have gone straight to the big house, and it would not have been difficult for the Earl to trace him. But the CO saw him alone. The carefree young subaltern, Boy Tallis, who had served under James Staffray before Kimberley, was now a prematurely aged man of thirty-eight. Twelve months on the Somme and a bad wound had sent him home and left their mark. He was now a Colonel. Jimmy came smartly to attention and saluted.

'At ease. I understand you're under age, Corbett?'

'Yes, sir. I wanted to get in, sir.'

'Do your people know about it?'

'Oh yes, sir. I left a note for my foster mother, Mrs Lyttelton.'

'Do you want to get out?'

'No, sir.'

'I have a request from the Earl of Louderdown to arrange for your discharge. What have you to say about that?'

'With respect, sir, Lord Louderdown is no relation of mine and has no legal rights over me whatsoever.'

'Can you explain his request, then?'

'Yes, sir. Mr Eckersley, a business friend of my step-father, was my guardian while I was being educated in England. Mr Eckersley was killed in France, so Lord Louderdown kindly agreed to look after me while I was still at school. Just before the outbreak of war he telephoned my mother and told her that he would do this. There was scarlet fever at school and I could not be sent back to Vienna. He was very kind to me. But, with respect, sir, I'm not really at school, am I? I'm in the Army now.'

Tallis managed not to smile at the endearing impudence. The boy had all Louderdown's charm. It was written all over him.

'And your family is still in Vienna? Your father is Austrian? And how about you?'

'My step-father is Count Eugene Erhmann. I am a British subject, born in Clapham. My mother is an Englishwoman born in Yorkshire.'

'I see.' Tallis permitted himself the ghost of a twinkle. He had known James Staffray and Viola back in 1899 when their love affair had scandalized London. Viola Corbett – Duchess. He had been one of her entourage of adoring young officers. He wondered how much the boy knew about all that. Nothing, he should imagine. But he was the image of Staffray – and something of his mother too. What a handsome couple they had been! A couple of mad beauties setting the town alight. All the chaps wild about her, all the women pretending to be shocked and dying of envy. Staffray would certainly have been asked to resign his commission if the war in South Africa had not broken out. Two years later he had married and everyone thought that had been the end of the affair. But now, here was this handsome lad trying to get himself into the Army at seventeen, and lying like a good 'un to do so. Every inch a gentleman and first-class officer material, which, God knows, was thin enough on the ground these days. Remembering the mud-drowned hell of Flanders he had to discourage the boy.

'It's no picnic out there, Corbett. If you choose to go back and work out your school time and come back when you are eighteen I shall think no worse of you.'

'Thank you, sir. I quite understand. I've been helping in a convalescent home and talking to wounded men. That's what made me so keen. Help to get it all over.'

As though, Tallis thought bitterly, this beautiful young life would make a pennyworth of difference. One more number on a casualty list. But they were taking anyone these days.

'Well,' he said briskly, 'we need every man we can get. It's up to you. Have you had OTC training?'

'Yes, sir. Three years, sir. At school.'

'Right. If you apply for a commission I shall see it goes to the right quarters when the time comes.'

'It won't keep me out of France, sir?'

'Probably get you out there a lot quicker,' said Tallis dryly. 'I'm giving you a pass for this evening. Lord Louderdown is staying at The Old Bell. I think you should see him and explain the position yourself. He is an old friend of mine and I don't want him to think I have ignored his request. Give him my compliments. All right. Dismiss.'

Jimmy saluted, turned smartly and marched out, collected his pass, set his newly acquired service cap at an angle and went into the town. He felt very grown-up and self-assured. The ill-fitting uniform was his certificate of manhood. No one could question his age now. He presented himself at The Old Bell and an elderly hall porter barred his way.

'No other ranks here, sonny. Try The Crown down the road.'

For a moment Jimmy was furious, then he grinned.

'I've an appointment with Lord Louderdown.'

The man's attitude changed immediately.

'Right, sir. His lordship is in the writing room. I'll show you.'

There was a glazed partition between the corridor and the writing room and James was sitting in a lounge chair before the fire, the only occupant of the room. Sitting there alone, there was an air of dejection about him which startled Jimmy, to whom he had always been a splendid figure of affable patronage and authority.

'It's all right,' he said to the porter. 'He's expecting me. I'll announce myself.' He tapped on the glass and James looked up, and his unguarded face was filled with love, pride and a terrible anxiety. They stared, blue eyes into blue eyes, for a long moment, and in that moment Jimmy guessed the truth. Chaotic thoughts flooded through his mind turning his world upside down. *This is my father. He is exactly as my mother described him to me. Tall, soldierly, handsome, a man of great family.* How could he have been so blind? Why else should the Earl have singled him out for such indulgent kindness? He was his father. And Bell – Bell was his half-brother, like Lorenz back in Vienna, and Lucinda was his half-sister, like Theresa and the new baby, Coralie, whom he had never seen.

Like thunder following a lightning flash he remembered Lucinda in his arms, her urgent young body pressed against him, her eyes brilliant in the moonlight. The colour flared into his cheeks. He had been more than a little in love with her that night. He had dreamed, as all departing soldiers dream, of a girl left behind, waiting for his return. There were other girls. A pretty young actress in London. One of the nurses at Louderdown. But that night Lucinda had taken precedence in his heart. He had been worried because she was so young, and he ought perhaps to have been more discreet, but now it was horrible. Something shameful and forbidden. He pulled off his cap and went in to meet Louderdown, who rose and stretched out his hand.

'Jimmy. We have been in no end of a stew about you. Sit down.' They sat down facing each other. James saw Jimmy's glance shift uncharacteristically and noted the burning colour in his fair cheeks.

'So, you've guessed why I'm so fond of you, Jimmy-C?'

'Yes, sir. Just this minute. I can't think why I didn't before. I thought it was – well, because poor Mr Eckersley was killed. You must have thought me a fool.'

'Of course not. People don't see the obvious, thank heaven. I wanted to tell you from the first. But it was not entirely my secret. Besides – I didn't know *how* to tell you.'

They sat in an awkward silence, wanting to say so much, unable to find words.

'You don't despise me then, Jimmy? I did let your mother down.'

'Oh no, sir,' Jimmy said, painfully polite. 'Papa – Count Erhmann – explained there were circumstances beyond your control.'

'I could have controlled them,' James said wearily. 'You must never, Jimmy, think ill of your mother.'

'That's exactly what Papa said. He said it was her choice not to marry you.'

'Her choice, and my weakness,' said James. Her generosity, he thought bitterly. Letting him off the hook, giving the Louderdowns a chance to escape. And he had taken it. He had even, for a little while, been grateful. Until the longing for her had returned to gnaw at his heart again.

He leaned back. His breast felt choked with unshed tears.

'You must try and forgive me, Jimmy. For not giving you my name. For not being able to acknowledge you. For not standing by her, and caring for her. I shall never forgive myself.'

Jimmy sat, turning his cap between his hands. Old tides of passion seemed sweeping over him. He felt very young and inadequate.

'Your mother is a unique woman. She has a courage I never had. Courage to face a barrage of rifle fire, to command men and risk my own neck, yes. But your mother can face the truth — about life, and herself, and those she loves. We were young when it all happened. I was obsessed with her marvellous beauty. She was so beautiful.'

'She still is,' said Jimmy proudly.

'I am sure. I have not seen her since she first left England. But people who have, have told me. It was only after she left and married your step-father that I began to understand her strength, her honesty and simplicity. I think he did from the start. But he was older and wiser than I . . . he knew she was a woman to treasure. I was just a young fool.'

A floodgate of relief was sweeping over James, relief that the boy had not rejected him. Pleasure at being able to speak openly to him about Viola. Memories of her that he had thrust away from his consciousness over the years came back. He leaned back in his chair as though he had made a great physical effort.

'Are you all right, sir?'

'Yes.' James pulled the tattered edges of his self-esteem together. At least the first barrier had been crossed, and Jimmy was still there. 'Touch the bell, will you? Will you dine with me?'

'Thank you, sir.'

When the waiter came he ordered drinks and reserved a table.

'Now, there's the small matter, Jimmy, of getting your discharge.'

'If I was your own son, sir, and not Mama's. If I was Bell, and had done this, would you try to get me out?'

James shook his head.

'No. I always wanted to be a soldier. My father was. I hoped my son would be too. But Bell is all Bellairs. No Staffray.'

'He's great,' Jimmy said stoutly. 'He's frightfully clever – and funny.'

'Jimmy, the child of the woman you really love is different. It's a thought to hang on to, when you're older. When you are thinking of marriage. I'm very proud of what you have done, but I'm sick with anxiety, not just for you but knowing what your mother would feel if she knew, and God knows I have caused her enough pain.'

'But she won't know. Or not until it is all over. And it's nothing to do with you. I chose to go. I told Colonel Tallis that I wanted to stay in the Army. There are plenty of chaps in of my age, and even younger. I'm afraid you can't get me out, sir, if I won't go.'

'I know.'

'Shall we drop it, then?'

'Is there anything I can do for you? You only have to ask.'

'I shall be glad of your advice and friendship.' He took a sip of the Scotch and soda James had ordered, trying to assert his manhood. 'I have things to arrange.'

'I shall be glad to help in any way.'

'I shall be writing to my father's bank in London. Now poor Mr Eckersley has been killed I must take charge of my own affairs. I must arrange for money to be paid regularly to Aunt Betsy . . .' he paused, then said stiffly: 'I assume now . . . now everyone knows, you would rather we moved away from Louderdown. It might be an embarrassment.' There was a long silence. 'You did tell Bell and Lucy?'

'No,' James said. 'Their mother did not wish it. She too realized the truth of the matter. She has taken it badly. I do not agree with her. I think there has been enough concealment. But she insists that they are not told, and that the friendship between you and her children should cease. No letters. No further communication. If she wishes it to be that way, I must agree. I must ask you to respect her wishes.'

'I quite understand,' Jimmy said stiffly. 'And perhaps it would be better if I didn't see you either. I have no wish to cause you embarrassment.'

James smiled and put a hand on his arm.

'Nothing, Jimmy, that you could do would ever embarrass me. To part from you, now I have found you, is something I cannot possibly agree to.'

Jimmy's eyes pricked with unshed tears.

'Thank you, sir.'

'But I understand there was some sort of flirtation between you and Lucy, and she imagines herself in love with you.'

Jimmy's face flamed and his blue eyes darkened with guilt.

'It was nothing, really, sir. A kiss. Lucy's just a kid. She's got one of those pashes that girls get on me and imagines I'm no end of a hero.'

'You've suffered from this before?' James was amused.

'Well, girls can be so terribly determined. I behaved badly . . . but I didn't know, and it was really nothing. She is only fifteen.'

The calm, experienced eyes comforted him. Perhaps it was not such a heinous mistake after all.

'My mother realized who you were and told my wife. She met your mother once. They were both, of course, horrified. Not just about your relationship with Lucy. Fortunately there is no harm there. But that a girl of Lucy's age should behave like that. Respectable women can make mountains out of molehills.'

'I swear to you, sir, that no harm was done.'

'I believe you. But, if it had been, whose fault would that have been? Mine. Lucinda will forget. But if her mother does not wish her to know, or Bell to know, that you are their half-brother, I must agree. My wife has been bitterly distressed by learning about this, and I do not want to hurt her any more.'

'Poor lady,' said Jimmy. 'She is very nice.' He burst out suddenly, 'It's all such a mess.'

'But it's not your mess, Jimmy. Not of your making. I hate to ask you not to communicate with the twins. Rightly or wrongly, it is what Lady Louderdown wishes. I know you were all great friends, and it is hard. But I must ask it.'

'Of course. But supposing one day I ran into them?'

'Then I shall have to rely on your discretion. Since you refuse to accept a discharge it should not be difficult. You will be difficult to trace, because all recruits are moved about at first. And Mrs Lyttelton will move as soon as it can be arranged. If they should trace you and write, you will not reply.'

'Very well, sir. I'm sorry about Bell, though. We got on first rate, right from the start. I am glad he is my brother. It is a pity he can't know.'

'And Lucy?'

'Oh, well, it's best she doesn't know. She'd feel let down – she's a bit romantic. It's different for a girl.'

James rose. 'Well, shall we go in? Let's hope there is something palatable, in spite of the rationing.'

The waiter hovered with the menu.

'There's very good jugged hare, sir.'

'Splendid. And a bottle of claret, eh, Jimmy? And afterwards, you shall try a light cigar.'

'Topping. Better than bully beef.'

Jimmy loved the aura of masculine authority, the confidence that James's presence always gave him. He treated him like a man and expected him to behave like one. And it was even better now that he knew the truth.

As they crossed the corridor to the dining-room they were quite alone. Jimmy stopped and Louderdown turned to him questioningly.

'I do understand, sir,' he said with grave young dignity, 'that, all things considered, it would be out of the question for me to see the twins or go to Louderdown again. But – I want to say that I am glad you are my father. I love Papa – Count Erhmann – but somehow this is different.' He coloured, said expressively, 'I don't know how to tell you how I feel.'

'My dear boy.' James put his one arm through his son's and they went in to dine together.

At Louderdown the remnant of the summer holidays dragged wearisomely after Jimmy's departure. Dank weather set in, with lowering clouds. No one had any heart to organize excursions or games, and it seemed to the three children left behind that a light had gone out of their world. They were told briefly that Jimmy had refused to ask for release and would be staying in the Army. James went back to London and his work at the War Office, and Florence did not mention Jimmy's name.

Lucinda was distraught and restless despite her pride in what she insisted was his heroism. She was the type who needed a *leader*. Someone to adore, follow and look to for guidance, and Jimmy was the first person to fulfil that role. Her father was too remote. Her mother too occupied. Bellairs tried to fill Jimmy's role in the hospital, very conscious that to the wounded men he was still just a boy trying a bit too hard to adapt himself to their rough, adult talk and not to flinch at their pain. Lucinda moped about the great house, or rode alone, and watched and waited for letters that did not arrive. Why did he not write and tell her his address? He could not have been sent to France already. The one thing she would not believe was that he did not love her.

Unable to stand it any longer, she turned her horse in the direction of Park Cottage one day. She had never been there before. She understood that Mrs Lyttelton, Amy's mother, was Jimmy's housekeeper, and had no doubt that if she demanded it she would be given Jimmy's address.

She tethered her horse on the grass verge and strode up the path, and Amy opened the door when she knocked.

'Hallo!' she said.

'Have you heard from Jimmy?'

'My mother has.'

'May I see her?'

She did not wait for a reply but went past Amy into the sitting-room. It was obvious from the packing cases and disturbance that the Lytteltons were preparing to leave. Betsy rose, peering short-sightedly at the handsome young girl.

'Mrs Lyttelton, I'm Lady Lucinda Staffray.'

'Good day to you, my lady.'

'Are you going away?'

171

Betsy regarded her apprehensively, tight-lipped and uncommunicative. She had heard from Lord Louderdown that Jimmy now knew about the relationship, but not the twins, and he had asked her to leave Park Cottage as soon and as quietly as possible.

'Yes, my lady. Now Mr Jimmy's in the Forces there is no point in our keeping this big place on.'

'But where are you going?'

A touch of colour came into Betsy's thin cheeks.

'That's not for me to say.'

'You mean you won't tell me? But why doesn't he write? Do you know his number and regiment?' She lost her temper. One would think the stupid little woman was Jimmy's mother instead of his housekeeper. 'Mrs Lyttelton, *will* you do as I say! Give me Mr Corbett's address at once!'

Betsy bristled. She had her instructions and she agreed with them. She knew that they should never have come to Louderdown; she had thought that, to do so, was courting disaster unless her ladyship knew the truth. Matthew would never have agreed to it, and she should never have allowed his lordship to persuade her. But times had been hard and the air-raids frightening. She realized she had put the cat among the pigeons by flying off to the great house with Jimmy's letter, but she had been beside herself with anxiety over the lad. She kept thinking of Viola and what she would feel if she knew. But there was no need for young Lucinda to ride her high horse.

Amy had just come back into the room carrying a pile of school books. Her big eyes blazed.

'Don't speak to my mother like that, Lucy!' she said. 'She is not a servant.'

Lucinda controlled her temper with an effort.

'I cannot see why I should not have Jimmy's address.'

'I've had my instructions, my lady,' said Betsy primly.

'From whom?'

'I am not at liberty to say.'

'I think it's impertinent of you. You're only his housekeeper. I don't understand.'

'In that case, your ladyship –' Betsy was now thoroughly ruffled – 'you'd best make enquiries nearer home.'

Lucinda stamped out of the house, untethered her horse, set it at the hedge, whipped it over and scorched back across the fields towards Louderdown.

'Ah, dear,' said Betsy, 'I'll be glad when we've gone from here.'

Amy did not reply. She knew her mother had heard from Jimmy and from the Earl, but she had been told nothing. There was a mystery, and she did not like mysteries.

Lucinda put her lathered horse into its box and went straight into the house. Bellairs was in the great hall playing chess with one of the wounded men – it had been converted into a games room for the hospital. A tall, attractive figure in her riding clothes, she strode through, emanating fury. He ran after her, catching her on the ceremonial stairway, lined with family portraits. She turned a distraught face to his question.

'What on earth's the matter, Lucy?'

'I've been over at Great Louder. Mrs Lyttelton is going away. She refused to say where Jimmy is or to give me his address or say if she had heard from him. She says she's been told not to.'

'By whom?'

'She wouldn't tell me.'

Bellairs whistled comprehendingly.

'Bell, I'm going in to see Mummy and Grandmother. I promised Jimmy I would write. He'll think I've forgotten him. As though I ever could. They've got to tell me where he is.'

'I wouldn't do that.'

'Why not?'

'Use your brains. Haven't you noticed that you've been under surveillance since the flannel dance? Mummy wants to know where you are, what you're doing, and hikes you about with her to meetings and calls?' He grinned into her furious eyes. 'You shouldn't hang about under cedar trees.'

Her eyes flared. 'Mind your own business! You don't know anything about love. You're only a silly kid.'

'Just a slow starter. I shall be known as the wicked earl by the

173

time I'm thirty.' She did not smile. She never laughed at his jokes like Amy and Jimmy. She was always so intense, always wanting to be best and first at everything. 'Look, Lucy, it won't do any good kicking up a row. You know what Mummy and Gran are when they get entrenched – even Dad gives in. You'll only make things worse. The only thing that worries me is that Dad didn't get Jimmy out of the Army.'

'You forget that Dad was a soldier,' said Lucinda loftily. 'He was decorated for bravery. If it wasn't for his arm he'd probably be a general now. He would understand Jimmy wants to fight for England.'

'Oh, cut it out, Lucy, you sound like a bally Boadicea.' He grinned again, his charming perceptive sidelong grin. He seemed utterly casual. No one could have guessed he was wracked with anxiety for his friend. 'You just want to shine in his reflected glory.'

'I'm British and everyone knows we're the finest nation in the world.'

He scratched his thick dark hair and gazed at her despairingly.

'Everyone in the world?' he repeated scathingly. 'I suppose you've asked the Laplanders? And the Bedouins? And the hula-hula people in the Pacific? You talk the most utter rot, Sis. You don't seem to realize he might get killed – or worse, wounded like some of those poor devils in the wards here.'

'I do – and so does he. That's why I am so proud of him.'

'Nuts. The best thing you can do is to be sly, stealthy and Machiavellian, and not provoke family rows. The less they notice you the easier it is to find things out.'

'You are a sly, cowardly brute, nothing but a wet little conchy. I'm ashamed of you and I *am* going to speak to Mother.'

Head held high and cheeks aflame, she went onwards to her mother's sitting-room.

Lady Louderdown was taking tea with her mother-in-law: the old Countess was in her wheel-chair, her knees wrapped in rugs, her sunken eyes peering brilliantly from the frame of her lacy shawl. They both looked at her without speaking and under that united disapproval she ran out of steam. Her grandmother said icily, 'Kindly go out of the room, Lucinda, and come in quietly, closing the door behind you, and bid your mother and I good afternoon.'

Lucinda took a deep breath and did so. Her cheeks burned and her eyes began to fill. She hated them both for being able to reduce her to a silly schoolgirl. She would have liked to throw over the delicate tea-table and shatter the china on the floor.

'Sit down, Lucinda.' She sat down on the chair indicated. 'You are behaving very tiresomely,' said her mother.

Florence had changed. She had never been affectionate, but she had never been harsh. She seemed to hold herself on a rein now, as she might an untrustworthy horse, as though she mistrusted her ability to control herself. And she had gone back to the horses again. During the war she had been so busy with the hospital she had no time for anything else. But during the past weeks she had been riding again, alone, hard, and dangerously.

'I wanted to speak to you. It is the height of bad form to go chasing after boys, especially boys older than yourself. Do you want the whole of the sixth form at Harrow talking about you?'

It was a palpable hit and Lucinda's lips trembled.

'Jimmy Corbett is a gentleman. He wouldn't say anything. He is a man now, and a soldier, and is not going back to school.'

'He is not a gentleman and you did not behave like a young lady. Flirting, publicly, like a *kitchen maid*. It is *unthinkable*!' said her grandmother.

'Did you tell Mrs Lyttelton not to give me Jimmy's address?' Lucinda cried. 'Or tell me where she is going? I'll ask Dad. I'll ring him up in London.'

'You will not,' said her mother, 'and if you did he would not tell you. If it were not for the war you would be packed off to Switzerland or France to school. You behaved appallingly on the night of the flannel dance. It is conduct I will not tolerate.'

'What did I do?'

'You made yourself conspicuous with – with that boy.' Florence could not bring herself to speak the name. 'Do you deny it?'

'Why should I?' Lucinda's head tossed proudly. 'I glory in it. I'm in love with Jimmy and he's in love with me. One day when he comes back from the war, I am going to marry him.'

'That is quite enough. I dislike these dramatics. You are much too young for that sort of talk. The boy is obviously a flirt and a rake; he behaved in an ungentlemanly way to encourage a silly schoolgirl. With his background, I suppose it is to be expected. You will not go over to see this Mrs Lyttelton again. I need not tell you that at school and home your correspondence will be watched. Now, go and wash your face and change, and come back here and I will ring for more tea. I do not wish to hear another word about this foolish matter.'

Lucinda rose, her pale blue eyes, so like her mother's, incandescent with anger, like blue sulphurous flames.

'I don't want any beastly tea. I'll never give him up. You can lock me up, it won't make any difference. You'll see.'

Florence was vividly reminded of the days when she had pursued James Staffray through the London drawing-rooms, getting herself talked about, until at last she had succeeded in capturing his amused, reluctant notice. Her family had been triumphant. He had not loved her. Love, her passionate heart had told her, would come with marriage. It had not. The shadow of another woman had always been there. Her face as she looked at Lucinda was so bitter that the girl shrank back.

'That's enough, Lucinda. I will not have the matter mentioned again.'

'One day I shall be grown-up and I shall choose my own friends. I shall do as I like, and kiss whom I like and marry whom I like, and it *will* be Jimmy Corbett. You'll see!'

She rushed out of the room, banging the door, back to the stables where she rubbed down her horse, sobbing against its quivering neck in despair.

'Florence,' said the old lady wearily, 'don't you think that perhaps James is right? The children should be told.'

'I cannot – she is too young. She does not understand.' The real reason came explosively. 'Do you want me to tell my children that James prefers that woman to me and her boy to his own

176

children? Why did no one tell me about her? I would have been spared so much.'

'If I had told you, Florence, you would have had him just the same. You made a good marriage. There is no finer man than James. Don't destroy everything over a woman you will never see and a boy you will never hear of again.'

'But James will not give this boy up!' Florence paced up and down, wringing her hands together. 'This is what I ask, and it is not so much. He could make other arrangements for his guardianship. There is no reason for him to be personally involved. In our sort of family this kind of thing can be arranged through solicitors.'

'It is not a matter of money,' said the old lady wearily. 'The boy is rich. If it were only money, it would be quite simple. Unfortunately it is a matter of love.'

'Love! What does either of them know of love? I will not give up, Mama. Until James promises never to see that boy again, nothing can ever be right between us.'

Old passions, old sins. The old lady rang the bell and when Castle came, asked to be wheeled away to her room.

Bellairs got out his bicycle. He knew his mother was not keeping an eye on him. Boys were different, and anyway he had not been copped kissing under a cedar tree. He wished he had. He longed to cross the barrier of adolescent innocence. Sex, he thought, should be something you acquired automatically at a certain age, like long trousers.

At Park Cottage, he did not go crashing in like Lucinda, but put his bike in the hedge and went round to the back of the house and whistled a shrill blackbird call, one of their secret signals. He did not want Betsy to see him. Presently Amy came out, prim and pretty in pink gingham, her hair tied back with a pink ribbon. Bellairs thought she looked charming – straight out of a Kate Greenaway book.

She carried a metal canister, which she waved as she came through the field-gate from the garden.

'Blackberries,' she said. 'Mother's making jelly. Says we won't get any sugar back in the South.'

'When are you going?'

'Soon. They're coming for the trunk in the morning.'

'Where?'

'I'm not supposed to tell anyone, but it's called Richmond. It's a flat, not a house. It's supposed to be too far out for raids. I don't know the address yet. I expect it's somewhere suitable for His Majesty Jimmy-C to come back to.'

'You're cross with him?'

'I hate being shifted about to suit his convenience. It means changing schools again.'

'But aren't you afraid he'll be killed?'

The intensity of distress in her clear eyes startled him.

'Don't say such a thing, Bell. It won't happen. I won't let it. I tell God every night that it mustn't.'

'*Tell* God?' Bellairs hooted. 'I thought one prayed to God.'

'I don't. I *tell* Him. I tell Him if anything happens to Jimmy-C I'll never believe in Him again. I'll never pray or go to church as long as I live. At least you know where you are with the Devil – he only does bad things.'

'You're a funny little thing.'

'And I'm sick of being called little, so please don't mention it. I'd better pick some blackberries. You pull down and I'll pick. I've got to keep my dress clean because I've to wear it tomorrow.'

He found a branched stick and pulled the loaded sprays down so that she could pick and he noticed how neatly her small white hands did so, very precisely, not getting scratched, barely bruising the juice on to her hands. The low September sun reflected the pink of her dress on to her pure childish face.

'D'you remember at the summer half when the hedges were full of wild roses, and Jimmy was telling us about the masses that grew round his home in Austria? And he said you were like one, and Lucy was jealous and asked what she was like and he said a bean-pole and she sulked all day.'

'She's more like Diana the Huntress, she's so fierce. Jimmy

says things like that – about the wild roses – to girls when he is trying to get round them. I expect he wanted me to do something for him that he knew I didn't want to do. He thinks all girls like to be told silly things, and that they are all in love with him.'

'Which most of them are.' He smiled. 'No, he just likes people to be happy. I told him so once and he said it was his Italian blood. One of his grandfathers was an Italian. Really only a few people mean anything to him apart from his mother and family. You and me, and maybe Lucy. He's very fond of my father, whom he thinks a great swell. He should have been Dad's son. He's just what Dad would like. He's always been disappointed in me.'

She looked at him curiously. 'You're much cleverer than Jimmy. I get mad with him but never with you. He makes me mad because, ever since his mother brought him back to England, our lives seem to be arranged round his. For *his* benefit. It's for ours too, I know, because Mother gets paid to look after him. She treats him like the master of the house. But his mother was only a shop girl, like herself, even if she is a Countess now.'

'Is she as beautiful as he says?'

'Oh yes. She's so beautiful she . . . well, she's different . . . sort of above other people.'

'She transcends them?'

'Yes, that's right. I mean she still speaks with a Leeds accent, like Mother, and Jimmy says her German is terrible, but she isn't ashamed of it and she doesn't care, so no one else does. She's like a queen. He adores her. I never saw anyone so gone on their mother as Jimmy.'

'I expect she's the same about him. That's what it is with him. Everyone loves him and he just can't believe that anyone could take a dislike to him – like my mother has done. D'you know where he is, Amy?'

'I'm not to say. I had to promise. What's it all about, Bell?'

'It's Lucinda.' He looked uncomfortable, and coloured a little. 'She's such a fool. She made a dead set at Jimmy on the night of the flannel dance. You know how families are about girls. Particularly Gran and Mother, who go on about what they

179

call "our position" and "suitable" friends of our own station. Well, Jimmy is illegitimate and Dad is an Earl, I suppose. Don't look at me like that, Amy. I think it's a lot of bally rot too.'

'It's insufferable,' said Amy. 'Snobs. That's what they are. A lot of stuck-up snobs.'

'Yes. But it's obvious they want to stop the whole thing, so they think if I know where Jimmy is I might tell Lucy, or enclose letters to her, or something.'

Amy listened expressionlessly, but there was a turmoil inside her. The mystery was still there. There must be something more than this in it. But the thought of Jimmy and Lucinda knotted up her puzzlement with jealousy in an uncomfortable way which she did not understand. Why should she care whom conceited Master James Cock-Of-The-Walk Corbett fell in love with? Or Lucinda? If she was stupid enough to fall in love with him when he had hundreds of other girls?

'You mean they really are in love?'

'Oh, *Lucy* is. She's always in love with someone. It used to be Lord Kitchener and Sir Lancelot. She's got a passion for heroes. I don't know about Jimmy,' he brooded, forgetting how young she was. 'Jim's known lots of girls . . . he's told me. He's actually done it with them . . .' He stopped, horrified at what he had said, staring at her pretty triangular face, which was now burning red. 'Well, you know what I mean, Amy. You're not silly. Grown-up people do.'

'I'm not shocked,' she said stoutly. 'You've only to watch the birds and animals and have a good read of the Bible to work it out. But people – they don't, do they, before they are properly married?'

'Oh, yes, they do,' Bell said airily. 'You've only to read Shakespeare, but I expect you have the Shakespeare with all the spicy bits cut out at school. If they didn't, Jimmy would know who his real father is and not be illegitimate.'

'Oh,' said Amy flatly. 'Of course, I see what you mean. I see now.' Her pale, pearly face suddenly became close and secret. 'Yes. I understand now. Look, I have enough blackberries. I must go in.'

They heard the back door open and Betsy call.

'Coming!' Amy called in answer. 'Good-bye, Bell.'

'I hope we meet again.'

'So do I. But it's not likely.'

'Well, good-bye, then.'

They looked at each other gravely – they had been good friends.

'I'll remember you always,' said Bell, 'and the four of us, and what fun we've had this last year. D'you mind if I kiss you?'

'Not at all,' said Amy primly, and put up a pink silk cheek on which he placed a friendly smack. 'Good-bye.'

She went into the kitchen, and he pedalled back to Louderdown. Next day Amy and Betsy left for London.

After an arduous two months' training Jimmy was moved south to an OTC training unit, on the recommendation of Colonel Tallis, who tactfully allowed the age he had enlisted under to remain unaltered. So far as the authorities knew, Private J. C. Corbett was approaching his twentieth birthday. He was given a brief leave at the new address which James had found for him and where Betsy and Amy were already installed.

It was a large, light mansion flat at Richmond, conveniently near London yet reckoned too far out to be a target for the air-raids. They had ceased over London since the destruction of the Zeppelins. The newspapers predicted a new frightfulness to come, the Gothas, but so far the nights had been peaceful. After the life in barracks it was a pleasure to sleep in a comfortable bed, enjoy Betsy's cooking and wallow in the modern American-type bathroom, where hot water flowed at the turn of a tap. He got in touch with the old school-fellows and enjoyed several days as a young man about town, including a day with James, ordering his new uniform. It was no use pretending they did not revel in each other's company. James loved 'showing Jimmy the ropes' and Jimmy loved to learn. James bought him a beautiful and expensive British Warm and showed him where to have his boots made to measure. Jimmy took James out to lunch at The

Cecil. Their mutual delight in one another was a pleasure to watch. Along the grapevines of servant and society gossip their meeting got back to Florence at Louderdown, increasing her despair. It seemed to her James was mad. It seemed to his mother that history was repeating itself, and James was as reckless about befriending the boy as he had been when he had flaunted the affair with his mother all over London.

James was absurdly proud of his promotion, although Jimmy was not so sure. He had been happy in the rough comradeship of the camp and had made a lot of friends. He was not sure he wanted to leave them.

'The experience will be good for you,' said James. 'If you have to lead men you have to know them. It's something I missed. I went straight in with a commission from Sandhurst.'

'It might make it harder,' said Jimmy thoughtfully. James noticed that some of the cocksure arrogance of privileged youth had rubbed off in the past months. 'If you mess with chaps, hear them talk about their homes, get drunk with them, it could make it more difficult to command them. Especially out at the front.'

'You share the experience.'

'But it's different. I was a messmate – now I shall be boss. I hope I don't have to command any of the chaps I've served with in the ranks. They'll think of me differently. A lucky sod, out of the worst of it. Not the danger. The daily grind. That's the hardest for them.'

'And I've always been one of the lucky sods,' said James, smiling. 'Yes. It's a different sort of war. Are you changing your mind about making an army career?'

'No. It's what I want – I've just got another angle on it. One of the fellows I liked best was a surface worker from a pit near Rotherham. What he earned at his job for a week wouldn't pay for this meal. But when we went out he'd stand his round although he needed the money. D'you know I've never known what it was to *need* anything, Dad?' James warmed to his easy use of the term. 'He was proud. Yet now he'll be on the other side of the fence. Out of bounds to other ranks. I could go into

182

his pubs or mess, but without permission he couldn't come into mine.'

'But you're a gentleman, Jimmy. You have the privileges of your class.'

'Yes. But I'm a bit of a mix-up really, aren't I, sir? One thing it's taught me – to understand my mother. I think she must have hated poverty and fought it like an enemy.'

'Sometimes,' James said, 'you're very like her.'

Jimmy was silent, then he said, 'May I ask how Bell is? And Lucinda?'

James's Edwardian duality preferred to keep his two lives apart. Jimmy always asked, although he had kept his promise and had never written.

'The twins are well,' he said stiffly. Jimmy saw the pained and embarrassed look on his face, and said quickly, 'I'm sorry. It was better before, wasn't it? When I didn't know.' He looked at his watch. 'D'you mind if I don't take coffee, sir? I'm meeting Amy and taking her to see *Chu Chin Chow* and then to Gunter's for tea.'

'You're fond of her and her mother?'

'Of course. They're my family, really. Amy's actually growing. She's over five foot now. And bright as a button – talking about going to university.'

'You're not getting too fond of her?'

'Good lord, she's only a baby still.' His face was very still, his blue eyes met his father's. 'Sir, even if I were, that doesn't apply to me, does it? I'm not going to inherit Louderdown. I can fall in love with whom I like, except Lucinda.'

Not said bitterly but reminding him of the truth. Reminding him there were two other children whom it was his duty to love. James felt heavy with guilt. But he could not bear to part with Jimmy. It was his last day in town before joining his regiment.

'Are you engaged for this evening?'

'I'm afraid so, sir.' Jimmy was charmingly apologetic, 'And I can't really get out of it. I'm going to dine with a couple of chaps from school.'

'That's all right, my boy.' They collected their hats and went

183

out into the cold winter sunshine, two handsome soldierly men, alike in feature and colouring. They shook hands. 'It's just that I didn't want you to spend the evening alone. Write to me at Whites.'

'I will. I'm stationed quite near town – I'll be up now and then. I'll be in touch.'

Jimmy went off in a taxi, and James walked slowly towards Whitehall. The war news was terrible. The armies were at a standstill again on the Western front, and it was known that the Germans were preparing for a new offensive. The Austrian victory at Caporetto had shaken everyone. He wondered how Jimmy thought about that? Whether he felt divided. Would it never end? The heavy shipping losses, the submarines harrying the merchant ships like sharks. The increasing shortages of essentials. The fear that haunted his dreams came to him in the daylight now. If ever he had to tell Viola the boy had been killed! It was something he could not bear to contemplate.

It would soon be Christmas. The fourth of the war. He must put in an appearance at Louderdown. He went more often nowadays, because his mother was failing. Florence kept up a courteous and correct front before the staff and the children, but she locked her door against him. He knew she blamed him for their separation – but he would not capitulate. He would not put James-Carlo out of his life. It was impossible now, more so than ever, when every day brought him nearer active service and the threat of the Western front.

Christmas came and passed, the food position became worse, the Allied offensive – the much publicized Big Push – had bogged down in the hellish rainfall of the Somme, creating a quagmire of impassable mud in which men drowned and over which the new armour could not pass. The Germans swept into their new offensive breaking the line nearly to the sea. In April the USA declared war and every available man was mustered to hold the enemy until the new American Army was ready, and James-Carlo Corbett, a subaltern in the newly-formed Tank Corps, was sent to France.

Lord Louderdown received a message at his club – Jimmy

would be passing through London and entraining at Victoria. He took a taxi to the station. The lilac was out in the parks and the sweet smell of spring in the air. The newspaper placards and the shrill shouts of the newsboys told of the weight of the German attack, and the courage with which it was being held. James knew of the appalling casualties which it cost to do so, which were not featured in the headlines. The station was packed with khaki-clad men standing patiently beside their kit-bags and haversacks as the train came in to be filled and take them to the ports. Some of them were talking to relatives, nervous and anxious, many in tears, saying the platitudes that meant nothing – 'Take care of yourself', 'Let me know if you need anything', 'Write often.' Some of the men were drunk and being solicitously looked after by their mates, almost tenderly heaved along the platform and into the train.

Even though James had now passed forty and had only one arm he felt ashamed of moving among these uniformed men, a civilian, not going to the war. He found a carriage reserved for officers and saw Jimmy talking to Betsy Lyttelton and Amy. His arms were linked in theirs and he looked at them with an affection which sent a foolish wave of jealousy through James. They were now more nearly Jimmy's family than he could ever be.

He had not seen them since they had left Louderdown. Betsy had already accepted middle-age with the docility of her type and class. Her neatly inexpensive clothes were in the same style that she had worn twenty years ago, her dark grey costume and black hat and gloves, her inevitable neatly rolled umbrella. But Amy was growing up. She was slightly taller than her mother. She wore her black felt hat with a school band and badge with an air which promised an ultimate chic. She looked at him warily, her cheeks pink, a touch of resentment about her pretty mouth. James hardly noticed them – he had only eyes for Jimmy, who came forward to meet him. They shook hands.

'It was good of you to come, sir.'

'I had to, of course.' He turned to Betsy. 'Will you excuse us, Mrs Lyttelton?'

They walked slowly along the length of the carriage. Jimmy

185

seemed a little pale, visibly excited, heartbreakingly young and splendid in his beautifully tailored uniform.

'Are these your chaps?' asked James, indicating the soldiers swarming up the platform.

'No, sir. Infantry. I'm joining the unit in France.'

'You'll let me know if there is anything you want? If there is anything I can do, or can get you, I will.'

'Thank you, sir. I don't think there is anything.'

They walked in silence. Like the families about them, James found nothing to say. Nothing but inanities. He envied an elderly, drunken Cockney embracing an apprehensive young private. He wished he was drunk.

'Sir, there are one or two things. If anything should happen to me . . .'

'Don't say that,' James almost shouted. 'You'll be all right. The Americans will be there within weeks.'

'Maybe. I hope it's not all over before I get a show. We want to see what the tanks can do. I've made a will, sir. It's at the bank. Papa – that is Count Erhmann, settled a considerable amount on me in England, and I have left it all to Mrs Lyttelton and Amy. I've named you as trustee. I hope you don't mind?'

'Of course not.'

'And if it should happen, you'll let my mother know?' The nightmare came so close it was almost reality. 'Could you do it personally? I imagine it might be possible. You have diplomatic connections.'

'Of course. But I know it won't come to that.'

'I'd have liked . . .' Jimmy hesitated, then recklessly broached the subject that had been taboo: 'I'd have liked to see Bell before I went. I'd have liked him to know how fond I still am of him, and that the split was not of my making. I'd have liked him to know we are brothers.' He smiled. 'If – if anything should happen, sir, it won't matter any more, will it? You can tell them then, the twins, and give them my love.'

Inside James was weeping. Imposed tradition would not let him weep in public like the parents of these Tommies about him, but inside the pain was like an open wound, the tears were

186

tears of blood, washing away everything but his love for this boy and his mother. He put his arms round Jimmy and was startled when he kissed him, on both cheeks, then raised his one hand, kissed the back of it, then curiously, his shoulder – and then he remembered that in Vienna this was the salute a son would give his father – that this was how Jimmy would have bidden farewell to Eugene. He could not trust himself to speak.

'Good-bye, sir. Keep an eye on the Lytteltons for me.'

'When you come back, Jimmy, I promise you it will be different.'

'Don't worry about that, sir.'

'I won't stay.' Whistles were sounding along the platform and the sergeants were shouting commands. Doors slammed and windows were jerked down, women were clinging to the men bending down for a last kiss. Mothers, wives, fathers. 'Good-bye, and God preserve you, my son.'

'You too. Don't be unhappy. Good-bye, Dad.'

He hurried back to his carriage, embraced Betsy. 'Good-bye, Aunt Betsy. Take care of yourself. Keep the home fires burning for me to come home to.'

He looked down at Amy. Her nose came level with the knot in his tie, and tears, large and noiseless, were slipping down her petal-smooth cheeks. In the dusky dirt of the station her face gleamed with a pure pearly quality. He lifted her until her face was level with his and she threw her arms about his neck, and the black school hat jerked backwards until it hung from its elastic.

'Don't be brave,' she said. 'Just keep alive and come home. I'll tell God every night. Good-bye, darling Jimmy-C.'

'You'll miss the great conceited oaf, after all.'

He set her down and jumped aboard, leaned out of the window, catching their hands and holding them until the moving train separated them. They stood waving until it slid round the curve, under the Pimlico Road bridge, and out of sight.

People began to drift away. Some composed and resigned, some tight-lipped, a few sobbing hysterically. Betsy put her

187

hand into Amy's arm.

'I remember,' she said, 'his mother telling me how she went down to Tilbury to say good-bye to his lordship when he went to South Africa. That was when he lost his arm. I remember her saying how she stood watching until the ship was out of sight. In a way I'm glad she's not here today. Whatever is happening out there in Austria, and they say it's bad, she'll still be thinking he's safe at school. She'll think he's too young to go, which he is.' She mopped her eyes, and then realized what she had said. 'Oh, love, I'm all upset. I should never have told you that.'

'It doesn't matter, Mother,' Amy said. 'I guessed anyway, a long while ago. When we left Great Louder.' It was strange that now she was sorry for Lucinda, who was so arrogant and proud, and understood why they would not want her to know. She held her mother's arm closely. 'The only thing that matters is that Jimmy comes home safely.'

'You won't tell anyone, Amy? I promised his lordship that no one should know. It was Lady Louderdown, you see, who wouldn't have the twins told that Jimmy was really their brother. I didn't tell you because I did not think you were old enough to understand.'

'But I did – one day it became very clear and very terrible. I understand why Lady Louderdown does not want them to know. It would be hard for Bell, because he would realize that, although he is Lord Staffray and the heir, his father loves Jimmy best. And it would be terrible for Lucinda, who is so proud – she would feel a fool. She would feel life had made a fool of her, and she would not be able to bear it.'

'Aye. If folks could see the consequences of what they do, happen they would behave better. But you won't say anything to anyone?'

'Of course not. I don't think I like the Staffrays, Mother. They push people around to suit their own convenience. And Jimmy's just like Lord Louderdown. More like him than Bell ever was. It's a funny thing, though . . .' She stopped, realizing she was probing her own feelings aloud. Why had Jimmy always meant so much to her when she really liked Bell so much better?

'What's a funny thing?'

'Oh, nothing. Just that people shouldn't be so sure of their right to privileges. But don't fret, I won't tell anyone. You know that.'

In August the American Forces went into battle, a fresh, vital young army, neither war-weary nor underfed, fighting with great heroism, stemming the German's last offensive at Chateau Thierry, so that the tide of arms lost its impetus and began to ebb backwards, north-east into Germany.

The bead-headed pins on the war maps began to advance. The war was not won. There was still fighting. But across Europe hearts began to lift and hope again, and to Betsy and Amy in Richmond and to James Louderdown there was the blessed relief that Jimmy was still safe. The hostilities staggered on with rumours and counter-rumours of surrender and armistice, until at last the sirens sounded and the bells rang, the lights went on and the country went mad with relief and joy.

CHAPTER SEVEN

During the last months of the war Die Kinderburg had been so quiet – no visitors or house-parties. Not on the main road to any strategical point, there were no troops or troop movements. It seemed to Viola that life had stopped. Only lately had fear come – as the Imperial armies collapsed, and the fighting stopped along the Russian Front a great malaise had set in, and men had begun to desert. In small groups at first, then larger bands, most of them armed, but ragged, starving and desperate, they struggled homewards like deserted animals. The *soldatska*, the brigand soldiers, without discipline, taking whatever came in their way. So far Die Kinderburg had been lucky. Only a few men had come through, and those small bands, and they had managed by feeding them, letting them rest and wash, finding them clothing and footwear and a little cash, to send them on their way. But, of recent weeks, the trickle had become a stream, and the villagers had begun to bring all their produce, food stores and salted meat to Viola at the castle where, in the big storage cellars and still-rooms, they thought it would be safe.

She wished Eugene could be with her but he could rarely get away from Vienna. Every separate state in the Empire was demanding autonomy. The government and the advisers who congregated round the new young Emperor Charles vacillated as they had always done, between right and left, between concessions and a hard line, and now with a bankrupt country and a worn-out, ill-fed army, there was no way in which a hard line could be imposed. The Emperor struggled to preserve his dynasty, and Eugene who loved reason and hated extremes, a convinced federalist, was being besieged to use his influence for this or that faction which was demanding autonomy, all deeply suspicious of the government and of each other. Inflation was running wild and in the poor, factory quarters of Vienna, children were beginning to starve. Every day more soldiers drifted homeward, some of them ravaging the farms and homesteads like hungry wolves.

Sitting in Eugene's study, at his desk, going over her accounts, Viola heard the crack of a rifle far away and rose uneasily. The two elder children, Lorenz and Theresa, were away at school. Only Coralie, now four, was with her. She had closed nearly all the rooms, and her only servants were Vatel, her old cook, and a young peasant girl from the village, who served as a housemaid and as a nursemaid to Coralie.

Eugene had wanted Viola to stay in Vienna, but she had refused.

'You are away so much. I see you just as often here. What could I do to help in Vienna, except serve soup to starving people? There are plenty of ladies who can do that. I cannot feed all Vienna, but I can help to feed the folk in the village. I can look after our own people, so that at least we are not a burden on the country, and have a surplus to send to the towns.'

He knew she was right, but it kept him awake at night, thinking of her with little Coralie in the remote village, and the only man old Vatel.

Viola pulled a fur wrap about her shoulders and went out on to the small balcony. It was a clear night bright with stars and frost was in the air. There was no further sound of shots. Perhaps it was only boys poaching – there were no men left in the villages now. Only boys and old men. They took pheasants, and deer occasionally, and she did not care. She was glad they had good fresh meat sometimes, and it did no harm to cull the herds.

She saw a light gleaming, far away, high up the mountainside. It must be at Adlerburg. The big country hunting lodge belonging to the von Retz family had been empty during the war years. Gottfried von Retz was in disastrous financial straits, for most of his fortune was invested in Russia and Czechoslovakia. The summers at Adlerburg, with the parties for the shooting and fishing and harvest home were things of the past. The extravagant food and wine, the fashionable company and the pretty spoiled children came no more. The men were in uniform and many were dead, and Viola knew that, without Eugene's discreet and generous help, Gottfried could not have kept on the Vienna apartment, nor the children at their expensive schools. But tonight there was someone at the house, and she wondered anxiously if it were robbers.

When she went back into the study Coralie came bounding in, straight into her arms with the impetuous confidence of a much-loved child. She was pretty and precocious, a daring, boyish child, and although she spoke German fluently, she and Viola always spoke in English together.

'Mummy, Maritska's in the kitchen waiting to see you. She's brought half a pig to store. They killed one yesterday. Poor old piggy.'

'Poor old piggy, indeed! You still like the bacon!'

Viola kissed her lovingly. She was a lovely child. A mass of bright, ruddy-gold curling hair, a skin like a wild rose, and Eugene's grey, sparkling, intelligent eyes. All her children were handsome, lovable and attractive – except Lorenz. She supposed virtuous people might think fate was punishing her, when she had wanted so much to give Eugene a fine son, whom he would have been proud to have carry on his name and the great business. But Viola had no time for such thinking. Why should Eugene, or for that matter Lorenz himself, be punished for her sins?

She picked up a ledger, and taking Coralie's hand went down the winding stone stairway to the old kitchens. These kitchens, cool and dry, were surrounded with still-rooms, pantries and wine cellars. The first thing Viola had done when she had first arrived at Die Kinderburg was to have modern kitchens built, level with the dining-room on the ground floor.

'I'm not having my servants running up and down those spiral stairs with trays,' she said indignantly. 'Maybe it was all right when the castle was built, but times have changed.'

The great stone arched kitchens, with bread and roasting ovens and rows of open grills, blackened beams with hooks for hams and herbs, and an iron spit which had at one time been turned by a little peasant lad sitting beside the hearth, were still there. Like a museum. They smelled of stored apples and the earthy smell of stacked potatoes. The old hooks were hung with smoked hams and sausages, and the vats against the wall were full of brine for salting. No jams, for there had been no sugar now for a long while.

A village woman, her head bound in a scarf, thickly shawled and petticoated against the cold, stood waiting, her gnarled, work-worn hands folded patiently. Her small light eyes were almost oriental above her high cheek-bones. Maritska, the swineherd's wife – she drove her pigs through the forests to forage, helped by her old father and young son. Her husband had been lost in the Italian snows. Before her on the enormous table lay a side of freshly killed pork.

'Sit down, Maritska.' The woman had brought the meat on a hand-cart; tomorrow she would come and smoke it in the old smoke house in the yard. The old artefacts, out of use since Eugene's father's time, had come back into their own in wartime. 'Only a half pig? Have you been having a feast in the village?'

'No, gracious lady.' She spoke a trifle indignantly, for she was a notoriously saving woman, selling or bartering all her surplus.

'I'm only teasing, Maritska. The pig is yours to use as you like. Whether you smoke or salt half or the lot, is not for me to say. I only keep it here for you until you need it. Just put your mark here. To say I have received it.'

Laboriously the woman put her mark in the ledger.

Viola unlocked a store cupboard and took out a small packet of sugar. Maritska's eyes lit with eager greed.

'It isn't much, I'm afraid,' said Viola. 'A friend of the Count's sent me some. It's enough to make a few cakes for the children.'

'Will the *Gräfin* not need it for herself?'

'Oh, I've kept a bit, and we still have honey left. A glass of wine, Maritska, before you go? Or some schnaps?'

'Schnaps, please, *Gräfin*.'

Viola carefully poured out the small glassful and Maritska downed it eagerly. She looked at Viola a little hesitantly, and then said, 'There is only half a pig because the other half has gone up to Adlerburg.'

'To Adlerburg? Is Baroness von Retz, there?'

'No, *Gräfin*, it is Prince Friedrich. He is back from the wars.'

'Prince Friedrich Schausenhardt?'

'Yes, *Gräfin*.'

'He is alone?'

'No, *Gräfin*. He has brought back men from his regiment. The Prince has been demobilized, because he was wounded. Here –' She ran a blunt finger down her face from forehead to lip. 'Ach, he looks like the devil. The women are all telling their daughters to hide if these men come into the village. They came into the village yesterday and said the Prince says we should all give them something to eat and in return, if the bandits came robbing, they would protect us from them.'

'You mean – they are forming a *Heimwehr*.'

'Yes, that is what they call it. They are all big, strong men though, quite young, not like the old men and boys in the village. They are not from round here.' She looked at Viola anxiously. 'They said that up north the *soldatska* are very bad, big gangs, and people have been killed. It will help to have young strong men with guns to protect us until our own men get back.'

'I wondered why so many people came for stores yesterday,' said Viola. 'Did you tell the men you had been storing your food in the castle?'

'I did not,' said Maritska slyly. 'I do not believe in telling where food is these days. But what others said, I do not know. Some are young girls, and they are always silly when young men are there.'

'I see,' said Viola.

Coralie stared up, puzzled by her mother's preoccupation. Usually Viola laughed and chatted with the village women, asking questions about their families and finding out if there were ways in which she could help them. But since the Prince's name had been mentioned a change had come over her.

'Mama –' she tugged at her hand – 'is something wrong? Why do you look like that?'

Viola started, annoyed that she had betrayed her feelings.

She had not seen Schausenhardt since that silly fracas with Jimmy, back in 1913. He would have forgotten all about her. He was not a man noted for fidelity, even to an idea.

'Maritska, I did not think we could see the lights up at Adlerburg from here. I thought the forest was too dense. But tonight I saw lights.'

'The Prince has had his men felling trees before the house. So they can look down into the valley and if trouble starts they will see where it is. And we are to ring the church bell if there is a raid, then his men will come down with their guns.'

'Well, let's hope it never happens,' said Viola briskly. 'Hungry men we can feed, and when they are fed they listen to reason. But I do not like bullets flying about, whoever is shooting. Good night, Maritska.'

'Good night, *Frau Gräfin*, and many thanks for the sugar.'

She touched Viola's hand with her lips, gave a small bobbing curtsey, and went out, a doll-like figure in her thick, many-layered petticoats and clattering wood-soled clogs.

Viola and Coralie went up into the main hall – there was no coal but a log fire was burning, for there were always plenty of fallen logs in the forest around. Eugene's two big hounds lay before the blaze, their noses grizzled now with age, and they lifted their great heads and lazily wagged their tails. In spite of the war Viola made her house look charming, because Eugene often arrived from Vienna without warning. There were clusters of red berries and autumn leaves in the vases – the sheltered rose garden had been cleared for vegetables, and in the hot houses they grew tomatoes and winter salads instead of orchids and rare chrysanthemums. The long brocade curtains were drawn, and the firelight glimmered warmly on the polished panelling and the gilded Erhmann quarterings. It was a place where Eugene could get a few hours' rest and escape from the grey capital, where the slums starved and the empire threshed desperately in its dying agonies.

Coralie brought a story book and Viola read to her. She had not started lessons yet. She was only four, but she was sharply intelligent and already beginning to string letters together. But the child needed other children to play with, and since the raids and rumours of marauding soldiers she dare not let her go running down to play with the village children.

They dined together, Vatel waiting on them as meticulously as ever at a table beautifully laid with lace and silver, fruit arranged on vine leaves, the simple meal of soup and grilled trout perfectly served. He was looking his age and was doing the work of three men, but he doggedly tried to keep up the standards his pride demanded. Viola understood his pride and did not interfere. His uniform was getting a little shiny at the elbows, and his once glossy black hair was snow-white without the rejuvenating attentions of his barber in Vienna. But Viola loved him, and he knew it, and loved her too in the only way he knew, with faithful and devoted service.

The telephone rang, and he went to answer it, returning with a pleased smile.

'The Count's secretary, madame. He will be coming tonight, but not until late.'

'Oh, goody, can I stay up?' demanded Coralie.

'No. Papa will come up if you are awake.'

Suddenly the evening was no longer lonely, the firelight seemed warmer, life gilded with unexpected joy. She put Coralie to bed, tucking her up, lighting the nightlight before the blue-clad madonna in a niche in the wall.

The hours crawled past and the silence and loneliness pressed down about the house. She put on her fur wrap again and went outside. The wind blew coldly along the river, and the ivy and pine trees were beginning to glitter with frost. She walked to the end of the terrace which looked down upon the courtyard, and, as if impelled, looked up and saw the light, far up above the serried pine trees, the light at Adlerburg like a yellow eye, staring down at her. She shuddered. The very thought of Schausenhardt was repulsive to her. She supposed that now the fighting was finished he had come home, and that poor Gottfried von Retz could no longer afford his brother-in-law's profligacy, and the old Princess, his mother, whose fortune he had whored and gambled away, was now dead. It would certainly be cheaper for them if he lived here, off the peasants and the land, than spend his time running up debts in Vienna.

The moon rose, making a glittering frosty landscape. There would soon be snow. The two older children would be back from school for Christmas. And Jimmy? Her heart contracted with longing. The war *must* be over by Christmas – every day the newspapers prophesied the end. Germany was beaten, and Austria in chaos. Russia in the throes of revolution. Would it be possible that she would soon see Jimmy again? Next year he would be twenty. She had heard, indirectly, that he was already a soldier. She prayed for the fighting to stop. That he and every mother's son would be safe. Keep him safe and let me see him again, my handsome, lovely lad!

Once again she heard the sound of a shot, far away. A dog or a wolf howled. Since the war a few wolves had made their way from the east through the forests and across the steppes. She shivered and turned back to the house, and then heard the sound of a car coming along the high road towards the village. Her whole face lit up with joy. It must be Eugene.

Ten minutes later he came into the house and she ran into his arms, startled by the expression on his face.

'What has happened? Is it over? The fighting?'

'Yes. Germany has surrendered.'

'Oh, thank God the killing has stopped.'

'Over thirteen million men are dead, and Austria has lost over a million. One cannot imagine all those corpses. And all so young.'

'But it is ended now?'

'And the Empire has ended too. The Emperor has renounced his rights in government, and a Republic will be declared.' He put his arm round her and they went into the firelit hall. The two big dogs rose to welcome him. 'We have to fight to win the peace now. To build something from this terrible wreckage.'

She took his hat, helped him with his coat, ministering to him, bringing as she always did, heart's ease and renewal.

'But it will not help if you kill yourself with overwork. Tonight we are at home together. Come and sit down before the fire. I will get you a drink . . . what would you like? A little brandy after such a cold drive I think.'

He took the glass from her hand.

'Ask Vatel to bring me something on a tray here,' he said, 'and to look after young Franzel.'

Franzel was his chauffeur, a young man invalided out of the army, jumpy with suppressed shellshock.

Eugene let her wait upon him and spoil him, and as always in her company his tension relaxed. Vatel delightedly brought a tray of light, delicious food which he set before the fire, and poured the wine. Viola watched Eugene, the ruddy firelight on his face, the clipped golden beard, just touched with grey, the light, Slavonic eyes, the face of a knight in a tapestry. He finished his meal and they sat together on the big settee before the fire.

'Now tell me all about you and Coralie?'

'We are well. I promised you would go up to say good night, but she is fast asleep.'

'No trouble? No *soldatska*?'

'One or two, quiet enough, poor devils, and glad to get a meal. Tonight I thought I heard shots in the high forest. Poachers, I expect.'

'I saw a light at Adlerburg. Who is there? I know von Retz and his family are in Vienna. I saw him yesterday.'

'Prince Friedrich is living there,' she said quietly. She must not let him see that she was afraid. She must not add to his anxieties. 'I heard tonight. Maritska, the swineherd's wife, told me when she brought a side of pork to smoke and store.' His face was alert with query. 'She says he has some of his men with him – ex-soldiers. She says the Prince has asked the villagers to give – to make contributions of food, and in return he and his men will protect them against the bandits.'

Eugene's face set grimly. 'A private army? It is something I have dreaded. The *Heimwehr* is necessary now, and men have a right to protect their homes, but that factions should form their own gangs of men is dangerous.'

'But surely it is better that the village should be protected?'

'If it stops there. But these are hungry men, ex-soldiers, used to death, used to killing? And with no employment. And not for a long while . . . we will not get industry moving overnight. Are you worried that Schausenhardt is there? He was once a great nuisance to you.'

'Oh, that was years ago. There is no reason why we should meet.'

He looked at the calm and lovely face. Men did not forget Viola. Schausenhardt was a dangerous man. He remembered that season in 1913 when Prince Friedrich had pursued Viola through the balllrooms and drawing-rooms of Vienna, making a conspicuous fool of himself, and embarrassing her with his persistence. The young officer with the bad reputation, and the crazy Schausenhardt eyes, blue, protuberant, in his tight-fitting white dress uniform, standing, watching her slender figure as she swayed past him, blind to glances and amused laughter, blinded with his primitive and uncontrolled desire.

He remembered Viola's distress over the sordid public incident when young Jimmy, goaded by the man's drunken insults, had struck him across the face. Diplomatically and quite ruthlessly Eugene had engineered Schausenhardt's posting to Galicia, far away from Vienna, from the dissipations he loved, and from Viola. But he was sure that the Prince, neurotically obsessive about his caste as an officer and an aristocrat, would not have forgotten.

He kissed her bright hair. There were a few silver threads over the temple, and they touched his heart absurdly – the signs of approaching autumn were as precious to him as Coralie's first bright curls. He could never imagine her growing old. But he was growing old himself. How long and how well could he protect her now?

'I am taking you and Coralie back to Vienna with me tomorrow,' he said definitely. 'I cannot leave you here any more. Now, no arguing.' He knew she felt responsible and protective about the village, helping the women to eke out an existence while their men were away. 'It is too dangerous here now. You must come back with me, and perhaps, until things get easier, I will

199

send you and the children abroad. The war is over. I could arrange it, I am sure.'

'Not without you.'

'We shall see.' He rang for Vatel and told him that they were returning to Vienna in the morning. 'Tell the girl to pack for Madame and Miss Coralie; we will close the castle and make an early start.'

Vatel beamed with relief.

It was after two o'clock and someone was hammering on the door of their room. They were both awake in an instant, Eugene dragging on a dressing-gown, and taking the revolver from the bedside table, Viola reaching for her wrap.

It was Vatel.

'M'sieur, wake up. There is a bad raid on the village. A boy has come to warn us. A big band of about thirty men. He says one of the women has told them that the food is kept here and they are coming to the castle. They are armed and they are marching the women and children before them.'

'Telephone the police station at Faldheim, Vatel . . .'

'Excellency, the wires are dead.' Eugene's face tightened. It must be a big raid: only an organized group would have thought of that. 'And, Excellency, as soon as the fires started young Franzel ran off with your car.'

'The devil he did!' said Eugene furiously, pulling on his clothes. 'Well, he was only a boy and has seen enough death for a lifetime. Here –' he gave Vatel a key – 'get a couple of guns from the rack, and undo the courtyard gate. We will see if they will listen to reason if we make them welcome. I'll go out on the terrace and see if I can parley with them. Viola, get dressed, and go to the child. Stay with her, and take the other women with you. Don't unlock to anyone but me or Vatel.'

She hurried to obey him, handing him a jacket and his boots, taking her own clothes out of the wardrobe.

'Eugene, take care, my darling, please. Take no risks. These men are desperate.'

200

'And hungry . . . we will feed them first and see if that helps.'

She was startled by his quick, youthful movements, and the speed and decision with which he moved. The weary heaviness of the long months of political negotiation seemed to have lifted from his shoulders.

'I am going to the end of the terrace which overlooks the forecourt. I'm going unarmed, and I'll talk to them. If they get food and drink, some money and a night's rest they may be all right. Vatel will be behind me with the guns, but we will not talk about shooting yet. Let us hope it will not come to that.'

As he reached the door they heard the sound of the church bell, loud and clear, hammering out a tocsin, unmelodious and insistent.

'That's the signal,' said Viola, 'to bring Schausenhardt and his men down here.'

'It will take them half an hour to get here,' he said. 'Let's try to get it settled first, and hope that they won't be needed.' He caught her up against him and kissed her tenderly. 'Take care of the baby and yourself,' he said, and went out of the room.

She dressed hastily, pulled on a woollen shawl and ran to Coralie's room. The old cook and the young girl who looked after Coralie were in the corridor, clinging together, terrified.

'Get dressed,' she said. 'The Count has gone out with Vatel to talk to the men. Don't be so frightened. Nothing has happened yet. Come to Miss Coralie's room, and be quiet. There is no need to waken her if she hasn't heard.'

The child was fast asleep in the deep sleep of secure childhood, sweet limbs sprawled, bright hair tossed across the pillow. The room was on the far side of the house, overlooking the rose gardens, and the gathering sound of voices and the beating of the alarm bell could scarcely be heard. The bell stopped as abruptly as it had begun. Someone had silenced the ringer.

The two women came in and sat down, the older one weeping silently, and wringing her hands.

'At Faldheim they burned all the houses,' she said. 'Everyone ran into the woods and hid until they passed. Why don't we do that, madame?'

'You can if you wish.'

The old woman hesitated, and then ran out of the room, but the girl stayed.

'Thank you, Anna.'

They looked out of the window; the red glare of burning thatch was reflected on the forest trees.

'They must have fired the village.'

Viola could stand it no longer. She gave the girl the key and told her to lock it behind her. 'Stay here, don't come out. Not until we come, or morning comes . . . I will come back as soon as I can.'

On the terrace she saw Eugene standing silhouetted against a fiery glow, Vatel behind him, holding two rifles. She crept silently to his side so that she could peer down into the forecourt. There was a crowd of men, rough, filthy and ragged, clad in torn uniforms and bits and pieces of sacking, some with blood-stained bandages, some with their feet wrapped in old rags, but nearly all of them were armed. Before them, hostages, stood the village women with children clinging about their skirts. She saw Maritska in the front, her square face half hidden by the dark headcloth, her arms held behind her by a thin, wolfish man.

'It's no use talking to this scum, Excellency,' she shouted. 'In a short while the Prince will be here with his men and then they'll get lead in their bellies, as they deserve.'

The man hit her across the head, sending her sprawling on the cobbles, and the women began to cry out loud. From some-where in the house the two big hounds began to bark.

'We want food,' shouted the man. 'We want it quickly now, before the *Heimwehr* get here.'

'We want booze and we want women,' yelled another, 'but we can wait for that.'

They all started to shout, and Eugene put up his hand.

'If all you want is food, let the women go, and put up your arms.'

'Open up, or we'll beat the doors in . . .'

'Let the women go, and we'll do just that. You can rest here tonight, and wash, and the women will see to your wounds. I will meet Prince Friedrich's men, and tell him you are making no trouble. If you go to Vienna and come to see me there I may be able to get you railway passes to your homes. That will be better than dragging through the forests. But you must put down your arms and behave peacefully now.'

A man shouted from the rear of the crowd, 'Don't trust him. He's a Jew and you can't trust Jews. He's keeping you talking until the police or the *Heimwehr* come. Open up the place and get at the food.'

Eugene saw the man – he was well back in the shadows. It was a German voice, a Viennese voice, and most of these men were Hungarians and Tyroleans, the furthest from their homelands. The man was neither ragged nor starving, nor wearing uniform. He knew at once that it was one of Schausenhardt's men, and that he was trying to provoke a riot.

'That man is not one of your band,' he shouted. 'He has not dragged across Poland trying to reach his home. He is one who would rather see you with lead in your bellies than the food you shall get here.'

The soldiers turned like one man on the intruder, and there was the crack of a rifle. Viola saw Eugene stagger and put his hands to his chest, staring over the mob into the darkness beyond, searching for the marksman before he heeled over on to the terrace paving. Men began pouring into the courtyard, and shots were being fired, the screaming women were trying to run away, trying to pull the children into shelter, through into the stableyard, into the gardens.

'Oh, Christ!' cried Viola. 'Oh, dear God, no . . .'

She and Vatel reached him together, dragging his body along the terrace and into the hall, laying him down on a rug before the hearth. She tore open his shirt. The wound was only a small one just below the ribs, but blood was beginning to pour from it. She ripped off her blouse, and pressed it over the wound, staring down into his face, frantically willing him to live.

'The telephone,' she said. 'Vatel, the doctor from the town . . .'

'Madame, the wires were cut when I tried to get the police.'

'Darling, darling, lie still . . . I will send Franzel in the car . . . you with him, and I will come with you . . .'

'Lift me, lift me a little,' he said. She put her arm beneath him, lifting his head against her shoulder. The blood ran down on to the frail white cambric of her chemise. 'You forget – Franzel went . . . he took the car. Poor boy, he has had enough of guns . . .' His voice wavered. When he drew a breath the blood from the wound bubbled brightly, soaking the blouse, running over her fingers. 'It's no use, *mein liebchen*, my dear one.' She bent and kissed his mouth with passion and despair. 'Go away. Take Coralie. Go away from here, from this country . . . go to England, take the children . . . to Jimmy. To Staffray . . . go away . . . do not mourn for me, *liebchen*, for you were made for life, my duchess, and I do not want sorrow to touch you . . .'

He stopped, and choked, and blood began to run from his mouth; his bright eyes suddenly dulled, and then – he was no longer there. She wiped the blood away, thinking irrationally how beautiful he was. Looking so strangely young. One of the big dogs raised its great head and howled, and the other growled uneasily, looking towards the door. Vatel's old hand with its swollen veins gently closed the silver-grey eyes.

'The Count is dead, madame,' he said, and he took Eugene from her, laid him down gently on the floor, placing a cushion beneath his head. He rose and went out of the room, and presently came back with an embroidered cape, an antique robe, a court relic of some past Erhmann, and covered the still figure. Then he put a shawl round Viola's bare shoulders, and held her, rocking her against him, while their hearts broke together for the man they had both loved. Outside there was silence. The firing had stopped.

Time passed, and they did not know how long it was. The sound of booted feet outside and the main door being thrust open made them turn, their arms still about each other, Viola's drained white face lifting from Vatel's shoulder with an unearthly, pallid beauty that made Schausenhardt feel as though he had never seen her before, and this ghost-like, pearly beauty was even more tormenting than the glowing Viola of five years ago.

As he came into the hall he was followed by three of his men, big, young, burly, crop-haired fellows, dressed in rough hunting clothes. They stood at the door as though forming a guard. Schausenhardt came forward and stood looking down at her. Viola stared at him blankly, without recognition. Vatel rose and helped her gently to her feet, but her hand still twisted tightly in his. The tall, strong man, with his high, ruddy complexion and prominent dark blue eyes seemed familiar. The look in the eyes still haunted her dreams . . . protuberant blue eyes. Her husband, Arthur Netherby, and his pale watchful eyes and strong cruel hands. But Arthur was long dead and he had been an elderly man. Schausenhardt lifted his hand to cover the new pink scar that ran down his face, lifting his harsh, sensual mouth in a perpetual sneer.

'You remember me, Countess?'

'I . . . you must forgive . . . I cannot . . .'

'Highness,' said Vatel, 'my lady is distressed and exhausted. The Count is dead.'

Schausenhardt bent, flipped back the embroidered satin robe and looked down at the still, golden-bearded face, so fine in death, the care lines smoothed away. He stared down at the man he had killed, whom he had wanted to kill for a long time.

'A stray bullet?' he asked.

'We do not know, Highness.'

'We came quickly from Adlerburg, but we came just too late, I see.' He offered his arm to Viola. 'Allow me, Countess, to help you to your room.'

'There is no need,' said Vatel quickly. 'I will assist the Countess. We must get a message to Vienna, and a doctor and priest.'

'A priest you *may* get,' Schausenhardt said cynically, 'though the old fool in the village has his hands full tonight. Nothing else can be done until the morning. I will take charge.' He gestured to his men. 'Help the Countess to her room, then carry the body to the dining-room and put it on the table there. Then

205

keep watch at the door in case any of that scum return. In the morning we will send to Vienna and get the police.'

Two of the burly young ex-soldiers took Viola between them when they began to lead her away, she cried out like an animal in pain, and broke away, throwing herself down by Eugene's body, bent, agonized, and kissed his lips. Schausenhardt's heavy face reddened, fraught with jealously of the dead man.

'The Countess is distraught,' he said. 'Take her to her room.'

'Do not touch her,' cried Vatel. 'Let me attend my lady . . .'

Prince Friedrich swung round on him, glaring, but Vatel did not waver. He was in his sixties, he was exhausted with grief and weariness, but he was not afraid.

'Get this old man out of here, to his bed or to the kitchen,' said the Prince, gesturing to the third of his guards. 'I do not let servants meddle with me.'

The tall young man led Vatel away, and he knew it was no use struggling or shouting. There was no one to hear. The other two men carried Viola up the carved stairway to her room. They looked at her white face furtively, but did not meet each other's eyes. The Prince had fed, sheltered and employed them since the fighting had ended, but they were afraid of him and his unpredictable moods, and they had heard him in his cups, ranting about the English whore, the Jew's fancy woman and what he would do to her.

He followed them upstairs.

'Keep watch,' he said, 'at the head of the stairs. I wish to speak to the Countess before we leave. I shall not be long.'

The two young men hesitated, and when he roared at them, turned with trained obedience, and took their stations at the top of the stairs. He went into the room and closed the door.

Viola was sitting on her bed. Although she had a shawl about her shoulders, she had torn off her blouse to staunch Eugene's wound. The fine white cambric of her chemise was stained with blood, and there was blood on her upper arms and on her white breast. The long seductive green eyes which had driven him mad held neither fire nor defiance, they were neither afraid nor accusing. She sat before him like a woman drugged or sleep-walking, and did not speak.

'So,' he said, 'your Jew is dead. His money cannot protect you now. He cannot send me out of Vienna, like a servant, at his wish.' Her stillness suddenly cracked some dam of obsessional desire, and he fell on his knees by her side, seizing her lifeless hand. A sound was torn from him, a groan of pain and longing. 'Viola, look at me!' His big hand forced up her face, making her meet his eyes. 'I have wanted you like no man ever wanted a woman before. All these years, all through the fighting, I have thought only that one day I would possess you. You have given me no peace.'

'Did — you kill him, then?'

'I should have killed him years ago . . . he should have fought me as a man of honour.'

For the first time a glimmer crossed the still white face. 'But you would not have fought a Jew,' she said, and her dead eyes mocked him and everything he stood for.

'Viola, come to me.'

Her brows drew together, childishly puzzled. She was numb with shock, frozen with horror. Bereft. If she thought, then she would know Eugene was dead, and she did not want to know that yet. Exhaustion was engulfing her like a black cloud. The man with his burning eyes, his heavy strong hands clamping on her bare shoulder wavered before her, like an object seen along the road in the glare of a heat haze.

'I want to sleep,' she said. 'Let me sleep. Tomorrow there will be much to do . . . let me sleep until tomorrow.'

'Viola, listen to me!' He shook her so that her head fell back and he was gazing at the long, fragile line of her throat, the curve that led beneath the laces to her beautiful breasts, and he felt his hands tremble and his breath become fast. 'Viola, I will marry you, if you will come to me. In Vienna you tormented me, but I will do anything to possess you.' His head bent until his lips rested on the long white throat, and when he raised it he said, 'I am Prince Friedrich Schausenhardt . . . I will make you my wife. You will be a princess.'

She did not move, and he dragged her upright, holding her

207

like a rag doll, trying to make her understand. 'I am Prince Frie
drich Schausenhardt. And I am asking you to be my wife.'

She came to life, and her eyes narrowed. She drew herself up
looking at him with infinite disgust.

'You,' she said, 'are shit and always have been!' And she spa
in his face.

He threw her on the bed and tore the clothes from her slende
white body. When he saw her lying before him, as he had s
often imagined her, naked and at his mercy, her tumultuou
hair streaming over the pillow, he was shaking, incoherent
beside himself with desire, and with cruelty, wanting both t
possess her and to stamp her out of existence. He took her wit
ferocious brutality, but she did not utter a sound. She did no
cry out with pain or with pleasure, she did not open her eyes, th
heavy long-lashed lids were closed against him and she was a
limp in his arms as a dead woman. When he rose from her he fe
neither triumph nor relief, but only an abysmal self-disgust. Sh
opened her eyes and they stared up from the sunken hollows a
him as though he was some filthy scum, something unmention
ably low and disgusting. He turned away. He could not bear it
She lacerated his pride. She destroyed his egotism. She was lik
some strange obstruction to his desire which he would neve
conquer except by death. For one crazy moment he turned o
her and took the long white throat in his hands. He could see th
red marks of his teeth lividly on her flesh. But she showed no ves
tige of fear and made no sound, only the burning, haunting eye
staring at him, telling him that he had not possessed her, no
ever would, and that what he had done meant nothing. He le
her go and left her, calling to his men, and she heard the sound
of boots down the stairs and the banging of the great oaken doo
below in the hall. The grey winter dawn began to show behind
the mountains.

Presently Vatel came in. At first he thought she was dead, she
was so white, and the dark hollows round her closed eyes so
dark. Then she put out a hand, and he saw the faint movement
of breath lifting her breast. He drew a cover over her. She wa
icy cold. He brought her brandy, piled the logs on the hearth.

'Help me, Vatel,' she whispered. 'I must be clean.'

He helped her to her feet and to her bathroom, adjusting the shower, tending her like a nurse while the water ran over her defiled body as she tried to wash away the feel, the smell, and the hideous memory of Schausenhardt. Then he wrapped her in a warm towel, drying her gently like a baby, fetching her a clean gown and wrap, slippers, as though his love and respect could heal her.

'I – I want to go to the baby now,' she said.

Very slowly they went through the house, knocked at the night nursery door, and the scared girl, Anna, opened it.

'I want to sleep with my little girl,' she said.

Vatel helped her into the bed, and drew the quilt over her. The child turned, warm and unknowing, and to his relief he saw a faint smile touch her face.

'I should have shot him,' he said.

She shook her head. 'My dear friend, you have done all you could and more . . . just one more thing. In the medicine chest there are some sleeping tablets. I must sleep or I shall die . . . tomorrow will have to wait.'

He found the tablets, gave her some with water, sat by her until sleep claimed her. Then he lay back in a deep chair near them. The Count had been a great man. Vienna must be informed and the funeral arranged. The other two children must be told, and brought home for it, and the lawyers contacted. All the rituals of life and death, which he knew so well how to stage-manage, must be attended to – tomorrow. Presently the old man slept, as his mistress slept, worn out with horror and with grief.

CHAPTER EIGHT

Jimmy got leave before Christmas, and came home, a tall, lean, young man whom Amy did not know. He seemed to have no relation to the boy who had gone away. The day after his return he went to meet James at his club. He was still in uniform, and James was inordinately proud of him. His soldier son who had fought with honour, and returned unscathed. But was he? The blue eyes had lost their careless gaiety. They had seen death near and often and had the edgy recklessness of a man who has come through but does not quite know how or why. He told James that, because of his fluent German, he was to be sent to Cologne with the Army of Occupation.

'I don't want to go. At least, not yet. Once you offered to get me out. Would you see if you can get me an extended leave?' He brought a letter out of his breast pocket, 'This came through my bankers. It's from Mama. Papa is dead.' He handed the letter to James. The big sprawling childish writing, the words occasionally mis-spelled, seemed so familiar to him that the years fell away.

> 'My darling boy,
> I think this will be the first letter to get to you, though I've sent many. I wish I had good news, but I have to tell you Papa is dead. Things got very short so I lived at Die Kinderburg, where we had food. Papa came from Vienna whenever he could get away. When the Russians gave up more and more poor soldiers deserted, starving and frozen, tramping back to their homes in gangs. At first we fed them, but then they got so threatening we had to hide the food, and the villagers brought their stocks to the castle and we hid it in the big cellars, and every day they came for what they wanted, so that if there was a raid their houses were empty. Then there was a raid on Die Kinderburg. Lorenz and Theresa were away at school, but I had little Coralie with

me. Papa tried to persuade the men to go away in return for food, but they began shooting, and we had to bar the doors, and protect ourselves. The Heimwehr from Adlerburg, the vigilantes, came to help us, but Papa was killed, how I don't know.

I stay here. Vienna is a sad city now and one feels guilty having money when so many people are so poor and have no food, and prices are every day higher. Thank goodness the children are all well. Your Papa used to say that the Empire was brave but not wise. Let us hope the new republic will be both. They will need to be very wise. I want to come home, Jimmy. There is nothing to keep me here now Eugene is dead. I want to bring my children back to England. Can you help me? Will you send for me? You must be nearly a grown man now. My love, ever, Mama.'

'You see,' Jimmy said, 'if it is possible I must go to her at once. She sounds afraid. I have never known her to be afraid before.'

The Repatriation Mission travelling to Vienna was made up of high-ranking officers from Administration and civilian experts in Transport and Supply. Second-Lieutenant James Corbett was quite the youngest member of the party. They had a reserved coach on a packed train filled with a miscellany of businessmen, soldiers and refugees. It was a long, tedious journey continually held up in sidings, and, across France, by shattered railway stations and narrow, temporary bridges thrown up by the engineers. They peered out at skeleton towns, struggling back to some kind of normality.

In Paris he was startled to find his elders and betters were anxious to spend a night there, sampling the hectic pleasures of that peace-drunk city, glad of his company because of his excellent French, and because his youth, and his lordly cosmopolitan sophistication, made him an admirable guide.

Jimmy felt tense with emotion; with memories that filled him with unshed tears. He guided his older colleagues through the pleasures of a city hell-bent on making up for four lost years, and his mother seemed to float by his side in the glory of her mature and tender beauty.

211

Had he really been that schoolboy, feeling so grown-up in his first dinner jacket, proudly accompanying her to the theatres and restaurants? The Madrid and the Cascade and Maxim's . . . full of rich, smart, carefree people and elegant women. Remembering his bursting pride because she was the most beautiful of them all, he could suddenly see her again, the little, tender, indulgent smile as she watched him coping with bills, with tips, with the gallant behaviour which was her due from men, and feel the appreciative squeeze of her white-gloved hand. What had happened to her now Papa was dead? Was she in danger, or afraid, or suffering? The delays irked him, and although he never forgot his manners or his rank he was irritated by what seemed to him wasted time.

He could not wait to get to Vienna. He wished he could have flown.

Even when war-torn France was far behind, and the mountain valleys were glorious with spring, the war had cast a blight over everything. The blossoming orchards and flushed mountain peaks gave an illusion of beauty, but in the stations and towns the weary, shabby drabness, the hungry-looking people, the quantities of war material, pushed into sidings, discarded, rusting refuse now the killing was done, all told their own story. And through Germany and into Austria they saw the haggard, half-starved men in uniform, moving somehow, anyhow, back to their homes.

Vienna – the station where he had been met by his mother and step-father on his journey home from school, travelling with Vatel in their own compartment, with every comfort. No laughing kisses, no carriage or Daimler waited now. An official met them, greeting them with the hostile courtesy of the defeated and drove them to their hotel.

Jimmy asked to be excused for the evening, and made his way to the house in Prinz Eugenstrasse. The lilacs were in green bud in the Michaeler Platz, and in the Burggarten the chestnut trees were already breaking into leaf. Along the Kartner Ring and Graben the cafés seemed just as full of officers and ladies as before the war, and the green trams clanged along exactly as he

212

remembered them as a child.

On the surface it appeared the same, but the surface was skin deep. Its superficial charm hid an undercurrent of desperation. In the tenements the people were starving as the men came back from the Front to find the factories closed, the food shops empty, their women lining up daily in the bread queues. At night shadowy beggars hung outside the cafés. The Vienna he could remember might have had poverty but it had been hidden by the flamboyant gaiety of the privileged. Now the other side rose like a black tide, invading the wide, tree-lined, café-lined streets, demanding the right to live. It was not just defeat. The heart of the country, the four-hundred-year-old Hapsburg Empire, had vanished. The city was drifting on a tide of despair like a rudderless ship and every day brought news of riots and demonstrations.

The house was dark and shuttered when he arrived in the early evening and the gates locked. A slogan was sloshed along the walls in yellow paint. 'JEWS EAT WHILE AUSTRIANS STARVE.'

He rang the bell at the porter's lodge and a man came out, eyeing his British uniform suspiciously. The city was not occupied and there were very few foreign uniforms in the street. He was wearing the pike grey breeches of a field uniform and a shabby army shirt. Jimmy spoke in German.

'Good evening. Is the Countess Erhmann here?'

'The apartment is closed, as you can see,' said the man sullenly. 'The Countess is in the country.'

'At Die Kinderburg?'

'Yes. D'you know it?'

'Yes. I was brought up there – and in this house too. Do you know if she is well? If the children are well?'

'Better than we are here. There's food in the country and the farmers keep it to themselves. She pays my wages. I haven't seen her since the Count died. They do well to keep out of Vienna who can.'

'Do you know if the Baroness von Retz still lives in the Herrenstrasse?'

'So far as I know.' Jimmy gave him some money which he took, resentfully rather than gratefully, but his manner eased slightly.

'You've seen active service?'

'*Ja wohl*. Three years on the Italian frontier in those blasted snows. Sometimes I think I'll never be warm again. Come back to find my business gone and my wife run off with a Hungarian. I'm lucky to have this. Vatel, the Count's old valet, got me the job.'

'Is Vatel in Vienna?'

'No. He is with the family.'

'Well, thank you again. I will try and find the Baroness von Retz.' He had a box of Players cigarettes in the pocket of his service warm, and he gave it to the man whose face lit up with more pleasure than they had at the money, which by morning could have again lost value.

'You are young, Herr Lieutenant. Were they calling babies up, too, on your side.'

'Pretty well.' Jimmy grinned. 'But active service makes old soldiers of us all. We must learn not to hate each other – at least we are alive and can see it doesn't happen again.' He saluted and the man drew himself up and saluted in return. Jimmy hesitated, and then said, 'Who scrawls these things on the wall?'

'Oh, all sorts.' The man looked uneasy. 'Street mobs. Men back from the front, starving and unemployed. Czechs, Poles, Hungarians, Germans – all blaming each other, and a lot of them blaming the Jews.'

'But why?'

The man shrugged and spat. 'Someone has to be blamed. They've got rid of the Emperor, and the Republic can't seem to cure their ills. And someone like Count Erhmann, who owned this house, and was a great man in the government and never saw a shot fired, he was still rich when the rest of us starved.'

'I see,' Jimmy said, then abruptly: 'He was my step-father. A better man never lived. Good night to you, and good luck.'

'Good night, Herr Lieutenant.'

214

Jimmy returned to the hotel and tried to telephone Die Kinderburg but was told there was no longer a connection with the castle. He walked along the Ring to the Herrengasse. His British uniform attracted curious glances, and an occasional muttered or shouted epithet. At the von Retz house he rang the bell of the apartment on the first floor and an elderly servant opened it a crack without undoing the guard chain, peering round at him suspiciously.

He gave his name and she retired without opening the door, but returned shortly, unhooked the chain and opened the drawing-room door.

'I am sorry, Herr Lieutenant, but one never knows who might knock these days. Will you wait here? My lady will not be long.'

Where was the noise, the bustle of liveried servants, the gossip of company, the cries of spoiled children at play? Of course the von Retz children would be in their teens now, like Lorenz and Theresa, his half-brother and sister. Here he and they had once been fed with cream cakes and glacé fruits, and he had made his first boyish attempts at flirting. There was dust in the folds of the heavy brocade curtains and the convoluted plaster work of the high ceilings. The valuable bric-à-brac of Meissen and Dresden, the many fine old pictures, had all gone. Although it was only early spring the big porcelain stove was empty and cold.

He remembered how warm it had always been, how clean and polished, how extravagantly rich and luxurious, with Baron Gottfried, large and red-faced, beaming indulgently at his spoiled aristocratic young wife and fair-haired children.

The door opened and Princess Charlotte, Baroness von Retz, came in. He would not have recognized the plump, vivacious, frivolous Tante Lotte, who had spoiled, petted and flirted with him in his budding manhood. A thin, apprehensive-looking woman, who looked at him guardedly, came into the room. Her clothes, although of expensive material and cut, were out of date and shabby. Her hair, which had once tossed in shiny black ringlets, was twisted negligently on her neck – the ineffectual effort of a helpless woman. It was obvious that Lotte had no ladies' maid now, nor an expensive hair-dresser.

215

'James-Carlo!' she exclaimed in astonishment. 'What are you doing here?'

Slowly, as though not quite sure of the correct approach, she held out her hand. He remembered how plump her hands had been, how vivaciously gesticulating, showing off her superb diamonds. There was only the one gold wedding ring now. Jimmy brought his heels together and kissed the outstretched hand in the approved Viennese manner. It seemed to reassure her, although no answering gleam of coquetry lit her haunted eyes. 'Well, sit down, sit down. It seems very strange to see an enemy uniform in my house after all my poor country has suffered.'

'All countries have suffered, and wars must end, Tante Lotte.' He was uncomfortably aware of pomposity but was at a loss for words.

'You are a man now. Do you still flirt as much as you did when you were a small boy?'

Jimmy smiled, his quick, warm smile, trying to reach her; to break down the hostile apathy. 'I do, when I get the chance. But I have been on the Western Front for twelve months, and now I am stationed at Cologne.'

'You are young – although you look a grown man. How did you come to be called to the army?' Her lips were suddenly scornful. 'Did not the Erhmann money protect you in England?'

'I volunteered, Tante Lotte.'

She looked at the lean, tanned, young face, hardened with warfare, and sighed. 'I am sorry Gottfried is not yet in. He would have liked to see you. He is not a Schausenhardt – he is not so sensitive as I am. The children are away at school. My mother, I regret to say, has passed away.'

Jimmy recalled the fat, greedy old Princess with difficulty, and tried to look sympathetic.

'My brother, Prince Friedrich, served most gallantly. He was decorated by the Emperor. The old Emperor.' She gave him a queer, probing glance, and he wondered how much she remembered of the old scandal, how he had loathed her brother and had insulted him in public. 'But why are you here, James-Carlo?'

'I am here with an Allied Mission. I am acting as interpreter. It is to do with repatriating prisoners of war.'

'*Ach*, they are not bringing more of them back?' Her face clouded pettishly. 'As though we have not enough of them. These *soldatska*. Brigands. Robbing decent people of the few possessions they have left and making riots in the streets.' Her dark-ringed eyes held the same sullen expression as the porter at Prinz Eugenstrasse had shown. 'I regret I cannot ask you to dinner. My servant has already done the marketing, and we were not expecting guests. It is not like the old days – then the servants ate more in a day than would feed us for a month.'

'I'm sorry. I know things are bad. Food is not easy in England either. Nor fuel. I was hoping – perhaps you and Baron Gott-fried would have dinner with me tonight. I presume there are still good restaurants in Vienna?'

'Oh, there are places for those who can afford it – the profiteers and the Jews. I'll be glad to dine with you, James-Carlo. But that's not what you've really come for. You've come to find your mother.' She laughed. 'Everyone looks for Viola. To protect her. To see she has everything. Even Friedrich, although she has treated him like dirt.'

He looked at her restlessly twining hands.

'I have been home, but the house is closed. I tried to telephone Die Kinderburg, but there was no connection. Is she well? Have you seen her?'

'I do not see her now. I believe she is well. The people at Die Kinderburg are fond of her. When are you going?'

'As soon as I can get leave of absence. Tante Lotte, tell me, how did Papa die?'

She rose abruptly, avoiding his glance. A high spot of colour appeared in her cheeks.

'How should I know? I was not there. There was some kind of riot – a food riot. The *soldatska* were always attacking country houses then. My brother was at Adlerburg and he took his men and went to their assistance. Freddi knows how to deal with such scum. He is organizing the *Heimwehr* out there.'

'*Heimwehr?*'

'Men ready to arm themselves to protect their homes – vigilantes.'

'Can I see your brother?'

'He is at Adlerburg. He is waiting to see what will happen. The so-called Republic is a farce, a rabble of socialists and Jews. Intellectuals. There will have to be a new party, he says. A party of decent people who will unite with greater Germany. We shall cleanse ourselves from all these excrescences and make one great German-speaking people. Friedrich is waiting for the time when he will be called to help to build such a Germany.'

'Would these be the people who paint slogans on Papa's house?'

She gave him a quick, defensive stare.

'But why? Papa was not a Jew. He was an Erhmann. A Count of the Holy Empire. An Austrian and Viennese to his finger-tips.'

'His mother was a Jew,' she shouted suddenly. 'A man is a Jew if his mother is a Jew. Freddi says this, and it is true, even if his ancestors fought with Charlemagne. Erhmann was a banker like his mother's people, the Mendels. Money everywhere, all over the world, as such people have. His business did not go bankrupt like Gottfried's. They never did without. Has Viola had to sell her jewels? Had Eugene to sell his pictures, his land, like we have had to? Has she had to scrape and get into debt? And she was English – an enemy alien. Why was she not interned as she should have been? Who knows that she was not a spy? No, she was protected by his money and his bribery . . .'

'Tante Lotte,' said Jimmy painfully, 'you are speaking of my mother.'

She stared at him as though she had not heard, her dark eyes glaring fanatically.

'And Vatel,' she went on, 'their manservant. A Frenchman. He too was not interned. People like us had no servants, but he still served them and was not interfered with . . .'

'But Vatel is in his sixties, Tante Lotte, and has lived in Austria almost the whole of his life in the service of our family.'

'What does it matter? Be sure he was a spy. And she . . . she is

218

not even a lady. She was a common girl, one of these little shop girls, whom men pick up for a bit of fun, and now she flaunts it down at Die Kinderburg as though she were truly the lady of the manor and not a jumped-up tart. . . .'

'*Lotte!*'

Baron Gottfried von Retz stood in the doorway. The anxiety and poverty that had overtaken him had not made him thinner, but his frame was flabby and his affable features pale and drawn. The eyes behind the thick spectacles were as kind as ever.

'Lotte! How can you say such things. It is *disgraceful!* You know well that Eugene kept things going because he was a brilliant financier, and that he helped me greatly before he died. You know that Viola helped us, and it is through their generosity that the children are still at their schools. You should be ashamed.'

'I am ashamed of taking Jews' charity,' she said, and burst suddenly into harsh, shaking sobs. Jimmy put out his hand and Gottfried grasped it.

'My dear boy. Such a man now! You must forgive my wife. It is hard for her – she was a little Princess. She has never had to stir a finger. At such times one can only be glad to be alive. You will dine with us.'

'I'm afraid not, thank you, sir. I had hoped that you and Tante Lotte would dine with me.'

'I – I do not think it would be suitable, under the circumstances. You being still in uniform. When are you going to see your mother?'

'I want to see if I can hire a car . . .'

'A car!' cried Lotte, as though he had struck her. 'He can afford a car! It must be pleasant to be a conqueror and spend Jewish money. We would not dine with you if we were starving!'

Her husband made a hopeless little gesture.

'I think I had better go,' Jimmy said with grave courtesy. 'Good-bye, Princess.'

She turned her back on him, but before he could reach the door, flew after him, and kissed him, touching his face, dabbing at her tears. '*Ach*, Jimmy-C, *liebling*, it is not your fault. Such a lovely boy. I cannot bear that you should not think of me as Tante Lotte any more . . .'

'*Auf wiedersehen*, Tante Lotte,' said Jimmy and kissed her.

Gottfried walked with him to the front door.

'My dear boy, she is not herself these days. She has lost so much, and her nerves are in a dreadful state. The doctor gives her calming drugs, but I think they make her worse – irrational. She listens to Freddi with his wild schemes of making the *Heimwehr* into a greater German party. At Adlerburg he drills the men like soldiers. He is full of hare-brained ideas. An extremist. Always was. These ideas of racial purity. The world has flowed through Vienna from east to west and back since time began. How can we have a pure race? They want a scapegoat, men like Freddi Schausenhardt, for their own inadequacies. He is a product of his class, I suppose, educated only for idleness or war. I don't know. Times are hard, but I would have come out of it better had I been more clever. But I am sorry that my poor *liebchen* should have spoken to you so . . .'

'It does not matter, sir.'

'But it does. You are going to find your mother?'

'That is why I wangled the job, sir!'

He smiled, but still glanced apprehensively at Jimmy from behind his pebble-glasses. 'You will find her somewhat changed, though still as beautiful. She is a woman of great strength. But – do not blame her . . .'

'Blame her?'

'I do not mean that. People say such dreadful things. That she was a food hoarder – but the people of Kinderburg were loyal to her, and she to them. She is one who looks after her own. Who can do more? We have all done things during these terrible times that would have seemed strange before. Well, good-bye, my boy. I hope it will only be *auf wiedersehen*. But who knows.'

'*Auf wiedersehen*, sir.'

They shook hands and Jimmy went slowly down the street of old mansions, built for the rich and aristocratic in days gone by. At the hotel he was relieved to learn that in the confusion and disorganization of these early days of the newly-formed Republic it would be a day or so before they could get the repatriation conference organized. His chief, who had been well briefed by Lord Louderdown as to his underlying reason for being in Vienna, told him it would be possible for him to have a car and go to Die Kinderburg in the morning.

It was nearing midday when he came in sight of the village and saw once again the little castle on its rock above the river. It was a sunny day with blowing clouds against a blue sky. In the orchards the apple trees were heavy with blossom, the pink and white petals blowing across the road like confetti. The picturesque timbered houses with their overhanging eaves, and the old church with the copper spire, turquoise blue with verdigris. The vine terraces beyond, and the woods rising to the skyline, and in the far distance, as the car mounted the winding road up to the castle gates, the white capped peaks of the Tyrol.

The stableyard was empty as he drove in. No blowing straw, no stamp and snort of boxed horses, the doors closed and locked. Beyond the archway he could see the gardens, once overflowing with his mother's favourite flowers, now planted with rows of vegetables, the lawns dug over, sprouting with early potatoes. Something moved with amused tenderness within him, a wave of confidence that his mother would be all right, somewhere within the house. She could never, like poor Lotte von Retz, be reduced to hysterical resentment. As Baron Gottfried had said, she was one who looked after her own. If there was a food shortage, she would grow it, or buy it, or even steal it for those who depended upon her. It was as though the flower garden spoke to him with all Viola's flat north country common sense, 'Aye, well, love, folk can't eat roses.' So there were carrots and cabbages and potatoes and onions where once her cherished flowers had grown.

As he got out, an elderly man carrying a gun over his arm came to the top of the terrace steps, and stood looking down at him. Jimmy recognized him immediately. The once carefully dyed black hair was snow white, and the neat, deft figure bowed, but it was Eugene's French valet, Vatel. As Jimmy bounded up the steps, he levelled the gun, and said, '*Attention, m'sieur.*'

'Vatel! Vatel, don't you know me?' The gun muzzle dropped. He ran up the remaining steps, and put his arms round the old man. So thin and small now, gnarled and bent like a vine root. 'It's me. Jimmy-C. There, Vatel, please don't cry. You'll make me cry too. The war is over, Vatel, and I've come for my mother. Where is she, and where are the other children?'

The old man could not speak for a moment. He gazed at the tall young soldier as though at a vision.

'*M'sieur. M'sieur* James-Carlo. A man. *Un soldat.* An officer . . . I cannot believe it.'

'Well, it's true. I tried to telephone my mother, but they told me there was no connection.'

'Yes, it is so. Since . . . since for some time. You must come in. Please to come in . . . This way, please *m'sieur.*' The highly trained upper servant had miraculously surfaced. *M'sieur* Jimmy-C had come back, a grown man. A man to take charge. To protect his beloved Countess.

'Vatel, will you prepare her . . . go ahead . . . I don't want to frighten her.'

'She is alone. *M'sieur* Lorenz and *Mam'selle* Theresa are away at school, and the small Coralie goes to the village school, and is not yet home. I will tell milady you are here.'

The old man had pulled himself together. He was wearing rough country clothes, gaiters and breeches, but from his manner now he might have been wearing his immaculate pre-war livery. He led the way to the library. Jimmy caught his breath. His mother was seated at her desk working on some papers. She was dressed in black, which enhanced her white skin, and wearing the long string of pearls which he had so often played with when he was a baby. The wings of her cloudy red hair were speckled with grey like a fox's pelt.

She looked up, shading her eyes against the bright afternoon sunshine which streamed across the terrace and rose, not recognizing him, her face suddenly cold, expressionless, frozen as she saw a tall figure in uniform silhouetted against the light, as though she expected someone else, someone who was not welcome.

'Madame,' said Vatel shakily. 'Milady, here is *M'sieur* James-Carlo, just arrived from England.'

She went white, and clutched the edge of her desk. She had only fainted once in her life before – when she had read that James Staffray had been seriously wounded out in South Africa. But now it was Jimmy who ran forward and caught her in his arms.

It was mid-afternoon when she took him to Eugene's grave in the churchyard of the village. It was a plain slab of local granite in a far corner, beneath some beech trees shrill with spring. It bore his name and rank and age, the Erhmann crest, his ministerial rank, and the date of his death. A village woman was bending over it, clearing something from the stone. Jimmy saw yellow paint, and his heart sickened.

'Again, Maritza?' said Viola.

'Again, *Gräfin*,' said the woman patiently, 'in the night some time. It was found early. I have cleaned it.'

'It was kind of you, Maritza.'

'Kindness for kindness, *Gräfin*,' said the woman, staring at Jimmy. 'He was a good man.'

'My son from England. Do you remember?'

The woman smiled with amazement. '*Herr* Jimmy? The bold one? *Ach*, I remember. How things change. Well, I will leave you to pray.'

She picked up the rags and bucket with which she had been cleaning the stone and left them. Viola sat down on the slab. She had wound a fine shawl of black lace over her hair and round her shoulders.

'What was it?' he asked. 'What was she cleaning?'

'The usual things. The muck these people write.' She put her hand gently on the stone, shrugged, and said, 'When he died the funeral was here, not in Vienna. But many, many people came. All kinds, ministers and princes, generals, simple soldiers, poor

223

people, representatives of the Imperial family. Ambassadors from abroad. The little church was filled to overflowing. None of these scum dared raise their heads then. But it doesn't matter. He isn't here. If he knew he would understand how frightened and unhappy they all are. It's not from the village. They loved him here. They come in at night these people, to deposit this refuse.'

'Who sends them?'

'Who knows?' she said guardedly. 'People who know would not tell. They would be afraid.'

'Mama, tell me how it happened? I heard there was a riot and a fight and he was killed. Was it an accident?'

'Who knows?' she said again. 'The brigands were very bad then . . . We tried to help everyone who came to the door, but it was impossible. It was as if we were in a lifeboat, Jimmy, and more and more poor drowning people tried to get in. We have big dungeons and wine cellars at the castle, so the village people brought their produce and I hid it for them until they needed it. But someone must have found out, and one night there was a big attack. They came out of the woods like hungry wolves. Papa was here that night. The only other man was old Vatel. Someone sounded the alarm bell, and Prince Schausenhardt's men came down from Adlerburg.'

'You mean his servants?'

'No, they were men from his regiment whom he had brought home with him. They were not like the local *Heimwehr* – more like a private army. The bands of brigands had been getting more threatening, and local people were glad to pay for their protection with food and wine.'

'Like – like feudal times?' he said unbelievingly.

'Yes, so Papa said. We did not like it. He went out because – he thought the *soldatska* would be reasonable and he could give them a few provisions to help them on their way. But as soon as Prince Friedrich's men appeared the shooting started, several men were killed, Papa among them. That was how it was.' She looked up with hard, sad eyes. 'I don't talk about it, Jimmy love. It's done. Nothing can bring Papa back. He was a

224

grand, lovely man, wise and kind, witty . . . I was lucky to have been married to him.'

'Prince Friedrich. He is an extremist. He – he wouldn't have attacked Papa?'

She lifted the black lace scarf, drawing it round her face as though cold. 'I did not see anything, Jimmy. I do not ask about it. My Eugene is dead – what would be the use? There has been enough killing. Let it rest. Come. We will go and meet Coralie from school. You have not met your little sister yet.'

They met her, small, copper-haired, blue-eyed, precise, Bobbing in the German manner to the tall young soldier whom, they told her, was her brother.

On the terrace Vatel had set the tea-table. There were cakes and there was real Ceylon tea. It had been sent, Viola said, from the New York office with a parcel of provisions, the moment the mails came through.

'It is as useful as money. Tea and sugar, for potatoes and flour.'

'Baron Gottfried said you were one who looked after her own.'

'You saw them? Poor Lotte. She hates me now. I didn't know until things got bad. Perhaps she didn't hate me until then. She hates me because, though I'm common born, I've got things she thinks are hers by right. She hates me because Papa loved me, and he was a very clever man, while her Gottfried, though a lovely fellow, is a fool. And because I don't give up. I fight to survive. I've worked like a peasant with the village women here while the men were away.' She took his hand in hers, and smiled, her eyes full of tears. 'I'm not a good woman, my Jimmy, but I'm loyal to those I love, and I'll fight for them and myself, and always will, I reckon, until I die.'

'Mama darling,' he said, 'you are splendid, and you don't have to explain anything to me.'

Little Coralie sat on his knee and asked questions until her nurse came to take her away.

'Let's go up through the woods a little way,' said Viola. 'I have not walked there for so long. It hasn't been safe. It's better now – and now I have a great strong soldier with a pistol to protect me. It will be light for another hour.'

They took a winding path through the woods where the bluebells were about to break into flower, and the very young bracken just uncurling. She paced by his side, all in black, her fine lace shawl about her head and shoulders, her hand in his arm. Her hands were not so beautifully cared for now, and she wore no rings except her wedding ring.

'I have my jewellery safely, but apart from these pearls, I do not wear it. There is no company, and planting carrots is bad for diamonds.' She smiled. 'Your father gave me these pearls, Jimmy, when I first met him. Now you've met him. Tell me – what do you think of him?'

'He is, as you always told me, a great gentleman.'

'But you like him?'

'It would be difficult not to.'

'But – you don't sound very sure.'

As a schoolboy, he had thought James magnificent, loved him, and still did. But now, having met and fought with men of all classes, he recognized his limitations.

'Well?' probed Viola.

'Well, Lord Louderdown is a great gentleman, and he was, and is, very kind to me. Papa was a great gentleman too – but he understood humility. I mean he thought he had to earn things, not take them as his right.' He glanced at her shrewdly, and said, 'But you loved my father more, didn't you?'

'No. It was – different. There are different kinds of love, Jimmy. You will find that out. But James Staffray will always act as though the world was made for him. You mustn't blame him too much; he was brought up to believe it. You're half me, you know. It's better to be a bit common – keeps your feet on the ground.'

They laughed affectionately together, back in their old close understanding.

There was the sound of voices ahead. She stopped, and the cold, stony expression came into her eyes, wary, watchful, unyielding. Her hand tightened convulsively on his arm, and she turned as though to go back down the path.

Ahead of them, four square across the path, was a tall man in the leather-trimmed costume of a German huntsman. He had a horn slung on his belt, and carried a rifle, and a gun dog ran at his heels. Behind him, in an open space, a group of similarly dressed men were skinning a deer.

'It is Schausenhardt,' she whispered.

'But this is your land. Has he permission to shoot on your land – and at this season?'

'He makes his own rules,' she said, and her hand tightened as Schausenhardt came down towards them. 'Say nothing. I do not care about the deer.'

Schausenhardt came slowly down the track towards them, stopping where it branched, one way leading up past where his men bent over the carcase, the other winding back to Die Kinderburg. He waited until they came near, then raised his hat to Viola, ignoring Jimmy.

Jimmy put his hand over his mother's and found it was trembling. He was glad that he was not the boy who had yelled defiance at this man six years ago. He was glad he was taller, young and strong, and that he was in British uniform. He stared with studied indifference into the Prince's hot blue glare. Calm in the face of the enemy. At least he had learned what that meant.

Prince Friedrich had aged. The puffy redness of dissipation had gone, leaving him pale, with deep, saturnine lines etched deeply round the mouth which a war wound had left with a perpetual fox-sneer. He looked at Viola just as he had when he had pursued her through the drawing-rooms and ballrooms of pre-war Vienna. The predatory look of a hunter whose quarry always just eludes him; a look of longing, fury and despair.

He gave a stiff bow, clicking his heels.

'*Gnädige* Countess, you have caught me poaching. The deer ran across our boundaries. You must allow me to send you a haunch.'

'Thank you, but tomorrow I am leaving for Vienna.'

His hand went up to his mouth, pressing it where the severed nerve began to shake.

'How long are you going for?' he demanded.

'That is no concern of yours, Prince Friedrich,' Jimmy said icily.

Schausenhardt jerked his head round, dropping the monocle he wore. Jimmy saw that the face injury had also affected the left eye, leaving it in a round, unblinking stare. The Prince's trigger hand moved, and for a moment Jimmy had an almost irresistible impulse to duck and pull his mother down with him. Trigger-happy. He had known men overstrained by long patrols react so. Certainly the Prince was trigger-happy.

'So you have your son back, and in enemy uniform,' said the Prince. 'His manners, I see, have not improved.'

'Nor yours, Prince Friedrich,' Jimmy said. He spoke with all the studied disdain of his Staffray blood. 'So far as I remember they are just the same. Do you still insult small boys with impunity?'

'You pup, if you don't forget, neither do I . . .' His voice rose, and the men around the bloody carcase further up the path rose, and looked towards them uncertainly.

'Jimmy,' said Viola, 'please don't make a scene. Let us go back to the house. Good day to you, Prince Friedrich.'

'Viola.' The name seemed to be torn from Schausenhardt; suddenly he was a man in torment. 'You are coming back here? You will be returning to Die Kinderburg? You are not leaving for ever?'

'My mother is leaving with me for Vienna in the morning. She is now under my protection. Although we were familiar friends with your family once, I prefer you not to use her first name. I understand you have been of service in protecting her and her house. For that I thank you, but I am here to do that now. I would be glad if you would let us pass.'

Prince Friedrich's face suffused with anger, but Jimmy's gaze did not falter. Schausenhardt fell back and they passed, turned down the winding path leading back through the beautiful woods to the little castle. The Prince stood, his gun between his hands, watching until they were out of sight.

'Has he been bothering you?' Jimmy asked.

'No, he's helped to protect me, and the village, from marauders since Papa died. I have been grateful, but he is a man who cannot take a refusal. It has been difficult.' She saw his eyes cloud with anger, and smiled. 'Oh, don't fret about him, love. Papa always said the Schausenhardts have a crazy streak. They have lost almost everything now, except the house, Adlerburg, which does not belong to him but to Lotte's husband. It is mortgaged heavily. Friedrich lives there alone. But I have no need of any help now you're here.' She looked at him coaxingly. 'And you've told me nothing about yourself. So you're over twenty, and you're a Captain, and you live in London with Betsy and Amy – but what about girls? Have there been a lot of girls, my Jimmy-C?'

'We-ell, there have been a few.'

'But so far no special one?'

'No, of course not. Give me time.'

He thought of Lucinda and Amy. Lucinda, his sister now, out of his life for ever, and Amy with her pretty, firm mouth and soft little chin, her big, mocking, grey eyes, for ever teasing him about his love affairs with sarcastic disapproval, a born little schoolmarm. He would have liked to tell his mother about Lucinda, but somehow he could not bring himself to do so, although he was sure she would understand.

'No, of course, no special ones. I'll think of that when I'm an old man of thirty and ready to settle down.'

Viola packed that night. They would take Vatel with them, and collect the other two children, Lorenz and Theresa, from their schools.

'I hope they like the idea of coming to England.' Jimmy said.

'Theresa will. She is still stage-struck; she has heard there are good theatre schools in England. We will see. Lorenz, I don't know. He is Count Erhmann now. The castle belongs to him and the house in Vienna. I think he will want to come back here one day.'

After dinner, just as the light was fading, they went out on to the terrace. The spring air was still chilly, and Viola was

229

wrapped in furs, bringing a hundred childish memories back to him, of her bending over his cot to kiss him before she went out; of cuddling into her warmth as their carriage drove through the lights of the city. High above he saw lights twinkling, and said, puzzled, 'That must be Adlerburg. We used not to be able to see it from here.'

'No. No. Prince Friedrich has cut a great deal of timber on this side of the house. There is a sale for timber. Besides, it enables him to watch the village. They can signal if danger should threaten again.'

'I'm sorry, Mama, if I was too ungracious,' said Jimmy stiffly. 'I understand now that he behaved so badly because he was in love with you, and knew he did not stand a chance, not while Papa was alive.'

'Love?' she echoed, and he was surprised by the harshness of her voice. 'A man like that does not know the meaning of the word. But, why do we talk of him? The war is over, and I must pick myself up and start all over again.' He could see her eyes were full of tears. 'Thank God I have children to help me.'

Tomorrow I shall have gone, she thought. All this will be in the past. That is how my life goes. In episodes. Happiness and near despair. It finishes, then starts again. It's always been like that.

She too looked up at the Adlerburg lights. Schausenhardt could be watching, even now, when it was dark, and nothing could be seen but the small lights on the terrace. She knew that in the daytime he watched her through the powerful army field glasses he always carried. She had never been free of his menacing presence since that terrible night when Eugene lay dead in the hall.

She had not told Jimmy everything, she had not told him that Schausenhardt had taken her weary body, when she had been too bereft, too shocked with grief and sick at heart to resist. He had not dared to touch her since. The frozen disgust of her rejection had penetrated even his insufferable egotism. He had protected her and the village with his men, importuned her with pleas for her forgiveness and almost hysterical offers of marriage, all of which she had

230

met with stony indifference. She knew that she had power over him; that had she chosen she could have made him suffer. She could have employed all the tricks of a triumphantly sexual woman to torment him. But she knew that was what he expected of all women, and that her indifference ground his arrogance like a millstone. There were some things that should never be told. And it was time the killing stopped. Jimmy was a man now, but still very young. He had the Staffray temper and the Staffray pride. Eugene had taught her the uselessness of revenge. Tomorrow could not come soon enough.

'I'm glad to be going away. It is beautiful here, but I am glad to leave it. Perhaps I shall only remember the happy times when I have gone. I am going back to England, my Jimmy, and I am going to have a nice, quiet, ordinary life with all my children, like any ordinary mother. Will you like that?'

She would never be ordinary – not to him, nor to the men who had desired her, nor to anyone. He was old enough now to understand the depth of her attraction.

'Mama, don't deceive yourself,' he said, stooping to kiss her, 'you'll never be ordinary – not in a hundred years.'

PART THREE

THE STORM BREAKS

CHAPTER NINE

The red drugget and awnings were stretched across the pavement outside a house in Grosvenor Square and from within passers-by could hear the steady percussion of a dance orchestra. It was late June, mid-season and the weather was hot.

A few late strollers and idlers hung about outside the large Georgian mansion hoping to see celebrities or publicized society beauties entering or leaving. It was already past midnight. By the railings of the square the cars were parked, the chauffeurs standing in groups, smoking, or sitting in the limousines dozing, waiting for the hired linkman to call out their employers' names.

A group of very young people in evening clothes came running out of the house, filling the square with the noise of their laughter, Lucinda Staffray leading them. She was always the leader. At twenty she was tall and slender, supremely confident of her position, always exquisitely dressed. Her hair was fashionably shingled, the highlights golden, smoothed round her head like a cap of shining metal. Her light blue eyes seemed to search the world hungrily as though she was continually in pursuit of something or someone who always evaded her, and indulged in the freakish excitements of her set, simply to fill in the time. The image she sought was Jimmy Corbett. She was twenty. She had never forgotten him.

Tonight she was wearing a white chiffon evening dress, the skirt short in front, showing her long elegant legs to her knees, and floating in ostrich fronds almost to the ground at the back. She wore a long string of pearls, and diamond slave bangles above her elbows. She ran across to a large open scarlet tourer parked among the more sedate family limousines and threw her cloak of flame-coloured velvet into the seat. The duty ball had been attended and now the night was beginning. She was the débutante of the season, one of the set who had been dubbed

235

'bright young people'. All the gossip columns reported her triumphs as a leader of the younger set, whose exploits became more bizarre as the season proceeded through its round of fashionable events.

Her mother was pleased with her success, and appalled by her notoriety. Florence did not like London life. She would be grateful when Lucinda was safely married, and she could return to Louderdown. James accepted the expense and fuss of his daughter's presentation year with generosity – it was to be expected that she should be launched with everything that money and position could bring to her aid. He put in appearances when he was required in his remote but kindly way. He was proud of her looks and her dashing competence in the hunting field. He was too tolerant, Florence said, but James shrugged it off. Young people needed to cut loose a bit after the war.

He did wish, however, that she would not get into the newspapers quite so much. Columnists were less discreet than in his young days.

His indulgence came from his sense of guilt over the twins. He had never really known them and he knew it was his fault, and since his breach with Florence the gulf was wider than before. He over-compensated by generosity, paying for their extravagant cars, Bellairs' bachelor flat, their bills and Lucinda's astronomical dress allowance. He was sometimes glad his mother, the old Countess, had not lived into the post-war era. She would neither have sympathized nor understood the ways of her grandchildren.

From the driving seat Lucinda regarded her friends disdainfully. The good-looking boys and well-dressed girls, all a little tight from the champagne they had drunk at the dance, all standing like fox-hounds waiting for the huntsman's whip to crack, and hoick them on to the next quarry. She despised them all. There was not a boy among them to whom she could have given a serious thought.

'What are we going to do now?' she said.

They all talked at once. Go to the Savoy, and dance to the

Orpheans. Go to a night-club, find someone's party and gate-crash it. Drive out to a road-house, go for a midnight swim. Drive down to Brighton for breakfast.

Bellairs tall, slender, like an elegant pierrot in the black and white of his exquisitely cut tails, hands in his pockets, opera hat tipped on the back of his head, slumped down beside her. He had drunk rather less than the rest. His laxily smiling, rather diffident manner concealed an abysmal boredom. The difference between him and Lucy was that he was not searching for anything. He knew what he wanted to do if they would only let him do it. That he wanted to leave Oxford and go to an art school had met with stonewall disapproval. His mother considered artists impossible people. His father had said, good-naturedly, that there was no harm in him messing about with it, but it really was not the kind of thing for the future Earl of Louderdown to take up seriously. So as Bellairs would not consider the army which, to the martial Staffrays, was a disgrace in itself, and as he did not, like Lucinda, care for country life, the best thing was for him to go to university and think again, which he was supposed to be doing. Actually he spent most of his days painting, and most of his nights roistering, and his fast sports Bugatti burned up the miles between Oxford and London. The lecture rooms saw very little of Lord Staffray.

But at least his father, in the face of his mother's furious displeasure, allowed him to have a flat of his own in London. But this year, Lucy's presentation year, he had had to spend a lot of time in town. It was only right, he thought, bored but loyal, to provide an escort when she needed one, and she needed him often. Not that she lacked admirers. She was considered the catch of the season, but the men of her social set bored her. Schoolboys and grandpas, she said. All the decent men had been killed in Flanders. So he accompanied her on her restless search for interest or pleasure.

'Where are we going?' he wailed. 'Couldn't we just for once be frightfully original and go home to bed?'

This was greeted with groans and catcalls.

'My God, Bell, it's only just after twelve!'

'I'm not going home,' said Lucinda. 'You go if you like. We've got to do *one* amusing thing first. We've wasted all evening at that frightful hop, bored to death. I'm not going home yet.'

There was an interval of noisy argument while Lucinda sat at the wheel glowering and Bellairs slouched, aristocratically bored. He gave her a cigarette, and brought a gold flask from his pocket from which they both took a nip. Everyone thought them both the last word in chic and assurance. In reality they were very young, very inexperienced, and scared of the post-war world they had inherited.

'You decide, Bell dear,' said one of the girls. 'Whatever you choose should be absolutely ripping.'

He looked at her with a jaundiced eye. The newspapers often named her as his favourite dancing partner. She was a pretty, painted, well-bred little doll.

'Let's go to the Can-Can, there's a good band, they go on until two, and I hear this new cabaret is worth watching.'

They all piled into the car, and the pretty little doll girl scrambled on to Bellairs' lap. He cuddled her obligingly, while Lucinda drove off with a grind of gears, bringing audible comments from the waiting chauffeurs as they scraped past the car in front.

'What a nerve!' said the painted doll.

They were men, they had fought in the war, and now, Bellairs thought grimly, they were lackeys to a lot of rich idiots like himself. They made him feel uncomfortable, like the ex-servicemen's bands busking the streets and the groups of unemployed miners singing for pence in the West End.

'Serve us right if they hang us all on lanterns,' he said.

The girl on his knee put his hat on straight, kissed him, and cooed, 'Oh, darling Bell, you must be drunk!'

They shot along Piccadilly, in and out of the traffic, across the Circus and down the Haymarket. The Can-Can Club was at that moment *the* late-night place for the younger set. Lucinda stopped the car with an abrupt grind of brakes, throwing everyone into each other's arms, making the girls squeal.

Bellairs' eyebrows went up quizzically.

'I think you've had too much champagne, Sis.'

'I know when I have. Everybody get out. Bag a table near the dance floor and order the drinks. I'm going to park the car.'

'I'll come with you,' said Bellairs.

They drove through the back streets and found a parking place. Bell put her cloak round her shoulders, and his hand through her arm. He tried to be her friend, to get through to her. Heaven knew he needed friends himself. It was as though something central and strong had gone from their lives when Jimmy had been sent away. He knew she still kept his signet ring on her key ring. He knew she was still looking for her lost love.

He could feel the muscles in her arm taut with tension under the smooth young flesh, and the desperate unhappiness which always seemed to overtake her at the end of the day.

'Oh, Lucy –' he gave her a little reassuring squeeze – 'what's the matter? Still thinking of Jimmy-C? Look, if he wanted to get in touch he would have done so. You've got to accept it. Forget all about it. It's dam' nigh seven years ago now. There are other chaps in the world.'

'Not for me.' She jerked her arm free and strode ahead, a shining figure in her flame-coloured cloak of ring velvet. 'And don't imagine I haven't tried.'

'Jimmy wasn't killed. That much I know.'

'No. That's it. That's why I'm still a seeking virgin. I'm sure he hasn't forgotten, and if we met again he would understand that I don't care who his family are, or what mine think. It's his beastly honour. I'm sure he gave his word not to see me again and he's keeping it!'

'He might be married, engaged, or in love with a night-club queen,' said Bellairs. But she was not amused . . . she never was. She was moody, self-absorbed, and rather magnificent.

They went down the carpeted steps – the night-club, housed in a large basement, was packed. The cabaret had started, the lights dimmed, the heads of the audience silhouetted against the footlights. Their friends had secured a table, and there was already an ice-bucket with champagne and the waiter was filling their glasses. There were token plates of sandwiches on the

239

table to satisfy the licencing laws. Bellairs sat down, and the little doll girl put her arm round his neck, and crooned with the singer on the stage.

'All alone, I'm so all alo-one, and there's no one else, but you . . .'

'You're tickling my neck,' said Bellairs.

'Oh, Bell, you are so horrid and unromantic.'

'I'm tired. Thank God Lucy only comes out once. Another season like this and I'd go into a monastery.'

Lucinda's hand gripped a champagne glass, and her pale, aquamarine eyes searched among the audience, moving over the tables, peering through the half-darkness. She felt very wide-awake. She had some tablets which a friend had given her to help her through the long, late nights of the season. In the morning she could sleep until midday, but she had a feeling that she must see the hours out until the dawn. The war was over. Jimmy was young. He had liked dancing and the London life. Somewhere, unexpectedly, she might see him again.

She wished she was twenty-one, free of family duties, able to live her own life. To travel. When Lucinda thought of travelling it was because, in her imagination, Jimmy was always waiting at the end of the road.

She was sure he would still be in the Army, because an army career was what he had always wanted. At first she had written secretly, addressing her letters to Army headquarters. She did not know whether he had ever received them, for she had never received any replies. But then her mother always checked the daily post.

She sighed impatiently, drinking down her glass of champagne, ignoring Bellairs' protesting smile. If only she could see him again, just once, and talk to him, she was sure everything could be explained. And then – *she saw him.*

He was sitting with three more young people at a table on the far side of the dance floor. Another boy, and two pretty girls. He looked older, and had filled out into manhood. But there was no mistaking the finely shaped head of crisp fair hair, the ears flat to the skull, and when he turned and the lights caught his face, the sweet rather teasing smile.

For a moment she felt as though she might die. Her heart seemed to stop, and then was pounding fast as though with terror. She *was* terrified. She had dreamed of it so often, and now here he was. She felt her breast would burst. She sat rigidly, staring across the room, hanging on to consciousness and self-control. Her shaking hand pulled at Bellairs' sleeve.

'Bell, look there. Look at that party near the dance floor. Two girls, two chaps. Bell, look, and tell me . . . isn't it Jimmy?'

Bellairs followed her glance, peering across at the party, lit up by the spotlights of the cabaret.

'I can see two frightfully pretty girls, and a fair chap with specs. Oh, yes . . . the other man . . . the older one . . . sitting sideways. Wait a bit . . .'

There was certainly something familiar about the well-shaped head. The cabaret ended in a spatter of applause. The lights went up, the dance floor cleared, the band on its circular stage came swinging into sight, beating out a rhythm. There was no doubt about it. The handsome, broad-shouldered young man sitting at the table on the other side of the room was Jimmy Corbett. The beautiful red-haired girl, exquisitely dressed in lavender chiffon, and the thin, stiff-looking fair boy in horn-rimmed spectacles, he did not know. The other girl, dressed in blue, petite and dainty, with long hair, parted *au ballet Russe*, with a white flower behind her ear, was Amy Lyttelton.

Bellairs jumped to his feet with a whoop of delight, discarding the pretty doll, who wailed with dismay. He seized Lucinda's hand.

'Excuse me,' he cried. 'We'll be back. We've just seen an old and dear friend.'

He was off across the dance floor, dragging Lucinda after him. Utterly shaken, more than a little muzzy with champagne, over-stimulated, it seemed to her the dance floor stretched out for ever. And then she was standing by the table, and Jimmy had risen to his feet, recognition dawning in his eyes. It was him. It really was him. The dream had come true at last, and happiness like a wave of glory swept over her.

Bellairs put out his arms, and Amy too rose to her feet.

'Oh, frabjous day,' he cried. 'Jimmy! Jimmy; and Amy too. When shall we four meet again! And here's Lucy, too. The famous four are together again.'

Lucinda was engulfed in the hugging, laughing, joyous welcome. It was not what she sought . . . not the unity of four friends. She wanted Jimmy alone. For herself.

The first flush of delighted recognition passed. Memory came flooding back to Jimmy. It was seven years ago, and it was forbidden territory. He had given his word. For the moment he was too confused to think clearly. He took refuge in introductions, in summoning the waiter for extra chairs, in ordering more champagne.

'Bell and Lucy, this is my brother, Count Erhmann, and my sister, Theresa Erhmann. There's another sister, but she's too small for night-clubbing. Lorry, Terry, these are old friends of mine, Lord Staffray and the Lady Lucinda. The terrible twins. I was at prep-school with Bell. Well, sit down, chaps, and have a drink and tell me what's happened over the years. Bell, did you ever get to study art? I remember it was always what you wanted to do.'

'You remember? Well, yes I do, but not officially. The parents are distinctly not keen. And you – you're still in the Army? A regular. I'll bet you're a General now.'

'Not quite. I'm a Captain. I'm stationed at Cologne with the Army of Occupation. I'm home on leave. It's Terry's birthday, so I'm treating the children.' Terry pulled a pretty, pouting face, and her green eyes glinted mischievously at Bellairs. They were both immediately very aware of each other, but Bellairs turned to Amy Lyttelton.

'And, Amy, what are you doing? My goodness, you're quite big. I thought you were going to be a midget.'

'Me, too.' Amy laughed. 'But I made five feet three.'

'Amy's the brainy one,' said Jimmy with a touch of pride. 'She's at Oxford.'

'So am I.' Bellairs was delighted. 'How come we never met? But we will now. Where are you?'

'St Hilda's.'

'I'll be round Monday morning for coffee.'

Lorenz looked disapprovingly at this gay, elegant and self-assured young lord, and made his resentment quite plain.

'Amy,' he said, 'has little time for anything but her studies.'

'You mind your own business, Lorry,' said Amy tartly. 'I'll make time for Bell. He's an old friend.'

Bell sensed undercurrents. He was longing to dance with Theresa Erhmann, with her sweet nymphlike figure, and her cloudy red hair, but he decided he would dance with Amy first. He wanted to talk to her. To get the lay of the land. Besides, he knew that Theresa knew she attracted him and he was too old a hand at flirting to capitulate straight away.

Lucinda had not spoken after the first tumultuous greetings. She simply sat, looking at Jimmy, terrified but ecstatic at the joy of seeing him again. She began to feel excluded as she had often felt excluded by the other three when they were children. She could never understand their casual, bantering, teasing affection for each other, and their deep loyalties. She had always hated sharing Jimmy, and wanted him exclusively for herself. Was it going to happen again? That once, that one night at the hospital ball she had felt victorious. Then he had been hers, loved her, as she adored him. Her hands were trembling. She searched his smiling face for some special recognition, but found only a good-natured friendliness.

'Amy,' said Bell, 'come and dance with me. Last time we met you were picking blackberries.'

Amy jumped to her feet, and they were off on the floor. The dance was a Charleston, and it was quite obvious that they were both experts. Lorenz watched with a face like a thundercloud, and Jimmy said, smiling, 'Would you like to dance, Lucinda?'

She felt that, if he touched her, she might faint. She did not trust her legs to hold her up. She gave a tight little smile, and shook her head, consumed with a hot, melting, frightening fire.

'I think I'll sit here a while . . . we've just come from a ball.'

She thought he would stay and talk to her, but he turned immediately to his pretty sister.

'Dance, Terry?'

'You bet!'

She was on her feet in a moment, and they were off among the dancers, leaving Lucinda with Lorenz.

They sat in silence for a moment. He looked at her lovely face with its tormented eyes watching Jimmy dancing with Theresa, and thought bitterly that here was another of them. Another of these girls who followed Jimmy like so many sugar-drunk butterflies.

'You do not care to dance, Lady Lucinda?' he asked stiffly.

She started, suddenly aware of him.

'I do, but not for a moment.'

'I do not care for this kind of dancing,' he said. Of all the family he was the only one with a pronounced German accent. He was a nice-looking boy, she thought, but so painfully young. Beside his half-brother he looked as unfledged as a young bird, with his round cropped head and the rather narrow shoulders.

She said, politely, but bored, and not in the least interested in him. 'And what are you doing in London, Count Lorenz?'

'Oh, please, call me Lorenz. I am not in London. I am at a college learning estate management. I have an extensive estate near Vienna, and I wish to develop it agriculturally.'

'I see,' she said disinterestedly. Her eyes still followed Jimmy's broad shoulders round the dance floor, quite unaware that Lorenz found her indifference intolerable. When Jimmy was home on leave none of the girls noticed him. Even quiet little Amy Lyttelton. Or so it seemed to Lorenz. Since he had been in England his jealousy had revived. It had been the same ever since he could remember.

'Eventually I shall return to Austria,' he said precisely, wishing that, just once, this handsome girl would evince some little interest. Wishing he, too, could smile and dance and joke and flirt like these other young people. Wishing his sight was good and his shoulders broad, and his smile sweet and melting like Jimmy's.

'Amy is learning sociology at Oxford. This too will be very useful.'

For the first time her interest was caught.

'How d'you mean?'

'When she becomes my wife, it is a study which will be extremely helpful in the rebuilding of my country.'

'You are going to marry Amy Lyttelton?' she said, astounded.

'It is my dearest hope,' he said stiffly. 'I am aware, of course, that socially it might be considered a mistake. Before my mother returned to England and took the house in Kensington, Amy's mother was Jimmy-C's housekeeper. But she is a very exceptional girl, and I have become very attached to her.'

'I see.' The music ended and they were coming back to the table. Lucinda lost interest in Lorenz. She moved quickly into the chair where Amy had been sitting, next to Jimmy.

There must be some way in which she could get close to him again. She could feel his withdrawal, courteous and charming, but after the first tumultuous shock of recognition, definite. He was playing the host skilfully, sharing his attention with the others, giving her no special sign. She was afraid of behaving like a silly flapper and saying something gauche. He seemed so experienced, so much older than the rest of them. But her heart burned fiercely in her breast, and she could not believe he had forgotten that evening beneath the cedar trees at Louderdown.

Bellairs, still wildly elated at the reunion, was flirting happily with the other two girls.

'Here we all are again,' he said. 'All these years apart and not a word and all because you and Lucy, Jimmy, had a necking session in the garden and Mummy found out.' Jimmy froze, but Bellairs went on unheeding, 'Well, we're all older and wiser, or at least, more careful. Amy's as pretty as a picture. In fact, she's just like a Kirchener girl picture.'

'How do you know,' said Amy mischievously, 'you've never seen me without my clothes?'

'Well, the bits that show look delectable.'

Lorenz glared at Bellairs, who was cheerfully indifferent to his anger.

'And what am I like?' asked Theresa. 'Another poster girl?'

'A Barrabal, green-eyed, and glinting like a pussy-cat. And Lucinda,' went on Bellairs. 'She's the deb of the season, or so they say. Can you imagine it, Jimmy!'

'Indeed I can,' Jimmy said, smiling. 'I've seen your pictures in the magazines, Lucinda . . .'

'Oh, that,' said Lucinda impatiently. Of course, she could not expect him to make any sign with these other idiots here. Why hadn't she danced with him when he had asked her? Why didn't the others go and dance, and this stupid Lorenz boy take Amy away? She looked at Amy, and drawled, 'I hear I have to congratulate you?'

Amy's big grey eyes blinked uncomprehendingly. 'What on? We don't get the mod results until August.'

'I mean on your engagement – to Count Lorenz.'

There was a frigid silence. Theresa gave a glance of mocking despair. Amy's small pretty face went rosy with fury. She turned an accusing gaze on Lorenz.

'Lorry, how *dare* you?'

'Amy,' said Jimmy protestingly, 'don't be cross and spoil the party.'

'Don't be *cross*? When this idiot goes around telling people I'm his property!'

'You offend me,' said Lorenz stiffly.

'And you offend me!'

'Oh, lord, rows,' said Theresa to Bellairs in an undertone. 'Lorry has a genius for causing rows.'

'What have I said to offend you?'

'You – you, oh.' Amy was bursting with indignation. 'Just because you asked me you think it's all settled. As though any woman could possibly refuse Count Lorenz Erhmann. As though *I* have no say in the matter. You and your German *kinder, kuchen, kirche*.'

Theresa and Bellairs began to laugh.

'I am sorry if you feel like that,' Lorenz said furiously, 'but you were flirting to provoke me. You came out with me tonight and you should not behave so.'

Amy drew in a long breath, striving for calmness.

246

'I came at Jimmy's invitation, because it is Terry's birthday. If I was flirting, it certainly was not to provoke anyone. I was thrilled to see Bell again. I love him, and always did, and he makes me laugh, which is more than you do, Lorry Erhmann.'

A boy seated with a party at another table who had been listening with amusement, rose, came over, and asked Amy to dance. She rose at once and went off with him, her pretty mouth set and her small nose in the air.

'Who is that?' asked Lorenz furiously.

'Relax, *Dümmling?*' said Theresa. 'It's an undergraduate she knows at Oxford.'

Lorenz rose, bowed stiffly. 'You will forgive me, but I think I will leave.'

Jimmy said quickly, 'Don't spoil Terry's party, Lorry. You take things too seriously.'

Lorenz glared at him angrily. 'I do not find life a game. I am quite aware when I am not wanted, Jimmy-C,' he said, and stalked out of the dance room.

'Oh, God,' said Jimmy, sitting down. 'Adolescent passions!'

'It's not breaking up my party,' said Theresa airily, 'Lorry makes everyone feel uncomfortable. I'm glad he's gone.'

'Poor boy,' Jimmy said good-naturedly.

'What was all that about?' asked Bellairs.

'Oh, family squabbles,' said Theresa. 'Lorry pestered Amy to go out with him, so she did, but when he got bossy and possessive she was fed up. He thinks it's because Beau Geste here is on leave, but it's his own silly fault, really.' She smiled affectionately at Jimmy. 'She's just not all that interested. Lorry is always jealous, and a great bore about it all.'

'Talking about interest, I am very interested in asking you to dance with me, Theresa. Will you?'

She gave a dramatic sigh. 'I was wondering whether you were ever going to ask me,' she said.

They rose and went on to the dance floor, two very attractive young people, amusedly taking each other's measure. Jimmy and Lucinda were left alone at the table.

Jimmy watched Amy thoughtfully as she danced with the

young graduate.

'It's funny,' he said. 'I've lived with Amy and Aunt Betsy so long I feel responsible for her, even now, when my family is here and I'm living with them, and they've gone back to Clapham. I still feel she's my responsibility. She's a splendid little kid, really, and terribly independent.'

'Are you in love with her?' Lucinda demanded.

'I'm sorry?' he said, puzzled. 'With little Amy? Of course not. I'm forgetting my manners. Would you like to dance?'

'I'd rather sit and talk.'

'Suits me,' he said equably. The tune ended, but Bellairs and Theresa were sitting up at the bar, and Amy had joined the Oxford group she knew at the other table. Lucinda knew her own friends were looking across at her and Bellairs indignantly, and chose to ignore them.

'Are you bored?' she said.

'No, I'm not. It's just that everyone – all of you, seem so young. It's being in France – like coming awake again, like Rip Van Winkle, and finding everyone so young. In Germany it's so different. Plenty of night-clubs, but they're not for people like you.'

'Who are they for?'

'War profiteers, occupying officers, tarts. England seems comparatively childish and innocent. But all of you seem hell-bent on having a good time. I brought the girls here to-night because I wanted them to have fun, but I feel out of place.'

'I do too,' said Lucinda eagerly. 'Everything is so silly. This year, being a debutante, has been dreadful. Mummy insisted that I came out. It's supposed to have been fun for me. I'm supposed to have made lots of friends. Look at them!' She scornfully indicated her deserted friends who, catching her eye, waved. 'Idiots! And all this is to get me married. To find someone of the *right* family. It's degrading.'

'I thought all girls wanted to get married,' he said lightly.

'I don't need to go through all this to find the man I love.'

Her pale eyes were burning. Suddenly she was reckless and determined to break him down. 'Have you forgotten everything,

248

Jimmy?' she asked.

'About Louderdown? No. Of course not. I never shall.'

'I have not forgotten either. Now, please listen. Don't, don't shut me up. Give me a chance. I'm not a kid any more. I'm twenty-one this year. Do you remember the hospital dance, the night of our birthday, before you joined up? When you gave me your ring? Look.' She opened her purse and took out the little gold signet ring with the Erhmann crest upon it, fastened to her key ring. 'I've always kept it.'

He picked it up, smiling, shaking his head. 'My mother gave it to me once for a birthday. I couldn't remember what I had done with it.' He slipped it on to his little finger, and smiled. 'It still fits. Are you returning it, Lucy? I'd like to have it again.'

She stared at him. She could not believe he did not remember. She did not realize that he was giving her a chance to withdraw. It was her nature to be reckless, not to look ahead, to ride straight at her fences. She had been waiting for him to come back to her for nearly seven years, and he was here. She had to grasp at him, and she was not afraid. She was sure of herself, of her beauty, and her position. Lucinda was not humble. She had wanted him and still did, and she could not and would not believe he might not want her.

'Jimmy, after you joined up I wrote to you. I wrote secretly and posted the letters to Army headquarters. They were not returned. Did you not receive them?'

He said gently, 'Yes. I got them. But Lucy, we were very young and rather silly. I thought it better not to answer, and that you would thank me for not doing so.'

'Did you – and be honest, Jimmy, did you promise *anyone* – my father or my mother – that you would not write to me?'

'Look, Lucy, yes. Yes, I did. I promised your father. And he was quite right. He told me that your mother wished it.'

Her face glowed. 'I knew it. It was right then, but how about now, Jimmy, when we are no longer kids? You remember how we said we would always love each other? I was so proud of you when you joined up. I read somewhere that you were mentioned in despatches and I was so proud. I told all the girls at school.

249

Mother and Father and Granny behaved ridiculously. I think it was Granny who made all the fuss. She was *really* Victorian. I mean, I *knew* I was too young. I *knew* we would have to wait until after the war. But there was no need for them to be so stupid and stuffy, to make you promise not to write, or anything.'

'Lucy,' he asked, 'why do you think they did this?'

'Why, because of your birth, of course. Because you were illegitimate. What my mother calls a nobody. A bye-blow. She has a very big idea of the family and the sort of person she expects me to hook. I'm sorry, but it doesn't interest me at all.'

He wanted to stop her, but did not know how, unless he told her the truth, and it was not for him to do so. It was the more painful for him now because it meant nothing to him. The breaking of the friendship with Bellairs meant far more. That had hurt – Bellairs was a brother he could have valued. More so than poor sulky, resentful Lorenz. But those kisses under the cedar tree at Louderdown had gone the way of other, more exciting kisses, into the limbo of boyhood and a host of forgotten girls.

'Jimmy,' she said, 'you made a promise to my parents, about not seeing me, and not writing and you're trying to keep it. It is very honourable, but don't you see that it doesn't matter now?'

'Lucy.' He took her hand and her heart leaped and her skin crept with pleasure at his touch. 'It's all so long ago, and we were only school kids. Let it stay in the past.'

'We're grown up now, and I haven't changed, and I don't believe that you have. Soon I'll be twenty-one, I'll have money of my own from my grandmother. She left all the Bellairs money to Bell and me. It's only a few months. Then we can do what we like.'

He relinquished her hand, and drew back, his voice suddenly edged with authority, though his eyes were still kind.

'I think, Lucinda, you are a flirt, like Terry. You're pulling my leg. Be honest. A pretty girl like you must have had all the opportunities in the world.' He waited, hoping she would take the chance of escaping from a situation he found unbearable. But her expression did not change. He remembered her fierce single-mindedness as a child, and her possessive rages when she was refused anything. Her lack of subtlety and humour, never able to see anything that was out of her ken. He went on, patiently, 'Those were very happy days for all of us, and you and Bell and Amy were all very kind to me. I missed my family, especially my mother, very much. But – it was only a boy and girl thing, if I remember. And it was moonlight, and I was a conceited, precocious young pup, just beginning to find my way around with the girls. Your people, quite rightly, put a stop to it. I wasn't at all a suitable boy friend for the young Staffrays – particularly the Lady Lucinda.'

She knew he was lying – Jimmy could never lie convincingly – it was not in his nature. She was sure he was still keeping to that old promise made to her father, which simply did not matter any more.

'I don't give up, Jimmy,' she said, and smiled with such heart-breaking assurance, he could have wept for her.

'Well, I think you should. I'm not really the sort of character a nice girl like you should know at all.' He rose, smiling, and so handsome she could have died with longing for him. 'I must collect those girls and take them home. I have to drive Amy out to Clapham, and Aunt Betsy will sit up all night if she isn't in. You see, other parents don't trust me either. But it's been great seeing you, Lucy. Have a splendid season and enjoy yourself.'

'I'll see you again,' she said desperately.

He shook his head. ' 'Fraid not. I'm off back to Germany the day after tomorrow.'

He shook her hand, but did not kiss it as he used to kiss ladies' hands when he was a boy, went over to the bar, took Theresa away from the protesting Bellairs, collected Amy from her Oxford friends, shaking hands as he went, and in a few minutes they had gone.

Lucinda sat at the empty table feeling as though the world had fallen in ruins about her. He had forgotten. She could not believe it. Bellairs came across disconsolately, took a bottle out of the ice bucket, found it was empty, and dropped it back.

'That's that,' he said. His clever, humorous face was puzzled.

251

'So that's Jimmy's Austrian family. That Theresa, isn't she a stunner? Going to be an actress, she says. Lorenz is a bit of a pip, poor chap. But wasn't Jim a bossy old so-and-so? What on earth made him whip the girls away like that? He was really pleased to see us at first. Then the freeze came on. What's got into him?' He looked at her still, self-absorbed face, and asked in concern, 'What's got into *you*, Sis? Feeling acky or something? You look as though you've seen a ghost.'

'I told him that I haven't thought of another man since he left.'

'Oh, Christ,' said Bellairs disgustedly. 'Sorry, Sis, but you are a fool. It's enough to send any chap running for cover. You're always so high-handed. Why don't you stop and think, and give him time, if you're really dead set on him? He's a fine-looking bloke – he's probably got women creeping out of the skirting boards. I never knew anyone like you for making an awkwardness.'

She seemed to surface from some inner hell. Her eyes cleared and she looked at him scornfully.

'We can't all be as trivial as you are. I know what made Jimmy change. He is a gentleman. He gave his word. But I don't care. I'll make him see it differently. Did you find out from that Amy girl where he's living?'

'In Kensington somewhere. His step-father, Count Erhmann, is dead, and he's brought his mother and her children, his half-brother and sisters back here. He lives there – when he's at home. But he's been in Germany for three years.' He looked across at the disgruntled friends they had arrived with. 'I'm afraid we've been a bit rude, we'd better go back to our crowd and mind our manners.' They crossed the dance floor together, of a height, handsome and elegant, the well-known Staffray twins, leaders of the younger set.

'I shan't take any notice of Jimmy's Anglo-Saxon attitudes,' said Bellairs on the way home. 'Nor of Lorenz's Wagnerian jealousy. I shall see Amy in Oxford and take her to some parties, and when I'm in London I shall pursue Theresa with all the lust in my hot-blooded Staffray soul.'

Lucinda did not laugh.

'Oh, Lucy, don't be so tense! Theresa said something very odd. She said any girls who fall for Jimmy will have a rival in their mother. She said that Jimmy has always been her favourite and that he'll never meet anyone more beautiful, or anyone who loves him more. Jimmy's a man now, she said, but Lorenz isn't. He's still so jealous of him, that anything Jim wants, *he* wants. That's why he is such an ass about Amy.'

'You mean that Jimmy is interested in her?' demanded Lucinda. She stared at him, then burst out laughing. 'I don't believe it.'

Jimmy's mother? She remembered how often he had said how much he missed her, how beautifully she dressed, how she always smelled of gardenias. He had always been talking about her. Countess Erhmann? If she could only make an ally of her! Surely she would be pleased? No son could make a better match than Lucinda Staffray. If she spoke to his mother, and told her about her feelings and made her understand that she loved Jimmy, and did not care about the past, or his illegitimate birth. If he was her favourite as Theresa had said, how could she help being pleased?

Lucinda found the address in the telephone book. For the first time in her life she did not dress to please herself. She wanted to please Jimmy's mother. She wore a long-sleeved marocain coat-dress of the fashionably mushroom pink beige, and a small cloche hat turned back with a brown suede flower. Were her skirts too short? Had she too much lipstick? She did not want to look like a fashion-plate. She wanted to look everything a wise mother would wish for in a daughter-in-law of her position.

She drove to Kensington and found the house, a pleasant, old, double-fronted mansion, standing back from the road, shaded with trees and with a large garden at the rear. The road was very quiet, and when her engine was switched off she could hear a child laughing and a dog barking somewhere behind the vine-clad walls.

When she rang, an elderly man with snow white hair opened the door, and she saw a flicker of surprise cross his imperturbable face when she gave her name. He showed her in to a large, comfortable, drawing-room at the rear of the house from which french windows opened on to the garden. There were white walls, good pictures and white peonies in Nankin vases scenting the air. It was a family room, of charming taste, with none of the splendour of Louderdown or Belgrave Square. A book and a pair of spectacles lay on a small table, and a child's toys were left on the floor. There were many books, a gramophone and a player piano, family portraits and photographs. One of Jimmy, Theresa and Lorenz, with a handsome fair, bearded man.

Outside the french windows the big London garden was full of flowers, and a small girl in a bathing costume was playing with a hose and a large lolloping puppy. A woman with red hair, wearing an azure blue robe, lay in a hammock reading. Her stillness and comfortable indolence startled Lucinda. Jimmy's mother? The fabled Countess Viola?

Lucinda's smart hat pressed down on her forehead in the heat. She envied the almost naked child and comfortably robed lady. The manservant crossed the lawn, the lady looked up, glanced towards the house and rose, balancing herself smilingly on her servant's shoulder as she slipped her bare feet into a pair of gold oriental slippers that lay on the lawn. She spoke a word to the child and then came towards the house, tall, unhurried, slender, with a curiously beautiful walk, like a tall flower in the breeze.

Lucinda felt a sudden sense of inadequacy. She had come to assure Jimmy's mother that nothing in her past could have any effect on her feelings for him. She had imagined a déclassée Viennese Countess, not accepted in her mother's circles, who would be impressed by a girl of her birth and fortune. The minute she saw Viola she was out of her depth.

Viola stepped into the room and smiled. Lucinda saw immediately the likeness to Jimmy, the slow lift of long lashes, the flash of perfect teeth, frank, engaging, a natural unstudied but dangerous charm.

'Lady Lucinda Staffray?' said Viola. 'Sit down, won't you?

Would you like some tea?'

Lucinda accepted quickly. Time. She needed time to think. Theresa had said their mother would be a rival. Viola ordered tea, and Vatel went to attend to it. Lucinda, who had been full of passionate and courageous words, sought desperately for an opening.

'You have a lovely room.'

'Thank you.'

'Do you prefer London to Vienna?'

'Yes. Vienna is a sad city now.'

'Things are bad there?'

Lucinda was not interested in Vienna. She wanted to say what was in her heart, but she felt convinced that the lady in the azure robe, who sat opposite, her cheek resting upon her hand, was not going to give her a chance. Questions stirred in the lovely eyes. Lucinda had come to her so she waited, speaking of other things.

'Very bad. Money is worth so little, and its value changes day by day. Folks do crazy things when they feel insecure.'

'You come from the North?' Lucinda recognized the homely accent.

'From Leeds.'

Vatel brought the tea on a trolley, which he wheeled to Viola's side. There was the small ceremony of asking, passing, offering. Lucinda put down the Meissen cup with a clatter that made Viola glance at her curiously.

The tall girl rose to her feet, and paced tormentedly down the long room. Trivialities leaped to her sight. The little trees woven into the Persian carpet. A honey bee buzzing drunkenly in the dusty yellow heart of one of the white peonies. The Countess's pearls were finer than her own mother's. She tried to think of the things her mother had once said about Jimmy. The son of a loose, immoral woman, dragged up from the depths, an affront to decent society.

'Has Jimmy said anything to you – about me?'

'You'd best drink your tea,' said Viola, with a sigh. 'Then tell me why you've come.'

'I know he has. I can see it in your eyes.' The Countess's delicate brows went up, but before she could speak Lucinda swept on. 'I know my family have been awfully rude and stuffy and stupid, and that Jimmy is the soul of honour and, having given them his promise not to see me, would never break it. I know. When we fell in love I was still at school. *He* promised. *I* didn't. I told them they couldn't make me. I'd die first.'

'Heroics,' said the Countess, sipping her tea.

'Don't mock me like they did. It's years ago now. I'm twenty. Believe me, all the time he had been away I have never thought of anyone else. I have never kissed anyone else. I knew one day we would find each other. And now we have. Last night, at the Can-Can. Suddenly – there he was. I know everything will be all right now we have met again. Of course, I understand that he couldn't say anything to me there. He still feels bound by his promise to my father.'

'Yes,' said the Countess, 'I can understand that. Don't you think you are making rather a fuss? It's a great while ago. Happen, my young lady, that you're thinking of a boy of seventeen, and not the man he is now. He's a grand lad, but he likes women. There have been many, and still are.'

'I don't care. I've been out with lots of boys . . . I was filling up the time until we found each other again. I expect he was too.'

'It's not *quite* like that with Jimmy.' Viola's smile was both sad and amused.

'I don't care if he's had affairs. It's me he loves. Theresa told my brother you would be a rival. Now I know what she meant.'

'Oh, did she?' the countess said dryly. 'Well, it's not quite true. All I want for any of my children is happiness and love. The rest of life can bring all kinds of pain, but folk get through if they have those two things. I'd only oppose anyone any of my children loved if I knew it could not bring happiness.'

'You don't know about me.'

'Yes, I'm sorry, Lady Lucinda . . . I do. Your parents did not want it. They are right. Before you go rushing ahead, don't you think it would be better to have a talk with them?'

'Oh, what's the use,' said Lucinda despairingly. 'They – the family – they think the family is so important. Well, I suppose they're right. But I know, if I . . . if Jimmy and I were determined, they would give in. Dad would. He's kind really. Mother is a bit stiff, and Dad never seems to bother, but he's really very kind.'

'Yes, I know. Very kind, very handsome, very charming. Like Jimmy.' She looked up and waited, but no suspicion touched Lucinda's eager eyes.

'You knew him, then? My father?'

'Once I knew him very well.'

'Then you'll know he won't go on being shirty and horrid about it.'

'You are very young,' said Viola.

'People always say that.'

'Well, if you want to stop them, you must grow up, and stop dreaming. Get hold of yourself, because you've got to. Not everyone has to, but you do have to. *You can't have Jimmy.*'

Lucinda burst into angry tears. 'Why not? That's all. Just tell me why not? Don't tell me he doesn't love me. I don't believe it.'

'Oh, my poor child.' Viola looked at her in distress. 'I am sorry. I know what it is to be twenty and in love. It's like a lovely death. The man has set you alight and you're sure you can have him. I did – but you can't. It's impossible. And they should have told you straight, in the beginning, and this would not have happened. What *did* they tell you?'

'Oh, they told me all the old reasons . . . at least my mother and grandmother did. My position as Dad's daughter. Is it my fault he's Lord Louderdown? Jimmy's illegitimacy. Is it his fault that he doesn't know who his father is? And what does it all matter?'

'He knows now who his father is, and it does matter,' said Viola. The small girl with the bronze hair passed the window, waving, pushing a doll's pram in which the puppy sat with a feathered bonnet on its head, tied under its muzzle, its front paws drooping ludicrously. 'That silly Mitzi,' said Viola, 'such a daft bitch.'

Lucinda flushed furiously, but the soft, deep voice went on

257

implacably. 'That is Coralie. My baby. I have two more children by my late husband, Count Erhmann. A boy and a girl. Lorenz and Theresa, Jimmy's half-brother and two half-sisters. The same as you.'

Lucinda's face went blank. Her mouth opened. She tried to speak and could not. Viola went to her side, took her hand, drew her down on to the sofa, sitting beside her. She had gone very cold.

'Poor little lass,' she said gently. 'Poor child.'

'I don't believe it. It's another plot to keep us apart.'

Viola rose and went to a big, old-fashioned ormolu *escritoire.* She unlocked a small drawer, took out a paper, laid it before Lucinda. Male Child. Corbett. James Carlo. 15th May 1900. Registered at Clapham Common. Mother Viola Marie Corbett, spinster. Father James Staffray, Gentleman.

Lucinda gave a queer, sucked-in little cry. Her hands clapped over her mouth. The sweat began to run down her face as though she was in pain.

'Jimmy did not know until he went into the Army. Then his father told him. But he did not tell you and Bellairs. It was, I believe, your mother's wish that you shouldn't be told. That was the reason – nothing to do with snobbery, or my not being married. Jimmy is your brother. It has all been very sad, very unfortunate, and in a strange way, fated, that you should all meet. Our sending him to school here, the war, and Lord Louderdown's fears for his safety – sending him to Yorkshire out of the raids. But you see now, don't you, why you must stop thinking about him in this way?'

Lucinda pulled off her tight hat. Her face turned from side to side as though she was struggling for breath. Inside she was one silent scream of pain. She could see it all now. The likeness that had made her love him. Her father's infatuation for the big, handsome, charming boy. And this was her answer? The end of all the longing, the waiting, the keeping herself pure and single-minded until her soldier boy returned. This – disgusting thing, like one of those sordid old bible stories that were always skipped over in scripture and the girls used to snigger over.

'Why wasn't I told?'

'At first it did not seem necessary. We lived in Vienna. After the war Jimmy would have returned to us. We did not expect my husband to be killed. Jimmy and Bellairs met by pure chance at school.'

'But – Dad brought Jimmy to Louderdown. And he knew?'

'These old sins,' said Viola unhappily. 'Yes. It was very wrong of him. But – Jimmy was my son, and James, I suppose, fell in love with him. A parent can with a child I know.' She touched Lucinda's shoulder. 'You must try to forget all about us, now you know the truth. It will be hard – but you have no other choice.'

'Don't touch me!' cried Lucinda. 'I feel filthy. I cannot bear it. I cannot bear you, with your prostitute's smile. Nor Jimmy. Nor Dad. I could kill you all for this. I understand my mother. I know why her marriage is ruined. I know why they no longer live together, why she hates Dad, and would not have Jimmy's name mentioned. It is because of you. You have made her a fool, and you have made me a fool.'

'If that's all you feel, it's easily mended. If it's only your pride,' said Viola gently, 'forget it. What I am afraid of is that it may have broken your heart.'

'It is my pride. And it's me.' Lucinda sprang to her feet. Her long, strong hands were pressed against her breast as though something inside was trying to escape. 'It's me,' she cried. 'The pain of it. The shame. The disgust. I will never forgive any of you. Not Dad, nor Jimmy. Nor you, and if I can hurt you I will.'

She drew herself up, summoning all the Staffray grandeur, fighting for her dignity and control, snatched up the discarded hat, and went straight out of the house.

Viola buried her face in her hands. This morning while she was taking tea, Jimmy had come to her room and told her about his meeting with the Staffrays at the cabaret the night before. He had felt distressed and angry, because he was so helpless in the matter. She had been warned. She hoped, as he hoped, that nothing more would come of it, but it had, and she was helpless too. What comfort or counsel could anyone give Lucinda now?

Until the hatred had burned itself out? She needed an arm to hold her while she wept, and who could she turn to? She was so self-centred, so proud, and she had been so sure of Jimmy and herself.

The poor child! Jimmy had told her about the separation from the Staffray children, but not this. But if he *had* told her she would still have been helpless to give Lucinda any comfort or counsel.

Coralie came in and leaned her curly head against Viola's shoulder.

'What's the matter, Mama? Are you sad? Has the lady gone?'

'Oh, my little love,' Viola said, drawing the child on to her knee. 'My little love, don't you grow up too soon.'

Lucinda started up her car and drove off. She did not know where she was going. She had engagements that night – a dinner-party at home, afterwards the younger members were to go to the theatre, and on afterwards to another débutante ball. She did not remember any of this. She just drove. Along high roads, side roads, through shops and markets, past trams and buses, parks and common land.

The stutter of the engine warned her of petrol failure and automatically she drew into the kerb. She had no idea where she was. She just sat, staring about her, trying to think. Trying to collect the shattered remnants of her personality together. She scrabbled in her handbag and found one of the tablets that she had been given, crunched and swallowed it. But when the lift came it brought no relief, only furious anger. She spoke aloud, stammering to herself. 'Damn him. Damn him. Damn Jimmy Corbett to hell. I wish he was dead. I wish he had been killed in France. I cannot bear to think of him.' Her lips began to tremble. 'He's spoiled me for every other man in the world.'

She had never been a weeper. She was a strong, fierce, passionately egotistical girl, and now she was broken. She looked at her small diamond wrist watch. It was after seven. She did not even remember the dinner-party. She drove into the first garage she saw and had the tank filled, and was directed back to the West End. She lit a cigarette and began to drive back to town, fast and furiously, cutting in and taking chances, the concentration on speed and co-ordination blotting everything else out of her mind.

Now the war was two years over and Staffray House had been opened for Lucinda's débutante year, James, at Florence's request, had moved back into residence. He had not wanted to re-open the house. If he had had his way he would have sold the lease. But Florence wanted Lucinda to have a launching becoming to her wealth and position in society, and a great London house, with all the necessary accommodation for entertaining, was an asset. And it was not as though they could not afford it. And she also wanted James there.

'Our private lives should not affect the children,' she said, 'and it is a help to a girl to have a father by her side occasionally.'

At thirty-eight Florence was still very good-looking in her imposing, rather grand way. She was not a great *élégante* or wit, with her position she did not need to be and an Edwardian childhood and girlhood had cast her in a firm mould. It was the duty of her class to keep up appearances at all costs. The children worried and exasperated her. They were tinged with the new restlessness. They did not seem to like their lives or want to do the things they should do. They went through the engagements of the season obviously bored, Bellairs making silly jokes and collecting silly girls, Lucinda impatiently discarding suitors like poker cards. Florence blamed the war. There were so few men – for Lucinda's age – just a little older than herself. Boys from university, or just out of school. A generation of young men had been killed. The girl only seemed to come alive after midnight, when she could leave the balls and parties and chase round the night spots.

James had tried once again for reconciliation. He considered Florence had been unnecessarily stubborn about the whole thing. He tried to be both charming and reasonable, and he was

261

very good at both.

'Flo, be reasonable, my dear girl' he had said. 'There is no need for you to continue to bar your door, or for us to be separated. The war is over. After Lucinda's year, let you and I take a trip. To Canada perhaps? I mean a real trip, over several months.'

Florence hated him because she desired him so much and because he thought no more of their quarrel than a tiresome and unnecessary inconvenience.

Other men of his generation had thickened or coarsened with the passing years, or if they had seen active service, become haggard shadows of their former selves. He was still handsome and youthful. She knew she was lucky; Bellairs had been too young to serve, and James was disabled. She knew this was an agony to him, a born soldier, not to be able to play an active part. She was glad something hurt him. She grudged James his life because she felt it should belong to no one but herself.

'You know I don't care for travelling,' she said abruptly. 'And nothing has changed. You still see that boy, don't you?'

He could not understand her. 'What difference does it make to you?' he said, good-naturedly exasperated. 'Jimmy is serving in Cologne now with the Army of Occupation. He is rarely on leave.'

'You see him when he is?'

'Very rarely. He is a great skier. When he can get off he goes to find the snow. He has kept his promise meticulously. I know it hurts him, because he was fond of the twins.'

'You went out to Switzerland to see him. I saw your photograph in the *Tatler*.'

James was silent. He had wanted to see the boy in the sport he excelled in, and it had done him good to see the war shadows ease from the young face as he skied in the sunlit mountains.

'My conditions are just the same,' said Florence. 'You do not see him at all.'

'It is like a childhood quarrel. Who will give in first. You never see Jimmy. You never will have to, or even think of him. You behave as though I was keeping a woman instead of very occasionally seeing my own son. He takes nothing away from you.

262

He asks for nothing. Come, Flo –' he put his arm round her shoulders, his hand tipping her face towards his – 'come on, my dear, let's get away together. Go on a real long trip. We could take a year.'

For a moment he thought she would give way. He pressed her flushed face against his shoulder as he had in their early married days, and he knew his touch aroused her. Her breast stirred with a quickened breath, and the pupils in her pale aquamarine eyes dilated. He remembered her first wild, possessive passion and bent to her lips, but before he could touch them she broke away, flushed, ruffled, angry.

'No. You think you only have to touch me, like you do your fancy women and I'll give in!' She gave him a burning, inquisitorial glance. '*She* is in England now, isn't she?'

'Yes.' He rose irritably, turning away, and again it was his indifference that stabbed her. 'But I have not seen her, and I do not intend to. If you wish I will promise not to, and you know I will keep my promise – that is, of course, if you come back to me.'

'No promise will stop you thinking of her. It never has.'

'I cannot understand why you should be so extreme.'

'It is in my nature. You cannot imagine how I feel. I am your wife, but to you I am just another woman. You could come back into my bed tonight as though this had never happened. But I need assurance. And the only assurance I will take is that you never see that boy or his mother again. Then, and only then, will I change my mind.'

'I am sorry, Flo,' he said simply. 'I will not give Jimmy up.'

'Then there is nothing more to be said.'

So the farce continued. He went back to Staffray House, the connecting doors between their rooms remained locked while the expensive ritual of Lucinda's presentation went on. If his valet and Florence's maid gossiped he simply did not care. He never thought about servants' gossip – he never had.

Jimmy telephoned him in the late afternoon. His voice sounded strange. 'Are you free, sir, for an hour or so? My mother wants to see you.'

263

He was totally unprepared for it. He knew Viola was in England. He even knew where she lived. By common consent, he and Jimmy, apart from conventional enquiries, did not speak of her. For a moment now, the very blood seemed to stop in his veins. He could not refuse to see her if she needed him. He had to go. Twenty years of stifled longing surged up within him; he knew it would be wise not to go but only once'had he had caution in his dealings with Viola, and that had been the greatest and most tragic mistake of his life.

'Has something happened?'

'Last night. I took the kids to the Can-Can. It was Terry's birthday. We ran into the twins.'

James came to earth with an ugly jerk.

'I hoped that would be the end of it. But this afternoon Lucinda came to see Mama at Campden Hill. She was very distressed. Mama would like to talk to you about it.'

'I'll come straight away.'

As he went through the hall, Florence came in, looking very attractive in a blue suit, and a small hat encircled with darker blue velvet flowers. She was with a man he knew slightly, one of her lame dogs, an ex-officer who had been at the Louderdown Hospital. A silent sort of fellow, taciturn and shy, devoted to the country life of dogs, horses and hunting that she loved. He was obviously in love with her, poor chap. Florence looked more relaxed, alive and animated than he had seen her for some time.

'Oh, James, are you going out? The car has just dropped me – shall we keep it for you?'

'Don't trouble. I'll take a cab.'

'You know Archie Hamilton, don't you? He was one of our patients at Louderdown. Major Hamilton, my husband.'

James extended his one hand, briefly affable, then took his hat from the footman.

'I've been talking about the stables at Louderdown,' Florence said eagerly. 'Archie has some splendid ideas for building up the stock again. As soon as the season is over I have asked him to come and stay at Louderdown and give me his advice. He bred bloodstock before the war.'

'Can't afford to now,' said Hamilton. 'Lucky to keep a hack on my pension. But Lady Louderdown wants to get your colours racing again.'

'An excellent idea,' said James, moving towards the door. 'Why don't you stay on for the shooting? Won't be much this year, with all the wartime ploughing, though they tell me there should be some grouse.'

'That's exceedingly kind of you.'

'Not at all. Delighted. I must go, if I'm to be back for your dinner-party at eight. Good-bye, Major Hamilton. Good-bye, my dear.'

As he went through the door he heard her ask if Lucinda had returned, and the footman saying, 'She is not back yet, madame.'

'Oh dear, that girl! And she takes such hours to dress. Well, come and let me give you a sherry or a cocktail, Archie . . . I can spare an hour before I dress.' They went up to the first floor talking animatedly, the shy man and Florence, but there was a moment when she paused, looked back over her shoulder at James's indifferent back going out through the front door. Archie Hamilton's unspoken devotion was at least a comfort if it was not what she wanted, but if she had hoped it would arouse the least uneasiness in James's mind she was disappointed.

At Campden Hill, James saw Jimmy's Napier standing in the driveway. Vatel opened the door and showed him into the drawing-room. There was a faint scent of gardenias, tormentingly reminiscent, and Viola rose from a deep chair in a shadowy corner of the room.

They stood quite still, looking at each other. She was older, and obviously made no attempt to hide her age. The turbulent hair was fading to a pepper and salt grey. Fine lines shadowed her mouth and the laughter creases about her glorious eyes had deepened, but she was still tall, slender, proud, moving as she crossed the room towards him like a lily in a breeze, or a wave of the sea. The long slender column of her neck emerging from a

265

tea-gown or kimono of dark silk embroidered with silver flowers and birds, and he remembered how she had loathed the fitted dresses and tightly-laced corsets of her girlhood, and how at home she had always worn these loose, lovely robes, so that when he had touched her he could feel the strong, soft body beneath the silk, and at the memory desire rose like a flame. Oh God, he thought. Oh, my God! Twenty years – more. She was now a woman in her forties, and it was just the same, just the same as when they had met, a boy and girl, travelling in the London express from Leeds.

He went across to her. The pearls he had given her all those years ago were about her neck. He lifted them, and they were warm from her body. He looked down at her lips, and kissed her, and she did not deny him. She never had.

'Duchess,' he said.

'My lord.' Then as his arm moved to encircle her she shook her head, and moved away. 'James,' she said, 'Jimmy told you? That he had met your children, quite accidentally?'

'Yes.'

'Lucinda came to see me today. I had to tell her, James. She is in love with him. Nothing would have persuaded her that they couldn't start where they had left off in 1917. Why wasn't she told then? It was cruel to let her build dreams all these years.'

'I had no idea it had gone so deep,' he said stiffly. 'I wanted them to know. It was my wife's wish that nothing should be said. She thought . . . well, I did too . . . that eventually he would return to Austria, and it would be unlikely that they would meet again.'

'James, she came to see me today – to see his mother, trying to make a friend of me. Get me on her side. Is it because of my Jimmy that you and your wife are separated?'

'Yes. I could not promise not to see him.' His voice was stiff and angry. She recognized the old arrogance; her eyes were both accusing and sad. James broke out passionately, 'Damn it, Viola, I could not give the boy up once I had met him. He is your boy and mine, and I loved him from the start. He is a son any man would be proud of.'

266

'But what about your other children – *her* children?'

'That is what they are, *her* children. I – I am fond of them, particularly Bellairs, although he is full of tomfool ideas about art. But she brought them up, and nurses, and governesses, and schools, and my mother spoiled Bell, as she spoiled me. I never knew them. But I knew Jimmy instantly. As though we had been waiting for each other.'

'And so we have this dreadful thing? Because you were indifferent, and your wife, poor lady, bitterly hurt. All these war years that child has been living on dreams that one day she would find him again, and all misunderstandings would be smoothed away. She is tenacious, and bold, and would not give up. And today I had to tell her the truth.'

'You told her?'

'You should have told her years ago.'

'But she was such a child. I thought she would forget the whole thing. And Florence insisted. We were both certain she would forget.'

'But she didn't, and so it came to me – the *cause* of all the trouble. I had to tell her. What will she think of me now? And I *had* to, James. She was in such a strange, exalted state. Afterwards, when she knew, she would take no comfort from me. Of course. She must loathe me. But now I think you should speak to her and try to help her.'

'I'll get my wife to,' he said stiffly, 'it is not a man's business.'

'It is a father's business,' said Viola.

'I tell you, Viola, I would not know how to begin.'

'But one of you,' she said inexorably, 'will *have* to – and very soon.' A little half-laugh, half-sigh, escaped from her. After all these years, at this first meeting, they were both angry. 'Ah, James, my love, all this is because of you and me. We're guilty of that old sin, not these children. If anyone can help her you can. She should have heard the truth from you. If you had told her how it all happened, how we were too young and crazy and thoughtless and selfish as all young people in love are, then happen she could understand and forgive us. Well, not me perhaps. But you. And our Jimmy, who is no more guilty than she is. Aye, dear, it's a mess . . .' She put her hand on his arm, and inclined her head so that it almost rested on his shoulder, then sighed, and moved away. 'There's another thing I've got to say. If it will make for peace and happiness in your family, I think you should promise not to see Jimmy again. I've spoken to him. He would understand.'

He was about to protest that it would cut him off completely from all he held dear. He could not conceal his pain.

'Not to see him! Nor you – now we have met again. Not occasionally . . . it could do no harm.'

'James, already it's done terrible harm. You're trying to have your cake and eat it, love, as you always have. This time it is your own children you are harming.'

He knew she was right. 'Yes. It is my fault, most of all. Yet, you know, Viola, I'd do it all again. Happiness is not a thing to be relinquished. You don't get a second chance. It's like in a battle, you have to hang on to what you can hold. It's been my tragedy that once I let you go . . . that's where all the evil stems from, Viola. Not from our being in love. All right. I'll do as you say.'

He thrust out his one hand.

'Just give me your hand. Once, for a moment. So I know that it did all happen, and you are still here, alive, in the world.'

She put her hand in his and he kissed it and let it go.

'I must go back now. I will speak to Lucinda – and to Florence. May I speak to Jimmy? Just to say good-bye?'

'Of course.'

He turned to the door, remembering she too had suffered loss. 'Jimmy told me about his step-father's death. And what a fine man he was. I am sorry.'

Her face changed, haunted, evasive. 'I cannot bear to talk about it.' The sharp memory of Eugene lying dead was unbearable. Eugene who, even now, in this crisis which was not of his making, she needed, whom she always needed now, in a way she had never needed James however much she loved him. 'He was a wonderful man. We were very happy. He gave me everything and protected me and loved Jimmy like his own children. They shot him down, for no reason, the people he was trying to help.'

'I'm sorry,' said James again.

The telephone in the hall rang and Jimmy came in, white and shaken, and went up to his father.

'Dad, it's Amy. She's with Bellairs. They just got back to his flat and they found Lucinda there. It seems she had a key. Dad — she's tried to kill herself.'

CHAPTER TEN

Jimmy drove James to Bellairs' flat in Chelsea. The evening was warm and many people were in the park strolling or lying on the grass. Children were playing, a few kites bobbed in the sky. The newspaper placards snarled about the war debts that the beaten Central Powers could not pay.

Lucinda had tried to kill herself because of him. Jimmy could not believe it. A young, aristocratic, rich, beautiful girl with her whole life before her. Because it was impossible that they should ever marry. He had seen death close at hand, and danger, but the desperate passions of the spirit had never touched him. Love to him so far had been a pleasant mutual game. Lucinda's action seemed extreme, unbalanced, outside the comprehension of his nature.

'Why should she do such a thing, Dad?' he asked helplessly. 'It's nearly seven years ago – she was only a kid and now she's grown up. I can't believe that it meant that much to her. I'm not even the great hero she expected then. I've not done badly in the Army, but nothing spectacular. Has she never spoken about it to you?'

'She's like her mother,' James said shortly, 'keeps things to herself. Tenacious. It's all a damned ugly muddle. She should have been told when it happened.'

Jimmy was not only horrified, he was deeply embarrassed. Like James he was, outwardly, deeply conventional, loathing public emotionalism or anything conspicuous. He had known men, with their nerves shattered by warfare, try to take their own lives when they had reached the limit of endurance and had understood, helped and covered up for them. But that anyone should find life unbearable because of a broken love affair did not seem credible.

'I understand that she must feel pretty shocked, and dis-

270

gusted perhaps. When you came up to Catterick that time to tell me about it, I felt pretty sick. *And* guilty – although it was not my fault. But I was three years older than she was then, and I should have had more sense, even if it had been all right. If we hadn't been – related. But for it to mean so much to her. It's not possible!'

James remembered the months after Viola had left him when life had seemed insupportable. When he had lost his arm and his army career had finished. He remembered in the hunting field, taking hard fences with the awkward balance of his single arm, and thinking it would ease things if he came off and broke his neck; but nothing could have made him do so deliberately. He remembered Lucinda's blazing eyes and stubborn young face and knew what she had done she had done to punish him. He did not know her at all. He had no words either to counsel or comfort her. What could he say to her?

They turned along the Embankment to a tall old house in Cheyne Row; he thought it was typical of Bellairs to have chosen such a district. Bohemian and artistic. But a young man of an age to sow wild oats needed a place of his own. He remembered his own flat in Half Moon Street. But his children ran contrary to his wishes. They wanted things he could not understand. Bellairs wanted to leave university and spend his time painting. He had never known what Lucy had wanted until now. She had always seemed to him restless, pleasure-seeking, unpredictable, surrounded by a lot of charming, foolish young people. Now he knew. She had wanted Jimmy-C. Apparently nothing else. Nothing else in life.

Lucinda's open tourer stood outside the house and a chauffeur-driven limousine just beyond. He recognized the Rolls of their family doctor: Bellairs must have sent for him. When they rang, Bellairs opened the door, his shirt stained with blood. James stared in horror, and Bellairs put a quick hand on his arm.

'It's all *right*, Dad. It's a mess but she's all right. Thanks to Amy Lyttelton. She knew what to do until the doctor came.'

'Does your mother know?' James asked painfully. Jimmy

stood in the background, apart from this family conference. The outsider.

'I telephoned,' said Bellairs. 'I told her that Lucy had had a bit of an accident with the car door but that she was all right and we were bringing her home. I told her to carry on with the dinner-party without us.' It occurred to James that he should be doing all this. He felt old and useless, and was grateful for Bellairs' quick thinking. The boy was suddenly unable to bear it that his tall, soldierly authoritative father should look so stricken and defeated. He put an arm round his shoulders, 'It's all right, Dad. It's not your fault. Lucy's a funny girl, really. Always has been. I'm her twin. I know.'

'I've never known either of you, really,' James said helplessly. 'Why was that?'

'You didn't have much chance,' Bellairs said dryly. 'With Mummy and Gran and nannies and governesses and boarding schools. It's the custom of our class.'

'It won't get into the newspapers?'

'Not if I can help it,' said Bellairs. 'Lucy's been hitting the headlines far too much since she came out. They'd make a circus out of this. We must get her home quietly. You know Mummy will loathe it if any of it came out. You'd better come up, Father, and speak to her. Sir Melvyn is still upstairs with her. I managed to catch him. He's brought a surgeon along.'

'A surgeon?'

'To put in the stitches.'

'Oh, Christ!' said Jimmy, and Bellairs looked at him as though just realizing his presence. Jimmy knew that Bellairs knew, that Lucinda must have told him. They looked at each other curiously, appraisingly, knowing they were brothers. 'I'd better cut along,' Jimmy said, 'unless there's anything I can do.'

'Well, could you wait until Dad and I have gone, and then take Amy home? She's been such a little brick.' Bellairs hesitated, then burst out, 'Jim, don't look so guilty. You're not to blame. Supposing it had been different? If there had been no relationship, and you could have married, and you'd kept in touch

272

during the war – do you think you'd have wanted to take it up again?'

Jimmy shook his head, comforted by the understanding in Bellairs' eyes. 'No. I had forgotten. It was part of childhood, before France. I haven't thought of it for years.'

'Well, if you had turned Lucy down she would have behaved in exactly the same way. I tell you, I know her. You remember her pony, Dad, Flyer? You gave us both ponies, when we were twelve?'

'The one that broke its neck?'

'*She* broke its neck. She wanted a thoroughbred horse, but you said she was too young. So she took that pony out and put it over jumps right outside its strength and range and it killed itself trying, and she could have killed herself too. I can remember standing watching and crying my eyes out and shouting at her to stop, and getting called a cry-baby. Everyone said what guts Lucy had, what a pair of hands, so she got put up on her first hunter and got her own way.'

'She managed it too,' said James.

'She can manage everything but herself,' said Bellairs crisply. 'She thinks life is like a horse and you can beat it into submission. Come along. Jimmy, when we've gone, you pick up Amy. She has been wonderful – but she is pretty shaken.'

'I'll wait in the car.'

They hesitated, then simultaneously shook hands. Somehow it was Bellairs who was in command of the situation.

'No more of this damned nonsense between us, Jim,' he said earnestly. 'It's funny – but I feel I've always known we were brothers. Right from the start, at school. I'll be seeing you. Come upstairs, Dad. Let's get it over.'

Jimmy moved the car further along the road under the shadow of some overhanging trees. He did not want Lucinda to see him watching. The light was beginning to fade. He remembered the incident with the pony, although he had not been present when it had been killed. Lucinda had expressed no remorse, triumphantly riding her big new mount, and showing off her prowess. Bellairs had scarcely spoken to her during that particular school holiday.

He saw the two doctors leave in their car and shortly afterwards James and Bellairs came out, supporting Lucinda between them. She had a man's light coat over her shoulders, and her wrists were heavily bandaged. There were dark rusty blood stains on her pinky-beige marocain silk dress. She was white but she walked with her head erect, the evening sunlight glinting on her cap of golden hair, her face proud, furious, beautiful, staring around defiantly. She could never understand a world where her will was denied. He remembered how, when they were children, her temper would crack like heated glass, and how she would shout furiously, 'I am the Lady Lucinda Staffray, and I can do what I like.' And if they laughed, she would fly at them in rage, picking up anything, sending them running until she threw herself down, beating her head on the ground, sick with anger, uncontrollably passionate, never giving in or giving up.

He waited until they had driven away, and then got out of the car and rang the bell of Bellairs' flat. He heard light footsteps dragging down the stairs and Amy opened the door. She was very pale and still trembling, he could see bloodstains on her pretty, crisp summer dress. Her face filled with relief when she saw him.

'Oh, Jimmy,' she cried. 'Oh Jimmy, it was so awful. It was so awful! Thank heavens you've come for me.'

He put his arms about her and held her closely against him; for a moment he thought she was going to faint. He picked her up and carried her upstairs into the flat . . . she was light in his arms, small-boned, limp as a drowned kitten. He set her down, looking round frantically for brandy, but when he found it she shook her head. He remembered that a hot drink was the thing for shock and clattered into the kitchen, feeling inadequate. When he finally found the cups and tea-pot and brought a cup of tea to her, it was luke-warm and almost chocolate brown. She drank it, pulled a wry face and sat up.

'It's *awful*!' she said. Her tension eased, and he was relieved to see a touch of colour in her face.

'Bellairs said you had been wonderful.'

'Oh, fiddle. I've just had a bit of training. If the war had gone on I was going to take up nursing.'

He sat down beside her and took her hand.

'Can you tell me – about Lucinda? What happened? Do you mind?' Her hand shook again, and he said, 'All right, don't if it upsets you.'

'No, you ought to know. Oh, Jimmy, I don't think – I don't think she's quite sane. Bell asked me to go to the National Gallery with him, and then come back here and see his pictures.'

'You came here alone with him? To his rooms?' Jimmy was very shocked.

The big grey eyes widened with amusement.

'It is 1923, Jimmy, you know. Did you think we came here to make love?'

'No, of course not!' he said hastily. But he did not like it. Amy was not the sort of girl who went to the rooms of young men alone, and in a way she was his property, under his care, having no father. She knew exactly what he was thinking and a tenderness moved within her, thinking that, for all his dashing looks and sophisticated charm, he was nothing but an old-fashioned simpleton at heart.

'It was like a bad dream,' she went on. 'We'd had such fun, a lovely afternoon, and we came along here to see Bellairs' pictures and have some tea. We were laughing a lot, because you know Bellairs is great fun. I didn't realize how much I had missed him.'

Jimmy felt Bellairs had stolen something from him – he had always taken Amy for granted. He was jealous and did not realize it.

'He is Lord Staffray, you know,' he said stiffly, 'and one day he'll be Lord Louderdown.'

'What's that got to do with being friends?'

There was a small impasse. The colour came to her cheeks and she rose sharply. 'Jimmy, take me home. I don't want to talk about it any more.'

'I'm sorry. Of course.'

'I don't want to talk about it' She turned to him again, 'But I must. Her car was at the door. She had a key. When Bell went in he called, but there was no answer, and then we found her in the bathroom. Thank God she had not locked the door! She was kneeling by the bath with her hands in the water, she had cut her wrists and the whole place smelled of blood. She tried to fight Bell off when he went to help her, but she was too weak. He got her arms above her head and held them while I tore up shirts, anything, and strapped them tightly, and all the time she said awful things. She told Bellairs that their father was your father, that he had always preferred you to either of them. She said terrible things about her father and your mother. She said she wished you had been killed in the war.'

Amy covered her face with her hands and began to shake again, still hearing the weak voice with its hysterical whispers of hate. 'Gas,' Lucinda had said, 'that's what he deserves. His lungs rotten, coughing them up, or disfigured . . . his face disfigured, so that no one would look at him again.'

'I don't think she knew what she was saying, Jimmy. I hope not. And all the time I felt it was not unhappiness, or sadness, but pride . . . as though life had made a fool of her, and she couldn't bear that.'

'Amy' – he put his arms round her, pressing her head into his shoulder – 'that's enough. Try to forget. It isn't your tragedy, or mess. You're so good and you've been brave. Now let me take you home.'

In the car on the way to Clapham he said, 'Did you know – before this, that Lord Louderdown was my father?'

'Yes. I'd begun to guess. It was obvious how much he loved you. Then Mother let it slip, once when we were seeing you off to France and he came to the station. I remember. I never saw a grown-up important man with tears in his eyes before.'

'But you've never said anything.'

'Why should I? As you said, dear Jimmy, it wasn't my secret.'

'You don't mind?'

'About what?' Her lovely clear eyes were full of surprise. 'Because your parents weren't married? It's not your fault. Mother said they were so much in love . . . she's not very imaginative, but she said your mother was so beautiful at that time she seemed to shine like a lamp. She didn't approve, of course, and neither did my father. My father did not even *like* Mother being friends with Aunt Viola.' She looked down at the ugly stains on her dress. 'In a way they were right. When people are young and do these lovely, wild things they always say they're harming no one but themselves . . . but that's not quite true. How can they know?'

'No one can know.' Jimmy smiled at her serious face. 'But happiness is now. The future may never happen.'

When Viola had returned to England and taken the house in Kensington for the family, Betsy and Amy had gone back to their little cottage in Clapham. Since Jimmy had come into the money Eugene had settled upon him, he had insisted on making Betsy a comfortable allowance. And the pretty little place was as neat and well-kept as a doll's house. He stopped the car outside. It was nearly dark now, and a moon was rising over the trees on the common.

'Why is it that there are some people who *won't* believe they can't make other people love them? They think it is their will that makes it love.'

'You're thinking of Lucinda?'

'And Lorenz. I am afraid I hurt him last night. I'm sorry. But I don't love him, and I never will.'

'I wish I wasn't going back tomorrow. I've hardly seen you on this leave.'

'Too many other adoring females.'

'Don't tease, Amy. I meant it. Will you come and see me off like you used to?'

She was surprised. 'But that was when you were living with us, and Mother was looking after you.'

'I'm asking you now. Please, Amy. Come and see me off tomorrow. I'll tell you now. Lord Louderdown won't come. After this he will not see me again. His wife wishes it. I understand.'

'You mean, for the first time, you've felt unhappy about your birth?'

'Yes. You know exactly what I mean.'

'All right, then,' Amy said calmly, although her heart suddenly raced within her breast. 'I'll come if you want me to. What time?'

'I'll pick you up. In the morning. We'll have lunch.'

'How grand.'

They sat together in silence. He very much wanted to kiss her and he was astounded, because such a thing had never occurred to him before. After the passionate ugliness of what had happened that night, she seemed to him very pure and cool, like a small pale flower. And yet she had not been shocked or disgusted.

She got out of the car before he could move towards her, looking down at her stained dress. 'I'll try and creep in and get this off so that Mother doesn't see it. I don't want her to know. She'd be upset. You know, Jimmy, when awful things happen, it does somehow bring people together. You and me. We've not really talked since we were kids. You've been nice, given me treats, but we've not ever talked until tonight.'

'We've *often* talked,' he protested.

'No. You've talked. You've given orders. I've listened and obeyed . . .'

'*Really*, Amy,' he began to protest, but she bade him good night and ran indoors.

Well, I'll be damned! thought Jimmy.

When he got home to Kensington, Viola and the girls had waited dinner for him, making a little family gathering because he was going back to Cologne the following day. Lorenz had gone back to College and was not present. It was no use pretending that the house was not more peaceful in his absence. He was not happy in England. When he was twenty-one he would come into his Austrian possessions. Although he had not been left an interest in the banking house of Mendel-Erhmann & Sons, Eugene had left all the Austrian land and real estate to him, and a comfortable fortune shrewdly invested in America

278

and Switzerland, which was not subject to the raging inflation now bedevilling the defeated Central Powers. Lorenz was not adaptable. He felt himself an Austrian-German, an alien in England, particularly where many of the students were older men who had fought in Flanders. The fact that Jimmy was a British officer, who had fought against his homeland, rankled. His deep jealousy of his half-brother ran beneath the surface. When Jimmy was away he tried to monopolize his mother, and dictate to his sisters. When Jimmy was on leave it took all his patience and tact to placate Lorenz and keep the peace.

Dinner was, as always, perfectly cooked and served. Vatel was fanatical about keeping up his master's standards in this London home. Everyone dressed for dinner. Theresa, a cooler beauty than her mother, had Viola's tumultuous red hair but the shrewd, clever, watchful Erhmann eyes. She had been stage-mad since childhood and was now attending a London drama school run by a famous English actress. In her natural element at last, she was already a star pupil, with offers of engagements before she had even finished her course. Tonight, free from Lorenz's frigid disapproval, for he considered it insufferable that his mother should have permitted his sister to be an actress, she kept them laughing with her description of the audition she had attended that day, and little Coralie's cheeks were pink and her eyes spellbound as she listened to Theresa's mimickry. Viola and Jimmy had not spoken of Lucinda before the girls. It was a relief to them when one of Theresa's innumerable admirers called to take her out, and Coralie went to bed, leaving them alone.

'How was she, Jimmy?' Viola asked anxiously. 'Was it serious?'

'Thank God, no. And thanks to Amy, who knew what to do.'

'I'm so glad. I wonder what she intended to do? Was it a cry for help or an attempt at revenge? I think, maybe, revenge.'

'On me? Or on our father?' Jimmy asked grimly.

'On you both,' said Viola. 'You for being unattainable, some people can't stand that.'

'Like Prince Friedrich Schausenhardt.'

'Why should you speak of him now?' she said and drew a shawl up about her shoulders with a little shiver.

'You are cold?'

'No. I — I don't like to talk of that time.'

'I'm sorry, Mama. It was just that, in a way, Schausenhardt was like Lucinda, and Lorenz perhaps . . . one of these people who can't believe they can't get their desires. To oppose them is to affront them. They can't understand that you can't force people to love you. Amy said that to me.'

'Amy? She's a curious, clever child. But Lucinda, I think, could not forgive her father for not telling her, nor for loving you best. Children have strong jealousies, and some can't leave these childish jealousies behind.' He knew she was thinking of Lorenz.

'If it was revenge she wanted, she certainly succeeded,' Jimmy said grimly. 'I'll never forget Lord Louderdown's face tonight. He seemed to age while I looked at him.'

'He told you — that you are not to meet again?'

'Yes. I think it's right. The position was always awkward between us. There were things we could not speak of. We were never completely frank. Although I knew he loved me, and I knew I could go to him in any kind of trouble. When I was separated from you and Papa by the war, it was good to have him there. When I came back from France I could talk to him about the stinking hell of it. I could not talk to Amy and Aunt Betsy. But he had known active service, so I could talk to him.'

'Did you know that he and his wife were virtually separated because of his refusal to give you up?'

'Now. He told me. I accept his conditions.' He smiled. 'I somehow don't think Bellairs will, though.'

They were sitting in the half darkness and he could not see her face, but he could feel the sadness that emanated from the shadowy, graceful figure.

'Do you still love him? My father, I mean. Lord Louderdown?'

'Oh yes,' the words were barely audible. 'Ah, yes.' It was a whisper, a breath, a sigh on the summer night.

'But – he hasn't behaved very well. To you – or to his family.'

The sigh was suddenly a small laugh in the darkness.

'My dearest boy, what has that got to do with love?'

Something in her voice made Jimmy feel extraordinarily inexperienced and very young.

There had been a moment's difficulty in getting Lucinda into the house unobserved. Bellairs ran up the steps ahead, and came down to say that there was no one in the hall but Bradman, the butler.

'Dear faithful old Bradman,' drawled Lucinda, 'always to be trusted. What have you told him, Bell? Lady Lucinda is drunk and not fit to be seen by her mother's guests?' It was the first time she had spoken.

'It wouldn't be the first time I'd told him that,' said Bellairs grimly. 'Come on, Lucy, cut out the drama. This isn't Louderdown with Nanny waiting for you. It's time you grew up.'

'Let's go in to Mummy's dinner-party,' she said loudly. 'Let's go in and tell them all that I tried to kill myself over Dad's bastard who is my half-brother. What a dinner table topic that would be!'

'Lucinda, for God's sake,' her father protested. 'If I had had my way you would have known from the start.'

'But you didn't tell me, did you? You let me make a fool of myself. The way Jimmy looked at me, while I raved on. He looked at me as though I was some sort of beggar and he was sorry for me.'

'Get it out of your head that you're so important,' said Bellairs. 'You've been hurt. You're not the only one. If you're thinking of making a scene and a scandal, everyone will be hurt too, and you won't feel any better.'

He half-helped, half-pulled her out of the car. She had stood, glaring round her defiantly, and for a moment they were afraid she was going to make a scene. But there were no people about. No newspaper men, thank God. They helped her up the steps and across the marble hall. The nurse ran down and took over.

James, watching, longed to atone, to comfort her and did not know how to begin.

'Is her ladyship all right?' Bradman asked anxiously, rather disapprovingly. Lucinda's exploits during the London season had shocked him considerably.

'She's pretty shaken.' Automatically James repeated what Bellairs had told him to say. 'A little accident with the car door, crushed her hands. Tell Lady Louderdown I am here and will be with them immediately. Send my man to me.'

The hall was decorated with a great display of flowers from the Louderdown glasshouses, sent down by train that morning. From the great dining-room on the ground floor he could hear the loud hum of voices, the slight clatter of plate and cutlery. He went upstairs to Lucinda's room. She was lying on her bed, white and pale, her eyes closing, her bandaged arms raised on a sling. His handsome, wilful, unknowable child. Bellairs and the nurse stood beside her.

'Is she all right?'

'Quite all right, your lordship,' the nurse said, professionally calm, inwardly agog at this scandal in high places. Sir Melvyn had, of course, not told her all, but she suspected a broken love affair. These wild young people! 'I've given her an injection. She will sleep. Sir Melvyn said he would be in first thing in the morning.'

The specialist had been the soul of tact. 'There has been a profound nervous trauma of some kind. These things can be triggered off by anything at her age. She has had a very hectic first season. Lady Lucinda has been keeping the press men busy. Does she take any stimulants, by the way?'

'Are you asking me if she drinks, man?' said James furiously. 'She's only twenty.'

'She doesn't drink any more than the rest of the crowd,' said Bellairs quickly.

'She doesn't take any tablets? To keep her going?'

'Drugs?' James was horrified. The press had been full of sensational stories of drug-taking in high society. 'Why should she do that?'

282

Sir Melvyn shrugged.

'She's been taking something. I'll find out in the morning. These young people, you'd be surprised. Rushing about, not eating or sleeping enough. Well, take her up to Louderdown – the season's nearly over anyway. Fresh air, exercise, quiet country life. That's the ticket for that young lady.'

James went to his room; the evening ritual was like an extraordinary nightmare. Dressing, putting on the crisply starched shirt his valet held for him, submitting to the tying of his white tie, the diamond studs and buttons, the white waistcoat and tail suit moulded to fit his superb figure. With his one arm, these things were difficult. He entered the dining-room when they were already at the savoury, making greetings and apologies, explanations, a slight accident with the car door. Yes, Lucy was all right, but sleeping . . . Bellairs had been clever to think of the car door.

Bellairs himself arrived when coffee was being served, having driven to Chelsea to change and back again. The strain of the evening showed a little in his long, sensitive face, but he gathered the younger crowd up to go on to the ball with his easy, debonair manner. It was ten o'clock before the last guests left. The footman closed the door, and James and Florence were alone in the big cream and gold drawing-room.

'Well,' she said, 'what sort of a scrape did she get into this time?'

'No scrape. She tried to kill herself.'

'Lucinda?' Florence was horrified. 'I don't believe you. She's wild, I know, and she drinks too many cocktails, like they all do. And she has a vile temper if she can't get her own way. But not that sort of thing.'

She made it sound as though suicide was a kind of middle, or lower-class activity.

'Florence, it is time we faced the facts about our children and ourselves. Sir Melvyn suspects that Lucinda has been taking some kind of drug to keep herself going.'

'Nonsense! She has the energy of two people. She can ride all day and dance all night.'

283

'Florence, please sit down and listen.' She sank into one of the gilded chairs, her face averted, her mouth disdainful. 'It seems that all these years she has still been thinking about Jimmy Corbett.' She made a small, disgusted sound, but he went on, 'She has imagined herself to be still in love with him, and was convinced he would feel the same. Well, it seems that last night she and Bell ran into him accidentally. He is home on leave. She would not believe that it was not a great romance. She went to see his mother this afternoon. I don't exactly know why . . . yes, I do. She wanted to – to ingratiate herself with Viola, to get her on her side, to assure her that his illegitimate birth made no difference to her.'

The colour had drained out of Florence's face. She sat very still, holding a long, single ostrich feather fan. The lights from the crystal chandeliers made the diamanté beads on her blue chiffon dress glitter, as did the diamonds at her throat, and a small diamond butterfly in her marcelled hair. She looked like a lady sitting for her portrait. Pale, aristocratic, perfectly still. He went on remorselessly. She had to be made to understand. 'You see what has come of your refusal to explain the truth to her? Viola' – Florence winced at the name – 'told her the truth today. In my opinion quite rightly. She could do nothing else. Lucinda left her house and drove off. When Bell got to his place late this afternoon he found her there. He had a friend with him, young Amy Lyttelton. Fortunately they stopped the bleeding and called Sir Melvyn. Lucinda had cut the veins in her wrists.'

Florence gave a little cry and rose to her feet, but he held her back.

'It is no use going to her now. She is asleep under sedation. But I want you to be with her when she wakes, because she will not speak to me about it.'

'Do you wonder – learning about this *filth*? Do you expect her to speak to you again?'

'I expect nothing. I know I am guilty,' James said wearily, 'but I am not alone. Viola and I were desperately in love and very young, and both free. I had not even met you. But your part – in forbidding me to tell the children that Jimmy Corbett is

284

their half-brother – *that* has caused the mischief, and *that* was because of your pride. I want you to know that I would do anything on earth to put all this right. Lucinda will recover and I hope will forgive me. I want you to ask her to forget it. To put it behind her. She is very young, and life can give her so much. I will promise you, Florence, that I will do as you asked me. I will not see Jimmy Corbett again, nor, of course, his mother. I will do as you wish. Let us write it off and try to build a reasonable family life.'

Her pale blue eyes flashed with a glint of malice.

'I am afraid, James, that you have left it too late. The harm has been done. I no longer care what you do. Go and see your bastard and your fancy woman if you wish. It is no longer any concern of mine.'

She left the room and went up to Lucinda.

Before the end of the week she and Lucinda had left London, going up to Louderdown. Lucinda was pale, but had apparently recovered. The car-door explanation was accepted by all her friends. Florence told them she would be sufficiently recovered to hunt.

The ubiquitous and adoring Archie Hamilton was in attendance.

Jimmy picked up Amy by taxi, and they drove to Liverpool Street where they lunched at Bishopsgate Hotel before he went across to get his train. Not a little girl's treat this time. Hock and sole and Amy in a pretty hat with pink roses with a new, and to him endearing, look in her big grey eyes. He could not imagine why he had never noticed how pretty she was, how witty she was, how she enjoyed things. She made him think a little of his mother in this capacity for enjoyment.

Jimmy too looked very splendid. He was twenty-three now, and the war had prematurely robbed him of the last shadow of boyhood. Broad-shouldered, slim, and so handsome that Amy was sure every woman in the restaurant was looking at him. He had had new uniforms made while he was on leave, and Vatel had polished his belt and buttons with loving care. His campaign ribbons were bright on his superbly cut tunic. His service cap was pulled down slightly to one side. The tense cynicism with which he had come out of the trenches had gone, and he had again a look of that very young, cocky, beloved Jimmy-C who had so irritated and entranced her as a little girl and a teenager. The old mischievous desire to take him down a peg rose almost irresistibly within her as she stood on the platform and surveyed his magnificence. He frowned questioningly at her expression.

'Now what, young Amy? Do I look funny?'

'You look superb. As lordly as your father. An advertisement for your tailor. In the *Tatler* – what the well-dressed young officer should wear. But that was ghastly tea you made yesterday, I'll bet you've never made a pot of tea in your life before.'

'Well, there's always been someone else to do it. Vatel, or my batman . . .'

'Or Mother. Or me.'

He smiled at her teasing. 'Well, you must teach me how to make it. But it seemed to do the trick. You did feel better.' He was suddenly serious. 'What a terrible thing to happen! Bell telephoned this morning. Lucy's all right. She's going up to Louderdown. You were splendid, Amy. Bellairs said you were splendid.'

'Yes. Well, I'm all right at that sort of thing. I don't faint or anything. If something's got to be done, I can do it.'

'Like my mother. It's the Yorkshire blood.'

'I wish I was like her, silky and beautiful, making everyone she meets adore her.'

'I don't want you to be any different,' he said abruptly. 'You're my Amy. Just as I want you to be. By the way, Bellairs sent his love. Do you like him?'

'You know I do. So do you. We did as children. We still do – don't you remember? It was only poor Lucy who did not fit in. When we met that night, at the Can-Can, it seemed as though we had never separated. Lucy wanting all the attention, you and Bell such friends, and me liking you both so very much. You two boys were wonderful to me then. He was so funny and clever, and you were so strong and brave.'

'Which one of us did you prefer?'

She shook her head and smiled.

'Will you see him while I'm away in Germany?'

'If he asks me to.'

'Don't get fond of him, Amy. Not too fond of him.' She gave him a quick, bridling, challenging glance, and he threw up his arm, smiling in defence. 'All right, I know, it's not my business. But it is' – he was smiling down at her, for even now the top of her rose-trimmed straw hat only came just to his chin. 'You're not like any of the other girls I've gone out with. You know I've a very proprietorial feeling about you, young Amy.'

'Pooh,' she said scornfully. She had been hoping he would sternly forbid her to go out with Bell or anyone, but if they were flirting now, for the first time, he was by far her master at the art. 'You don't mind my seeing Bell?'

'And if I did, what notice would you take? You with your perky independence? Telling me to mind my own business. That I'm conceited and selfish, and imagine all the girls are in love with me.'

'Well, so you are.' She sighed, and her eyes were suddenly misty with tears. 'So they are.'

'Why, Amy,' he said. 'Why, Amy darling, what is it? Yesterday? That's past. Like the war and the trenches. Horrible things pass and the good things seem better then. I mean the war . . . I came through all that and found you here still. Wonderful!'

'*Me*?'

'You, my own little Amy. So sweet and good and sensible.'

'I didn't think you cared for good girls.' He started to laugh. 'What's so funny now?'

'Well, I didn't. Not until this leave – this moment. I didn't like them at all, so why am I so suddenly, Amy, quite crazy about you?'

He was teasing, but his eyes were serious. Jimmy's sweet sensuous, smiling eyes. Her cheeks went very pink and her breath was a little fast. They stood silently, not knowing what to say.

The station seemed full of sunshine. He bent and kissed her, full upon her fresh young mouth, feeling her lips tremble and sigh under his.

'I'll write to you as soon as I arrive. You'll write to me, Amy?'

She always had. All through the war years, and often; incredibly, he had not bothered to reply.

'Will you read them?'

'It will be different now. Tell me about yourself. That's what I want to hear.'

He felt distracted. He wanted to say so much to her, but the train was about to start. He looked at her as though he was seeing her through a magnifying glass, wondering at the pure texture of her skin, like a child's or a flower petal, wondering at the clearness of her grey eyes.

'Amy, when the schools break up this year, Mama is taking Theresa and Coralie to Italy. She has a farmhouse near Lake Como. Lorenz is spending the summer in Vienna. Would you and your mother come to Como too?'

'Foreign parts!' Amy mimicked her mother's horrified refusal. 'I should say not, my lad. You'd find all sorts there!'

'Amy, don't tease. The train is going at any minute. Would your mother let you come, if Mama asked you? I could get some leave. It's a lovely place. Papa gave it to her. They were very happy there.'

'If Aunt Viola asks me, then I'll come.'

'She will. I'll see to that. It's settled then.'

He went into his compartment and pulled down the window, reached down and lifted her up and kissed her as he had done before. But this time it was different. Achingly, beautifully different. This time it was no longer just little Amy, but a warm, sweet young girl, whose lips responded, and whose heart beat beneath the grip of his hands. He set her down and they watched each other until the train slid out of sight and she turned, dawdling back along the platform, her hands clasped, joy singing in her young heart like a rising lark.

Jimmy took the memory of her with him. Now he really felt he had come through, clear of the grey horror of the trenches, the killing and maiming of comrades, the awful thunder of the guns. The ghastly, hysterical business with Lucinda seemed part of that. Now he was through, catching some of the youth he thought had gone forever. He was his father's son. He loved the texture and beauty of life. He loved gaiety and laughter and good things. He was his mother's son. He disliked the irrational, lack of humour, unnecessary suffering or pain. He felt the war years slide away. He was alive, he was twenty-three, he was rich, he was a soldier, which was all he had ever wanted to be, and now, surprisingly, he was in love.

At the farm above Como the grapes were ripening and the lake with its reflected islands was as blue as the Madonna's veil beneath the Italian summer skies. But it was all rather like a school outing when Viola brought her party of excited girls ashore, and they drove up the mountain in an ancient plodding barouche to the farm. Viola had not been there since those last weeks of deep happiness before the war, when her baby Coralie was conceived, and Coralie was now a mischievous nine-year-old, spoiled by them all.

It had not changed much up in the mountains. Remote, beautiful, simple, the people who served her and Eugene in the old days still there, a little older, running to meet them, welcoming her back with smiles, saying how sad they were that the Signor Count was no longer with her, but how glad they were to see her, and how beautiful the *Contessa* still was and how lovely all the young *signorinas* were. The *Duce*? They shrugged. He was in power, of course, but up here in the mountains, little had changed. The *sindaco* was Fascisti, but a man they had known for many years.

The hay smelled sweet in the upland meadows, the small high-growing patches where only a mule and a man could get, the scythes whistling as they worked to get it in before the vine harvest, the really serious business of the year.

Jimmy arrived from Germany. He was out swinging a scythe with the men and getting blisters from the unaccustomed work,

Coralie was playing with the peasant children among the hay-cocks. Theresa, not too fond of the country, had that day driven off with a rich young Italian from Milan who had arrived in a resplendent car to take her out for the day. When she returned to London she would begin rehearsals for her first professional part.

Viola and Amy had loaded a picnic in donkey panniers and took it out to the fields. All Viola's memories of this place were happy ones. The life she had loved to share with Eugene when he could escape from affairs of state and finance, and away from the round of Viennese society. The farm held no dark memories for her, no shadow of violence, of terrified women and rifle bullets, and Eugene lying dead and bleeding in the snow. No memories of Schausenhardt's cruel hands and hot, hungry eyes, of her frigid shame and agonized submission. It was a place where she had only been happy.

It was quite obvious to her that Amy and Jimmy were in love. She was not surprised. Jimmy had written to her about it, and with all a young man's impatience he was afire to become engaged and get married. It was Amy who insisted that she should finish her university course. Viola had been startled — she had not imagined anyone could keep her splendid son at arm's length. She began to have a deep and amused respect for Amy. When they came to the hayfield and saw him, stripped to the waist, tanned and handsome, she said involuntarily, 'Do you want to marry him, Amy?'

'No,' said Amy, her small, pretty face very quiet and grave. 'No. I didn't *want* to love him. He's not at *all* the sort of man I want to marry. I *don't* want to be a soldier's wife. The person you fall in love with isn't necessarily the person you want to marry or ought to marry.'

'You are not afraid another girl will come along?'

'Oh, yes, all the time.'

'Two years before you get your degree. It's a long time to keep a boy like Jimmy waiting.'

'Time for him to get tired of me. If he's going to . . . better now than later.'

Viola burst out laughing. 'Oh, Amy love, what a way to fall in love.'

'Not your way?'

'No, indeed.'

Amy looked very slim and small, the upland wind blowing her blue summer dress and the strands of her long brown hair. Jimmy was bounding up the path to meet them, pulling on his shirt. A look came into Amy's eyes, loving and tender, almost maternal, strange in one so young and totally inexperienced. Viola was moved. Amy was a steadfast little thing, like her mother, but with a witty mind and a valiant heart. Jimmy was lucky.

'Off you go,' said Viola. 'I'll follow.'

Amy raced down the mountain path, jumping across the big boulders like a gazelle, until Jimmy met her, caught her and swung her up aloft like a child in his strong arms.

The summer and autumn social rounds at Louderdown were not interrupted that year. Lucinda's wounds, beautifully stitched, hidden with long sleeves or the fashionable cluster of bracelets, healed quickly, and so apparently did she. If she drank a little more than was good for her, it was not noticeable among the hard-riding, hard-drinking hunting set in which she moved. James, still shaken by the disaster, rushed to make amends with suggestions for a world cruise, a suggestion Lucinda would not hear of. She had too many engagements she said, very bright, cold, glittering with an apparently tireless energy and appetite for pleasure.

There was the grouse shooting and soon the cubbing would start, and all the plans for the twins' twenty-first birthday in September, the anniversary of that fatal hospital dance when they were fifteen. Florence had made extensive plans. The marquees had been hired and caterers engaged, for the garden party and tenants' luncheon. Village children were already dragging wood up to the top of Beacon Crag for the traditional bonfire when the heir to Louderdown came of age. There would be fireworks, and a ball with a London dance band, and all the county present. A world tour? Go away and miss the fun? Not likely. Not yet, declared Lucinda. Her eyes were always as cold as blue glass when she looked at her father. She filled the house with young friends of whom the current expression 'madly gay' was very appropriate. She was their leader, but she seemed to despise them more than ever. Especially the young men who fell in love with her. The newspapers loved her, reporting her every exploit, but she filled father with despair.

James had genuinely tried to make Florence happy again, but it was, as she had prophesied, too late. It was as though Lucinda's attempted suicide had cut the final bond between them. The door between their bedrooms had been unlocked, but all Florence's passion for him was spent, and in the face of her acquiescence all his experience and subtle sexual skills could not avail. He did not love her, and she knew it and now she did not care. James drank just a little more than he used to with the gentlemen after dinner. He looked older than his years, still the picture of a fine country gentleman, but there were shadows beneath the handsome dark blue eyes, and the still luxuriant hair was almost white. The worshipping, protecting Alex Hamilton now lived on the estate, managing the racing stable. He was part of the household. Never far from Florence's side.

With bleak deliberation Lucinda made her father suffer. She was, on the surface, everything a charming, spoiled good-looking daughter could be, the soul of every event that crowded summer. But in private she never spoke to James. If their paths crossed she would not look at him. She took everything he offered, money, a new hunter, a diamond bracelet and a powerful red sports car for her birthday but she would never let him forget her hatred. She could not make Jimmy pay – he was beyond her reach, but she could punish James, and she did. He was glad when Bellairs arrived for the birthday junketings – the one good thing that had come out of the whole unhappy business was that for the first time he had come to know and find a friend in his other son.

Lucinda and Bellairs were the centre of the activities, a

handsome couple, typical English aristocrats, or so everyone said. The Staffray twins. Lucinda tall, slim and fair, Bellairs courteous, a little diffident, rather shyly making the right kind of amusing speeches. Florence and Lucinda made speeches and accepted flowers. Gifts arrived from all over the county, and the final night arrived with a dinner-party for close friends and relations at which two Royals were present, a ball afterwards in the great hall, ending with the bonfire at midnight and the fireworks.

The family gathered to receive the guests. The two women looked splendid in what Bellairs called 'full fig'. New gowns, family jewels, Florence in blue, Lucinda in white, tall and glittering, an ice princess. On each wrist she wore a row of glittering bracelets. The huge drawing-room was hung with saffron brocade, lined with family portraits, furnished with priceless armchairs covered with Beauvais tapestry. Flowers were banked before mirrors; the chandeliers glittered, the long french windows were open to the late summer night. Bellairs wondered if it was the end of an epoch, the last great occasion at Louderdown. Even with his father's great wealth the estate was becoming a burden to maintain. The death duties on his grandmother's estate had been prohibitive. Would his son want to come of age like this – and if he had a son, would *he* want it for him?

His mother and father and Lucinda stood silently waiting for the guests. That other birthday, the flannel dance in 1917, seemed to haunt them all. As on that night, the big hunter's moon was rising, turning from orange to silver, painting the gardens with its light. But tonight there was no black-out, windows blazed, coloured fairy lights hung in the trees. At midnight he would have to drive to the Beacon Crag and light the bonfire that proclaimed the heir to Louderdown had come of age. Bellairs suddenly grinned to himself, wondering if anyone really cared a damn.

The first cars began to come down the mile-long drive.

It all went very well. The family twitched to life with inbred charm and graciousness. A hundred people sat down to dinner at a table decorated with orchids from the hothouses, peaches,

293

grapes and nectarines in gold Restoration porringers, tall white candles glittered in gold sconces, gifts for some dead Earl for victory in some famous battle. Footmen in full livery waited at table. James, charming and affable in his place at the head, had a sense of unreality. It was like a scene from a film, one of those spectacular Hollywood films. The thread, the purpose of the family had broken.

Afterwards he slipped away into the garden to smoke a cigar. He could not stand the emptiness of it all. They were no longer a family. What would happen to them after tonight?

He heard footsteps behind him and turned to find Lucinda, glittering in her white dress and diamonds in the moonlight.

'I want to speak to you,' she said.

For a moment his heart warmed eagerly. 'Of course, my dear. I was hoping that tonight you would.'

'It's nothing sentimental. I would not unless I had to. It's about money. I suppose from tonight I have my own money?'

'Yes. The money your grandmother left you. And you will have an income from the estate. There are the jewels, too. You'll be a very comfortably off young lady.' He attempted lightness. 'And, of course, there will be another settlement when you are married.'

'I'm not likely to do that.'

'Lucy,' he implored, 'try not to be so bitter. Of course you'll marry. You are young and very beautiful.'

'Oh, don't talk about it. I haven't a duty to breed for posterity, like Bell. I just want to know where I stand. How do I get hold of this money?'

'The solicitor will be here to see you and Bell in the morning.'

'I want money right away. I've decided to go away. I've finished the season and done all the expected things. I'm going to take a flat in Paris and travel from there.'

'What does your mother say?'

'I haven't asked her, actually. I'm starting right away. I'll take the car and drive. I'll let you know where I am through the solicitor.'

'You're going alone?'

'No. I'm taking a friend with me, at first, unless I get bored with the set-up.'

He remembered the good-looking, hard-drinking young man she had been seeing lately. He was here tonight. Well set up, a good rider, not much money; a bad reputation with women.

'Lucinda, don't do anything crazy. This is your home. You are independent now, but your mother and I love you . . .'

'Yes?' Her voice was icy. 'You never loved anyone but that woman and Jimmy-C. We need not speak of it again. We need not meet, really. It won't be necessary. If I run into you I'll be polite. I'll keep in touch with Mummy, I don't blame her.'

'Lucy, I am your father. I am not asking you to forgive me, although I feel you are being irrational and extreme about the whole thing. If there is anything, anything I can do to help you at any time, you know I will.'

She turned her head, looking at him over her bare shoulder, her eyes cold with dislike.

'Like what? Through you I was put in a position where I was disgraced, humiliated and made a fool of . . . I went pleading to that whore of yours for her son's love. Can you make me forget that?'

She turned and went back into the house.

Just before midnight the guests came crowding out of the house on to the terrace and Bell left for Beacon Crag in his car. Everyone waited. James, Florence and Lucinda stood with their guests. The church clock chimed midnight and up on the Beacon a small flame flickered and in seconds the huge fire was leaping against the sky, illuminating the crag, throwing up showers of sparks, and faintly, far distant, could be heard the sounds of cheering. A few seconds later the fireworks began to explode their coloured patterns against the sky.

James remembered when he had lit the bonfire on his own coming of age, riding horseback up the hill to the crag, feeling so proud.

The band struck up the birthday tune, and the young people encircled Lucinda singing it – to see her laughing, one would have thought she had not a care in the world. The handsome

295

young waster called Cowdray was by her side.

Bellairs came back, smiling, slightly soiled with wood smoke, to receive congratulations beside Lucinda. They were twenty-one now. Adults. They seemed to James so young. Presently Bell came to his side, put his arm through his and said, 'Come out into the garden, Dad,' and as they strolled out, added in his offhand way: 'Thanks for everything. I know it's not always been easy,' and the unexpected sympathy touched James's heart.

'This fellow Cowdray,' he said gruffly, 'who's always with your sister. What's he like?'

'Like Jimmy a bit, isn't he? To look at? That's all. He's a bit of a cad, really.'

'What does he do?'

'Ex-officer, no money, gambles a bit, looking for a rich wife.'

'Lucinda's not going away with him?' James asked in alarm. All his Edwardian prejudices rose to the surface. His daughter! Behaving like this.

' 'Fraid so, Dad.'

'Does your mother know?'

'I think Mummy hopes they'll marry. I think Mummy would like to see Lucy married to almost anyone at the moment. But she won't. She's already bored. Cowdray's only a make-believe Jimmy . . . not what she's looking for.'

They walked to the end of the terrace, their cigars making red glows in the dusk. Couples were drifting down into the garden. Lucinda passed with Cowdray, down over the lower terrace, across the lawn towards the cedars. His arm was round her, her fair head, a little muzzily against his shoulder, but when they reached the cedars she stopped, pulled away and ran away from him, back into the house.

'When you saw the bonfire go up, Dad,' asked Bellairs, 'did you wish it was Jimmy who was lighting it, and not me?' His perceptive grin was full of affection. 'I'll bet you did. So did I. He would have been so much better at this sort of thing. He'd have enjoyed doing it. He enjoys responsibility and he can command men. I don't and can't.'

'Have you seen him?'

'Yes. I'm through with all that nonsense as I said. I went out to Cologne where he is stationed for a few days. We had a good time. It's good to have a brother again.'

'And what have *you* decided to do, Bell?'

'I've enrolled at the Slade, Dad. I was lucky to get in.'

'But – you must have some occupation.'

'Dear Dad,' Bellairs said affectionately, 'that will be my occupation.'

'There's no girl? Nothing of that sort? You should get married.'

'Oh, plenty of girls, Dad. It's a habit with Staffray young men, playing the field until the right one comes alone.'

'You've plenty of time.'

'Yes.'

It was true there were plenty of girls. And there was Theresa Erhmann, tantalizing, growing more beautiful every day. Bellairs thought of Lucinda, railing at him as he and Amy staunched her bleeding wrists, and his mocking lips set in a hard line.

'One thing,' he said, 'I'll never try to *make* anyone love me.'

So this, Lucinda thought, is Vienna. This was the city where Jimmy Corbett was born and reared. James-Carlo Corbett, the adopted son of Count Eugene Erhmann, bastard son of the Earl of Louderdown and his mistress, her half-brother, whom she hated more than anyone in the world.

This was the city which, in spite of defeat, crippling inflation, massive poverty and the collapse of its empire, was still so charming. Where the trees in the square were purple with lilac, and the crowds strolled along in the sunshine or sat and gossiped in the coffee-houses as though the war had just been a bad dream and their present explosive politics something that would pass, leaving only a ripple of bad memories on the surface of this urbane, delightful and self-satisfied city.

This was the city which had made Jimmy just that much

different from the average, good-looking English schoolboy. Lucinda remembered the day when Bell had first brought him home for the holidays, so big and handsome for his age. The Austrian boy, they had called him. They had all been fascinated by him, laughing yet intrigued by his command of language, his charming manner with women and girls which had made him stand out head and shoulders above the other schoolboys of his age. She had adored him. Not a suspicion of the truth had ever entered her head. The agony of her humiliation faded, like the scars on her wrists faded, but it was still there eating away inside her, giving her no rest.

The past two years had passed hectically and uselessly. A flat in Paris, a horde of friends, travel and the high spots of the society year. She went to Louderdown in the autumn for the hunting and to see her mother. She never, if she could avoid it, saw her father. She had had love affairs, she had been engaged, nearly engaged, once nearly married, breaking it off at the last moment. Her reputation as a heart-breaker was spectacular, like her red sports car and her clothes. She was photographed by Beaton, she attended first nights, she was a fashion leader and a beauty and she was bored, restless and alone. She longed to go home to the old familiar things and to stay there. But stubbornly she would not give in. Somewhere there must be a man to fill her mind and heart, and to make her forget.

She sat at the café terrace of her hotel waiting for a young Englishman of her acquaintance, a gilded junior at the Embassy who had been at university with Bellairs. She was quite unconscious that her beauty, her assured upper-class Englishness and her superb clothes made her conspicuous.

Some young men, wearing armbands with a Swastika emblem, moved among the tables, selling what seemed to be party pamphlets. Some people bought them, some pushed them away with laughing or derogatory comments, when the young men would glare aggressively, raising their arms in a stiff-elbowed salute before moving on.

A very slender fair boy approached her table. There was something familiar about his cropped head, and the horn-rimmed spectacles on the youthful, rather unformed face, and the shy smile was unexpectedly and chillingly familiar. He put a pamphlet on the table before her, and she shook her head, briefly.

'No, thank you. I don't speak German.'

'But I speak English, Lady Lucinda.'

She stared.

'Don't you remember me? That night in the Can-Can. Two years ago. Lorenz Erhmann. Jimmy Corbett's half-brother.'

'Oh!' The colour flamed in her cheeks, remembering the dreadful nightmare of her humiliation. 'Oh, of course. Well —' she opened her handbag, but he said quickly, 'Please. Allow me to give you one. It is for the National Socialist Party.'

'I've read that you are a lot of young thugs,' she said.

His fair skin flushed indignantly.

'That is false propaganda put about by Communists and Jews!' he declared. 'You must read our programme before you make your judgement, *Fräulein*.'

'Well, I will, if you can offer me something in English or French.' She wished he would go. She was not interested in his propaganda. He reminded her too poignantly of things she longed to forget. He had no attraction for her. He was a boy, not a man.

'Are you staying in this hotel? If so, I will bring you some literature in English to read.'

'Well, thank you. I can't promise to read it. I haven't much time. I'm motoring. I don't know how long I'll stay.'

She saw the Embassy acquaintance and waved to him. He came threading his way between the tables, immaculately correct in his black jacket and striped trousers, the black 'Anthony Eden' homburg, the trademark of the successful young diplomat, set at an angle on his well-brushed head.

'Hallo, Lucinda darling, lovely to see you again. Hallo, Lorenz. D'you two know each other?'

'Yes. We met once, briefly, in London. He has been trying to sell me Nazi literature.'

'Oh, Lorenz, *really*! It is a bit much, swinging this tripe on your acquaintances. Now, don't get into a huff. Sit down and have a drink.' He pressed Lorenz down into a chair, took the one beside him and summoned the waiter, saying airily to Lucinda, 'The worst of these fanatical blighters is that they're never off duty.'

'No one can be off duty,' said the boy fervently, 'if the German people are to be saved.'

'Yes, well, quite, but don't be so intense, old boy. Drink up and go and sell your papers, there's a good chap.' The boy coloured furiously and Lucinda said conciliatingly, 'I'll really be very interested to read your literature if you can find me something in English, Count Erhmann.'

'I will do so. This evening. With your permission I will bring them to your hotel. Perhaps you will do me the honour of dining with me, when I can tell you more about our cause, and our splendid leader.'

When he had gone, her diplomatic friend said, 'He means Hitler of course. You don't really want to dine with that little tick?'

'Well, perhaps.' She wanted to see Lorenz again, and suddenly she knew why. 'I am interested in his family.'

'The Erhmanns? It's funny, because Lorenz's grandmother was Jewish and his mother English. Can't understand why he has a passion about this pan-Germanic tosh. I think the party tolerates him because he supports the funds. His father was a brilliant man, both as a statesman and financier, and he wisely kept sonny-boy out of the business, but invested money abroad for him. He's very rich by Viennese standards today. Anyhow, he's pretty harmless. He's not one of the bully boys who break up other people's meetings and Jewish shops. You sure you won't do the town with me tonight?'

'No. Tomorrow, perhaps, if you will give me a call.'

Lorenz arrived at the hotel punctually. He had changed into a dinner-jacket, English made and beautifully cut, and looked what he was – a wealthy young gentleman. He greeted her eagerly. He was not wearing his armband, but a small swastika badge was fastened into his lapel. He had brought flowers as well as propaganda.

'I am so glad you are free. It is of great importance to us that the English and Germanic people should be friends – the Aryan Nordic peoples. After dinner I have arranged for you to meet a friend of mine. A neighbour, too, at my country house at Die Kinderburg. Prince Friedrich Schausenhardt.'

'A member of your party too?'

'Not openly. Not yet. He cannot declare his sympathy with our party yet, but the day is soon to come. He was an organizer of the *Heimwehr*, the party that protected homes and frontiers immediately after the war. But they contain many opinions, and are an Austrian party. He is using his influence to bring as many of them as possible behind us. Into a greater German party, behind their wonderful new leader, Adolf Hitler!'

Over dinner he talked incessantly about his friend. It was obvious that he idolized him. He had been a great soldier, Lorenz told her, fighting on the Russian front, and afterwards the terrible Italian front in the high snows. He was an aristocrat and a patriot. His family had become impoverished during the inflation.

'I help him all I can. I am honoured to be able to. The Prince is a lot older than I am, of course. When I was a little boy, he was my hero, although my half-brother, Jimmy, always hated him. The night Die Kinderburg was attacked by the bandits the Prince came with his men and drove them away. He saved our lives and the lives of the village – all except my father who was shot by one of the Bolshevik deserters.'

'I shall look forward to meeting your hero,' said Lucinda indifferently. She was wondering how she could have seen any likeness to Jimmy in this intense, boring boy.

A tall man came into the restaurant and stood by the entrance, his glance searching the room. Heads turned, people glanced and whispered, some greeted him eagerly, some turned pointedly away. Whoever he was he was imposing in a curiously malevolent way. His height, the brutal mouth, one lip lifted by an old scar, the intensity of the slightly bulging blue eyes. He was about the same age as her own father, and his closely cropped hair was grizzled, the forehead bald. He raised a swagger cane to acknowledge Lorenz and the prominent eyes raked her as though she was an animal brought for his approval. Then he came over, bowed correctly over her hand, and took a seat at the table. Lorenz, to her surprise, rose, made some halting excuse about a telephone call and left them together. Friedrich Schausenhardt looked at her with cold amusement.

'So – you are the aristocratic English beauty whom Lorenz described to me. You are no doubt aristocratic, and you are certainly quite charming, *Fräulein*, but I am no longer interested in little girls.'

Lucinda swallowed her fury. She did not like him and he frightened her. His attitude was insulting. And yet she wanted him to stay.

'I'm afraid Lorenz was over-anxious that I should meet you,' she said casually. 'I'm sorry. He says you know his family. His half-brother?'

He gave her a quick, piercing glance.

'That puppy who was the apple of his mother's eye? You know him?'

'I've – met him.'

'Lorenz tells me he is to marry.'

She felt her heart catch in her throat with despair.

'Who is he to marry?

'The daughter of a servant, Lorenz says. A fitting match. He is angry. He says his mother has lost all sense of their position. You know his whore of a mother?'

'Yes. I have met the mother.'

'She is getting old?'

'No, she is middle-aged, of course. She is still very beautiful,' and then she knew why, in spite of her dislike and fear, she wanted to talk to this man. She wanted to know everything about Jimmy's family. Everything he could tell her. Hidden there might be the thing she wanted. The weapon with which she could strike at him.

302

'Tell me about them,' she said eagerly. 'Tell me about them all . . . about Die Kinderburg, and why you hate Countess Viola so much.'

CHAPTER ELEVEN

It was a beautiful day in May when Jimmy and Amy were married. Amy's idea of a small, quiet ceremony with just the family was swept away by Jimmy's lordly insistence that family ceremonies should be done 'properly', by which he meant a guard of honour of his fellow officers and all the large circle of friends acquired by the Erhmanns since his mother had returned to London.

A marquee had been erected in the garden in Kensington, and Vatel was buzzing about like a perturbed June-bug in charge, chivvying the caterers' men, checking his lists, fussing over the flower arrangements and worrying over the temperature of the champagne.

Up in Theresa's room there was a froth of lavender tulle and a gaggle of dressmakers with the bodices of their dresses stuck full of pins as they tried to keep the excited Coralie still enough for last-minute alterations to her bridesmaid's dress.

It was going to be a nice, ordinary, happy wedding. Viola tried not to feel desolate. She tried not to blame herself for caring so much. She was glad he was marrying Amy. She was happy they seemed to be so much in love. And yet she felt oppressed. A feeling of endings, of future loneliness. She supposed all mothers of much-loved sons felt like this when they married, and presently, when he came down into the drawing-room for a glass of champagne with her, her heart nearly burst with pride and love. Six feet tall, and resplendent in his dress uniform, and so heartbreakingly handsome and dashing. So like James that the years slid away, and she was a wild girl again, deeply in love with her soldier lover.

'Don't cry, Mama,' he chided her, pouring her a glass of champagne. 'I want a happy wedding.'

She took the glass and they drank. She set it down, turning to him, brushing a non-existent speck of fluff from the gold-laced epaulette. He was a man now, and about to be married, this boy child whom she had so greatly loved. They had had such a special and close relationship, and now he had someone else. A small, quiet, clever girl, with big grey eyes, a girl who had all the qualities which she had never had. Patience and humility and learning. A girl restrained where she had been reckless, a girl who had learned to hide her heart's secrets. It would be months before she saw him again. As though guessing her sadness, he kissed her.

'D'you remember our first visit to Paris, Mama, when you let me take you out to the Cascade, and I had my first dinner jacket, and you let me pay the bill? And we went to the Opera and the Folies? I felt no end of a swell. I was so proud of you.'

'I remember, Jimmy.'

'I don't suppose any fellow, anywhere, had a more satis-factory and gorgeous mother.'

'And now you must make a satisfactory and gorgeous hus-band. You've been very spoiled. Amy is quite different from me.'

'I know,' he said ruefully. 'Sometimes I'm a bit scared of her. For one thing she's so tiny. I'm afraid she might break. And another thing she's so determined. She's just not like any other girl I ever knew.'

'And there have been plenty,' she teased.

He chose to ignore this.

'Except for the times during the war when we were apart it's all been so good. Mama darling, thank you for everything.'

'Thank you, for being born.'

'And you're happy now?'

'About you and Amy, yes. I just wish Lorenz was here. The girls are here. I wish things had been different between you two boys.'

'I do too. But he wouldn't come. I wrote, and I telephoned, but he said that he could not leave Vienna at the moment. He still thinks I came between him and Amy. It was not so at all. But he blames me. He always did. Perhaps you could go to Vienna to see him.'

'No.' Her rejection was positive. 'I don't want to go there. I'm hoping he'll come and see me soon.'

'When Amy and I have gone?' Jimmy asked ruefully. 'Yes, that would be best. I tried, Mama. I honestly did try with him.'

'You were always very patient and kind.'

'Don't be too sad, Mama. When we're settled in Egypt and have somewhere to live you must come out to us for a while. There's lots to see and I believe the season in Cairo is very brilliant. You'd be in your element.'

She smiled, shaking her head — that kind of ballroom brilliance had no attraction for her now. Somewhere quiet with happy memories and blue skies. 'We'll see. I think I'll spend more time at the farm.'

Vatel came in to announce the best man, a brother officer, also resplendently magnificent and stiff in his uniform. The two bridesmaids, Theresa and Coralie, came billowing down the stairs into the hall, Gainsboroughs in lilac chiffon, with beribboned and flowered leghorn hats. Viola listened to their excited chatter, wishing that life had spared her Eugene for a few more years. Wishing that Lorenz was with them, wishing that she did not worry about him more than all the rest. Wishing, absurdly, that James could be present to see his son married. She always wanted everything from life — she always had. It had given her most things, but it had also taken hideously away.

'Mama, for goodness sake, go and put your hat on,' said Theresa. 'We shall be late. Amy will be at the church before us, and that would be terrible.'

Jimmy kissed her and his sisters and went off with his best man. She went up to her room to put on her hat, regarding herself seriously in the mirror. In three years' time she would be fifty. She felt, curiously, a little old-fashioned. She belonged to a more spacious age. She could not bring herself to shingle her long hair, or shorten her skirts, or wear these headachy tight cloche hats. She put on a toque of yellow roses which went with her golden-bronze dress. She had always loved these golden-bronze, amber colours. They flattered her hair. But it was going grey now. She was middle-aged.

306

There was a knock at the door and Vatel came in.

'May I leave now, milady? Everything is in order. I will leave the church immediately after the service to be back here before the guests arrive. I have the taxis waiting for the dressmaker and her assistant and the house staff.'

'Of course, Vatel, you must get off.' The years had bent him, and he was becoming a little wizened. He had spent his whole life in their service. She bent, for he was a small man, and she was a tall woman, and kissed him. 'Thank you for everything, dear Vatel.'

'I wish milord could have been here.' He saw the swift pain darken her eyes, and said hurriedly, 'I mean Count Lorenz. It seems a pity. His only brother. But they are no longer boys – and their lives will be separate now. But it is a pity they could not be friends.'

'Yes, Vatel.'

He bowed himself out, colliding with Coralie, who came flying in, ribbons and curls whirling about her.

'Mama, come at once. Theresa said the bridesmaids must be there before the bride.'

'Ah, yes, I'm coming.' Her lips twitched with rueful amusement. 'I mustn't forget. I didn't have that sort of wedding, you see.'

Coralie raced out again and Viola followed her – as she went the headline of the morning newspapers caught her eye. It had been brought folded on her breakfast tray, but she had not had time even to glance at it.

'Louderdown divorce. The Countess of Louderdown has commenced divorce proceedings against the Earl, naming a Mrs Davina Smith of Brighton.'

Viola stood still. Davina Smith? She gave an involuntary laugh. Poor James. Some unknown woman in a hotel room. Doing the 'right thing' for Florence. How he would have hated it. He who so valued elegance and style! So he was free – and what would that mean? Free to come and see Jimmy again? And to see her? She went out, adjusting her gloves, joining the girls in the car. As they drove away the mid-morning post came, bringing a large packet of well-wishing letters. Among them one for Jimmy, from Austria.

Amy arrived with Betsy at the church. Betsy was visibly nervous. She had to escort Amy to the altar and was praying for strength to carry it through. Only Amy's obvious happiness sustained her. She looked so radiant, and so very pretty, in her high-necked white dress, a small coronet of white flowers on her smoothly parted hair. Her big eyes shone – it was Theresa and Coralie who were fussing about the train, and the bouquet, Amy did not care – she just looked through the pointed arch of the church entrance to where she could see Jimmy's fair head and broad, uniformed shoulders, silent with his best man, waiting for her. The trappings, the lovely dress Viola had helped her choose and insisted on paying for, the diamond brooch, the pearls, his presents, all the rich and lovely things he gave her so generously, meant nothing. She was afraid and she was wildly happy. So happy she was more than afraid.

Viola kissed her, and kissed Betsy. There was a sudden stir and a clicking of press cameras outside.

'Vi,' Betsy whispered, 'it's Lord Louderdown.'

James and Bellairs, immaculate and correct in morning dress, came into the porch. James took Betsy's hand.

'Mrs Lyttelton,' he said, very formally, very much the great gentleman, 'I have been told, or at least Bellairs told me, that you would be going with Amy to the altar. Would you let me do this for you? Since dear Matthew is no longer with us – I'm sure he would have wished it.'

'Oh,' Betsy said faintly. 'Yes. Thank you, my lord.'

James looked at Viola, and said, 'You'll let me attend our son's wedding, won't you, Duchess?'

'Oh, James. I'm so happy, my love, that you came.'

When the wedding march sounded, and Jimmy's head switched round to greet his bride, he saw it was his father, with Amy on his single arm, leading his bride to their wedding.

It was all too happy, too beautiful. The sun shone, the orchestra played, the guests wandered through the garden among the May blossoms. Bellairs flirted with all the prettiest girls, but pursued Theresa. She was, he said, the most beautiful girl he had ever seen, a remark Theresa had often heard before but always liked to hear again.

'Also the most conceited,' he added, and loved the furious flash of her pretty eyes.

'You may be Jimmy-C's half-brother,' she said, 'but you're no relation of mine. If you're going to be stinkingly rude I shall go and flirt with your father. He's quite the best looking man here.' But she did not go.

'I saw you in a play last month. You were very pretty, and terribly bad.'

The lovely, challenging, provocative face was suddenly serious.

'I *was* very bad,' she agreed despondently. 'It's not until you get on to the professional stage you realize how bad you are. At the Academy I was always top girl, winning all the prizes. Now I know I'm just a raw beginner.'

'But you'll go on?'

'Until my dying day.'

'I can understand that, Theresa' he said. The toasts were drunk and the speeches made, Amy and Jimmy had gone upstairs to change for their journey. 'You know,' he said, 'once I thought I was a little in love with Amy.'

'Oh, everyone falls in love with Amy,' said Theresa pettishly. 'My brother Lorenz was off his head about her. She's so good. I mean right down honest-to-God-good. She'd never play you up or let you down. I'm not a bit like that. I'm very ambitious and selfish and ruthless and want my own way, and will tell any great fib to get it.'

'A woman after my own heart,' said Bellairs. 'Do you know when I look at you I understood how all this happened . . . my father and your mother, all that time ago. She must have been like you. People like that are bound to cause chaos and even disaster. Will you sit for me one day, Terry? I'd like to do a portrait of you.'

'I'm going to New York soon.'

'I might come to New York too.'

They sat, smiling at each other, measuring each other's sincerity. Coralie, already a victim to Bellairs' charm, came and sat on his knee and put her arms round his neck. Her one permitted glass of champagne had slightly glazed her eyes, her picture hat was sliding down her back, and the billowing lavender chiffon was already rather the worse for wear. She was growing into a gangly, thin girl and an incorrigible tomboy.

'Will you marry me, Bell?' she demanded. 'It's been such a lovely wedding I think I'd like to marry you.'

'How old are you?'

'Eleven next.'

'Well, it seems a safe sort of age. If not –' his side-long smile teased Theresa – 'perhaps one of the family.'

The suitcases were packed and in the car. Vatel was helping Jimmy to change. Jimmy submitted as graciously as possible, but his schooldays in England, and the Western Front, had made him independent of personal service. He knew the old man was enjoying himself. Everything had been packed with meticulous efficiency, passports and papers all checked and in a special case, as Vatel had once packed for Eugene on their travels throughout Europe. This rushing off in a car had no appeal for him. He liked to arrange everything – his master should only be concerned with a comfortable, leisurely progress from train to ship to train.

He packed the overnight case, morocco slippers, silk pyjamas and dressing-gown, ivory-backed initialled brushes, ebony razor case. Jimmy coloured and his pulse quickened unexpectedly. It would be his wedding night and he was filled with a dread and delight which he had never experienced in all his sophisticated young life. There had been other girls, and pretty girls, and jolly girls who had been good company. But this time it was Amy and for her it had to be right, to be wonderful, to be tender and gentle and happy – this time it was a different kind of rubicon he had to cross.

'Oh, come on, Vatel, there's a dear chap,' he said impatiently. 'I'm sure nothing has been forgotten.'

He hitched on the pullover in which he was driving down to the coast. There was a pile of letters on the dressing-table. He flipped through them and saw the letter from Austria. He flushed with pleasure, thinking it was from Lorenz, hoping the boy had thought better of his harsh words of jealousy, but it was not his writing. Curiously he slit the envelope and read it, and as he read the colour drained out of his face and the happiness out of the day. It was from Lucinda Staffray.

He read it through, made to tear it across, and then read it again. He looked at Vatel standing, holding his sports jacket ready for him to slip on, and it seemed as though hours had passed since he had opened the letter. He snatched the jacket and dragged it on, stuffing the letter into the pocket. He was overwhelmed by the terrible murderous rage and anger that possessed him. It was as though his whole nature changed.

'Captain Jimmy . . .' Vatel suddenly looked very old and frail.

'Yes.'

'Captain Jimmy, you must not blame milady.'

Jimmy stared at him with Staffray arrogance, but Vatel went on. He was not to be quelled by a boy he had held on his knee.

'I saw that the letter was from Austria. If it is about milady, destroy it and say nothing. Perhaps she did not tell you everything. Why should she? When you came to fetch her from Die Kinderburg it was behind her, you were bringing her here to a new life. It was a terrible time for her.'

'Will you tell my mother, Vatel, I would like to see her alone? I will be in the morning room.'

'Sir,' pleaded Vatel, 'it has been such a happy day for us all, and especially for her. To have your father with her . . . such a joy. She is a rare lady. She had suffered greatly, and she has always come through with courage . . . do not bring it back to her now.'

'Vatel, will you do as I say?'

311

The old man went out. Jimmy looked blindly at the packed overnight case, at his dress uniform on the stand. He had forgotten Amy, and his wedding . . . across the years he heard Schausenhardt using foul words and names about his mother, in a public place before other officers, and he was hitting him across his sneering, drunken face, and saying, 'If I was a grown man I would challenge you and kill you for speaking like that of my mother.' The murderous hatred filled him again until he could have choked with it. If it was true – if what this letter said were true, then he *would* kill Schausenhardt as he had said he would when he was a boy.

Vatel came back into the room.

'Milady is waiting for you.' His composure broke. He could not bear the cold young face. He wanted to protect her. 'Please, Master Jimmy-C, don't. To be hurt by one one loves is so terrible. It is your wedding day. She is so happy. Let it go away with the rest of the past . . .'

Jimmy looked at him as though he had not heard.

In Theresa's bedroom Amy was taking off her wedding dress and getting ready to go away. Betsy sat with her workworn hands folded in her familiar way, watching. She did not change. She looked as she had always looked, patient, humble and innocent, and these other people, whose lives involved hers, even her daughter, seemed grand and strange but not quite real. As though, since her first meeting with Viola, as working girls together, she had been watching a play unfolding, glamorous, exciting, sometimes tragic, but not quite real. And now Amy was joining the company, going on to the stage of the great world. Her little quiet matter-of-fact daughter, dressing in a cream tweed suit from Paris, chosen by Viola and costing heaven-knows what, wearing a big ring of sapphires and diamonds, and a pretty jacket of summer ermine, one of Jimmy's gifts to his bride.

Amy kissed her anxiously. Since her father had died she had taken his place in her mother's life, making the plans, taking responsibility.

'You'll write often, won't you, Mother? You'll go and see

312

Aunt Viola. You won't just be alone all the time? When we're settled you must come out to us.'

Jimmy had been posted to Egypt and they would be there for the next two years.

'Oh, don't fuss, lass,' Betsy said testily. 'I'll be all right.' She touched Amy's smooth face. 'But will you be? Young Jimmy's a great gentleman now, rich, grand relations now his father acknowledges him. Will you manage, Amy? Their ways aren't ours, you know.'

'Yes, Mother, I think I will. I've got to try. It's all anyone can do when they're committed to love.'

Betsy shook her head, a little bewildered. Words? She wanted to say so much but she had never been able to find the right words. Affection, tenderness and honesty had sustained her and Matthew through their short and loving marriage. Between two people, they were the things that counted in the end; even Viola had discovered that.

They heard the slam of Jimmy's bedroom door across the landing – the sound was so sharp and peremptory that Amy opened the door and went out, thinking that he was impatient to get away. He was standing in a shaft of light from the high domed skylight over the well of the staircase, his hand on the banister, about to descend. The light shone on his broad shoulders and crisp fair hair.

'Are you ready, darling. . . ?' His head switched round and the words faltered on her lips. It was a stranger's face, a beautiful face, but a stranger's. The smiling mouth was set and harsh, and the beautiful laughing eyes blazed with a look of hatred and anger. She ran forward, hands outstretched, shocked, and bewildered, but Jimmy went past her without a word, down the stairs, and she heard the morning-room door close with the same, angry slam. Vatel came out of Jimmy's bedroom, his thin face looking old and drawn.

'What on earth has happened, Vatel?'

'Ah, Madame Corbett . . .' She realized it was now her name. He shook his head, as though finding it difficult to speak. 'It is past ugly unhappy things . . . why should someone write to tell

313

him of them on this day of all days?'

Amy went downstairs and opened the morning-room door. Viola and Jimmy faced each other across the pretty little room. At her entrance they turned simultaneously – Jimmy's face the same stony mask she had passed on the stairs. Viola's was stricken with sadness.

'Jimmy,' Amy said levelly, 'will you please tell me what has happened? It is time we left to catch our boat at Dover. Everyone is waiting to say good-bye.'

'We can catch another boat,' he said abruptly, 'and please go away. This is not your business. It is between my mother and myself.'

The colour rose in her face. She shut the door and went and stood by his mother, unconsciously allying herself with the woman against the man. Her big grey eyes blazed. 'I'm not one of your troopers to be spoken to like that,' she flared. 'I am your wife now, Jimmy, and if this is a family matter, then I should hear it too.'

Viola gave a shaky little laugh, and put a hand through Amy's arm, looking at him, wondering how he would take it.

'So,' she said, 'we have another fighter in the family.' She sat down on the settee and pulled Amy down beside her. She had a letter in her hands, turning it between her long, slender fingers, where a big diamond glittered in the afternoon light, and once again Amy was fascinated by the unstudied grace of all her movements. If she was afraid, she did not show it.

'Lady Lucinda Staffray,' she said, 'is in Austria, and she has written to Jimmy. She has been seeing my poor Lorenz, who these days keeps dangerous company. A man who has always been my enemy, but whom Lorenz can only see as a patriot and a hero. A man whom my husband, Count Erhmann, Lorry's father, considered a brute. He has told Lucinda things about me, and she has passed them on to Jimmy. If she wanted to hurt us both, and she does, she could not have chosen a better time. Today was my happiest day. To see you and Jimmy married – but most of all to have his father present. And now James's daughter has done this. I am sorry for her, poor child.' She looked up at Jimmy. 'If I could wipe out that time, Jimmy, between Eugene's death, and your coming to find me after the war, I would. I can't. But I implore you not to let it hurt your life – or Amy's.'

'Mother, it says that the very night Papa was killed you became Schausenhardt's mistress. That he boasts about it in Vienna. Is that true?'

'You have no right to ask,' said Amy fiercely. 'You have no right to judge. It is *not* your life!'

.'Ah, love, yes, he has,' said Viola gently, 'because he loves me . . . and I love him. Too much. It's been my fault – to love him too much. We loved each other too much when he was a little lad. It's not right for a lad and his mother to mean so much to each other. If I could have loved him less and Lorenz more – it would have been better for us all. Love is the only thing that gives anyone rights over others, Amy.'

'I said I'd kill that bastard one day when I was a kid. And, by God, if this is true, I will.'

'It's not just *you*,' cried Amy. 'It's your mother, and it's me, and all of us. I cannot bear you to be like this . . . like Lucinda. Is it the Staffray in you? The pig-headed pride? You want to kill a man and hurt us all because *you* have been hurt.' She sought for words, and burst out against him. 'It's base of you, Jimmy.'

'You women talk as though nothing had happened. As though it did not matter. But is it true – that you slept with this man, this brute, in the same house and on the same night while Papa lay dead?'

'I did not want you to know,' said Viola. She was very calm. 'I wanted no revenge.' Her lips curled with scorn. 'I do not value myself so highly. I was half dead from grief and weariness, and when he came and told me that the fighting had stopped and the raiding *soldatska* had been driven away – I hardly heard him. I saw what he wanted, and I knew that he was beyond reason or pleading, and so he had his way. What use was it to scream and fight? In my life there have been two fine and great gentlemen who loved me, and two monsters. Years ago, when you were all children, and he was making a nuisance of himself in Vienna,

315

Eugene said to me, "You attract extremes, beloved." It is true.'

'But afterwards, Mama.' Jimmy's fierceness had abated 'Afterwards . . . the letter says you were his mistress for many months . . . until I came and took you away.'

'That is not true, Jimmy. Schausenhardt is like a mad dog, trying to destroy me. He destroyed my happiness when he took your father away. It is the only means of revenge he has now, to try and pull me down . . . to kill your love, and the other children's. His revenge is like Lucinda's when she wrote this letter, but she is young, and she loved you – that I can understand. But he cannot love. He never ceased threatening me. He never ceases. You saw your father's grave desecrated. It was at his orders. My children have Jewish blood he says, and one day he and his kind will destroy the Jews in Austria. He is deep in this new movement which this man Hitler has begun in Germany, and moves between Vienna and Munich, spinning his webs of intrigue like a spider. And people listen to him. His sister Lotte, who was once my friend, is now a fanatic for his cause. And my poor Lorenz worships this man. He writes to me that Schausenhardt will be a leader of the German people one day.'

'Lorry knows nothing of this?'

'Not unless Lucinda has told him – as she told you. It is very possible.'

'If I had known that day when I came for you to Die Kinderburg I would have killed him.'

Viola leaned back, her face weary, looking suddenly old.

'And what good would that have done? What did he have from me? For one hour – one night? A cold slab of flesh that could feel nothing. A mind that was beyond understanding, and a heart that no longer cared. He himself was covered with shame and horror, and the next day he came bullying, pleading, weeping, imploring my forgiveness, asking me to marry him . . . I did not even answer him. Why do you think he wants to destroy us? Because he cannot touch us, even if he killed us all. Because we have had love, and he has never known it and never will. I have said before, Jimmy, I am not one of those vain women who considers her body all important. When one loves one gives everything. Without love, what is sex? A transaction? A fleeting pleasure? But this, that Schausenhardt took was nothing to me and a humiliation to him which he will never forget, however much he threatens and bullies and boasts. I have told no one – no one knows but my dear old Vatel and me. I did not want it spoken about. I wanted no revenge – revenge is for fools and bullies. Now you know, and I prayed you never would. Try and forget. Wipe it from your mind. It's best that way.'

'What would Papa have done if he had been alive? What would my own father have done?'

She could not answer, because she knew what those two great gentlemen would have done. They would have shot Schausenhardt like the mad animal he was; Jimmy read it in her eyes.

'But Papa was dead, and your father does not know, and I hope will never know. I suffered, but in the end, when he grovelled at my feet, I knew it was my victory. I do not want murder, Jimmy.'

His young face was stern, withdrawn and cold. He had been reared by two proud men and he could not even try to put the matter aside. He could not understand her total simplicity.

'I would give myself to Schausenhardt now, like throwing a bone to a dog,' she cried passionately, 'if it would save one of you children any hurt or pain. Nothing but more suffering can come of revenge. Why do you think I was so afraid that you might know about this?' She turned to Amy, her eyes desperate with appeal. '*Help me*, Amy. Help me make him understand.'

'You were the most precious thing in all the world to me,' Jimmy said slowly. 'You were so beautiful, and so kind and loving and generous. You remember Terry once said you were like a holy icon. I cannot bear to think you should have suffered this disgusting thing. That this brute should have degraded you and the memory of Papa.'

'He has degraded no one but himself,' said Amy fiercely.

'But it is not right that he should go unpunished. Mama knows that Papa would have killed him, and that Lord Louderdown would kill him, if he knew.'

317

'Well, then,' Viola said flatly, 'we won't tell him. No one can hurt my Eugene now. A holy icon, indeed!' She laughed, but her beautiful eyes were tragic. 'What *nonsense*! You have only seen the side of me that all men see, Jimmy. I thought we were closer than that. Oh, I know I'm beautiful! An object of desire. No one sees the other side of me. I'm a fighter, Jimmy. I survive if it's possible to. I don't believe in crying over spilt milk. If I had, I'd have given up long ago, when you were born, and I had no money and no one to turn to. What is the use of yelping because this happened to me? All over Europe women were suffering the like – hunger, rape, starvation. I'm not so special! Revenge is for folk like Schausenhardt.' Her lips curled with fastidious distaste. 'For princes and aristocrats who fancy themselves important. Not for plain folk like me. We just pick ourselves up and get on with life like my mother did, when she scrubbed floors to keep me out of a factory. It happened, and nowt on earth can wipe it away, or make it any different. Not revenge. Not suffering. That's how it was, and it's past, so forget it. You and Amy are in love, so get on with your young lives while they are good. Take every happy day and bless it. It's all anyone can do.' She rose, and took his hand, her eyes gentle, sweet, seductive, old as the world, wise as the sphinx. 'You just forgive me, Jimmy love, for not being a saint, and then forget it.'

'Ah, Mama darling.' He bent and kissed her and for a minute she thought she had won. 'There is nothing to forgive you for. I'm sorry I was uncivil.'

'But what about forgetting?'

His hand fell away. 'That is a different matter.' He was suddenly very urbane, very charming, 'Amy, you forgive me too, for being so rude. And go and get your hat, and we must be off.'

She rose, doubtfully, but he kissed her and she went upstairs to do his bidding, misgiving deep in her heart. She did not believe this new face of Jimmy's – he was too transparent to lie, and yet, that was what he was doing now.

'Jimmy,' said Viola, 'you must not speak to your father about this. Lucinda is his daughter, remember. And Lorry – *don't* tell him if you see him. If she has told him, there is nothing we can do. But if he does not know, it is better so.'

'Mama, of course, whatever you wish.' He kissed her hand formally, and then her cheek. 'We must be on our way, darling. Thanks for everything.'

They went out into the garden to say good-bye, to be surrounded by guests throwing rose petals and confetti. His brother officers were tying an old shoe to the back of the car. Everyone was waving and calling good wishes as they got into the car. Jimmy was smiling as he left with his bride. But in his heart he knew that he was going to Vienna to kill Schausenhardt.

They spent their first night in a fine old hotel in a small village near Rouen. It was all it should have been. A copy-book honeymoon night. A delightful dinner, a room overlooking the wide bend of the moonlit Seine. Two young married lovers alone together, for the first time. Amy went up to their room alone. Jimmy had been charming, but she felt cold and afraid. She undressed and went to bed and sat up waiting, and the minutes ticked by. He did not come, and the coldness in her heart filled her whole being. She drew the covers up and in their warmth fell asleep. When she woke the moonlight was sending stripes of white light across the dark room and somewhere in the distance a cock was crowing. She switched on the light and looked at her watch. It was four o'clock. And Jimmy was not there.

She rose, pulling a wrap over the pretty blue chiffon nightdress she had chosen for this night of nights. The hotel was strange, large and empty about her. She could not go wandering the corridors in search of him. She drew the curtains and looked out at the terrace below that overlooked the river, where the white chairs and tables gleamed in the light. Beyond the skyline there was the pale light of dawn. She heard a footstep on the gravel and Jimmy came on to the terrace, his hands buried deep in his pockets, walking slowly like an automaton, as though he had been walking for hours.

She opened the window, and the small sound roused him; he

319

lifted his face and she saw the quick, mechanical smile, the flash of white teeth in the moonlight. He waved and went into the hotel, and in a few minutes came into the room.

'Where have you been?'

'You were asleep when I came up. I went out. I've been miles . . . up to the castle and along the river.'

'You should have wakened me.'

'I hadn't the heart.' He began to take off his things, yawning. He looked tired, but with a glittering kind of exhaustion that could not sleep. 'It's the responsibility of being a married man. And you were sleeping – like a little rosebud so tightly curled up, so I crept out.' He went into the bathroom and came back, changed into the silk pyjamas which Vatel had packed that morning. 'Come along – no one keeps awake on their honey-moon night. Let's get some sleep . . . we've a long drive tomor-row.'

'It's not so far to Paris.'

He drew her against him, running his hands through the long brown hair, streaming across the pillow.

'I've changed my mind,' he said. 'I thought we'd give Paris a miss and go east to Rheims and Strasbourg. I've decided to go straight to Vienna. Now, let's get some sleep. After all, we've got a lifetime in which to make love.'

The wedding guests had all gone. The caterers were taking down the marquees and carrying the gilt chairs out to the vans. James Louderdown had kissed her hand, and departed, the bridesmaids had gone off with a group of gay young people, organized by the debonair Bellairs, and including Coralie whom they promised to return by eleven o'clock before going on to the inevitable night-club. The house seemed very quiet as Viola sat alone in her drawing-room. She had letters to answer, but she sat with her chin on her hand, gazing into space.

Vatel knocked and entered to ask where she would like to dine.

'Oh, on a tray, Vatel. In my sitting-room upstairs.'

'Milady is tired?'

'A little. It has been a weary old day. We're alone now, Vatel, you and I. What shall we do, we two old people?'

Vatel smiled deprecatingly – in his eyes she would never be old.

'Vatel –' she shivered – 'grey geese are walking over my grave tonight. Sit down and talk, like we did at Die Kinderburg during the war and we only had each other. What should I have done without you?'

He hitched his tight black trousers up at the knees, drew a chair to a respectful distance, and sat down on the edge. She looked at him with loving amusement, as she looked at Betsy, and all the simple, humble people who had been devoted to her during her spectacular life. He was old, and she must find a way to ease his life without hurting his pride. Soon she would be caring for him more than he for her. Old friend, old comrade, who knew all about her life, about the happiness and the black tragedy, but had kept his counsel and loyal love. But he still would never sit down in her presence without permission.

'Have a cigarette, Vatel, with me.' She offered him one of the small black Russian cigarettes which he loved and she, very occasionally, smoked after dinner. He lit them with an air and great pleasure.

'Dear old friend. It was – very nearly – a grand, happy day. It's a pity that letter came. You don't think, do you, that Jimmy-C will . . . that he'll do anything he might regret . . . do you. . . ?'

'*Mais non*, milady. Not the *Capitaine*. He is far too disciplined – and too good-natured. Why never have I seen him to lose his temper . . .'

'Until today?'

'He might be angry, but he is a real soldier. He wouldn't do anything extreme, milady.'

'Not like my poor Lorenz?'

Vatel rushed to make excuses for the children who had grown up around him and whom he loved.

'The young Count is impulsive and sometimes wrongheaded. He had no father during formative years, because before his death *m'sieu* was away a great deal. And his brother was away. A too feminine *milieu*, perhaps, milady? But I am certain that he will be a good young gentleman, when he is a little older. He is still very, very young.'

'Everything was against him, Vatel. Jimmy-C, whom he envied and whom I loved so much. His own father, who was so clever but who could not hide his disappointment in his boy, nor his admiration for the boy who was not his own.' She was talking half to herself, reviewing her mistakes in the spring twilight. 'And then he had to fall in love with that little Amy. You know I believe he thought – here was a nice little thing, who would be overawed by his rank and his money, and whom Jimmy could not possibly fancy. Jimmy always was after the spectacular girls.' She shook her head, smiling. 'How wrong he is. That is a strong, staunch little girl, a fighter, who will be a match for my big handsome Jimmy any day. But that poor Staffray girl. She must have been so hurt to do this dreadful thing. I hope she will be sorry. I hope she will forgive Jimmy for what was not his fault . . . I hope she will forgive her father and herself.'

'Time passes, milady.' He rose stiffly, 'And about dinner?'

'Anything, Vatel. In the autumn, Vatel, Miss Coralie is going to school, and Miss Theresa to America to act in a play. We shall be alone, you and I. For the first time. What shall we do?'

Vatel permitted himself a liberty.

'You have many friends in London, Madame. Will not the Earl of Louderdown call?'

Viola coloured, and rose. He had asked if he might, and now when the ashes of their lives lay all around them, there was no reason why he should not. Who cared whether two old lovers met and talked again?

Vatel shook his head and permitted himself one of his hoarse, half-stifled chuckles. It was the nearest he ever got to laughing.

'Milady will never be alone,' he said.

•

It was a nerve-wracking drive to Vienna. Jimmy drove fast and direct, and the roads not yet recovered from the neglect of four years of war were bad. Life was recovering, although Jimmy scarcely noticed. He drove as through a long tunnel with Vienna waiting at the end. Battered Europe was beginning to repair, rebuild and re-sow. Amy watched the new strange landscapes, the towns and the snow-capped mountains, the forests and villages, all beautiful with spring. But Jimmy drove hard, his beautiful profile like an iron mask beside her, concentrated and set, driving with the smooth efficiency of a machine. They made brief stops for meals, and brief over-night rests. They lay together in strange hotel rooms, but they did not make love. It was as though he could not love her without tenderness and he had no tenderness left.

They had planned to drift slowly through Europe, staying in beautiful places, lingering in small lovely towns. But they drove as fast as the powerful new Bentley would go. Rheims, Nancy, Strasbourg, Ulm, Ausberg, München, Salzburg, Linz. Faceless cities, silent meals, hotel bedrooms and on the road again, driving towards Vienna as though the city was an evil magnet that drew Jimmy irresistibly towards it. No talk of the farm above Lake Como now, and long days of love in the mountain silences, before leaving for Cairo and his new duties. No mention of the future. They were suspended in an emotional limbo together, yet not together, for it was obvious that Jimmy had to follow this road alone.

They arrived in the late afternoon and were shown to their room – as always in the very best hotel. Lord Staffray's son and Count Erhmann's step-son always chose the very best. Ormolu and gilt, and satin brocades, everything very large, opulent and splendid.

Amy felt exhausted and very small, something of no account, brought along for no reason, except that she was Jimmy's property, and it would have been ungentlemanly of him to discard her.

She thumped the huge lace-trimmed down pillows of the royal suite, and lay down on the bed. Above her head golden cupids held the satin brocade hangings away from the bed-head, Jimmy stood looking out at the Ringstrasse, his back towards her.

'What a hideous great room,' she said. 'It looks more as though it was decorated for some Viennese tart than a respectable married woman!'

Jimmy turned and looked at her with unseeing eyes, and then suddenly became aware of her, sunk into the great flamboyant bed, small face burning with suppressed anger. He went across and dropped down beside her.

'My poor sweetheart, what a brute I've been. Shall I ring for some tea.'

'Yes, please. Isn't it enormous? The bed? Doesn't it stink of power and riches and corruption in high places? No wonder the Hapsburg Empire collapsed if they were impressed by this sort of thing.'

He laughed, and it seemed such a long time since she had seen his eyes light, or even a shadow of that young, gay and endearing Jimmy who had captured her heart. He rang for tea and came to sit beside her. He pulled off her shoes and her foot lay in his hand, tiny and vulnerable.

'I shall lose you in this great bed.'

She reached up and touched his face, and he bent down over her, and drew her into his arms.

'Would it make any difference, Jimmy?'

The wary look came into his eyes.

'What do you mean?'

'D'you love me?'

'You know I do.'

'Jimmy, we have been married for three days now. You have scarcely been aware that I am here. I am like some tiresome parcel that you had to bring along. What are you waiting for?'

He rose, and began to move restlessly about the big room.

'Amy, soon it will all be quite different. I promise. When we get away to Italy by ourselves, and come to rest.'

'When you have found this man Schausenhardt and killed him?'

'I have to go out,' he said, ignoring her words. 'I have to find

Lorenz. I am going to our old house, where he has an apartment, to see if he is there. You have a rest and some tea and I'll be back shortly.'

'Jimmy, please, *talk* to me about it. Or are you afraid that, if you do, you will not do it? That it won't bear talking about and you'll come to your senses. I thought you were grown up. A man. That it was Lorenz who was still a baby.'

'Amy, I will not talk about it with you. It is my affair and mine alone.'

'Oh, men!' She sat up, banging the pillows with furious fists. 'What good will it do? What are you going to do? Challenge him to a duel, in the high Austrian fashion? The sort of blustering, stupid old-style thing your mother hates, and your step-father despised? Once you told me what a wonderful man Count Eugene was, and how wise, and how much you owed to his teaching. How he sent you to England, because you wanted to be a soldier, and he said the Austrian officers, the arrogant, privileged aristocratic louts were the curse of the country and the Army. Now you want to be *like* this man you hate!'

He stood quite still, listening, but the meaning of her words did not touch him. They were like water or mist, running over and around him, not penetrating to any understanding.

'I have to find Schausenhardt and settle this account.'

Helpless tears poured down her face. She was choked with frustration, terrible anxiety and fear. Nothing she said could penetrate, nothing distract the cold hatred of his will.

'I can't make you hear. But remember I am your wife. I'm not just your – your little sweetheart. A plaything. I am your wife and I love you. I do not want to be married to a murderer. If you destroy this man you destroy yourself, you break your mother's heart, and you destroy our love.'

She saw the glint of stubborn anger come into his eyes, but when he reached the door all her anger evaporated, and she sprang up, ran across the room and threw herself into his arms.

'Jimmy, Jimmy, darling, please . . . please don't go.'

He kissed her swiftly, his young mouth hard against hers.

'Jimmy, please think . . . please think and take care . . . he might kill you.'

He put her gently aside and went out of the room.

He went quickly along the old familiar way across the Kartner Ring towards the Belvedere, the way he had walked home from the von Retz house and from school.

The old mansion looked much the same, the writhing stone caryatids supporting the huge stone archway by the porters' lodge, the stone courtyard beyond.

He rang at the lodge, but it was a new porter. He listened warily when Jimmy asked if Lorenz was in, and said he was away, and had been away for some days.

He took a taxi to the von Retz house, where the maid came back with his card, and said stiffly that the Baroness was not in.

'The Baron, then,' Jimmy insisted. 'I am sure he will see me.'

After a short while, Gottfried came hurriedly down the hall, glancing a little apprehensively about him. He was in evening clothes. He was as stout as ever, but the rather charmingly foolish expansiveness had gone.

'My dear Jimmy, how good to see you once again! I am so sorry that Lotte is engaged, but we are expecting guests very soon. Have you been to the hospital? How is that poor boy? It must have been a great shock to you?'

'Hospital? Why? Is Lorenz ill?'

Gottfried changed colour.

'I – I naturally assumed you had been informed, and that was why you were here.'

'What has happened?'

'Lorenz met with an accident two days ago. There was a demonstration and the rival gangs were fighting, and he was hurt. Badly hurt. It is a terrible thing to have happened, but it is common nowadays. The factions fight, and many criminals who belong to neither side take advantage of the disturbances to rob. The streets are never safe at night.'

'Uncle Gottfried, where is he?'

He gave the name of the hospital and Jimmy was in the street signalling to a taxi, when he found Count Gottfried pulling at his sleeve, his ruddy face pale, his eyes uneasy behind their thick glasses.

'I cannot talk here, Jimmy. When you have seen Lorenz, go back to your hotel. There are things which you should know. I will come to you there.'

Having given him the name of the hotel, Jimmy drove back there and went to find Amy. She was as he had left her, lying on the bed, wide-awake.

'Lorenz is in hospital. He has been hurt – in a street fight.'

'Lorenz!' she said blankly. 'In a fight? I don't believe it.'

'I am going to him now. Will you come with me?'

In a moment, she was up, pulling on her shoes, twisting up her hair. There was a note in his voice that she had longed to hear – he needed her.

When they arrived at the hospital, they found that Lorenz was unconscious. The doctor told them he had been brought in late at night. He had been found in the street near his apartment. His condition was causing some anxiety, but they could see him if they wished.

He led them into a private ward and Amy drew a horrified breath. Lorenz's thin, over-sensitive, boyish face had been beaten into a purple, bloody mass. She looked at Jimmy, and put her hand on his arm, frightened by what she saw in his eyes. The colour had drained from his face as he looked at his brother.

'Who did it? Does anyone know who did this?' he demanded.

'No. The police are making enquiries but I doubt if they will get very far. Unless someone informs, and people are unwilling to do that.'

'You mean they are intimidated?'

'It is possible.'

He was a kindly, sensitive young man, distressed at their distress. He told them what he knew.

'He has multiple injuries, but the worst is the skull fracture. There is some brain damage, not extensive, but severe.'

'Will he recover?'

The doctor's eyes flickered, he hesitated, then said, 'It might be better if he did not. Time could bring about a complete recovery, but at this stage no one can tell. In six months you will know.'

'And this was done in a demonstration?'

The doctor glanced at them curiously. 'Who told you that? There was no demonstration that day. Count Erhmann was found in the street not far from where he lived. I am glad you have come. No one has been to see him, or enquire. I find that strange. No friend or relative.'

'He has no relatives in Vienna. I am his brother. Should I – should I send for our mother?'

'It would be best,' the doctor replied.

Amy and Jimmy went back to the hotel, and changed, but neither of them could eat. They were taking coffee in their sitting-room when Count Gottfried was announced.

'So, this is the new small wife,' he said, bending over Amy's hand with old-fashioned punctiliousness. 'I wish you every happiness, gracious lady. I wish I could have shown you my city in the old days, when we were all so happy . . .' Behind his spectacles his eyes were moist with sentimental tears. He was conscious of Jimmy, his tall, slim, powerful figure and cold, enquiring gaze.

'Will you now tell me what happened, Uncle Gottfried?' he said.

'Yes, yes . . . You understand I was not present. There was a meeting at my house, and the meetings are secret, you understand. I never mix myself up with them. I implore Lotte not to, but she will not listen. They wish to join with Germany – to make a greater Germany under the National Socialists. Lorenz was one of them. You must understand he adores Freddi. He always has, even when he was a boy, you remember. He believes every word he says, and thinks he could lead the country to salvation. A future leader who will unite the German Empire. While I know he is a brute and a blackguard, whom I or his mother have kept all his grown-up life.' He paused, his eyes wandering, shaking his head. 'How can such men come to power? I tell Lotte it is because fools are infatuated with them.

But someone, I do not know who, told Lorenz how Friedrich treated your mother after the war. He came to our house that night, and implored Friedrich before all of them to deny the story. Friedrich was drunk, and as always when drunk, unpredictable ... he laughed at him before everyone, he insulted Viola, boasted that he had . . . had possessed her, and he called Lorenz a little Jewish swine.'

Jimmy turned away, his hand across his mouth. Amy went to his side but he turned abruptly away. It was as though he could not bear anyone near him.

'It was so dreadful, because Lorry had worshipped him. He had been devoting all his time lately and a great deal of money to the cause – or so he thought. In my opinion most of the money went into Friedrich's pockets. But – at this gathering, he challenged Friedrich. It was absurd and pathetic. Lorry, who was always hopeless at that sort of thing, and Friedrich a crack shot, once champion of his regiment – before the war a famous dueller. Friedrich laughed in his face and had him thrown into the street. Lotte told me. She told me her brother could not accept a challenge from such scum.'

Gottfried suddenly broke down, sitting in one of the ornate gilt chairs with the tears running down his plump pale face. 'What am I to do with her? And with him? He infects everyone, even my children believe this poisonous rubbish. They look for someone to blame for our defeat and poverty, and people like Friedrich give them the answers. He is an evil man, always has been. Your mother and father loathed him. They would never receive him. But he loved your mother – if it can be called love. He never stopped desiring her. He never forgave her for rejecting him. He never forgave your step-father for having him sent away from Vienna. He waited many years to take his revenge on them.'

'On Papa?' burst out Jimmy. 'But surely he was killed by the raiders at Die Kinderburg?'

'Once, when Friedrich was drunk, he boasted that he shot Count Erhmann. There was, he said, a great deal of shooting that night, and who would know who fired the fatal shot? There was one Jew less in the world, he said. But to Lorenz he had always been the hero who had come to his mother's aid. This week he learned the truth.'

'Schausenhardt killed Papa?'

'It may not be true, Jimmy, my dear boy. When he is drunk he says these things. I do not think it true that he made your mother his mistress. He has lied and boasted all his life, and who knows which is truth, which lies.'

'My mother told me of – of his treatment of her,' Jimmy said stiffly, 'but what happened to Lorenz?'

'I know no more than you. He was found near his house; he had been thrown out of a car, and he was taken to hospital. If Friedrich ordered it, who can say? He can command a troop of young bullies here in Vienna. He would simply deny the whole thing. In all his life no one has ever made him pay for his misdeeds. No one but Viola could bring him to his knees.'

'And where is he now?'

'He has gone to Adlerburg. To shoot, he says. The police have been making enquiries, but of course nothing points to him. No one will breathe a word about the quarrel here . . .'

'Not you, Uncle Gottfried?'

'Jimmy, do not ask me to do that. I am no longer young. There is Lotte and the children . . . shall I see them treated as was young Lorry?'

'No, Uncle Gottfried, I shall not ask you.' He rose, very politely. 'Will you take coffee, Uncle Gottfried? And a glass of cognac? You must forgive me if I ask you not to stay – I have a long day ahead of me tomorrow.'

'You are leaving?'

'I shall not leave Austria until my brother's attacker and my mother's persecutor is brought to justice.'

'My dear boy, I doubt if the police can help you.'

Jimmy's blue eyes were as cold as ice.

'I was not thinking of the police,' he said.

He left for Die Kinderburg in the morning, leaving Amy at the hotel. A call at the hospital told them that Lorenz was no better, and Amy telephoned Viola. An accident, she told her, and Viola said she would leave for Vienna that day.

Lorenz had not regained consciousness, but the disfiguring swelling was beginning to subside. Below the heavy bandages his weak, fair, boyish features were slowly becoming recognizable.

'I don't think we should leave Vienna,' Amy said. 'We ought not to leave him until your mother comes. He might die, and no one would be near.'

'You will stay here,' said Jimmy, 'but I have to go. I shall be back tonight.'

'I will wait for you at the hotel, but I'll come here to see Lorenz again this afternoon – and I will leave instructions for them to call me if he should recover consciousness.'

It seemed extraordinary that they should be speaking to each other in this cold, businesslike manner. It did not seem possible that four days ago they had been passionately longing for their wedding, and being together. But tragedy and evil had touched them like a shrivelling frost.

It was not until he turned to leave that she said, compulsively, 'Jimmy. Don't go.'

He did not reply.

'All right – then remember what I said.'

'About what?'

'About being a murderer.'

'Oh, that!' He smiled, as though she had said something absurd, but his eyes did not smile.

'Well, remember it . . . please . . . and remember that I do love you. And your mother loves you . . . and whatever you do now, we are involved. We will be hurt too!'

He looked at her gravely, and said again, 'I'll be back tonight.'

She sat beside Lorenz for some time. Before she left at midday he opened his eyes, pale blue slits between the bruised lids, and she called the nurse and the doctor. She smiled, bending above him, but no recognition dawned and in a few seconds they closed again as though even that effort was too great.

Jimmy reached Die Kinderburg by midday – the village and the little castle looked as beautiful as ever in the late spring sunshine. High up in the gap made by the lopped pines Adlerburg looked down the valley at the village, river and castle below.

He left his car in the courtyard. He had been so happy here as a boy. It had been a fairy-tale place filled with loving and laughter. He had wanted to bring Amy here, but now he thought this would never happen. It was infected with evil as though it needed to be exorcised.

The caretaker in charge was a middle-aged man who had been there in his boyhood but had only recently returned from the Army. He welcomed him, a little embarrassed and distressed when he led him through the great hall, which was hung with scarlet banners with white circles on which were printed large black swastikas. There were photographs of meetings and rallies with Schausenhardt predominating, often with his sister, Lotte von Retz, and many with the Austrian, Adolf Hitler, leader of the German party, striking heroic attitudes, glaring into the camera with his pale fanatic eyes.

Jimmy looked at the empty shelves.

'Where are all Papa's books? And the pictures?'

'Count Lorenz sold them all. He said he needed the money for the party. This is where they hold meetings when Prince Friedrich is up at Adlerburg.'

'Is he there now?'

'I believe so. I could see smoke rising from the chimneys and I have heard shooting in the woods. They are culling some of the stags in the upper forest. I was sorry to hear of the Count's accident. Is he better?'

'Every day makes recovery more hopeful. The Countess is coming from London to be with him.'

'I'm glad to hear it, sir. He is a young man. Too young to have so much money, and live alone. Will you be staying, Herr Captain Jimmy?'

'No. I must get back to Vienna. My wife is there. But I thought I would like to see the castle, and take a gun through the woods before we leave for Italy. I suppose the guns have not been sold?'

'Oh no, sir. The Count would not part with them. I'll get the key of the gun room, sir.' He bustled away, and came back with the key, leading the way, shaking his head, and muttering, 'The poor young gentleman. It's a mistake to get mixed up in politics, in these times. They say this Dolfuss will steer a middle course, but who can tell? Can I get you some lunch before you go out, Herr Captain?'

'Just a sandwich – and some of our good wine.'

He unlocked the rack and chose a gun, balancing it in his hands, a beautiful American rifle, which had belonged to Eugene who had taught him to shoot and stalk when he was a boy. He strapped on the cartridge belt, ate his sandwich, and drank a glass of wine, and then went through Viola's gardens, neglected now and weed-grown, and up the steep path into the woods beyond the stream where they used to picnic in the old days. There he waited, listening, until he heard a shot in the valley where the deer came to drink.

He descended in the direction of the shot, swift, light and silent as a panther, and came out on a rock where he could wait, hidden by thick growing shrub, watching the water meadows on the far side of the stream. He prayed that Schausenhardt would be out alone. He waited very patiently as the afternoon sun crept across the sky. Occasionally there were shots high in the Adlerburg woods. Then the deer began to cross the meadows, but not to the water to drink, hurrying, pausing with uplifted ears and alert heads, knowing they were being pursued.

He saw Schausenhardt cross the meadow to the stream. The carcase of a stag was slung across his pony, which he tethered to a branch. He had obviously just cleaned it for his big hands were red with blood. He went to the stream, put his gun down on a rock, and began to walk across the flat stepping stones, the ones he had crossed the first time he had ever seen Viola, lifting her petticoats from her bare feet, running down to the water with the children laughing about her. He bent down and began to rinse his hands in the clear mountain water.

Jimmy raised his rifle until Schausenhardt's head was squarely in the sights, then lowered it again. He wanted to kill him, and he was going to kill him, but he wanted him to know his executioner. He stepped out of the concealing bushes on to the ledge of rock, and raising his rifle, sent a shot chipping the rock on which Schausenhardt bent, half-kneeling, washing his hands. He looked up, rose, stumbling, shading his eyes against the bright light, not recognizing the man who stood on the rocks above him.

'Are you trying to murder me?' he yelled, and then he recognized him. The tall boy, with the fair hair and his mother's eyes. But these eyes held more than hatred. They held his death. The face, so handsome, was the face of an angel of death, the face of his executioner. He told himself that it was only a boy who would have no chance once he reached his gun. He began to move back, sliding on the wet stones, towards the bank.

Another shot cracked in front of him, striking the rock just before he put his foot upon it with a marksmanship as brilliant as his own. He turned furiously.

'What the hell do you want?' he bellowed.

'My brother is unable to meet you, Prince Friedrich,' Jimmy called. 'So I have come in his place.'

'And I tell you, as I told him, I don't fight any whore's puppy.'

'But this time you have no choice. I will allow you to pick up your gun.'

Schausenhardt scrambled towards the bank, furious with temper, shaken by a rising tide of fear. It was impossible. He had never been afraid. People could accuse him of many things, but never of fear. It was outside his knowledge. But he wanted to run for cover. The nearest was sixty yards away, and the boy could pick him off like a running deer. His men were nowhere near, and would take no notice of the sound of shots. His hunting horn lay near the gun, but as he reached for it, another bullet smacked into the rock, inches from his hand.

He picked up the gun and looked across at Jimmy. It was an easy distance. An easy shot. He grinned recklessly, one-sidedly, the scar pulling his ugly mouth down as his lips stretched, and raised his hand in agreement.

'It's your choice.' He shouted. 'On the count of three?'

Jimmy nodded, but without counting Schausenhardt swung his gun up to shoot, missed, and before he could fire again felt the bullet crash into his right shoulder, shattering the joint. He spun round and fell to the ground, his jacket already red with blood. He was helpless. He flung an arm up as though to ward off a blow.

Jimmy sprang down from the rock and came lightly across the stream, jumping from rock to rock until he stood over the wounded man, looking down at him. Through glazed eyes Schausenhardt could only see Viola, Viola looking at him through the boy's eyes with implacable repulsion and disgust. He clutched at Jimmy's ankle.

'Help me. Help me, Corbett. I shall bleed to death.'

Jimmy's boot spurned the clutching hand.

'That was for my mother,' he said quietly. 'I owe you another shot – for my step-father, Count Erhmann.' He raised the gun and looked down the barrel, and his heart leaped at the fear in Prince Friedrich's eyes. He lowered it again thoughtfully. 'But that was a swift death.' He clicked the safety catch into place, and reversed the gun, holding the barrel like a club. 'My brother Lorenz, you had beaten to the point of death. Perhaps I should beat you as he was beaten, with clubs and feet and fists, and leave you with broken limbs and a cracked skull.'

He raised the rifle above his head.

'Will you murder me?' gasped Schausenhardt.

Jimmy dropped the gun, and the devil's mask vanished. He looked round at the smiling water meadows, the tree-clad mountains and the little *schloss* of Die Kinderburg dreaming against the blue sky. People seemed to be standing round him – the people who loved him, his father and mother, Eugene Erhmann – and Amy. He could hear her saying, 'You want to kill a man, and hurt us all because you have been hurt. It is base of you, Jimmy.' He shivered blindly, as though he had just awakened, the reality of what he had so nearly done sweeping over him. He picked up the hunting horn and threw it down within

335

reach of Schausenhardt's uninjured hand and strode away across the meadow. The small field flowers jewelled the grass and the air was pure. He heard the sound of the horn calling men to Schausenhardt's aid. He was, after all, not a murderer, and he was nearly weeping with relief.

'I couldn't do it,' he said aloud. 'I *couldn't* do it,' he repeated. The sweat was pouring down his face. He retched suddenly and vomited, and stood wiping his face and hands, staring about him, as though he just realized where he was and his purpose there.

'Didn't you have any luck, then, Herr Captain?' the man asked as he returned the gun.

He shook his head, bade him good-bye, and drove back towards Vienna.

It was evening when he parked the car. The lights were on in the city and along the Ringstrasse the cafés were full after the warm day. There was a lovely sky behind the monumental buildings and avenues of trees, the spring smell of violets and coffee, the double trams clanging along, taking the workers home.

The exclusive and expensive café terrace before the hotel was full of a crowd of chattering, well-dressed people, incongruous in a city which was only just moving back from the abyss of starvation. As he threaded his way through the tables towards the entrance he saw Lucinda Staffray sitting alone. She was as always, beautifully dressed. She saw him and her hand clutched round her glass convulsively. He went heavily across. His limbs seemed to weigh him down. He sat down at the table.

Lucinda started to get to her feet, and he said harshly, 'Sit down and listen.'

He put his hand on her shoulder, not urgently, pressed her back into her seat. They sat silently, blue eyes looking into blue eyes, so alike in feature that their relationship was obvious. She thought, how *could* I not have known? The dark blue Bellairs' eyes, her father's frank, endearing smile. But her face was expressionless, carved as though in stone, her eyes like ice.

'Lucy,' he said and his voice was kind and familiar; the old Jimmy-C of their childhood, chiding her, not condemning. 'Lucy, when you tried to kill yourself I pitied you, but I did not understand. It was so extreme. But today I understood, because I went out to murder a man and nearly succeeded. It only wanted one blow, one shot to smash Schausenhardt's filthy face in for ever. It was Amy who stopped me. I remembered what she had said about revenge solving nothing, hurting the people you loved, making you worse than the person you hated. Making you base and evil. But – I *wanted* to do it. I *wanted* to kill him for the outrage he had done to my mother and to Papa's memory. Your letter made me do it. Your letter sent poor Lorry challenging Prince Friedrich, only to be thrown into the street and beaten up by his thugs, almost to death. You exacted a dreadful payment, Lucy.'

She tried to rise, to get away from the quiet, inexorably compassionate voice, saying these things without bitterness or condemnation, but his hands caught hers, forcing her to stay.

'You and I, Lucy, are both Staffrays. When our pride is hurt and our tempers roused we can do terrible things. I learned what I can do today. You've had your revenge. I hope you're satisfied.' She turned her face away, convulsed with shame and pain, the ice in her heart breaking with a dreadful crack of agony, tearing her apart. But the pain was a relief after the numb hatred of the past months. She had been so unhappy, and she was still unhappy, but it was different. Unconsciously her hands clung to his. 'Lucy, try to forgive us all. Me and my mother, and Father and yourself too.'

She put her head down on their clasped hands and wept.

'Oh, Jimmy! Jimmy-C. What have I done? Why had this to happen to us?'

'I can't answer that one.' His smile glinted, briefly and grimly. 'It would need someone far wiser than me. But it is all over. Let it really be over.' He released his hands from her

337

desperate grip and rose, briefly touching her bent head.

'I've got Amy now. But you've got Dad, if you'll only go to him. He's strong. He'll help you. He's been there too – down into despair. He'll understand. Good-bye, my dear. What does Bell call you? Oh, *yes* – Sis. Good-bye, Sis.'

He straightened up. He felt drained, empty, exhausted, but he smiled comfortingly into her distraught face before he left her.

Jimmy went upstairs to the suite and found Amy waiting for him. He went blindly across to her, dropping on his knees beside her, reaching for her silently, burying his head against her small, soft body. She held him closely, silently, terrified at what he might have to say, and yet filled with joy that once more they were close together. He looked as though all the vitality had drained out of his strong body. Through her thin dress against her breasts, she could feel his face wet with tears and desire for him rose overwhelmingly within her. She pulled his head back so that she could look into his eyes, and he answered her unspoken question.

'No. I didn't kill him. I could have killed him, but I didn't. I couldn't do it. When I had him there, wounded, helpless, pleading for his filthy life, I couldn't.'

'Thank God!'

'I feel as though I've been ill. I was sick with hatred. I've fought in a war, and had to kill men or be killed. But this was like being possessed. I know now what Lucinda felt when she sent that letter. Since I opened it at home I have thought only of finding Schausenhardt and killing him . . . and then I let him go.'

'Hush, my darling. I've been praying you would.'

'I suddenly remembered all the things you had said, as though you were standing beside me. I thought of Mother, and all she had endured, and what she would have to endure if I did this.' He leaned back on the settee, holding her against him, feeling her cheeks and mouth with his lips and fingers, as though trying to recognize her again. As though he was renewing himself with the feel of her skin and hair. 'Stay good, Amy. Always love me. Always be as you are. Mother is the most beautiful woman I have ever known, but beauty like hers can be a destructive thing. Everything that has happened to all of us, Lorenz and Lucinda, and Papa, was because of her beauty. I used to think that expression – fatal beauty – was just a silly thing sentimental writers say. But it can be true. Even that mad brute did what he did because he desired her and could not possess her. And never really did. It was as though her face and body built up a tension about her, like the electricity that builds up in the mountains, and we were all caught up in the following storm.'

'But she could not help being beautiful, Jimmy – and who would have her other than as she is? Not me – and not you, I know. But now it's over. It's our life now. The past is behind us. You're with me now, my darling.'

Presently he lifted her up in his arms and carried her into the bedroom. They did not leave the room that evening. They made passionate, demanding and forgiving love, the aftermath of the ensuing deluge that washed the evil away. They lay close together, naked in the darkness, and the lights of the city winked and twinkled their reflections on the high baroque ceiling, picking out the glints of gilt, the flashes of cut glass, the sheen of satin. They lay entwined together, Amy holding him in the healing shelter of her love.

'I said Mother was the most precious thing to me in all the world,' he said, 'but now it's you.'

Viola arrived in Vienna with Vatel in attendance and they took her immediately to the hospital to see Lorenz. That day he recovered consciousness, and she sat beside him, holding his hand, her face on the pillow beside his, talking to him gently until he fell asleep. He knew her, and managed to smile, but he could form no words.

'I will stay here with him,' she told them. 'Vatel and I. They say it will be a long slow business, but we will manage. You must go on – go to Italy and be happy. Then when he can be moved I will take him there, and make him well again. You'll see.'

Nothing seemed to shake her optimism. She kissed them good-bye, and saw them drive away south towards the sun. She was sad for them. Sad that these things should have happened. But they were young, and the young were resilient, and they had each other. Already they had the look of lovers brought closer by disaster, tempered by fire. She knew she no longer held the first place in Jimmy's heart – and she was glad.

She ate alone in the big hotel and then walked round to the hospital to sit with Lorenz. To sit beside the boy whom she had not loved quite enough, whom she would nurse and shelter, teaching him to return to life again; the boy who, now, of all her children, could at last claim her for his own.

James left his office at the Ministry of Defence to walk through St James's Park to the Ritz, where he lunched most days. It often seemed ironical to him that he, a soldier bred and born, an aristocrat and a landowner, should end up a desk wallah. One must serve as one could, just as one must eventually live as one could. The great house at Louderdown was open to the public since Florence had married Hamilton, and he kept just one wing there for himself as a country place, and as a home for Lucinda, where she spent most of her time now.

He walked on through the sunshine, carrying his hat and cane in his one hand, a tall, handsome, middle-aged gentleman of the old school. Very upright, soldierly and slim. Near the Ritz he saw Viola sitting on a seat in the sunshine. He stopped, delighted, and went across to her, and she stretched out hands of welcome. 'You are back in England.'

'You needn't think, James, that this is an accident,' she said, smiling. 'I'm staying at the Ritz and I've seen you pass two mornings. Today, I thought I'd wait for you.'

'You have made me very happy. But why didn't you tell me

you were in London?'

'I thought it best not to, perhaps. And then, when I saw you marching by, I thought, why not? Do you hear from Jimmy?'

'He's not much of a correspondent. I hear from Amy mostly.'

She laughed. 'Me, too.'

'He's all right. A bit fed up with the exotic Egyptian society. Says it can't last. I think they've got a good marriage.'

'Yes. A battle of strong wills. Amy has social conscience, and the state of the Egyptian poor appals her. She's not exactly the perfect Army memsahib.'

'They told you their news?'

'We'll be grandparents in the spring.' She shook her head, smiled, and sighed. 'I'm looking forward to that. And Bellairs?'

'Oh,' James said, with a touch of exasperation, 'still at this painting. Quite a success they tell me. I know nothing of such things. Is that girl of yours going to marry him?'

'Theresa? James, I don't know. I leave them to get on with their lives. They're not my babies any longer, worse luck. I said once I'd like a dozen.' She met his eyes, and the colour touched her cheeks. 'Yes. Long ago, when we were together. But I've had four, and I think that's enough.'

He sat down on the bench beside her.

'Viola, I've made a lot of mistakes, and I've caused you much sorrow – but the most terrible thing that happened between us was that Lucy should have brought you this tragedy, and at a time when you had come through so much, and life seemed good again . . .'

'Ah, James, don't talk about it.'

'She told me everything, Viola.'

'Everything?' Her eyes were suddenly haunted with memory, like a cloud shadow across the sunny day. 'About Schausenhardt?'

'Yes, *everything*. When I think of it, I could. . . .'

'No.' She was angry. 'No. Don't. I cannot stand it any more. We have come through. That is all that matters now.'

'I'm proud Jimmy went to kill him . . .'

'Ah, dear Christ, *men*!' She sighed.

341

'I'm prouder that he found the strength not to. I don't think I could have done that. He's a fine boy.'

'You must forgive Lucinda, James and try to understand. My poor boy is mending, and who is to say that if it had not happened, he was not destined for something worse. At least now he knows Schausenhardt and his followers for what they are. I'm glad she told you. Tell her to forgive me for the past, and try to forgive herself.'

'She came back to me,' said James, with a touch of wonder. 'Not to her mother, but to me. I seemed to be the one she needed. When she came to me in distress, and I comforted her, d'you know it was the first time I'd held her in my arms, as my child.' He paused a moment, his voice a little unsteady. 'Not even as a small girl had she come to me. Perhaps it was because I was the sinner and she knew I would understand. Poor child. But she seems all right now, changed, but all right. I hope. Up at Louderdown they call her the Little Earl. Well, she adores the place, and runs it . . . Bellairs has no real interest. She's still young. I hope one day she'll find the right chap. It's a lot of luck – isn't it – how it happens? A meeting somewhere . . . at a dance –'

'Or in a railway train?'

He smiled, and she was glad she had made him smile.

'But you, Viola. What brings you to London?'

'Searching for another doctor for my poor Lorenz. He mends – but so slowly. He walks, but is only just trying to speak again. I look for doctors and therapists . . . anyone who will help. There is a man in London people say is good. At a hospital in Maida Vale. I have an appointment to see him. Then I'm here to see my solicitors. Die Kinderburg has been sold, and I am selling the farm at Como. Lorenz has taken against Vienna, and I do not like the way things are going in Italy. They are ruled by a bully, and I cannot bear bullies. The people at the farm are just as kind and good, and still love me, but politics change, and now even in our little village the Fascists extend their power. I am taking an apartment in Montreux. My little one, Coralie, is at school in Switzerland. It is very quiet, and very pretty, and very unexciting – and this, I think, is what I need.'

She looked so mischievous that he started to laugh.

'After all, I am fifty-one,' she protested.

'You are still a child, Duchess.' The old name slipped out, drawing them together. 'You'll lunch with me?'

'That would be grand, James.'

She took his arm, and they strolled towards Piccadilly in the sunshine.

'Viola,' he said, 'I have to ask you, and now, at last, I can. With Eugene Erhmann – did you love him? Was it ever like it was between us?'

'Yes, it was. Before the end. Before Coralie was born. We had been happy, and I was content, but then, that last time together in the mountains, suddenly all the glory came, and we were like young lovers. He was fifty then. I am so grateful, James, that it happened, that I could give him a true happiness before he died.'

He was silent. How could he be jealous? He could only be grateful that here, in the autumn, they could walk and talk together again.

'Viola, when you are settled, perhaps in the summer next year – about the time of the cherry harvest, if I travel to Switzerland, may I come and see you?'

She pretended to consider.

'Florence has remarried. She married Hamilton in the spring.'

'Yes. I know, otherwise I should not have waited for you here. Well, love, all things considered, I really don't see why not. Who is going to take any notice of two romantic old has-beens, or care whether they meet?'

He laughed, and they walked towards the door of the Ritz beneath the arcades, a handsome and distinguished couple, wearing quite unconsciously the elegance of a generation that was already becoming history.

If you enjoyed COUNTESS, you'll also want to read...

THIS TOWERING PASSION
by Valerie Sherwood   (33-042, $2.95)

500 pages of sweet romance and savage adventure set against the violent tapestry of Cromwellian England, with a magnificent heroine whose beauty and ingenuity captivates every man who sees her, from the king of the land to the dashing young rakehell whose destiny is love!

THIS LOVING TORMENT
by Valerie Sherwood   (33-117, $2.95)

Born in poverty in the aftermath of the Great London Fire, Charity Woodstock grew up to set the men of three continents ablaze with passion! The bestselling sensation of the year, boasting 1.3 million copies in print after just one month, to make it the fastest-selling historical romance in Warner Books history!

THESE GOLDEN PLEASURES
by Valerie Sherwood   (33-116, $2.95)

From the stately mansions of the east to the freezing hell of the Klondike, beautiful Rosanne Rossiter went after what she wanted —and got it all! By the author of the phenomenally successful THIS LOVING TORMENT.
